Cardinal

ROSE CHASE

Copyright

Dedication

To those who suffer with silent demons and feel like they are drowning, you are not alone.
You are worth everything, so don't stop fighting. Someone is out there with their arms open for you, so don't stop searching.
Healing is not a race or a straight road, so don't rush or go a way that doesn't work for you.
I hope you can find a safe space with Luciano as I have.
I hope that you will one day find your Luciano.
Don't ever stop fighting.

Dedication

To those who want to see the mafia boss get on his knees and grovel to his bratty submissive, it's in here.
And to those who want a sweet dark romance with lots of Dom guiding a new sub, this will rot your teeth. Hope your dentist is hot because you're gonna be seeing them a lot.

Content Disclosure/Warning

This book is a contemporary dark romance that contains content that some may find triggering or disturbing.

Contents include: explicit language, explicit violence, sexual violence, abuse, alcohol and drug use, explicit sexual scenes, dubious consent, consensual non-consent, BDSM elements and tones (pretty heavy in this book), assault, edge play (knives, guns, breath play).

THE FMC STARTS OUT UNDER 18 BUT TURNS 18 BY CHAPTER 2!!!

MENTIONS OF/DISCUSSIONS ABOUT/IMPLICATION OF OFF-SCREEN CHILD ABUSE DEALING WITH A SEXUAL NATURE. NO GRAPHIC DETAILS ARE INCLUDED IN THIS BOOK!!!

If such content triggers you then please do not continue any further or be mindful of skipping areas of trigger!

P.S. There is a glossary in the back with all the foreign words used :)

Cardinal

East Coast Syndicate Book 1
Rose Chase

Blurb

"The Devil you know is better than the one you don't."

The night I escape the hell of the brothel I was sold to, I run straight into the arms of The Devil of The Syndicate and accept his hand.

Luciano Agosti is dangerous, and I shouldn't want him for many reasons. But, it is impossible to resist the handsome devil with a charming smile and eyes full of warmth for me. And only me.

I fall into the safety of his embrace and let him care for me. I let him mend my wounds and let myself become my enemy's fear. The ones who destroyed my young life before I had a chance to live it will pay.

They showed me no mercy, so they won't get any from me.

I will unleash The Devil on them.

Contents

Chapter 1
Juliet

"DON'T WORRY, WE GOT Momma Juliet here to keep us in line."

Instinctively, my eyes rolled at Hailee's comment about my serious and cautious personality. "Someone has to make sure you stay out of jail and actually graduate high school," I remarked with a snicker, squealing out a soft laugh when another friend of mine smacked my arm.

With a roll of her eyes, my friend leaned back in her seat. "Oh, please, none of that really matters. We all know that school is just a formality. My parents basically have the papers drawn up and ready for me to sign the moment I turn eighteen."

My life is over the moment school is over. Doomed to be a trophy wife for some old business mongrel.

The grim comment tightened my lips into a thin line as I held my tongue. All of us, me included, were set for life. Hell, everyone at this private school had their lives set in stone for success. Many of us were expected to keep up our family's businesses, so we were mostly set on our paths in life. School really was a formality to obey the law; a good portion of us really didn't give a shit about our education because we didn't need the grades for college or university—yes, a lot of us already had our way paid for by our parents.

"You okay?" Gale looked at me with a concerned frown. He was a sweet country boy who was here on a scholarship—aka a charity case for the school—and was someone I considered a true friend.

My emotions were in turmoil due to the recent family drama in my life. "I just... I don't know..." It was the honest truth.

"Listen, if you need a place..." Gale was one of the few friends who knew about my personal life—the full brunt.

Flattening my lips into a grim smile, I reached over and squeezed his hand. "I can't do that to you and your parents. You know the hell my parents would raise." They already made a huge deal about me having friends in general. If they were ever to find out I hung out with a boy, and a 'poor boy' at that, they'd probably have a stroke because it wasn't proper for a lady like me.

Honestly, I wouldn't have friends if they had things their way completely. I'd be cooped up at home, learning to be a good wife and a quiet and meek girl. Too bad they couldn't go against the law. Granted, they tried to pull some strings and homeschool me, but things flopped horribly because they failed to meet the checks and balances. So, in the end, they sent me to public school.

Gale's arms wrapped loosely around me as he sighed. "You shouldn't be letting them treat you like that. I mean, come on, it's the 21st century, and you guys are in America. I know you have things set, but would you be happy? Haven't you often told me and Haven about how you hate business? You have a knack for math, but it's not exciting for you and all of that. I mean, come on, you have the grades, the connections, the money, and everything to go to nearly any college or university you want and make a life for yourself. Just cut yourself away from your family, make your own life." Gale made it sound so simple, and maybe, in a sense, things were clean-cut how he presented them.

If only I had the strength to stand up for myself.

Given everything, my parents weren't horrible by any means. They might not be the most affectionate or attentive, but they kept me fed, clothed, and sheltered. I mean, it could be worse, but compared to my younger brother who was the sun and moon, I was the dying star galaxies away.

"I'll be fine..." I had to. Otherwise, I'd lose it all.

I thought about ditching the family business and living my own life. Needless to say, I nearly got kicked out just for considering it. To keep my trust fund and avoid ending up homeless as a teenager, I had to follow their rules. So, I let go of any dreams my ambitious mind had imagined.

A good, obedient daughter, one who held her head down and obeyed every order without question.

Easy enough, right?

Unfortunately, life wasn't so simple.

Being all my parents asked for and wanted wasn't nearly enough, something I found out that night.

The buzz of the spring break celebration fizzled out when I returned home to my parents standing rather darkly around a suitcase near the front door. Their eyes held such a heaviness to them as they stared at me in a dead silence that made my stomach churn into an endless pit of despair. My despair twisted sickly when I was refused further entry into my home by some guards.

The dreaded questions weighed my tongue down until my mouth opened from the pressure to let them out. "Ma? Ba? What's going on? Are you guys going on another business trip?" It wasn't uncommon for them to be here one minute and gone the next, but I doubt that was the case here with how they bore their grim eyes into me as if I were a dead person.

"No." My mother's blunt answer chilled the tense air more, sending a shiver down my spine.

"Then what's going on?" My survival instincts screamed at me to bolt back out that door and never look back, but years under my parents' thumb made me freeze and fawn.

"You're going to your new home," was the only answer my father gave before nodding in my direction.

Suddenly, hands wrapped themselves around my arms, causing my body to struggle instinctively. "Let me go!" My legs kicked and thrashed around, kicking at the legs of the two men on either side of me to no avail.

My heart could have been mistaken for a racehorse on the track with how violent and fast it beat in my chest as my frantic eyes looked to my parents for help, but the sight of them solemnly standing there with their arms by their sides and their faces unmoving threw my body into a state of limp defeat.

Why aren't they helping me? Why are they sending me away? What's going on?

I opened my mouth to say something, but my father held out a hand for me to stop before I even began. "Just accept it and be good. It's the only thing you're of use for. Be good, and they will treat you decently." Not even a goodbye from either of my parents as the men dragged my struggling body out of the house and into some SUV parked right outside the front door of a mansion where a driver waited.

An endless stream of questions and tears flowed from me, but I was met with nothing, not even a word, in response. Sensing my impending doom, I lunged for the door, only to be stopped by the man sitting beside it. I managed to slip the tip of my finger under the handle and budge it, but the door didn't open even though the lock was disengaged—child-locked. My escape attempt didn't amuse the guard; his hand meeting my face with a harsh slap had made it clear enough.

The man in the passenger seat snapped at the one who hit me right after the impact thundered the silence in the car. "Hey! No damage to the goods unless you want your hand gone." Then, he turned his flat face toward me, "Quit it. Behave and make this shit easier for yourself."

"What is going on, please," I begged through my sobbing tears as I held my stinging cheek with a hand.

"You'll find out soon enough." He gruffed out before turning back around in his seat and ignoring me along with everyone else.

Tension held my breath for longer stretches of time as we entered the bustling city. By the time we reached our destination, a building with a flashing red sign, I was about ready to pass out from the lack of oxygen.

Champion's Lounge

Why did we stop here?

Although I've never been here, my gut told me to fight, to do anything, not to enter this place. Unfortunately, my refusal to leave the car was useless as the men manhandled me out and in through a backdoor to the building. Squeaks of pain slipped through my grunts of effort as my body—particularly my shins—banged against the stairs as the men dragged me up to some office area that overlooked the whole club lounge.

The moment we entered the office, a brunette woman in her late forties looked up at me from her desk with a crooked smile. "Ah, there she is, such a pretty thing, even better than the pictures."

"Please, I am not supposed to be here. There's some mistake." I wasn't even close to 21 years old, so I shouldn't be anywhere near an adult establishment, let alone in one.

"Poor thing, there's no mistake," The devious coo in her voice as she eyed me made me shrink away from the fear and disgust gripping my body. "You belong to me now."

The lady crooked her finger in my direction, and the men dragged me closer and dropped me by her feet after she got up and rounded the desk. "I don't understand, please. I'm really not supposed to be here." I continued to beg, hoping this woman would see some sense and send me away.

Leaning down, the woman grabbed my face with her manicured nails, digging them into my soft flesh until I hissed from the pain. "Your parents made some bad deals with me, and now you have to pay the price for them, simple as that." The bite from her nails harshened with her tightening grip. "But, judging by your reaction, you had no idea about any of this, huh? Poor thing." Talk about an ice-cold bucket of water to my face.

"What?" I didn't want to believe it, and perhaps I misheard.

Letting go of my face, she patted my cheek a few times before standing up and looking down at me with a flat smile. "Doesn't really matter. Just know that your parents had bad deals with me, racked up quite a bit of debt, and their way of paying it off was to have you work off their debt for them. If you do well, then you might be able to pay it off in a few years."

"Work? Years? How much do they owe you? What are you even going to have me do around here? Clean? Work in the kitchen?" Walking around clad in nothing and chatting to men was off the list because I was underage.

Cracking a brief, amused smile, she burst out laughing for a good second before looking at me to see if I was serious. When I made no notion to change my confused and concerned expression, her face straightened back out. "Putting a girl like you into the back would be a huge waste of profits. No, you're going to be paying off your parents' 5.3 million debt with your body."

I visibly paled and physically winced at the number from the lady's lips. What she said before that didn't register until after the fact. "Wha? I can't... No, I won't. I'm not eighteen yet!" I needed to get out of here, get to the cops, report this, and get this place shut down or, at the very least, stir something up.

"Would you be here if I cared about your damn age? I don't care if you are eight. You were sold to me, therefore, I will put you to work. While you are in my possession, you will have no choice but to do what I say. Which, right now, is to spread those young legs of yours and bring me in the big bucks before you become too old to be much use." This lady was sick! There's no way any of this was serious! Things like this didn't happen in real life!

The contents of my stomach churned and threatened to spill out all over the floor.

This is some fucked up nightmare. There's no way something like this is happening to me.

I wasn't some piece of property to be sold and used like this.

All the pent-up anxiety snapped the moment sets of hands grabbed at my arms and dragged me.

I probably sounded and looked like someone mid-exorcism or a person amid a psychotic break as I threw every ounce of my adrenaline-fueled energy into thrashing, biting, and hitting the men who manhandled me down a hallway to throw me into some room.

"No! Please! Let me out! Please!"

Chapter 2

Juliet

~5 days later~

Time ceased to exist since my banishment to this desolate room. I literally couldn't tell time—no clock, no calendar, nothing. The only indication was my clockwork meals. Judging by the three meals a day, I guessed it had been about three, four, maybe five days. I couldn't confirm because anyone who entered—bringing food or supplies—ignored my pleas for answers and help.

It was clear that either they didn't care or had orders not to pay me any attention. I still had no idea what the plan was for me—okay, scratch that, I had an inkling of an idea given what the lady, Lady Heral, as I came to learn her name, told me the first night here. It was the fact and thought of being able to work like *that* which unnerved me to no end.

The lingering scent of rancid bile did nothing to settle my nerves. Even though this dingy prison of mine had an attached bathroom, I was pretty sure the acid from all my vomiting the past few days wore away at the toilet's protective coating and embedded the sour scent of bile into the ceramic. No amount of flushing and scrubbing from the cleaning crew could rid the air of the nauseating scent.

Oh, and the lack of windows didn't help my nonexistent grasp of time. The room had nothing but a small closet, a single bed, and an attached bathroom, all dimly lit with a yellow ceiling light. At least it was better than an actual prison cell, but at least prisoners got yard time and natural light.

But I was no prisoner, so I couldn't accept these conditions, hence why my clothes still sat in my suitcase and strewn about it and not in the closet. If I unpacked and settled, it would mean I accepted the situation, that this place would be my new home. All of which I refuse to do because, like hell, I would let this become my new life. I needed to get out of here, somehow, then go to the cops because this was all highly illegal.

I refused to settle, refused to break.

Question was: how long until I broke? How long could I last until it all becomes too much?

The thought of someone touching me in such violating ways made my skin crawl already.

God, I don't know if I can handle it.

Echoes of the pounding door broke my anxious train of thought to look at the person entering the room. Was it mealtime already? Honestly, maybe it was, couldn't tell because I literally have no way to do so.

Unfortunately, it wasn't some worker to drop off my scheduled meal—though I wished it was. "Good to see you haven't tried to do anything stupid." Lady Heral's cruel voice sent a wave of unease through me. "Get up." The clicks of her obscene heels sounded like nails against a chalkboard. "Get dressed in something good, and put some makeup on. You look dead." Lady Heral barked at me, scowling at the sight of my room.

"No." I hunkered myself down into the bed with my arms crossed. "I'm not going anywhere except out of here." I tried to hide my nerves, which crawled under my skin like spiders. "I'm not going to have my body defiled."

A few long strides were all she needed to close the distance between us with her lanky legs. Scowling deeply, her hand shot out and snatched my face. "Too bad you have no choice in the matter, so you better change your tone and get used to it, or these next few years will be hell for you. So, be good and listen, or we do this the hard way where I have to get some help in here to get you ready."

When I made no indication of complying by glaring back at her and keeping my mouth shut, she slapped me across the face and dragged me off the bed by my hair. "I need some assistance in here!" She shouted towards the door before going over to my suitcase and picking through it with a scowl of disgust. "Ugh, I told them to pack you right. How hard is it to pick the right clothes for a whore house."

"Maybe because I'm not a whore. Therefore, I don't have such clothes. Ever think of that, you bitch?" Wow, I have no idea where the fuck that came from. Honestly, I had no idea that side of me fully existed or was capable of coming out to that extent.

If I ever dared to speak like that to my parents or anyone, I'd be slapped across the face, just like now, by Lady Heral, who darted back to me with a face full of fury. Usually, this would be the point where I apologized profusely and held my head down, but guess I wanted to lie in my grave today. I locked my burning eyes right back at her as she glared at me with anger and disbelief. "You better watch that fucking tongue of yours before I cut it off, and that would be a real shame to lose a part that could make you money while you are here."

Another sharp sting bites my cheek before she stands straight up and throws a white dress at me. "You shouldn't talk bad about whores because that's what you're going to be after tonight. You're not even going to be a person. You will be nothing but a set of holes for people to use for their pleasure until your parents' stupid debt is paid, and by that point, you'll be so far gone you won't know what to do with your life besides this. So, better get comfortable and used to it, you fucking brat."

"Get her washed up, dolled up, and into that dress in the next hour. Don't make her look like a complete whore, though, keep it light, keep that innocence for the men to see and break. It'll also get them to bid more." Okay, now the fight in me ebbed upon hearing that last part.

Pooling the blood up in my mouth, I spat it out at Lady Heral, covering her stocking-covered leg with a bloody spitball. "Wait, bid? What do you? Are you seriously going to put me up like some cattle to be sold at an auction?! You can't do that!"

That's so messed up! There's no way this is happening!

Hissing, Lady Heral grabbed my hair and shoved my face into the ground. "I can do whatever the *hell* I want. I own this damn place and everyone in it, including you. You're lucky you're a virgin. Otherwise, you would have been put to work the very first night. I have lots of men lined up and eager to bid for your stupid unused cunt tonight. Your only saving grace is all the money it will net me."

"You—!" An angry, strangled cry escaped me as I made a lunge for Lady Heral, only to be held back by the workers.

No! Nonono!

I fought the workers tooth and nail; even if it was pointless, I had to try. Every person's worst nightmare, my own included, was about to happen to me. Call me stupid or a hopeless romantic, but I wanted my first time to be special—not like this. I wasn't asking for Mister Right to have my first time with; I was just asking for someone who I was comfortable and willing with.

Everything was for naught, though, because I still ended up on the dreaded stage down on the main floor in a short, skimpy white dress and heels that I tripped over with every step. My useless pleas were quickly silenced by a few more slaps across the face from Lady Heral, who only used my spunk and tears as a further selling point for higher bids from the deplorable men in the crowd.

Waves of numbered signs rose and fell from the crowd as the amount kept growing and growing—my eyes could barely keep up with it all. Combined with the numbers flying out of Lady Heral's mouth, I became overwhelmed easily to the point where I mentally shut down and became numb to everything around me. Lady Heral's voice muffled out to background noise as the crowd became a blur of spots and dots.

Bang!

"Item X483 sold to lucky number 32! Please go claim your item off stage!" We weren't even human anymore. Reduced to being objects labeled by numbers. Livestock were treated more humanely!

Bang!

Shit. When did another bid go by?! I barely even blinked!

Bang!

No! Stop! Stop banging that stupid hammer!

Bang!

No! Shit! Wait! Why was the girl next to me leaving the stage!? No!

Bang!

My heart exploded with the sound of the gavel banging. I felt like a criminal on trial who just got sentenced—might as well have been the case here. Every fiber of my being fell away from me as the severity of my situation stripped my freedom. Each breath scratched at my throat, burned my lungs, and every inhale and exhale felt shorter than the last.

My mind severed itself from my body as I numbingly watched the guards come up to the stage and retrieve me, and my body reacted instinctively to the touch of the men, instantly kicking into fight mode. Unfortunately, no one twitched an eyebrow in my direction when the men dragged me off, kicking and screaming.

Heartless bastards, every single one of them!

A sharp chill of fear straightened my spine at the sight of the room filled with men when the guards hauling me kicked open some doors and shoved me in. "There she is, boys. Better be sure to get our money's worth tonight." Some middle-aged man with thinning hair and dead gray eyes grinned at me with a dark glint as his lanky form approached my crumpled one on the floor.

Swallowing the nervous lump in my throat, I slowly scanned the rest of the men, instantly regretting it when their presence made me feel pathetic. "What's going on? Why are there so many of you in here?" Why were there so many men in here? And why were they looking at me so wickedly like I was some meal to be torn into?

The man ignored my question as he reached down and grabbed a fistful of my hair. "Look at her, so terrified, *fuck*, it's going to be so fun breaking you." His alcohol-laced breath burned my face like warm acid when it hit me from how close he lowered his head down to me. "You belong to me for the next three hours to do and use however I want, and I decided to be nice to my men for being loyal to me and share you after I make you bleed."

"No, please, please don't, please, I don't want to, I don't want it, please." I hated how pathetic I sounded and felt with my pointless pleading. Did I want to shed tears and feed that evil burning fire in his eyes more? No, I didn't, but I couldn't control my reactions as the situation fully sank into me.

Sobbing, I tried to lean away from the man when he leaned in close and sniffed the length of my neck, but his grip held me firm. Then, instinctively, my hand lashed across the man's face when he suddenly licked my tears off my cheek with a chuckle. His hand reacted to the impact by returning a slap that rattled my brain in my head. "Go ahead and fight. Makes it more fun." Tightening his grip on my hair, he dragged me over and onto the ratty-looking bed.

Even when my limbs felt like they would pop out of their sockets from my violent struggle, I didn't let up one bit. Pretty sure I dislocated a shoulder from jerking my body against the man who joined and held my arm down.

Fucking cowards, assholes, bastards.

At least the fact that this pathetic man needed four of his helpers to subdue a girl like me gave me some pride.

Unfortunately, it didn't last long. I thought I could remain strong and keep whatever dignity I had left intact, but everything shattered like glass when his disgusting hands touched my bare and exposed body. "No, no, no! Please don't, please! Please!"

Pain. Pure pain and torture for the next. Well, I don't know how long it actually was, but it felt like an eternity in Hell for me with what my body was put through. I thought having my innocence ripped away by the disgusting bastard was bad, but he was the least painful. The other men jerked my broken body around like I was a ragdoll, not caring one bit about leaving marks or hurting me as long as they could get their disgusting dicks in any hole they could.

I honestly thought it would be over the moment they were done, but if only it were just physical.

Psychologically, they broke me as well.

My mind and body didn't feel like my own after they were done and left. I was so disconnected that I barely registered my body moving.

Deep down, I knew trying to run away would be pointless; they would find me sooner rather than later and drag me back to the hell hole until my sentence was served. Yet, the moment the men left and stupidly left the door ajar, the last of my fight spurred my body forward. There wasn't a single thought behind my actions when I grabbed my tattered dress haphazardly, pulled it onto my body, and forced my pained body through the hallways and out some backdoor.

I was alive; the freezing night air hitting my shivering body as I mindlessly dragged myself into the streets was a good indicator of my live body. Yet, I felt empty, void of everything. I felt like a shell.

My wobbly legs threatened to give out any second as my body continued to push itself forward with no certain direction in mind. I needed help. But where?

Where do I go from here? Where can I go?

Like a broken dam, my once-empty mind flooded with endless trains of erratic thoughts. Between trying to figure out what to do and where to go, there was a constant and unconscious thought to keep on moving. No matter how much my shaky legs ached, my body pushed my limbs out of a basal need to survive.

My choppy steps continued until a hard impact threw my body to the ground.

Thankfully, I was so out of it that I barely felt the car.

Chapter 3
Luciano

THUD!

It was impossible to discard the sound of a body hitting a car after all these years in my line of work. Well, at least it wasn't my fault since I wasn't driving.

"Sir, I'm so sorry, she came out of nowhere." My driver, Marcos, apologized profusely, with a worried look at me.

Holding up a hand, I unbuckled my belt and opened the door to step out with Marcos. "It's fine. Let's just check the person and make sure they are fine. Get them to an ambulance if need be." Hopefully, the person would be too drunk to remember anything, or better yet, dead. A dead body would be a lot easier to deal with than a live body that could turn back and press charges.

"*Merda!*" Needless to say, my mind quickly changed about the person wanting to be dead when my amber eyes landed on the beat-up girl. Squatting down, I picked the female up into my arms, being careful to be extra gentle when I felt how tiny she was.

"Oh shit... I barely hit her." Marcos commented, his wide eyes running down her body to take in the damage as mine were doing until I snapped at him with a growl.

Shifting her in my arms, I shed my suit jacket to wrap it around her barely decent body. "Hey, calm down," I tried to soothe her shivering body, "I'm going to get you an ambulance—"

Her dazed eyes instantly clamped shut as her head shook violently. "No! No, please don't, they'll—"

A faint thud rang out in the distance, followed by approaching footsteps and heavy breaths. "Found her!" A male voice echoed off to the side of me.

I didn't like the urgency and irritation in his voice.

"Damn it." Another voice joined the first. "Sir, step—"

Before the man could fully address me, I drew my gun out and pointed it at both of them. "If I hear any more interruptions tonight, I'm gonna make sure you never get the chance to do it again."

The two men looked at me warily with their guns lowered next to them. Judging from their attire, they're guards for the club behind them. "Listen, we don't want any trouble. We're just doing our jobs. We just need the girl back." The one I cut off before spoke up with a nervous swallow as he tucked his gun away.

My eyes broke away from the workers when the girl in my arm struggled and freaked out. "No, please, no, no, no." The fear in her voice flipped something within me, making my body fill with an urge to put myself between her and these men.

"Hey," I said in a firm voice, tightening my arm around her to keep her body from twisting around too much. "Stop, you're going to hurt yourself more. I won't hand you over to them." I assured her with an unwavering expression.

"Just kill me, please... They'll find me and take me when you leave. Just kill me, please. Please, I don't, I can't go back there." The girl—well, I guess she wasn't a girl if she came from the club—broke down completely in my arms. It was sad to see all the fight from her leave in an instant, and the fact she so readily begged for death irked me.

My jaw ticked as my finger twitched towards the trigger. I kept myself from unloading into the two idiots who'd come to retrieve this poor, battered woman. "You two are going to march straight to Lady Heral and tell her I want to see her at my office tomorrow morning at 10 o'clock sharp." She'd be lucky to leave the place alive.

The two men who looked at each other and me for a few seconds with uncertainty. Then, when they showed no signs of moving, I looked at my driver. "Marcos, go tell Lady Heral—"

"We'll do it, Mr. Agosti." Even though I got a response from one of them, I wasn't fond of him cutting me off. So, I pulled the trigger and sent a bullet by his feet.

Deepening a scowl on my face, I kept my hard glare trained on them as I spoke up in a gravelly voice. "I already warned you. *Never* interrupt me lest you want your tongue removed." My eyes narrowed dangerously with a grave warning. "Do I make myself clear?" The men were quick to nod in response. "I don't appreciate your lingering and hesitance with my order. Carol might cut your checks, but do not forget who funds her and who is in charge at the end of the day. Now, get out of my sight before I have a different message sent to Carol Heral."

After the two men scrambled away, I turned my full attention back to the trembling female against me. "You should've just killed me. She's going to come after you and cause trouble." Did nothing of what I said before sink into her mind? Well, it wouldn't surprise me if nothing got through with her being in such a shocked state.

What did surprise me was her sudden lurch for my gun, which remained drawn but lowered at my side. "Hey! Stop that!" The way she flinched at my slightly raised voice had me frowning in regret as I felt her shut herself from me.

Taking a deep breath, I flicked the safety back on before tucking my piece away to use both arms to pick her up and hold her close. "I'm not going to let anything else happen to you. You are safe now. She won't touch you nor will anyone touch you with me around. I will protect you."

The reasonable thing to do would be to take her to the hospital and let things go, but I couldn't, not after that little exchange. Granted, if this were anyone else, then I would've taken them to the hospital and left them there. Yet, the way her dull, broken, cooper brown eyes flashed with hope and desperation for a split second when she looked at me clawed my heart. I couldn't get those haunting eyes out of my mind when I tried. I knew if I left her, I'd regret it for the rest of my life.

Carrying her to the car, I settled her into the back seat next to me before instructing my driver to take us home. "Why? I'm nobody." Her soft voice squeaked up as she curled her legs up to her chest. "Should've just killed me."

"That'd be a waste, for one," I replied curtly before softening my voice. "I am doing this because it is right, and something about you, something deep under, is reaching out for some salvation." I may be a killer, but women weren't high on my list of easy kills; she didn't need to know that, of course. "Rest, we can talk more when we return to my place."

"Just dump me off a bridge. I don't need or want your pity. Save and use it on someone who matters." Her melodramatic attitude made me want to roll my eyes and snark at her, but I held my tongue.

Unfortunately, this was not the time or place for any of that. It was clear she'd been through a lot, and whatever happened broke her. I would be a monster to add more to her troubles. Besides, attacking vulnerable women wasn't my forte.

Mobster, not monster; a very fine distinction.

Relenting to a tiny, broken girl like her was laughable. I was a feared mafia boss who showed no mercy to anyone. I should be telling her to suck it up and let her fend for herself because what else did she expect from a place like Champion's Lounge? You don't go into a place like that and expect easy work. Judging from the men who came after her, she was a worker who left mid-shift. Lady Heral didn't send her men after patrons for leaving.

On the other hand, this woman shouldn't be so beat up looking. Yeah, some people loved it rough, but from how she acted, there was no way she consented. I've seen my fair share of the aftermath of rough encounters, but they were tame compared to her ghastly state. It was hard to tell the full extent of her injuries in the dimly lit car—and the dark streets from before offered little insight, too—but I could see a badly busted lip, something at her eyebrow, and honestly, most of her face seemed fucked up.

She was probably beyond exhausted with how easily she knocked out after a few blinks of her eyes. She shouldn't think so lowly of herself because she could be in the worst position in life right now. At least she had a roof over her head working at the lounge, money coming in.

The more I thought about it, the more I wondered why I was even bothering with this ungrateful brat.

Simple, really: I was a good person at heart.

Yeah, laugh it up. A ruthless mafia boss having some goodness in his heart. It was ironic that I turned out how I did, given my name, Luciano. Granted, I don't think my mother foresaw this future for me when she named me.

I might not have much—or any—light in me, but I definitely had rage and lots of it, especially when I saw the damage done to this woman's body in the full light of the guest room. Regret was something I seldom felt, but it hit me hard when we'd gotten home, and I carried her up to the guest bedroom, where I settled her on the bed and flicked the lamp on. Yeah, I felt a little bad about thinking ill of her. Sex worker or not, she didn't deserve to be in such a state.

Most of her delicate body remained swallowed up by my jacket, but her face, hands, and shapely legs perfectly displayed to me. If only they were in pristine condition as they should be. "Gia!" I didn't mean to sound so loud, but my anger slipped through as the sight of the blood and semen staining her thighs burned itself into my mind.

"Yes, sir? Oh my!" The sharp gasp from my loyal housekeeper sliced into me as sharply. "Luciano! You better—"

"Oh God no, Gia, you raised me better." If it were any of my other staff members, then I wouldn't let them have such a tone with me. Gia was different; the older woman had been a part of my life ever since I could remember. She practically raised me after my mother passed, so I have a special place in my dead heart for her. Besides my biological mother, she was the only other motherly figure I knew and had in my life.

After a few deep breaths and gripping at my hair, I turned to leave. "I found her like that... I couldn't leave her... Listen, I can't—can you get her cleaned up and changed? I'll have Leah check her out in the morning while she's still here." I feared my anger would build and explode if I saw any more damage to the poor girl's body.

"Of course, I will take good care of her. You go change and eat. Dinner is on the table for you." Gia told me with a sad smile as she kept her eyes on the slumbering woman, who really did look more like a girl.

What happened to you?

Who did this to you?

Chapter 4
Juliet

THIS CAN'T BE HEAVEN; there's too much pain for it to be paradise.

I'd rather be hit by that car again than wake up, *if* I can even wake up. Everything felt so heavy, almost like my body was out of my control. My eyelids refused to open, and they felt like they were super glued shut.

"...Wa...ing..." Well, at least the soft voice sounded like an angel.

A wave of needles assaulted my body at the feeling of something touching my arm, and a whimper of pain left me instinctively. "Sorry." I heard the same voice apologize as I forced my eyes to open against their will. "Good morning, sweetie."

It took a few heavy blinks for the face of the Asian woman to come into focus, but her gentle smile sent a wave of ease through me even though she was a complete stranger to me. I opened my mouth to ask the flood of questions in my mind, but my parched throat refused to cooperate. The only sound that came out of me was my own coughs as I went into a tearful fit.

Instinctively, I sipped at the water when I felt the rim of the cup press against my lips. "Slow, slow, and small sips." The woman maintained her soft and calm demeanor as she spoke to me. "It's okay. I'll keep things as simple as possible. I'm Doctor Nguyen, but you can call me Leah if that makes you feel more comfortable. Luciano called me in to make sure you're okay and to look you over. Is that alright with you? It looks like you've been through a lot, so if you want a moment to yourself and want me to come back in a bit, then that is completely fine with me."

Digging through her bag by the bedside, she pulled out a notepad with a pen and handed it to me. "Here, your throat's probably killing you, so go ahead and use that to communicate for now until you feel comfortable to speak." I didn't want to see a doctor or anyone right now, but she didn't seem too bad. "Are you fine with all of this right now?"

Taking a deep breath, I nodded before gripping the pen. Might as well get this done and over with, and I can have some peace and quiet after all of it. "What's your name?"

"Juliet."

"Okay, hello Juliet, can you write down your birthday for me?" She continued with a kind smile on her face.

"04/21/2005."

"Oh, happy birthday..." The smile on her face quickly faded with her voice when the dots connected for her. Regret instantly filled her eyes, and she looked at me apologetically and sympathetically, "I am so sorry."

Unable to help it, I let my full body break into a full sob when it hit me fully. I had no concept of time in the place, so naturally, I had no clue about the date. I don't know exactly if it passed midnight before I was brutally raped repeatedly, but either way, it probably happened into or on my birthday despite the start time.

Fucking happy birthday to me.

A fucked-up way for me to go into adulthood.

Completely lost and helpless.

The feeling of warmth slipping into my palm made me jump from the surprise, but I didn't pull away from Leah's comforting touch. Even though Leah maintained a smile on her face, I saw a slight twitch at the corner of her lip. "Do you feel comfortable telling me what happened to you?"

Hesitating, I wanted to nod my head because I knew it needed to come out sooner rather than later, yet I froze up. I couldn't bring myself to agree to write out my ordeal. Well, to be fair, I didn't want to recount and relive the trauma of it all. I wanted to forget. I wanted to shut it all out, lock it away, shove it in a black hole, burn it to ashes, and pretend it all never happened.

"Hey." Her hand grasped my trembling one. "We can come back to this when you're ready. I understand it's not an easy thing for me to ask of you."

Unable to hold it in, I broke down again. Tears burned their way down my cheeks before landing on the notepad, and my whole body ached and shook with my sobs. Every blink of my eyes brought me back to that damn place. My stomach started to churn with the flood of memories. I knew I wasn't there, that I was safe elsewhere for now, but it felt like some hole sucked me back into the middle of everything.

I nearly jumped out of my own skin when the door suddenly slammed open to reveal a familiar man. Only this time, his face was taut, and his wide eyes searched the room until they landed on me. "What's wrong? What happened? Is she okay? Why is she crying?" His questions flew out with his hurried steps as he dropped by my bedside and searched my body with concern.

"Luciano!" Leah gave the man a scolding glare. "Some privacy, please." She wasn't asking with that hard tone.

Clearing his throat, he put on a straight face. "I heard crying."

"Wow, didn't know the Devil of the Syndicate had a functioning heart." Leah snarked with a roll of her eyes before turning her attention back to me and hugging me tightly. "Ignore him, he's a big idiot." She whispered in my ear with a snicker.

Yeah, no, not after hearing what she said. The comfort from her hug did little to settle the chill that stiffened my body. Don't know whether or not this situation was any better. I ran away from hell, but straight into the Devil's arms. I never thought I'd say this, but I think I would have been better off at the lounge.

Anyone who knew about the East Coast Syndicate knew about the reputation of its members, particularly the Devil of the Syndicate. Now, I never bothered with the mafia because I never had any inclination to get involved in crime, but I wasn't blind or deaf to the rumors and stories. Word on the street—well, in the whole state—was that they basically ran the city. Everyone was in their pockets, and of course, they're not the nicest of people around with all the illegal shit they do.

From what I know, The Syndicate has five members: Luciano, Aidan, Sebastian, Ares, and Cornelia. The five of them effectively and collectively ran all of New York and Florida. I knew Luciano and Aidan resided in New York while Sebastian and Ares kept business going down in Florida; I don't know much about Cornelia, though, but not much was known about them in general because they kept to the background.

Considering his fame, I probably should've recognized Luciano, but I also didn't pay attention to many things, including the media. He may be rich and famous, but I gave no care for any of that because he ran in a completely different circle than my family or me. My family would probably be considered lower middle class to him if we were to compare our net worth and wealth. Also, I never paid attention to him because he was like my parents' age, I think.

But Luciano Agosti, aka the Syndicate's Devil, had a reputation for being cruel beyond human comprehension, from what I've heard. He was the most feared among the five for his savagery. I think I once heard that he tore a man apart with his bare hands and brute strength, which I can somewhat see given his hulking figure. Hell, he could probably break my spine with a flick of his finger and stomp me to smithereens without much effort.

A ruthless bastard. The Devil incarnate. The one who fucking saved me when no one else would bat an eye in my direction.

God, how fucked up is the world that the Devil saved me?

Guess the shock of the situation won over my sanity because I started to shake with laughter and uncontrollable tears. This was beyond absurd.

"Oh, for fuck's sake, leave, you're triggering her." From the corners of my eyes, I watched Leah reach over and whack Luciano with the notepad after snatching it from me. "Get! Go to your stupid meeting. I've got her all taken care of, so get!"

Luciano's jaw clenched with a scowl before he clicked his tongue and relented. "Fine. You're lucky I have that meeting." He grumbled with a scoff before shooting me a quick look of concern, which hardened back up to dullness in a split second right as he turned to leave.

"How about I leave you for a moment to get you something to drink and eat. Then we can take this nice and slow, alright? Do you think you can do that? Or do you want to try this in a few hours? Maybe tomorrow?" At least she sounded sincere and didn't look at me with eyes full of pity.

Slowly, I grabbed the notepad to scribble my answers down. "Food please. Soup? Something warm? I feel icky. Try after food." I sounded like a toddler, but I couldn't find the strength to write out full sentences. I just wanted to lay back down, curl up under the blanket, and sink into a black hole of nothing.

"Alright, sounds good to me. Lay down and get comfortable while I'm gone." The warm smile on her face eased me some before everything came creeping back in when the sunshine left with her out the door.

The safety net snapped under me as I lay there and wallowed in my own thoughts. I was so lost. What the hell was I supposed to do now? The thought of going back home to my parents crossed my mind, but I quickly burned the idea to ashes because they're the ones who put me into this damn situation. What's to stop them from sending me back to the lounge if I went back? Especially if they owed money that I was supposed to be paying off with my body. But God, how fucked up could they be to send their underage daughter to be a prostitute? Well, scratch that, not underage anymore, but I was still their own flesh and blood.

Those dead eyes of theirs still haunt me. When I looked back for help and saw nothing, they looked at me with such a void in their eyes, as if I meant nothing to them. They're my parents, and they're supposed to care and protect me, not discard me like trash or toss me to the wolves.

I didn't know what to do now. The cops seemed like a good idea last night, but now I have my doubts. What would the cops even do? They couldn't arrest Lady Heral based on my word alone, and I doubt they'd find anything from searching the place. Maybe I could ask Luciano—no, I can't. I can't get involved with the mafia. Besides, what do I even have to bargain with?

I literally have nothing. I don't have clothes of my own, no phone, no wallet, no ID, nada, zip, nothing. I don't even know if I had my own mind and sanity intact. Well, at least I had some dignity left, I think. My own broken body didn't feel like my own anymore after those men forced themselves on me repeatedly for what felt like hours on end. I felt dirty, soiled, ruined. I wanted to peel my own skin off and get a new one—shed everything away.

Tears of anger and sadness burned at my beat-up face. This was pathetic of me, but I couldn't control it. I didn't want to cry, to be weak, but the tears just came and came and didn't stop.

Hopelessness clawed and dragged me down into the abyss until unhealthy thoughts of wanting to leave this life consumed me again.

Maybe it would be better if I ceased to exist.

Chapter 5
Luciano

"Are you sure I can't kill this bitch?" Leah's voice rang into my ears.

Sighing heavily, I rubbed my temples and peered over my hand at Leah, who flitted around the kitchen, throwing a meal together. "Not without a damn good reason, and even then, I get to take out the trash because it's my problem. Her damn business is within my territory, so the fact something like this happened right under my nose." Yeah, that got my blood boiling.

Like the others in The East Coast Syndicate, I ran a clean business. Every business within our territories had a set of laws they had to abide by, lest they want to face our wrath. Our concrete laws were simple: elderly, children, and innocent bystanders were never to be involved in any kind of illegal or illicit activities; no trafficking humans; any and all underground and illegal activities were to be run by a standing Syndicate member; and pay your damn fees to The Syndicate.

We were only dirty because we ran illicit weapons and drugs, had our hands dipped into the underground and black market in the state, and partook in some trafficking of goods, but that was about it. Still, with everything going on, we held the reins. Black market or not, there were things never to be sold or used. It was ironic for a ruthless mafia to talk about morals, rights and wrongs, and whether things were humane. But what was the point of having total power and control if it can't be used for our desires?

Besides that, we were all fucked up people in our own ways.

"At least let me cut up her face and let her suffer for a few days before you kill her." Leah's grumbling pulled me from my thoughts with a chuckle.

"Tempting, I'll think about it." I honestly might because some shame and humiliation before a brutal death sounded lovely.

"She deserves worse. I mean, there's no way this girl is the first. Lady Heral's been in business before we took over, so imagine how much has happened before and probably after." Leah, having the most heart out of all of us, was rightfully upset and probably correct.

There's no way this girl was her first offense. Which pissed me off because, again, it meant she'd been doing this right under my nose. It made me wonder just exactly how long she'd been at this until this little slip-up. How long would things have gone on if this girl hadn't escaped and my car hadn't hit her? What if I hadn't been held up at the meeting? I could have easily missed her, and things would have gone on.

Gritting my teeth, I took a deep breath while deepening my scowl. "Has she said anything? The girl. How is she doing?" Therein lies my second problem.

What the fuck am I to do with her?

"Juliet. Her name's Juliet." Leah corrected me with a stern look before going back to tossing stuff onto some food tray. "But no, she hasn't said anything. She hasn't been able to. I wish I could say she's doing fine, but I haven't been able to examine her yet. Clearly, she's not fine. No one is ever fine if they come out one end looking like they got jumped in an alleyway. Poor thing literally just turned eighteen, as her birthday is today."

"What?!" I hadn't meant to snap, but hearing the last bit caught me off guard.

"She was seventeen up until now based on the birthdate that she gave me." Leah gave out a heavy and sad sigh, shaking her head in shame as she passed me with the food tray. "She wasn't legal when she entered that place."

As I was about to offer Leah a helping hand, one of my men appeared to let me know of Lady Heral's arrival. My already sour mood rotted and turned foul as I entered my office, where the baneful woman and her guards occupied. "You know why I called for this meeting, Caroline?" I wasn't in the mood for any bullshit, and my curt, sharp tone meant I was in a foul mood.

"You can't just send your men barging into my business like that." Maybe she lacked far more brain cells than I credited her for.

"I can, and I did." I raised my voice a little to put myself higher in the room. "It may be your business, but do not forget who you work for at the end of the day." Giving her a pointed look, I continued, "You know the rules, Caroline, and you're lucky I didn't blow your brains out last night. I suggest you start coming up with excuses and ways to beg for your life while my men tear apart the lounge from the basement up." Gives me more time to think of ways to deal with her. A quick death would be too easy. I needed to send a message to everyone else with her.

"Listen, I don't know—"

Caroline flinched at the sudden boom my hand made against my desk when I slammed it down. "Don't fucking bullshit me, Caroline. That girl came from your club, and your men went after her to collect her. She's seventeen. Seven. Teen. Not only is she underage, but you also broke the rules." Okay, she *was* seventeen, but Caroline didn't need to know that—besides, I wanted more reason to set fire to her right now.

"She snuck in, got into something she shouldn't have, and threatened to go to the cops. That's why I sent my men after her. I needed them to collect her so I could deal with her correctly." A plausible story, but she shouldn't be in such a state if that were the case.

Surely, if something *that* unsavory happened within the walls of Caroline's business, then she'd know and put a stop to it before it got out of hand. Besides, Juliet was much too broken to fit the story Caroline tried to weave with me. Juliet's eyes were filled with fear and desperation before they became desolate when her light faded to almost nothing.

Honestly, I wouldn't have bothered taking her back to my home if she were anyone else. But something about her reached deeply into me and gripped at my soul the moment her warm, brown eyes landed on me. Even though she remained in a flighty state, I saw the way her eyes relaxed upon the sight of me.

Usually, the sight of me brought fear and terror, but she looked so relieved, comforted, and safe. She marveled at me as if I was her salvation.

"Why do you even care about some stupid little teenager anyway? Just release her back to me, and I'll deal with it all so you can keep your hands clean and happy. You already have a lot on your hands, and surely you don't need this nuisance either." She seemed a little too eager to get her hands on Juliet, though. The over-stretched smile with the taut eyes plucked at my nerves that already stood on end.

Seething out a low growl, I gripped the desk's edges and narrowed my eyes at Caroline. "Because she came stumbling out of your establishment like a damn zombie. No, wait, let me rephrase that: because that *teenager* came stumbling out of your establishment beaten, bloodied, and halfway to Death. Obviously, you're incapable of handling a damn child because if you had a handle on her, then she wouldn't have gotten into the lounge in the first place, and if you somehow did, then she shouldn't have gotten into such a dire situation to end up in the state she did. Since it's blatantly obvious that you cannot handle her, I won't be handing her over to you to fuck things up further. Why was she even there? Children like her don't exactly break into lounges at that hour of the night for shit and giggles." Time to see what I could pull from her.

Remaining tight-lipped, Caroline averted her eyes from me until I pounded a fist onto the desk to snap her attention back to my stern face. "Quit wasting my time, Caroline. I have much better things to waste my time on than you." I seethed through a scowl. "Whether you leave here in one piece is up to you. I am prepared to dispose of you right here, right now, and deal with the bullshit of your pathetic death." Taking in a deep breath, I kept a lid on my rising anger. "So, if you want to leave here alive, I suggest you start telling the truth."

The older woman's shoulders deflated with a long sigh, and her eyes averted from me to the side for a split second. "Her parents owe me money, bad deals, about 5.3 million. She was just there to work it off however she could. They told me she was going to be eighteen in a few days." It wasn't a lie, but I sensed she held something back. "Listen, she knew her reason for being there, and how she worked off the debt was up to her. There are plenty of things to do at the lounge. She's seventeen, so she's legal to work—"

I quickly snapped at her with a snarl, "Only in certain establishments and to a certain time only. You have to be at least eighteen to work in an adult-only establishment. So, your point is moot and rounds us back to the point of the fact that she should have been nowhere near or in the lounge. Which, again, brings us back to my point of you being irresponsible, so no, I won't be handing Juliet over to you."

I wanted to swipe the smirk off her face with a knife. "Oh? First name basis, are we? Is there another reason why you won't return her to me? I don't see why else you'd be making such a big deal unless you're involved with her." Damn snake, trying to turn this back around on me. "You and I both know debts need to be paid by any means, and don't act as if some of your staff are here of their own volition."

"Of course, I'd be on a first-name basis with my betrothed. I'm making a big deal because you touched what is mine. She was promised to me to relieve a debt owed to me, and we are to wed once she is of legal age. I wasn't allowed around her until she turned eighteen and graduated high school, but given the new circumstances, my presence in her life is needed now. She is payment to me, my possession, my soon-to-be wife, mine."

What. The. Fuck!

I mentally strangled and scolded myself for the uncontrolled words that flew out of my mouth without a single thought. Why the hell had I said such a lie? It was beyond stupid and unbelievable... Or so I thought.

Now, I couldn't fucking believe that she fell for it. "You two are arranged to be married? Since when? I've never heard about this." Disbelief and anger twisted at her frowning face.

Seeing her anger made me want to smirk because it meant I got under her skin. We strongly disliked each other; that was clear to nearly everyone in the territory. I didn't care; she could despise me all she wanted, but that didn't change the fact that I remained in charge and that she answered to me. I hated her because she liked pushing boundaries with me and fighting my rule.

Caroline was older than me by a good chunk of years and wasn't too keen on having someone dictate her ways. She, along with some others, resisted the syndicate takeover. Though they complied now, I could feel their burning eyes whenever I turned my back. They wanted me gone so things would return to the Wild West ways of before. Caroline and they wanted to be the top dogs again, which will never happen while I'm alive.

She was a snake poised to strike, just waiting for the perfect opportunity—one I couldn't afford to give her. It was clear Juliet was different based on the fact that I saved her last night, which was something out of character for me. Truthfully, Juliet was different, whether I wanted to admit it or not. I knew she was in good hands with Leah, and there was no one else I'd trust more than Leah when it came to anything medical. Yet, I couldn't help but worry about the poor female.

I could barely sleep last night because every time I shut my eyes, hers would flash to the forefront of my mind. Those helpless eyes pleading with me with such stark desperation before relief melted her eyes when I told her I'd protect her. Although short-lived, her lips had curled softly into a happy smile when she leaned into me for a split second; she had felt safe before everything came crashing back down on her, making her shut herself down and pull away from me.

I wanted to deny it; deny that Juliet was just another girl, but I couldn't. I felt this need to shield her, shelter and protect her, and keep her safe and happy. One hit was all it took for me to be entangled with her.

All of that had to be hidden, though. I couldn't let my enemies use Juliet against me. Putting her under syndicate protection without any valid or good reason would make it too obvious that she meant something to at least one of us. Since I would be the one to make that order, the target would be painted on my back with a flashing sign above my head. So, the next—and only—best thing I could think of was marriage. If I made the marriage seem arranged, then that would just look like another business deal, something predatory businesspeople like Caroline would clearly understand and not question.

"It happened a little over five years ago when her parents made some bad calls at Galewood Casino and bit off more than they could chew. Owed me more than their worth, and I guess slimeballs will be slimeballs because they offered me their sweet little daughter." Taking a deep breath, I settled back in my seat and swept a hand across my stubbled jaw. "Now, if I were truly a fucked-up bastard, then I would have taken her then and there, but I'm an honorable and proud man. So, the deal was that Juliet would belong to me, and after she turned eighteen, then, she was to officially become my wife before the end of the year. In the meantime, she'd remain in the care of her parents, grow up like a normal kid, graduate high school, and the wedding would take place sometime before the year is over."

After another brief pause to breathe, I continued my deceit. "I didn't want to impede on her life, nor would it have been healthy for me to obsess over some child because I'm not some pedophile. I kept my distance throughout the years, focused on my own and Syndicate businesses. I didn't recognize her initially because I hadn't seen her since her younger teen years, but when it hit me, let's just say you're lucky I didn't storm your place and burn it down to the ground after ripping your head off your body. I thought I could keep this under wraps and make everything seem seamless, but you provoked me."

I could see the gears turning behind Caroline's irritated eyes as she glared at me. "And the Chau's have said nothing to you or reached out to you regarding their debt to me?"

"No, they aren't exactly the most cooperative people. They barely manage to keep up their end of the bargain of giving me updates about Juliet throughout the years. Guess we should stop doing business with them because they're not too trustworthy." I lied smoothly through a fake, charming smile.

"Well, I hope you forgive my discrepancy this time. I was unaware that she is your betrothed. I look forward to your upcoming nuptials and will be awaiting the invitation." She might as well have said that with a nasty scowl on her face rather than squeeze her venomous words through a saccharine smile.

My pretend smile quickly turned twisted in response. "No, you are not forgiven. How much of your profits will go to me over the next year will depend on what my men find in their sweep and after I am done with my own personal investigation. I suggest you go back to business as usual and follow the fucking rules before you sign your death warrant indefinitely."

"Now, get out of my sight. I've wasted enough time on you today. I need to attend to my future bride."

Chapter 6
Juliet

"Is he really The Syndicate Devil?"

The rawness of my abused throat made me grimace with my words. Even though the dryness and aching dulled out after some fluids and the warm bowl of soup that Leah brought me, it still hurt to talk.

Leah didn't pause her physical examination of me as she replied, "Yeah, but don't let that stupid moniker get to you. He really is a big squishy underneath it all. He is literally the cuddly bear personified. Really, don't let him intimidate you. Not gonna lie, yeah he is as ruthless as people make him out to be, but only to those on the wrong end of it all. He doesn't go around eating children for meals or anything. I mean, he's kinda rough a little under the surface, too... But deep, deep down, he's mushy. He has a very good heart, though, or at least it's right where it counts."

Yeah, not sure how to take all of that because their definition of good could very well be different from mine. "Is he safe for me to be around?" I peered up from my lashes while nervously fiddling my fingers.

He felt safe last night, and if I was honest, he still felt a little safe. Yes, his huge size scared the fuck out of me, but there was this hardness in his eyes, this determination when he looked at me, that made me feel safe in his presence. Yet, I didn't want to be around him out of fear of his capabilities. Besides, what if he wasn't this 'good' man Leah made him out to be? What if he was an actual devil without other people around? He could very well be my next tormentor, my next abuser, assaulter, and I wouldn't be able to stop him.

"He's the safest option for you right now besides the others in the syndicate. While you are under his protection, no one, and I mean *no one*, will dare look your way, let alone think about touching you again." Leah's confidence in her words made me feel a little better about being here.

Unfortunately, I couldn't help but feel out of place still. This wasn't my home; I felt like an intruder, an unwanted guest. "Why is he even putting up with me? I'm a stranger to him, a complete nobody. I mean, I'm thankful for him saving me last night and bringing me here and having you check me out, and I don't know how I will repay him because I literally have nothing." My words trailed on when my rambling picked up until tears streamed down my face again.

I didn't shut up until Leah pulled me into a tight hug and soothed me. "Hey, don't think about all of that. If Luciano didn't want you here, then you'd be at a hospital or one of our shelters. He isn't one to pick people off the streets and bring them to his private home. And don't think badly about yourself like that. You are somebody. You might be a little lost, but you exist. Don't let what happened define you because it doesn't. How you respond to it all does."

"I really am nothing, though. My parents abandoned me, fucking sold me to a damn brothel, basically. I have no money. I don't even have my own clothes or anything. Whatever self-respect and dignity I had was taken last night by those monsters along with my body." Dejected, I exhaled heavily. "I just... I don't feel like a person anymore, just some shell, some dirty and used thing. I feel worse than trash. I don't even want to live anymore."

My own body felt so disgusting to me, and my mind was constantly plagued with the horrors of my ordeal. Phantom pain lingered and flared at the memories until they felt real again. Even if those men were no longer here physically, everything they did lingered. No one would want me after this. Used goods, trash, junk, that's what I was now.

Even though the marks on my body will heal, seeing all the bruises in the shape of hands and fingers from where they held me down or forced my body into positions against my will made me want to hurl. Bruises, abrasions, and lacerations littered my body, and they served as a constant reminder of my assault whenever I looked at myself.

I couldn't escape it even though I escaped that damn place. Every time I closed my eyes, I was sucked back to the place. Hell, every time I blinked, I would be back on that vile stage. Every thump of my heart reminded me of the gavel banging against the podium.

Even my own body served as a mocking reminder with all the bruises, scrapes, cuts, and aching pain that refused to go away.

Leah smiled at me sadly as she helped dress me back up into the oversized shirt and boxers. "We'll make sure you make it through this. I will leave you to rest. You seem like you need it. I'm going to make some phone calls to get a therapist set up for you as well. Unfortunately, mental health isn't my forte." Leah softly chuckled with a warm smile.

"What do I do now?" I shrunk into the bed, bundling myself tightly in the soft sheets.

"I'll let you and Luciano talk that one out. Technically, you can do whatever you want, but I feel like that's a conversation for you and Luciano to have." Leah flashed me another smile before packing her stuff up. "I'll have the test results over the span of the next few days, and I'll call you, err well, I guess I'll call Luciano and have him give the phone to you since you don't have a phone right now. Either way, I'll get the results to you as soon as possible. I'll be back around a few times over the next week or so just to check on you and make sure you're okay with everything. Of course, to be sure, I'll come around in about a month for that repeat pregnancy test." Placing a hand on my shoulder, she gave it a comforting rub and squeeze. "Well, I'll leave you alone for now and let Luciano know to come in later after his meeting."

All I could do was meekly nod my head in return and bury myself deeper into the bed until I was nearly obscured. The thought of being alone in the room with Luciano made my nerves go haywire with panic. I didn't want to be alone anywhere with any man, let alone be in a room with a brutal mafia boss.

My breath caught in my throat when a knock came from the door. I nearly damn well shot out of bed to go hide when it opened, and I saw Luciano appear. "Hey, it's just me, just here to talk." I didn't think his deep voice would soothe me, but it was soft enough that I didn't want to run.

Honestly, he would be less daunting if I didn't know about his mafia background and moniker. "T-thank you... For last night. For helping me." I kept the sheets tightly wrapped around me, a barrier almost between him and me. "Leave the door open! ...Please..." I grimaced at the stinging pain from my sudden panic when I noticed him pushing the door closed.

Removing his hand from the door, he held them up in the air while slowly approaching me. "Is it alright if I sit on the bed? Or would you rather me keep my distance?" He asked after stopping between the bed and the door in the middle of the room.

"B-bed's fine... But not too close...!" It felt weird to think about having him at a distance, but the thought of him close threw me off kilter, too. I didn't know what I wanted.

Warily, I followed his cautious figure as he sat at the foot of the bed. "Leah might have told you already, but I'm Luciano." Don't know if it was purposeful, but I was thankful for him keeping his deep voice smooth and low.

"Luciano Agosti, right? The Devil of The East Coast Syndicate?" I felt stupid for asking, but I needed to hear it from him.

Chortling, he gave me a grim smile with a nod of his head. "Yeah, and I'm not going to lie or sugarcoat any of it for you. I know of my reputation and what they say about me on the streets. I will not deny any of it because it's all true to some extent. I'm not a good person in terms of what I do. I'm a ruthless and violent man, but only towards my enemies. I would like to say that I am a fair and honorable man, though. You have nothing to worry about from me. I don't hurt children or women unless it's really an exception, which has only happened a very small handful of times. But you have nothing to fear of me, Juliet. You are safe here in my home and with me."

It should be illegal for him to say my name with how smooth it rolled off his tongue, and I should be locked up in a mental ward for thinking anything of it after what I've been through and the fact he's at least twice my age. "I don't know what to do now... I don't want to bother you more than I have, but—"

His hand immediately cut me off, and he shook his head. "You are not a bother, so stop thinking that and get it out of your head. I wouldn't have brought you to my home if I didn't want to bother with you. As far as what's going to happen next and what you're going to do, you're going to get comfortable here, make this place your home because it is now. I've spoken with Caroline—"

Hearing her name made me go frozen with fear. "No! Please don't send me back to her, please! I don't want anything to do with her anymore, please." My wheezing became distant as the room closed in on me with my tightening chest. I couldn't focus on anything else but the heavy dread dragging me under.

A tight warmth constricts around my rocking body, smushing me into something fleshy but solid. Incomprehensible words slowly penetrated my panic as my breathing became more paced, but I wasn't sure how or why because it felt out of my control. "...In...t...slo...got..." Slowly, the words came out clearer. "In and out, slowly, you got this, you can do it, you're not alone, I've got you, I'm here, I got you. You're safe here."

A part of me wanted to scramble away and put as much distance between us as possible because it felt so dirty to have a man touch me right now, but the comfort and safety anchor Luciano brought me right now was too good to let go. "I'm sorry," I muttered against his chest, peeling my head away and frowning out of embarrassment at the tears and snot on his shirt.

Reaching over the nightstand, he snagged some tissues and wiped at my face. "Don't apologize. It's not your fault. You didn't ask or want any of this to happen. So, don't ever apologize for your reactions to your trauma, understood?" Grasping my chin, he locked his stern but soft eyes with mine.

After I nodded my head in response, he nodded over to the bottles of pills on the nightstand. "Do you want some of your medication?"

"No, don't like meds." And after hearing the whole spiel of side effects from Leah, I wasn't too keen on wanting to take them. "I'm sorry about your shirt. That was so nasty of me." God, the first decent man in my life, and I slobber all over him.

"Juliet, it's just a shirt, I don't care. Besides, this isn't the worst I've been covered with." I sensed a story there, but he didn't elaborate any further.

Pulling back, Luciano pulled the sheets back up because he'd pushed them off me to hold me and bundled me back up before moving away to the end of the bed again. "I'm not handing you over to that bitch, nor am I handing you back over to your parents after hearing the story. So, you're staying here until further notice."

I opened my mouth to say something, but he held out a hand to stop me again. "I won't hear any arguments. You're staying here with me. I will provide for you and protect you." Luciano let out a heavy sigh, "And right now, staying with me is your best and possibly only option. The moment you go out there, I can only do so much to prevent Lady Heral from getting her claws into you, but while you remain fully under my care and protection, she and everyone else won't dare look your way."

His pitiful expression gazed down at me. "You've no one else to turn to. Sad to say it to you, but it's true. As I see it, you only have two options: stay with me or leave and risk the lounge again. And this time, you won't be able to escape, nor will anyone save you. You used your one miracle of a lifetime, so I suggest you don't push your nonexistent luck now. If you leave, I can guarantee you that it will only be a matter of time before Lady Heral snatches you up again to work off your parents' debt."

Screw him.

Unfortunately, I couldn't argue with him because I was on the losing side. His points were valid, sadly. If I left his place, his protection, I'd be a lost rabbit in a sea of wolves. As strange as it was, staying really was my best and only option if I wanted to go back to a somewhat normal life—if I survived that long. I hated that I even thought about ending my own life when I was being tossed a saving line, but the fact Luciano was willing to help me wouldn't stop the trauma from rearing its ugly head, nor would it change the fact that my body had been defiled.

No matter how raw I scrubbed at my body, no matter how hot I turned the water up, and no amount of soap could rid the phantom feeling of their disgusting hands. It made me feel gross and disgusted in my own skin.

Then the fact that the men—no, bastards—who did this to me were roaming around out there as if nothing happened. I didn't feel normal any-more, and I hated it. Thinking about returning to school after all of this, I don't know if I could. What if someone found out? I'd be the outcast and lose everything completely regarding friends and social standing.

"I don't know what to do..." I felt stupid for uttering those words, but it was the truth.

With a sigh, Luciano slowly moved back over and unwrapped me before hugging me tightly. "That's fine. That's what I am here for. What you're going to do is recover. You'll stay here with me, let me take care of you, and obey my rules for you. Alright?" All I could manage was a small nod in response because I had no other choice, really. "Once you and Leah find a therapist, I'll have home visits set up twice a week until you are ready to move it to once a week and so on. You are going to attend therapy because that's the first step to working out your inner turmoil. The second thing that is going to happen is a visit to your parents."

Mentioning my parents made me flinch involuntarily as my anxiety rushed me again. "I don't... No..." Their betrayal stung me like a poisonous knife to the chest, and I didn't want to see them ever again. I mean, how could they disregard me so easily like that? Like I meant nothing to them.

"Yes, we're going. I need to have a nice little chat with them, and you need to get your stuff unless you really have nothing sentimental there. I am fine replacing all your stuff, but this will be your only chance to get anything personal unless you plan on returning yourself some other time. You won't be alone. I'll be there with you and some of my men." He remained firm in his decision, and his unmoving expression meant nothing would sway him.

"I don't want to see them." I bit out defiantly and stubbornly with a shake of my head.

Sighing softly, he looked down at me and patted my head. "You won't have to if you don't want to. You just have to go in and straight to your room to grab your stuff while I occupy your parents. I promise, unless you want to see them, you won't, not with me around." He assured me with a slight smile before letting me go.

"I'll punch you if I see them," I grumbled to myself as I bundled myself back up in the sheets.

"If that makes you happy, then sure." He chuckled with a slight roll of his eyes, making me wonder if he was serious or not. "Either way, besides the things I've listed so far, you're going to attend school as usual, graduate, then go to college nearby if you wish, or we can discuss more on what you want after graduation." A slight tension and dip in his voice towards the end made me wary of him because it sounded like he withheld or omitted something important. Then again, I could just be overly paranoid and on edge after everything.

Pursing my lips, I sat there silently, letting everything fully sink in with much confusion. Luciano befuddled me greatly with all he put forth. Clearly, he wasn't going to let me leave, but why? I was just another petulant teenager, surely, and he seemed like a busy man who probably couldn't or shouldn't be bothered by me. Yet, even though he gave me the option of fending for myself out there, he made it seem grave to the point where remaining with him was the only real option.

"Why are you doing this? I mean, I'll accept all your conditions and all, and I'm grateful for it all, but at least tell me the truth about everything." Yeah, I was more than fed up with being kept in the dark about shit involving my own life.

Luciano looked at me pensively for a few seconds before sighing softly. "Honestly, I don't know fully. Just something about you and how you looked at me that night." He shrugged me off with his seemingly half-assed answer. There was some truth to it, but it felt as if something was amiss again. "I mean, initially, I was going to let you go after you recovered, but given the light of new information regarding your situation, I just don't feel comfortable one bit, letting a young woman like you out there with no experience." Again, it was truthful, but I sensed something was omitted.

"Kind of hard to believe a man like you would have trouble letting some-one like me go fend for themselves given your ruthless reputation," I remarked with a roll of my eyes.

"Have you done something to deserve brutality from me?" He questioned with a raised brow, crossing his arms and leaning back against the bedpost.

"No... I just... A man like you..." I didn't know how to put it nicely without possibly offending him.

"Shouldn't have a heart?" Well, he didn't sound too torn up about it. If anything, he sounded like he made a joke of it. "I've heard it all, princess. Nothing phases me anymore. I might not seem like it, but I still am a human at heart. I might not have much of a heart towards my enemies and those who break the rules of the syndicate, but if you're innocent, then you've nothing to fear from me. I'm not some bastard asshole who treats everyone as worms beneath me. My parents raised me better than that."

"I'm sorry... It's just so weird... Not to offend you or anything, but I'm somewhat fearful of you because I don't know you, yet you're so kind to me despite all I've heard about you. It's just a little confusing for me." I should be afraid of him, and I was, but not fully. His act of goodness taking me in and doing all of this really caught me off guard.

"No need to apologize. I'm more surprised at how well you're taking this given how your life got tossed into a pile of shit out of nowhere. I assure you, though, you have nothing to fear of me unless you wrong me. As long as you follow the rules I set forth, then consequences won't come to you." At least his soft little smile was genuine and comforting enough to settle some of my nerves.

"What are the rules?" And back under lock and key I went.

Brushing a hand across his jaw, he let his eyebrows furrow together for a second before replying to me. "Besides not wrecking my place, you are allowed nearly everywhere in the house except my office and all of the business wing unless stated otherwise. You will always have at least two guards with you unless you are in your private room. You're welcome to anything and everything in the place and on the property BUT the cars." Luciano paused and gave me a very pointed look, making me shrink a little with my nod in response.

Softening his face back up to a somewhat friendly smile, he continued. "Don't throw crazy parties. Ask me beforehand if you plan on throwing something with more than ten people. You are to inform me about your whereabouts. I don't particularly care where you go as long as I know where to find you. If I do ever tell you to do something, then I expect you to obey me without question."

Is he going to have me give myself to him? Kill someone? Oh god, what if he wants me to be his slave or something?

The thoughts sped through my brain and hung on my tongue, but before a word could come out of my mouth, he held a hand out to stop me. "No, I won't ever ask you to do anything illegal, immoral, or anything you'd find uncomfortable. I am not a complete devil, like what people make me out to be. If anything, I will tell you to stay home on certain days, stay safe in your room for certain times, or avoid certain areas."

"How will I get around then if I can't touch your cars?" As if I would even dare in the first place.

Luciano answered me casually with a soft shrug of his shoulders. "Your bodyguards will take you nearly anywhere you please without question. Keep in mind, I will give them orders not to take you anywhere unsavory or illegal for your age, so don't think about going out to any clubs or bars."

"Don't worry, I'm not that kind of person." And as if I wanted to do any of that after what happened. The last thing I wanted was to get roofied and dragged into some alleyway. Also, the thought of grabby hands on my body made me want to hurl. "But if you ask something of me that makes me uncomfortable—"

"Which won't happen." He assured me sternly with a curt expression.

"IF, like big if, then I get to refuse it or at least get an explanation before refusing it." Despite not being able to give my full trust to Luciano right now, I felt pretty confident that he wouldn't be some despicable man in *that* regard.

"Just know that if I ever tell you to do something, then it's for your safety. I wouldn't have you do something just to be an asshole, but fine, not as if I'd ever tell you to do something uncomfortable." He agreed with a wave of his hand.

"How am I going to pay you back for all of this? Or what's the catch?" No such thing as a free lunch is what my parents grilled into me; well, they grilled me on the fact that nothing in life was ever truly free.

"You be a good girl and live here with me, that's it. You don't have to pay me back for any of it. I'm doing this because I want to and because I want you to have the good life you were almost robbed of." There was that unsettling feeling again. Something went amiss, but what?

"Can I be alone now? I'm tired and want to nap." I needed some time to myself to process everything fully and accept it all.

"I'll be back later to wake you for a late lunch then and give you the stuff Leah's gonna drop off later. If you need anything, the guards are right outside your door." He seemed reluctant to leave as if he had something to say but didn't.

Great, how the hell am I supposed to live with him when he wasn't being fully transparent with me?

Men like him—mafia men—always had secrets, which I hated. Granted, there were probably some things he couldn't tell me because they weren't his to tell, or maybe he was just an asshole and didn't want to tell me something... Or it was to protect me... But I was fucking tired of being in the dark when it came to my life, and I was a nosey little shit.

Huffing out a loud sigh, I ruffled around on the bed to get comfortable, which was easy to do because the bed felt like some soft cloud—if a cloud could be solid. I thought my parents had nice beds, but fuck, this beat it by a long ass mile.

Curling up into a ball, I lifted the front of the shirt up to my nose and inhaled deeply. It was so embarrassing and weird, but I couldn't help myself. The rich, deep scent of warmth, whiskey—I think—and amber flooded my senses and body with a warm comfort.

Well, at least he smelt nice, or at least his clothes did.

Sighing heavily, I buried myself further into the bed with another huff before letting my eyes flutter closed.

Rest and recover. I could do that... I think...

Chapter 7
Luciano

"You did what!?"

Leah might as well have physically slapped me with how harsh she sounded. There weren't many people in my life who scared me, but Leah was definitely one of them. Yes, I was terrified of the little 5'4 Asian woman. To be fair, she could very well lay my ass out without breaking a sweat.

"Luciano! You fucking... Argh! Go fix that shit!" Leah seethed, whacking me with her bag. "I knew you were a fucking brainless gorilla, but even this is beyond for you."

"Would you stop?" I grunted while deflecting her hits. "Of course, I'm going to fix this. It was my stupid mouth and brain that got me into this situation. Just... I'll tell her later when she's not processing through the trauma of her heinous rape and torture. You're the doctor. Do you really think right now is a good time to break that news to her?"

Letting out a brief huff of relief, I straightened myself back out after Leah stopped punching at me. "Besides, if things go accordingly, then I won't even have to tell her because this marriage scheme will be buried before it surfaces to her."

I had it handled, hopefully. The plan was simple: get rid of Lady Heral. A very simple plan because if Juliet was in the establishment, then there were other skeletons hidden and waiting for me to unbury them. If I could uncover all her dirty secrets, discredit her, and shut her down before she blew this thing up, then I'd be golden. I would just have to figure out some other lie about why Juliet wasn't my bride by the end of the year.

Well, I could wed her and divorce her, but that wasn't right. My dad would have my head on a pike if I were to dare do such a thing because of how religious he is, and I'm sure my mother would rise from the dead to beat my ass for being a bad son and shit. I had my views on divorce, but if it was the only way to keep Juliet safe, so be it.

"You better hope she doesn't find out about it before it gets resolved. She already has been through too much for someone her age, and this would just be another slap to her face." Leah huffed and rolled her eyes after hooking her hands on her hips.

Maybe I was being a little overly confident, but only because I knew I could pull this shit off without a hitch. "It should be fine in the end. Two months is more than enough time for me and my men to dig up more than enough dirt and filth on Carol to drag everything related to her by name to Hell." I waved a dismissive hand at Leah before drifting my gaze back to Juliet's medical file that sat in front of me on my desk.

For her sake, I shouldn't read through it, but a part of me needed to know in order to fuel my sick, and twisted revenge plan. "There's no going back once you open that file," Leah warned with a heavy sigh and forlorn expression.

"I know, but I need more fuel for my hatred against Caroline." Anger never blinded me. No, it always cleared my mind, strangely enough.

Blinding red rage was something I'd never come to know in my life. Ever since I could remember, rage had always given me a sense of clarity. Everything would come into hyper-focus, my thoughts would go a mile a minute, but everything would make perfect sense, and the thrill and pleasure from letting the rage explode out of me was something beyond what words could describe.

Yeah, I was a little fucked up, but I loved and craved the control my anger gave me.

Leah spoke up again after a deep breath. "Six men, that's how many were in that room, according to her. They took turns holding her down and sodomizing her. I'll run whatever fluids Gia collected last night, along with what I got during my exam, and maybe we'll get lucky with some hits in the database or something." Though calm, I could feel and hear the rattling anger in her voice. "Can I at least kill them if something comes back?"

"No." My blunt denial came rather tersely. "If something comes back, I want them captured and brought to me. I want answers from them before you slice them into oblivion." I wanted to know who to go after and who to punish.

"As long as I get a swing at them," Leah grumbled with a roll of her eyes.

"You know, for a doctor who is supposed to be healing and shit, you are very violent and sadistic," I commented out loud with a chuckle while picking up the file and opening it.

"I care when it matters." Leah chuckled under her breath before letting her eyes grow wary of me.

My stomach churned at every word on the page, but not in a way where I wanted to vomit. I was thoroughly disgusted, yes, but I mostly grew angry at the fact this all happened to Juliet. She seemed like an innocent and precious little thing, someone who didn't deserve this level of assault; well, no one deserves this level of assault besides the assailants themselves. Of course, that gave me an idea about how to make these bastards suffer when I'd find them. Yes, when, not if. I wasn't doing it out of revenge for Juliet. No, it was for my personal benefit. People don't end up in these situations without some kind of connection, ones I needed to shut down if they were in my territory. No doubt Champions wasn't the only place in the city to get access to these asinine taboo acts.

On second thought, maybe it wouldn't be so bad to let these rotten scumbags rot in jail; they'd definitely get more damage done to them long-term. Paying off the guards and some prisoners wouldn't be too hard. Actually, maybe I should just have them tossed in prison after I was done with them, have them suffer through and through. Yeah, I should do that to get my dose of fun. Of course, Leah would be able to have a go at them as well; I'd just have to make sure she didn't kill them afterward.

Scowling deeply, I sighed heavily as I slammed the file shut and threw it onto my desk. "Let me know if something from the swabs comes back. I'm going to do some of my own digging in the meantime." Probably gonna be a pain in the ass, but fuck it; I would have my men comb through the lounge's camera feeds to narrow down my victim pool.

"Can you check on her again and make sure she's ready?" I asked with another sigh while running my hand down my face.

"Why don't you go check in on her? You're gonna have to get used to interacting with her since she's basically going to be living here for lord knows how long." Grumbling briefly under her breath, she rolled her eyes. "Besides, if this plan of yours goes belly-up, then you are gonna need to know your future wife at the very least." Leah bit out the last part rather harshly with a scowl and glaring eyes that made me flinch a little.

"It's not going to get to that point, and I can easily avoid her at all costs." Once she got back on her feet and groove, it wouldn't be hard to learn her routine, so finding out what hotspots to avoid and what times would be child's play to me. Also, I could shut myself in my office and live out of it if I wanted to.

"You better hope it doesn't get to that point, or else I'll help her cut your balls off and feed it to you." Yeah, the mental image of that made me instinctively close my legs tightly and cover my private area with my hands. Unfortunately, I have no doubt she would make good on that promise either knowing her. "Now, go check up on her and make her less scared of you."

"Well, I'm not exactly a lovable person," I grumbled with a roll of my eyes, not that I intended to because I didn't give a shit about if people found me approachable or easy.

"Well, dial it down a notch for her sake, please?" Leah pleaded with a pout.

Unbelievable. "Fine, I'll fucking try." How the fuck was I supposed to dial something back I was unaware about? Not like I tried to be an asshole to her, and not that I was.

"Even the devil disguises himself as an angel of light," Leah remarked with a chuckle before packing her things into her bag.

Sighing, I slumped in my chair for a bit to ponder how I'd go about this thing with Juliet. Honestly, avoiding her seemed like the best course of action, but there was no way Leah would let me do that. So, after a long while in my own mind, I reluctantly pushed myself out of the chair and carried myself down to Juliet's room, which I stupidly placed right across from mine.

Knocking softly against the door, I leaned against the doorframe. "Juliet, are you ready?" I asked with a wince when I realized how loud my terse words came out.

"I don't know." Her muffled reply came back after a moment.

Sighing softly, I wrapped my hand around the doorknob. "Can I come in?"

"Yeah..." Her shaky response returned, making me sigh again because it made me wonder if this was a bad idea after all.

Upon entering the room, I couldn't help but frown a bit at the sight of her curled up on the small lounge chair in her room. She looked so vulnerable and scared, and if I weren't in a time crunch, I'd cancel the plan of going to her parents today. "I know it's not something you want to do this soon, or ever, but it's better for you to remove yourself from their life completely sooner than later." Cautiously, I took a few tentative steps toward her to test the waters. "And like I said, you don't have to see them, let alone interact with them, at all during the whole time unless you want to." I continued to approach her slowly with my soft voice until I could kneel before her. "I will make my conversation with them as quick as possible, promise."

"Promise I won't see them?" It was fleeting, but a blip of anger darkened her soft, chocolate-brown eyes for a millisecond before her fear chilled them when she returned to her shell.

Confidently, I assured her with a nod and smile. Then, slowly, I reached an open hand out towards her, "Is it alright if I touch you?" She looked ready to bolt with how her eyes nervously darted around the room. "You have every right to say no as well. It's all on your terms."

Seconds passed before her erratic breathing evened out when she realized I would make no move until I got an answer from her. Too bad a simple nod wouldn't suffice for me. "Juliet, I need to hear it. It's simple to mistake a motion of your head, so I need to hear it, please."

Breathing deeply, she gingerly reached her hand out towards me, just a little. "It's okay to touch me." She spoke up in a small, shaky voice.

I needed her confidence to build again if I was to help her recover, and having her full autonomy is a major part of rebuilding it all. The sooner she realizes that she has full control of everything regarding her body and decisions, the easier it will be for her to gain her footing.

Smiling gratefully, I took her delicate hand into my own rough one and pulled her up as I stood. "You can do this, and I'll be right there with you if you need any help." She may be a scared little thing, but I sensed more underneath her turbulent waves.

"That's a lot more faith than I have in myself." She grumbled as she let me drag her out of the house and into the garage. "Holy shiiii... Are these all yours? Wait, never mind, stupid question, of course, they are, but god damn... Oh my God, is that a Bugatti Mistral?!"

I couldn't bring myself to stop her from darting off toward the car; her excitement was too rich to kill. Also, I don't think she's gotten this peppy since I rescued her, so I'd take what I could get. "I am *not* going to let you drive, so don't bother asking." I cracked a somewhat awkward smile with my joke as I approached her while she ogled the luxury car.

"I can't even legally drive anyway, so you don't have to worry about that. Besides, I don't feel worthy of driving such a beauty. Hell, I'm too afraid to touch it." It was kind of adorable at how awe-struck she was as she bounced happily on the balls of her feet.

"What do you mean?" Did she just not have her license? It's kind of strange for someone her age not to have one, I think. I wouldn't know; I drove way before the legal age.

Frowning, she let her gaze drop to her shuffling foot. "I don't have a permit or anything like that... My parents won't let me have one or let me learn to drive or anything like that. They say there's no need or point in me learning because I don't need it. The closest I've ever gotten to driving anything is through a video game, and the few times I hacked the family car." A heavy sigh deflated out of her before her mood fully dampened.

Well, this turned awkward fast.

Sighing softly to myself, I nodded to my housekeeper with a lopsided smile and thanked her when she approached me with the keys to the car.

"We'll talk more on the drive." Or maybe we shouldn't for the sake of keeping things relatively fine between us. The last thing I wanted to do was have some awkward, half-assed conversation for the sake of it.

The air in the car instantly became suffocating when we buckled in, and I pulled out into the street. "What else did your parents not let you do?" I strained out a bit because the awkward tension killed me a little with how uncomfortable she seemed. Seriously, she was almost as stiff as a statue in her seat, even though she'd been ecstatic about the car just a few moments ago.

"No driving, no parties unless approved by them or it was one of their parties, no going to friends' houses or places with them unless it was the library, no friends could come over unless their parents were acquainted with mine, no more than three meals a day, no sweets, no coffee..." Juliet pouted sadly in her seat as her words trailed off. "There's more, but it's just all a blur to me right now... It was basically school and home, and obey my parents." Great, think I just made her sadder with how she slumped in her seat. "I'm sorry for sounding so pathetic... I didn't really ever think..." She seemed to trail off into her head with a deepening frown.

Maybe I should have dragged Leah along. Being nice and shit was her thing, not mine. I mean, it was too late now because we were on the road. Hesitantly, I reached over and patted her shoulder—yeah, fucking awkward. "Get out of your head. Don't drown in your own darkness. You're still young and learning, so don't take it hard on yourself. Stop me if I'm wrong, but I'm gonna assume you had a sheltered life, or at least forced to have one by your parents. They controlled and manipulated you, and you wouldn't have known any better."

Well, she didn't stop me, but her long silence didn't bode well for me either. I opened my mouth to continue but promptly shut it when her soft voice filled the air. "I feel dumb for letting them pull the hood over my eyes like that, though. I just... I never thought I'd be one of *those* girls. I mean, I've read about them in books, articles, and whatnot, and it just feels foolish because I always thought, 'Oh, I'd never let myself be played like that' or 'I'd never let someone control my life like that' when in reality that's what happened. Just so fucking stupid." And the tears came—fuck.

Huffing out a sigh, I quickly pulled over and threw the car into park before turning in my seat to face her fully. Reaching out, I gently cupped her face and lifted her gaze to me. "Stop that," I commanded sternly yet softly, making her shudder in response. "Look at me," I demanded when her eyes drifted away, making her snap them back to me. "Don't do that to yourself. I was young and stupid once, and yes, it's embarrassing to think back on those moments now, but I grew from those experiences. As long as you learn from it all, that's all that matters." Smiling at her proudly, I brushed my thumb gently across her cheek. "At least you came far enough to recognize and accept that your parents are idiotic bastards for what they did to you, and I really hope that you don't fall back into the cycle as you have before. This is your one chance to have a life of your own, Juliet, so take it. You made your mistake. You recognized it. Now learn from it and move forward."

Okay, that was exhausting.

If she weren't some fragile woman (as in if she were a man), I probably would've just punched her in the face and told her to quit bitching and get over it. Yeah, I was a bastard—sue me. People didn't call me The Devil for no fucking reason, and I didn't earn that title by being nice. Something about Juliet, though, something about her makes me go soft.

Nothing about Juliet made sense to me, and I didn't want to try and figure that out right now when I needed my mind steeled and ready to deal with her parents in a bit. I'll just vent to Leah later since she was the one who was insistent on me being 'nice' to Juliet and spending time with her. Yeah, I had no plans to let Leah off the hook *that* easily.

"Now, no more frowning and moping. And for fuck's sake, relax. I am not going to rip your head off or do anything bad to you." Not that I could blame her for the last part because if I were her, I'd probably be wary of any man within a mile radius of me.

Then again, if I were her, I'd just go on a revenge-killing spree. Or at least, I'd like to think that to be the case. It was one thing to think and say something, but it was a whole different ball game to actually act it out. We all liked to think we were rough and tough, that we'd laugh in the face of danger, but life wasn't that simple.

I remember when I was her age and thought I was at the top of the world. Then, I got jumped one night by a rival mafia and completely froze at the sight of the gun when it trained on me. Even if my father had trained and prepared me for many different situations, having it happen outside a controlled training scenario was something else altogether.

Obviously, I wasn't the shit I thought I was.

"How about I make you a deal?" She perked up briefly at my words before she withdrew herself again. I didn't wait for her answer to continue, "No more sad Juliet for the rest of the car ride, and I'll take you out for some ice cream afterward. How does that sound?"

What the hell am I doing?

I shouldn't care about her feelings like this, nor should I bargain with her to make an attempt at lifting her feelings. The car shouldn't be pulled over, nor should her precious face be in my hands. I don't have time for this gentle guiding shit. I should be telling her to suck it up, drive to her parents, and let what happens happen. Yet, for some stupid reason, the thought of treating her like everyone else made my heart twist uncomfortably in my chest.

"I'm not a child... But fine, deal." She strained out with a defeated pout to her face. "But only because I've never had ice cream and want to try it." She quickly threw out before she pulled herself away from me and got comfortable in her seat while wiping away her stray tears with the sleeve of her sweatshirt.

"Okay, you have had to have ice cream in your life at least once." She couldn't have been that repressed and deprived of life under her parents.

Sighing softly, she shook her head with an ashamed frown on her face. "No, and the one time I tried at school when we had an ice cream party, one of the teachers on their payroll slapped it out of my hand. Next thing I know, I'm magically allergic to all things dairy, even though I can drink milk perfectly fine and eat cheese just fine. Unfortunately, since it's technically on my records as an allergy, no one could ever give me anything from then on out. But I swear, I'm not allergic to anything, at least nothing I'm aware of, and I'm gonna have an allergy test done with Leah after some more of my labs come back to make sure." Puffing her cheeks out in a pout, she huffed, crossed her arms, and slumped in her seat.

Unable to help it, I let out a soft chuckle and ruffled the top of her head before straightening myself back out in my seat. "Well, ice cream later if you behave, and once you're cleared, then we can slowly lower you into the waters." The last thing I needed was for her to be amped up on sugar or make herself sick by going crazy with trying new things.

"Can I pick whatever ice cream I want?" Though muted, the sparkle in her eyes was lovely to see. This was a breath of fresh air compared to the empty, scared eyes I'd somewhat gotten used to.

"Juliet, you can pick whatever flavor you want, though maybe stick to three max today so you don't get overwhelmed, alright?" Gotta keep it as a way to motivate her, too. If she tasted everything today, she wouldn't look forward to the next outing.

Wait, next outing? Why the fuck was I thinking about our next outing? There can't be another next time with any of this.

The rest of the car ride was silent, but not awkwardly so. It was a calm silence with how Juliet went into her own little world while staring out the window. Even though she had a small smile on her face, I could see the tension in her shoulders and her anxiety slipping through with her fiddling fingers. I thought about reaching over to ease her some, but she relaxed a little by the time I worked up the nerve to act. So, I kept to myself until we approached her parents' place.

Her body wound up like a spring ready to be sprung when I parked in front of the place, right outside the front doors. "Hey." I kept my voice low and soft as I reached out and grabbed her fidgeting hands in one of mine. "Look at me."

I felt her shiver in my grasp before her head turned towards me and her wary and fearful eyes fixed on mine. "I don't think I can do it. I want to throw up." She spoke in a broken voice, frowning at the end with an apologetic look.

Reaching my other hand out, I gently lifted her gaze back at me with a finger curled under her tiny chin. "Hey, remember, they can't touch you, and you won't see a ghost of them, not while I'm here. You can do this, and I know you can. I believe in you." They were a little too sweet for me, but they were words she needed to hear. Strangely, it didn't bother me as much to provide such reassurance to her, even if it wasn't my forte. Honestly, the most encouragement I've ever given someone was 'Don't die out there' or something along those lines.

"C-can you go to my room with me? I don't want to go alone." She asked sheepishly, chewing on her bottom lip in anticipation.

Smiling warmly at her, I softly pinched the tip of her chin. "If that is what little Juliet wishes." The sight of her bright smile caused a wave of warmth to burst within my chest. It kind of amazed me at how simple it was to lift her spirits and make those pretty eyes of hers light up with such wonder and excitement.

"Let me go deal with your parents first, then I'll come back to the car for you, alright?" Her smile faltered for a split second before she responded to me with a nod of her head. "What is on your mind?" A loaded question since there was probably the whole world on her mind right now.

Averting her eyes, she stared out the window momentarily before looking back at me with furrowed eyes. "You're not gonna kill them or harm them, are you?"

It confused me how worried she sounded. How could she worry for her parents after everything? Why should she even worry? Did she not want me to harm them? Even after all they did to her? Why?

"No, not unless they do something stupid to force my hand," I assured her through a forced smile and gritted teeth. "Why?"

"I don't know... I hate them, but I don't want them dead." Juliet paused and struggled with a wordless, gasping mouth.

But when she did get her bearings again, her next words truly surprised me.

"I don't want them to die. I want them to suffer... And I want to see them suffer, but I can't bear to face them right now... So, all that has to wait. I want them to see me thrive and be successful and regret their choices."

Guess Juliet had more of a fire in her than I credited her for.

Time to feed it and turn it into a raging wildfire.

Chapter 8

Luciano

LEAVING JULIET IN THE car proved harder than I expected.

I knew she'd be safe, but seeing her tiny form behind the tinted window of my car caused a wave of worry to wash over me as I ascended the stairs to the front door of the gaudy mansion.

Whipping my head back, I took one last look at Juliet before turning my full attention back to the front doors and kicking the heavy, intricately decorated wood in. The poor workers who were nearby jumped at the sudden crash that echoed throughout the foyer. "Arnold and Ana! Your pathetic asses better be here as you agreed, or we're going to have major problems!" I shouted into the place, hoping the small threat would be enough to pull them out of their pathetic hiding holes.

The head of a balding man darted out from around a corner. "M-mister Ag—" The shaky voice of a fearful man barely dented the thick air.

Scowling, I raised my deepened voice, "Did I say you could speak up? I only demanded you show yourself, not run your stupid mouth. Where is your wife?" She was nowhere in sight from a quick sweep of my eyes. "The agreement was for *both* of you to be present." The fewer questions and pushback from them, the better, and what better way to ensure their cooperation than a healthy dose of fear. "Here is what's going to happen. You and your wife are going to take my men and me into your stupid home office where business will be discussed. Then, you are going to ensure that *everyone* makes themselves scarce. If I catch a glimpse of someone, I will shoot them on the spot." Now, that last part wasn't an empty threat, and they should know better, given my reputation. "Understood?"

Arnold's head bobbed rapidly in response before he scampered away up the staircase with me right on his tail. In the background, I could hear the others scattering like rats for a few seconds before dead silence filled the place, and our footfalls against the marble floor filled its place when we resumed our trip to the office. Once inside, I made myself right at home behind the desk, even taking some extra effort to kick my feet up onto the flat surface after I leaned back in the chair.

"I'm not going to waste any more time here than I should because I have much more important matters to attend to, so do me a favor and sign the papers that my men are going to hand to you without any arguments. After the papers are signed, I will give you ten million along with a set of instructions." Oh yeah, this was highly illegal, but we were gonna make it legal in our fucked up little underground mafia world.

"But wha—"

Juliet's father—Arnold—quickly shut his mouth with a pointed glare from me. "Sign. No questions, no looking, just sign your name on those lines as if your life depends on it because it does." It'd be a lot easier to twist their arms once they essentially sign their life away to me.

Minutes passed, and the sounds of papers shuffling around and pens scribbling across the fibrous surface scratched the air. Once the lawyer gave me the okay after looking over the papers—I had to make it look somewhat legal to scare her parents some more—I threw the case of money onto the desk and opened it to reveal stacks upon stacks of bundled bills. "From now on, if anyone asks, Juliet was promised to me at a young age because of poor decisions on your part at a casino establishment of mine. The deal between us was that you sold your daughter to save your own hide, and we are to wed in the year after she turns eighteen. You were shitty people and never kept me in the loop about her growing up, and now she's in my safe hands after all these years. Deviate from that story or try to say anything else, and you'll be less fortunate than the rats that scour the city's sewers. Everything you ever owned or touched, anything with your name tied to it, will be fully transferred to me before I smear your name to all of the world."

The fury on the Chau's faces made me crack a twisted smile as I continued after holding up a hand to stop their outburst. "Oh, and if you try to say anything, those papers you just signed will say otherwise. Maybe you should have fought more to read what you were signing your life away to." As if I would've let them; I just wanted to rub it into their faces. "The ten million should be sufficient enough to keep you quiet, and if you try to extort me for anything more, then I'll just pull the papers out and proceed to ruin you for ten lifetimes."

"Y-you can't do this! We've done nothing to you! And you tricked us! Coerced us into signing!" Ana practically wailed in an unpleasantly cracked voice. "There's no way it'll hold! What does Juliet even have to do with any of this? She's not our problem anymore, so talk it out with that brothel owner!"

"Oh? Do you have any proof that you were coerced? All my men here who witnessed this would say otherwise." I remarked snidely with a cocky smirk, running my hand across my jaw and holding it there to hide the crazed grin that spread underneath. "And you may have done nothing to me, but you defiled and wronged Juliet as much as the bastards you sold her to for your stupid debt. She is mine now. Therefore, any slight against her is one against me. You fucked up, and my attention came to you the moment I found Juliet battered in the street after she was raped by scum who deserve worse things than death."

If she couldn't take her revenge, I'd do it for her. Her parents would forever look over their shoulders as long as I lived; they would never know a moment of peace starting now. "I know there are shitty parents in this damned world, but you manipulated her and lulled her into a false sense of twisted affection, then wronged her. You're supposed to be her parents. You are supposed to care and cherish her like the most precious thing in the world, yet you did none of that and took it a step further by discarding her like trash. If I hadn't given her my word that I wouldn't dispose of you, then you'd be dying in a pool of your own blood by now."

I didn't think I'd get so riled up about this, at least not to this extent. Sure, I knew I'd feel some anger toward her parents for how they utterly wronged her. But seeing their stupid, terrified faces mere feet from me struck a different chord in me. It pissed me off how they weren't worried one bit for Juliet, not even a simple 'how is she doing' or anything remotely about her well-being.

Yeah, I barely knew her for two whole days, but I was never wrong about people. *If*—for some odd reason—I was, her being a total bitch of a brat still wouldn't be a remotely acceptable excuse for what her parents did to her. Nothing shy of maybe her being some deplorable abuser herself—and even then, it was a huge maybe—would possibly warrant such a thing from her parents.

"Are you really so fucked up that you don't even care for your own flesh and blood?" I wanted to know what went on in their empty heads because I honestly didn't fully grasp it. Well, more like I didn't want to understand and accept it. I've heard stories and knew things like this happened, but Juliet was the first case for me where it was right there in my face. Juliet was the physical proof of the aftermath I've held, touched, and connected to.

Nervously, Arnold chuckled as he stood up warily and held his hands out to calm his wife down while smiling at me with such a sickly, sweet, but fake smile that made me want to rip his mouth off his face. "She knew what was expected of her. She was only of use to us as a commodity." His lips twitched as he struggled to maintain himself. "Listen, I don't know what she's told you, but she knew what her life was to be growing up. We're not the bad guys here. She's just played you." Chuckling nervously, he rubbed his hands together. "I apologize for my wife's outburst. She's been very distressed about Juliet's disappearance, and you know how women are and how they tend to overreact without thinking." The liar couldn't keep his eyes on me as his words flew out of his mouth.

Clicking my tongue out of annoyance and anger, I pulled my gun out and slammed it on the table with a clenched jaw. "I don't like liars or rats, both of whom you are right now. Not only do you not give a damn about your own daughter, but you dare call Lady Heral a liar? And you dare lie straight to my face despite the dirt I have on you and try to manipulate me?" Slowly,

I drummed my fingers on the desk as I spoke angrily. "You must really have a death wish. Lady Heral has already told me everything before I bought Juliet from her to save her from the hell you put her in."

"Then why are you bothering us? Why the lie you are forcing us to sell?" Arnold snapped back with a little too much gusto for my liking.

Slamming my hand down on the desk, I stood and picked up my gun to hold it menacingly in front of me. "It's not a lie. It is what is going to happen. I have my reasons, and you don't need to know it. Just muse my whims." Unloading the lie for them would possibly give them ammunition against me, so like hell, I'd explain myself to them. Besides, I had different plans, and explaining it all to them was an unneeded headache.

"What about after you marry Juliet? She is still our daughter, so we will be—"

I had a good guess as to where she headed with her words, and it ground my gears the wrong way. "Juliet will be an Agosti. After we leave here today, your ties with her are severed and buried, and vice versa. You two will have nothing to do with each other. There will be no joined family, no in-laws, none of that bull crap. Our business with each other is done the moment I leave that door, and don't even think about contacting me or her for anything unless it's to grovel for your actions. And before you try anything, I suggest you read the copies of the papers you just signed. I wouldn't want you and anyone related to you in name to lose everything." Lowering my gun, I kept my finger on the trigger just in case as I made my way to the door.

"That's it? You're just buying us off and cutting Juliet out of our lives like that? What kind of monster are you to do that to a family?" The audacity of this woman. Never before have I ever wanted to physically lay my hands on a woman until now. It'd be so easy to lash my hand out and catch her face, but fortunately for her, my parents raised me better than that.

"Unlike you, I am doing what is best for Juliet," I remarked with an arrogant smirk before throwing the door open. "Don't expect a wedding invitation." I chuckled before exiting the room and slamming the door shut.

Taking a deep breath, I ran a hand down my face before looking at one of my men by the door. "Make sure they don't leave this room until Juliet and I are off the premises. If they even so much as stick the tip of their finger under the door crack, cut it off." Or smash the digit to pieces to make them suffer, but I didn't want my men and I to spend any more time in this damned place than we needed to. "If anyone else tries to peek their head in on Juliet while she is here, make sure they're locked back up in a room but do *not* harm them. The only ones who can be harmed are the Chau's, understood?"

I waited for my men to respond to me before leaving the mansion to retrieve Juliet, who sat curled up in the seat of the car. Seeing her all scared and vulnerable made me want to turn back around and rummage through her room myself, but then that would defeat the purpose of me dragging her here and forcing her to do this herself. I wanted her to remove herself from her family's home and physically move herself and her belongings into mine.

Slowly, I approached the car and opened the door before reaching in and placing my hand on her shoulder, "Juliet." Regret quickly pulled me into the depths of the chilly ocean when she flinched and shied away from my touch. "Sorry." I should have been more mindful about physical touch and her after what she recently went through.

"Promise I won't see them?" She asked while uncurling her tense body.

Smiling confidently, I nodded in response before holding a hand out to help her out of the car. "I'll be right behind you."

Then, to my surprise, she shook her head, quickly darted behind me, and started pushing me forward. "No, you go first, just in case." I heard her quiet whisper as I let her steer me into and throughout the house until we reached a closed room.

It was so stupid, letting myself be pushed around—literally—by a girl half my size. If it were anyone else, I would've snapped at them, but I tolerated it for Juliet. If it made her feel better, then so be it. I'd deal with my snickering men later.

"Wait right here," I instructed her after pressing her flat against the wall next to the door.

When she showed no signs of disobeying me, I carefully opened the door after drawing my gun out and stalked into the room. Quickly, I swept her room, the connected bathroom, and the walk-in closet to ensure no vile surprises awaited her before returning to retrieve her.

"Was that really necessary? It's just my room, not like someone's gonna bug it or put a bomb in it." And that right there proved her to be too innocent for my fucked-up world.

I needed to find a way to shut Carol down before the end of the year and then clean up the shit with my lie before it blew up. No way in hell could I let it come true. I couldn't do that to Juliet. I'd be no better than her parents and those who've wronged her in life thus far. Besides, she still had her whole life ahead of her. It'd be somewhat wrong of me to chain her to someone more than twice her age and throw her into the mafia life when she had no place in it.

"I would argue with you otherwise, but I want your naïve innocence to remain intact," I replied with a sigh as I stood there and watched her whip through her room in a flurry.

The way she zipped back and forth with the occasional object being thrown onto her bed looked rather comical, and if the situation were different with a lighthearted feel, then I'd chuckle a bit. For her sake, I wished it was different. She shouldn't be packing to move in with a mafia boss because I was the only safe option in her life; she should be packing for college or some fun trip with her friends.

Speaking of college, what if I twisted things a bit? Alter the agreement? That should work. Well, that'll be plan B for now. If for some reason, I couldn't deal with Carol in a timely manner, then I'll just continue to lie and say Juliet and I came to an *agreement to wed after she finishes college. Yeah, that'll be a good plan.*

Everything will be fine.

Juliet deserved a good life, and I intend to give it all to her.

Chapter 9
Juliet

Everything, and nothing.

Whenever I thought I might not want or need to take an item, I did. Even though I made a mental list, being physically in my room threw me for a loop. I kept swinging back and forth between wanting to take everything to wanting to leave it all and start anew.

"Juliet." Luciano's concern broke my chain of anxiety as I looked over at him with a small frown. "What's wrong?" His comforting presence consumed me in his soothing scent when he approached my side.

Even though I pulled a good armful of items and tossed them on the bed to be packed, staring at it all made me want to turn away after throwing a match to it all. "I just... This feels weird. A part of me kind of wants to just forget it all and start anew because it feels wrong to bring bits and pieces of my old life with me to your place. It also feels like I'm tainting your place with my junk.

On the other hand, there are some things that have a lot of sentimental value to me." I hated how indecisive I was.

The feeling of his hand on my lower back caused a bloom of warmth to engulf me. "You're not going to tarnish or cramp up my place. Besides, it is now your place as well, and I want you to feel at home." With a soft nudge, he urged me toward the bed, where I had a growing pile of items. "Just because this is part of your past doesn't mean it's all bad, so just bring the good with you and leave the rest to rot with time."

Swallowing the lump in my throat, I slowly made my second round with my room, this time mindfully looking at everything, unlike before, when I went at everything mindlessly. It didn't take me long to go through everything, as I thought. Soon, I was packing my things away into boxes with Luciano's help.

"Who's this?" It was an innocent enough question, but the grave tone, ladened with seething jealousy, chilled me to my very bones as a fire lit itself in my chest.

Warily, I turned my attention to Luciano, who held a picture frame of Gale and me at the library. One of our friends snapped the picture of me falling asleep on Gale's shoulder because I'd grown so exhausted from studying for our finals. It was rare for me to have pictures of my friends, at least the ones that meant the most to me. I had a shit ton of pictures on my social media, but they were all for show or with the 'it' crowd because it was what my parents wanted. The only pictures that mattered to me amounted to exactly five photos, the one in Luciano's hands being one of them.

"That's Gale... He's just a friend. We were all studying late for finals last year, and I'd fallen asleep on him without knowing. One of our other friends thought it was cute and snapped a picture of us. It's the only copy I have because my parents made me delete the one I posted on social media and the one on my phone. They also made my friend delete the original, too." Yeah, my parents controlled my life very tightly, and with the wealth they wielded, they got away with nearly everything.

Grumbling, Luciano briefly narrowed his eyes at the picture. "Friends don't look at each other like that." I barely heard his low words as he tossed the picture into the box.

I knew that look and reaction all too well. "Gale is just a friend. Besides, why does any of that even matter to you anyway? What difference would it make if Gale and I were dating? Hm?" Luciano's jealousy was wrongly placed, in my opinion. I mean, it was kind of fun to see a man like Luciano getting jealous over simple 'ol me.

Gale was nothing more than a friend, even if it seemed otherwise at times. Honestly, I had no romantic feelings toward him, nor would I ever. By society's standards, Gale was a perfect man, and he would be a great partner to anyone lucky enough to win his affection.

"Sure, just a friend. Soon, it'll be just my husband before you know it." He grumbled as he continued packing things away. "You're too young to be dating anyway. You have college to get through, and a whole life to live before you even begin to think about settling."

Scowling, I softly 'tsk' while crossing my arms. "I am 18, that is not 'way too young' in this day and age. I'll have you know, a lot of my classmates are already engaged. Besides, I can date whoever I want because I can... I just don't want to." My eyes softly glared at him as I nervously tapped my foot.

Scowling softly, he rolled his eyes before giving me a stern look. "You shouldn't date whoever just because you can. If you're going to date someone, then it better be for serious intentions. Just focus on yourself and learn to love yourself again before you try to love someone else." He replied with a soft sigh. "I'm not trying to control you or anything, but I'm not going to let you do stupid shit."

Gritting my teeth, I huffed and scowled in response before giving him the silent treatment as I continued packing the rest of my stuff.

I didn't want to engage with him further because I felt it would get nowhere. Luciano was firm in his decision to keep me around and steer my life right, and I would be a complete fool to let this chance pass me because of my own stupidity. But he was up to something, though; I could feel it in my gut, and I'll damn well figure it out.

Luciano's little snickering chuckle made my attention snap back to him. "Cute, looks like I have a little nerd on my hands." He commented while waving a ratty textbook up in the air.

Dropping whatever was in my hands, I rushed over to him and grabbed the old book, only to have him hold it out of reach. Asshole. "Hey, be careful with that! Give it back to me!" I pleaded with a cracked voice.

Immediately, his playful demeanor changed to a concerned one as he handed the book back to me. "Hey, I was just teasing, no need to get upset. Besides, I can get you a new and better book that's probably more updated, too."

Snatching it from his hands, I hugged the precious book tightly. "I don't want another book." I snapped at him with a glare.

"Juliet, don't be silly. It's just a book." Luciano scoffed dismissively with a roll of his eyes.

Frustrated, I let out a low growl and kicked my leg out at Luciano, aiming for his shin.

"Whoa! Hey!" He quickly stepped back and caught my leg, stopping my kick. "You have a mouth, Juliet. Use it." He said sternly with hard eyes.

"Come here so I can use it to fucking bite you." Okay, that might have been uncalled for, but I felt a little spicy right now.

Luciano's jaw ticked as it tightened, his eyes darkening with his deep breaths. "You better change that fucking attitude of yours, or else." He left the threat hanging as his grip on my leg tightened.

Hopping up to him, I got right up in his face, or at least as much as possible with our height difference. "Or else what?" I challenged him with a defiant glare.

Taking a deep breath, he grabbed my neck firmly with his other hand, making my breath hitch at the sudden flare of heat exploding throughout my body. "Juliet, I am trying to give you the space and time you need to recover from your ordeal, but I am still only human at the end of the day. Push me enough, and you'll find that bratty mouth of yours occupied in ways you might find unsavory." He warned me lowly.

Reality quickly snapped me in the face like a taut rubber band. "L-Luciano, let me go, please." The phantom feeling of all the disgusting hands grabbing at my body crushed my nerves, and the room started to close in on me.

Choking on my own breaths, I desperately clawed at his forearm to be released. "Let me go, let me go, let me go!" Breathing felt almost impossible with how much my chest tightened, and the edges of my vision started to blur and close in.

Chapter 10
Luciano

Shit, shit, shit.

Immediately, I released her and took her into my arms, stroking her hair and shushing her soothingly. "Hey, breathe. In through your nose, out through your mouth." I instructed her in a calm and steady voice.

Tightly, I held her struggling body as she tried to control her breathing. "You can do it. In and out, slowly." I encouraged her again softly. "You are doing great so far. Keep it up, *principessa*."

Any edge I felt with Juliet's brattiness disappeared as fast as it came the moment her body froze up in my hold. The switch in her was enough to flip that protective side in me. I would deal with the guilt of being an inconsiderate asshole to her after I got her through this anxiety attack.

Remaining firm yet soft, I continued to soothe her. "Focus on my voice. Whatever is going on in your mind is just that. It's not a reality anymore, nor will it ever be again. You are safe, Juliet. You are here and safe with me." And a dandy fucking job I did with making her feel safe.

I felt like a complete bastard for triggering her with my actions; I should have thought about it before grabbing her neck like that. I should have known better, but my Dominant side came out before I could reign it in.

Would she be safer without me around?

I couldn't help but wonder if being around Juliet would be more detrimental to her recovery than beneficial. She could easily find comfort in someone else, right?

No, she's mine! There won't be anyone else. Only me.

The thought of her seeking comfort in someone else's arms made my blood boil. The only arms she belonged in were mine. Only I could hold her and touch her.

God, what is wrong with me?

I shouldn't be feeling this way towards her. I couldn't.

Reluctantly, I let go when I felt her body relax with her even breaths. "That's it, that's my good girl." I praised her with a smile.

Holding her at arm's length, I softly rubbed her shoulders with my thumbs. "I am sorry. I shouldn't have grabbed you like that. It's... A habit..." Nothing took control of a situation faster than a neck grab, no matter who I was dealing with. Uppity sub? I'd have them melting under me within seconds. A target? I'd have them shaking beneath my feet and begging to spare their lives.

Her neck bobbed with her nervous swallow as she nervously fiddled with the edges of the worn pages. "I-I shouldn't have gotten in your face like that, and I shouldn't have snapped at you." Looking down at the ground, she shuffled her feet a bit. "It's just... The book's a gift from my cousin, who put it together with a good friend of his who he went to school with, and it's been one of the few things I've managed to keep hidden from my parents to enjoy."

Well, this whole thing could have been avoided had she told me that in the first place. I couldn't fault her, though. I remembered how I was at her age, going silent on my parents and snapping at them for stupid shit—I apologized in the end, of course. But, point being that communication was the last thing on my mind in my teenager and early adult years.

Besides, her life was in turmoil right now. I had to give her props for handling things as well as she has been. If I were in her situation, I would have gone mad and let my anger take over to bring ruin to anything and everything around me.

Against my better judgment, I pulled her into a tight hug, rubbing her back. "Do you want to have the whole book copied and laminated so it can be preserved for the long run? I can have one of the men do that or get you what you need to do that." I offered with a curious look down at her.

The happy smile slowly worked its way onto her face as she looked up at me with bright eyes. "You'd do that for me?" Her body jerked a bit in my arms from her happy little bounce.

Chuckling softly, I brushed and tucked away her stray bangs behind her ear. "I would do anything for you, Juliet, as long as it makes you happy."

"What about letting me have one of your cars?" She asked with a cheeky little grin and giggle.

Rolling my eyes, I leaned in and softly kissed her temple. "Okay, there may be some stipulations to that." I knew she was joking, but I couldn't let her have some slack. "I'd sooner kill someone than let you get behind the wheel with no experience." The last thing I wanted was for her to crash.

A small shiver pricked my spine at the sight of Juliet's dark eyes hardening. "So, if I asked you to kill my parents right now, you would?" Her voice was mixed with wariness and hope with how her voice lifted at the end.

Cradling her face with a hand, I stroked her cheek with a twisted smirk. "If that is what you wish and would help you sleep better at night, then yes, without any hesitation." Granted, I never had any trouble with murdering anyone in general.

Killing was a part of me like breathing, and even though I found a sick joy in it, the thought of killing at Juliet's request brought a new fire of life to the activity. I shouldn't be leading her into my dark waters, but the dangerous edge to her eyes was too tempting and exciting.

Chewing her bottom lip, she looked at me for another moment before shaking her head and returning to how she was before. "W-we should finish up and leave. I am sorry for even bringing something like that up. I don't know what came over me." Her voice had a fearful tension, but it didn't feel like it was directed towards me.

"Nothing to apologize about, they did an awful, shitty thing to their own daughter." Pulling away, I comforted her with a half-smile. "They'd be shark food by now if it were up to me." I half-joked with a chuckle before releasing her fully to return to packing.

Honestly, what the fuck was I even doing? I shouldn't be encouraging her bad behavior. She needed to stay on a good path, the one which led *far away* from me.

The sounds of shuffling boxes filled the tense atmosphere. "So... Coding and hacking?" Fuck, why did I have to sound so awkward?

Chuckling nervously, Juliet didn't bother looking in my direction as she replied. "Yeah, it's simple and fun. I find it so amazing how I can have access to nearly everything from a simple computer, and I love how the most mundane changes could alter a program so much." Smiling, she grinned happily to herself. "And don't even get me started on all the shit I can control with some simple keystrokes."

Soon, a small smile made its way to my own face as Juliet prattled on excitedly about all the little things she could do with fucking around with lines of codes on a computer. Little of it made sense to me, but I couldn't find it in myself to put a stop to her brightness. I don't think I have ever seen her this excited since I brought her back to my home, so it was very refreshing.

After ordering some of my men to carry the boxes out to the vehicles, I interrupted her with a question. "Do you want to stop by an electronics store to get a computer after ice cream?"

I didn't think she could get any more excited today, nor did I think I would ever enjoy the sounds of anyone squealing. Yet here we were. "Yes! Please! Yes!" Giggling, she practically jumped in her spot with delight as she grinned at me gratefully.

Unfortunately, her happiness didn't last long. "You're so disgusting. I can't believe you're my sister." Juliet's face immediately paled, and her smile turned upside down at the voice of a younger male.

Chapter 11

Juliet

WHIPPING AROUND TO FACE the door, I frowned at the sight of my younger brother, who stood there glaring at me with utter disgust.

Boldly, he trudged up to me with Luciano right at my backside. Protectively, he wrapped an arm around my waist and held a gun out at my seething brother. "Don't, please." I quietly begged Luciano, placing a hand over his and urging him to lower the weapon.

"This is the bastard you chose to abandon our family for? To cut all ties for? Do you know who he is? What he does? What he just threatened ma and ba for?" A mere foot away from me, he glared up at Luciano and jabbed a finger in his direction. "You are disgusting and cruel. Walking in here like you own the place and demanding things of my parents like that. How fucking desperate must you be to force a mar—"

"That is enough!" Luciano's booming voice trembled in the air, making both my brother and I flinch. "You are lucky I don't put a bullet in you because

71

your sister still has a heart after your parents plucked it out and stomped over it."

"Gerald, leave, please. I'm just getting my stuff and leaving right now. I have nothing to say to you, nor do I want to see you. So, leave before something happens." I pleaded with my brother with a tired sigh.

As annoying as he was, my parents were to blame for how shitty of a brat my brother had turned out. They spoiled the absolute fucking shit out of him; treated him like he was some king set to rule the world. Unlike me, he got everything he ever wanted. If he mentioned something once, no matter how small, it was given to him the next day or less. He was treated like royalty, while I was a peasant on a good day.

Yeah, my parents were really big on the whole notion of boys being better and treasured and shit. It didn't matter if I was the oldest; I had the wrong parts, so I was seen as trash in my parent's eyes. I also kind of deluded myself into thinking that if I gave in to their demands and were the obedient child they wanted, then they would give me some affection and respect.

The tiny part of old me wanted to hang my head and beg at my parents' feet to forgive me and go back to them. But the new me knew better and fought against it. I couldn't go back to my old life. The old me was too weak and vulnerable, and if I wanted to live a happy life, then I needed to grow up, put up some walls of steel, and guard myself.

The next words to fly from my brother's mouth stung me as he called me every name in the book and under God's green earth in Vietnamese. Then, he started to spew more nonsense that drowned out in my muffled ears as I shut down.

The warmth from Luciano left my side, snapping me back to reality as the fear of him hurting my brother jolted me. "Alright. That's enough." Luciano growled as he shoved my brother back out of the room. "Guards! Why is he not locked away with the others!"

Approaching Luciano, I tugged at his sleeve lightly. "Luciano, I want to leave now, please." I hated how tiny my voice came out when I spoke.

I shouldn't let my brother's words get to me since they were thrown at me out of anger and resentment, but even so, there had to be some truth to it. What he said about me as a person didn't bother me too much because I knew they weren't true, but when he said something about Luciano and me, I couldn't help but pay attention.

Why would he say something about Luciano and I being in a relationship? Something about me being a gold-digging bitch to a bad man like Luciano and being his woman and whatnot. It was a jumbled mess, but I got some points from it.

My brother's protests and struggles faded down the hallway into some room as some of Luciano's men dragged him away. "Why does he think that you and I are together?" I asked Luciano in a wary voice, looking at him with a furrowed expression.

Sure, I stuck to Luciano, but he was the only other person besides Leah that I trusted and felt somewhat comfortable around right now. If Gale or one of my other close friends had been here, then I would have clung to them more tightly than Luciano. Well, maybe not. Luciano had this radiant energy that made me feel safe, something I had never felt from anyone before.

Not looking at me, Luciano answered, "I don't know. He might have just said stuff out of the moment. Also, he could just be bad at making inferences. Seeing a young woman like you cling to me and such could have given him the wrong impression in his haze." I didn't buy his words, none of it; his voice was hollow and avoidant like his eyes.

He fucking lied to me, but I couldn't call him out on it because how would I even begin to argue that? But what if he was telling me the truth? Maybe he sounded off because he was annoyed from dealing with my brother.

Sighing, I tucked the thoughts away for later, not wanting to possibly get into it with Luciano over possibly nothing. "Leave? Please?" This place felt heavier and heavier by the second, and I didn't want to run the possibility of running into a worker or, God forbid, my parents.

Taking my hand, he gave it a comforting squeeze before taking one last look around the place. "If you are done here, *principessa*, then we can."

Slowly, I went over every inch of my room for the last time to make sure I didn't miss anything before nudging Luciano to leave. I hated how my mood dampened so quickly from my brother's outburst, and I wasn't even sure if I wanted to go out and do anything with Luciano anymore.

Numbingly, I followed behind Luciano, letting him lead me out to the car. "Juliet." His deep, smooth voice beckoned my full attention to him as we stood at his car.

Pulling me into a comforting hug, he rubbed my back as he spoke. "Do not let what he said get to you. People can say things they don't mean when they are emotional. Besides, this will all be behind you, starting now." I could feel his arm move a little before the sound of the car door opening hit my ears. "Now, let's get out of here and cheer you up with some ice cream."

Ice cream didn't sound as tempting as it did earlier. All I wanted to do was go home and crawl into bed to wallow in my dark thoughts. Guess I didn't have much choice in the matter, though, because Luciano gently nudged me into the passenger seat and secured me with the seat belt before shutting the door.

By the time I worked up the nerve to protest, he was pulling into a parking spot in front of a gelato shop. I didn't want to trouble him now if we were already at the place. Well, a scoop of ice cream never hurt anyone. And after I got a whiff of waffles and sweetness, my mouth watered with a yearning to taste the unknown.

So, with a quiet smile on my face, I let Luciano help me out of the car and into the busy little business. "Ah, Luciano! How are you doing?!" A jolly old man with a heavy accent greeted us with a welcoming grin. "Come!" He eagerly waved us in. "Pick what you want!"

Even though the place was bustling, the old man pushed his way through to Luciano after rounding the counter. The next few minutes consisted of me standing there awkwardly as the man and Luciano exchanged some words and laughter with each other in Italian.

While they conversed, I peered around Luciano at the glass display that housed tubs of various ice creams. There were so many that the big U-shaped counter looked like a delicious rainbow.

The more I appreciated the frozen treats, the more my anxiety rose. Surely, I couldn't eat them all today, but I didn't even have an inkling of an idea as to what flavor I wanted as my first-ever frozen treat. I didn't want to pick something I would possibly hate and have that be my first experience with ice cream. Plus, some of the flavors sounded so fancy. I mean, what the heck was island sangria gelato supposed to taste like? What the heck was an island sangria?

"Juliet?" Luciano's voice pulled me from the muffling waters of my anxiety. "Do you see something you want?" His deep, accented voice sent shivers down my spine when it hit the shell of my ear.

Nervously, I picked at the cuff of his jacket. "I can't decide, and I don't know where to start."

Luciano turned his head to the old man and said a few more words before dragging me to some storage closet in the back. "Hey." His voice was soft yet firm as he commanded my full attention to him. "If this is too much for you right now, we can get a little of everything to go." He suggested, squeezing at my shoulders softly.

I wanted to shake my head and refuse, but my head remained stiff on my neck. I needed to push myself back out into the world, but I couldn't do it. The thought of going back out to the semi-crowded shop got my heart racing to the point where my stomach flipped, causing me to become nauseous. "Can we do that? I don't think I can handle being around so many people right now in an enclosed space."

"I can have everyone leave." Luciano chuckled softly, earning a concerned look from me because I couldn't tell if he was serious or not. "Mister Romano won't mind."

Quickly, I shot him down with a shake of my head. "We can't just send his business away like that." He seemed like a nice man, too, so I definitely didn't want to dampen his business for my stupid anxiety. "Let's just grab some to go. I really don't feel like being out anymore."

Humming, he gave a soft nod of his head before leading me out to the car, saying something to Mr. Romano in Italian on the way out. "My men will bring a little of everything back to the house for us." He informed me as I got settled in the passenger seat.

"Uhh, isn't that a little excessive? There were like so many in there." Granted, I wouldn't even have an idea of where to start. Excessive, but maybe needed. Still, I didn't want him to have tubs of ice cream sitting around, especially if I didn't like the flavor—I didn't want food to go to waste.

"Well, how else are you going to find what you like or don't if you don't try everything?" He mused with a chuckle, raising an eyebrow as he leaned against the open car door. "It's just a pint of everything."

"That's a lot of ice cream still." I protested with a soft pout. I couldn't argue anything else with him because he had a valid point. "What if I don't like something? I don't want it to go to waste."

Amused, he chuckled and reached out to ruffle the back of my head. "Then either I'll eat it on a cheat day, or one of my men will pick it up. Between all who work for me, someone will take the free treat." With that, he shut the door and rounded the car to his side.

"Luciano?" I waited until his head turned to me before smiling softly and brightly at him. "Thank you."

"Don't thank me for treating you as you should be, *principessa*."

Chapter 12

Juliet

~1.5 weeks later~

"Juliet, come here." Luciano's deep voice summoned me to his office just as I passed it.

I nearly tripped over my own feet from how fast I stopped to spin around on my heel. Standing at the doorway, I smiled at him apologetically. "Sorry, I know I'm not supposed to be in this wing, but they said you were over here, and I wanted to say bye before school." I also might have wandered a little too far in my daze.

Smiling, he forgave me with a shake of his head as he beckoned me over with a wave of his hand. "It's fine. Just be a little more mindful from here on out. It's not that I want to ban you from this wing just because." Once again, he had this reluctant edge to his voice that made me wonder if he held something back, but I didn't push it as I slowly approached his desk and stood across from him on the other side. "I am doing it for your own safety and sake. There are lots of things that happen in this wing that are unsavory, things I don't want to expose and taint you with."

His studious eyes looked me over before his face softly bunched up with a soft frown. "Are you sure you want to return to school? It won't hurt you to take more time off to recover, and my offer of homeschooling is also on the table." He inquired as he got up from his seat and rounded the table until he leaned back against the desk before me.

Uncertain, I frowned and twiddled with my fingers. "I don't know. I feel like I should try to go to school. I mean, it might help to be around my peers again... But it also just feels overwhelming to think about being around all those people." Chewing my bottom lip, I exhaled heavily through my nose. "I also can't stay cooped up in your place forever... But I'm so scared."

The thought of going back to school and pretending I didn't get trafficked by my own parents, gang raped, and now tangled with the biggest mafia on the east coast was unnerving, to say the least. On the other hand, how would other people see me if they managed to find out what happened?

Reaching out, Luciano took my hands into his, brushing his thumbs comfortingly over my knuckles. "You don't have to do this if you are not ready. It has barely been over a week since your traumatic event, and you have only had one therapy session so far." Settling my hands back down, he reached out and tucked my hair behind my ear. "You don't need to push yourself so much. You have only started the healing process, and if you overexert yourself, you can undo your progress."

He was right, like always, but being home with him felt suffocating with how he bounced from being caring and supportive to giving me a cold shoulder. I know he was a busy man, but over the past few days, he locked himself away in the office wing and felt as if he tried to isolate himself from me.

"I'll be okay... I have to be." I couldn't stay broken and weak forever. I had to pick my life back up sooner than later.

Sighing softly, Luciano shook his head as his hands cupped my face. "No, Juliet, do not force yourself to be okay when you are not. If you are not ready, then that is okay. You are allowed to take time, especially since you can." His thumb softly brushed my cheekbone as he looked at me with sympathetic eyes.

"Listen, I know you want to try and get your life back, take some kind of control back and all, but if you are not fully prepared to try and face the consequences, it will end badly. You have already gone through enough, and I do not want you to get hurt again so soon or ever." At least his voice was comforting to my nerves.

Just as I opened my mouth to protest, he held a finger to my mouth, "If you want to try today, then I will support you like always. I just need you to agree to a few terms, alright?" His voice sweetened just enough with his little smirk as he tilted my face up a little.

"Do I get to know the terms before I agree?" I asked warily as my body tensed up. The last thing I needed to do was blindly agree to something and get myself in a shitty situation. I doubt Luciano would do something like that to me, but I couldn't help but feel wary about any kind of agreement after everything.

Huffing out a soft chuckle, he gave me a proud smile of sorts. "Good girl, never blindly agree to anything." Letting go of my face, he placed his hands against the edge of the desk. "Go for half the day for the next few days. Give yourself some breathing room. *If* you feel like you can keep going by lunchtime, let me know so I don't have someone pick you up. If I do not hear from you, then I will assume you are not comfortable and will have your ass dragged home to decompress." Tilting his head, he urged me to answer with a raised eyebrow.

"Fine." It wasn't some ridiculous request. He was being more than reasonable, and it was for my sake and health. "What are your other terms and conditions?"

"If you feel uncomfortable and want a break at any point in the school day, then let me know ASAP. You will also let me know of any plans before or after school just so I know of your last known whereabouts if anything were to happen, not that they should, but just in case." After giving me a moment to process his words, he continued, "I am not going to control your life much if I can help it, but for you to have such freedom, you have to be safe, responsible, and reasonable with me. Your bodyguard will take you to and from school every day, and they will hang around the parking lot until it is time for you to go home."

Pouting a little, I held my complaint back as I reluctantly nodded. I didn't want a bodyguard around to draw attention to myself. Then again, pretty sure showing up to school in an expensive ass car with a new driver would draw eyes to me already.

Maybe Luciano had a point about taking a few days off, but even when I would go back, the situation wouldn't be any different. So, might as well suck it up now, I guess.

Resigning to my fate with a sigh, I looked down at my foot for a moment before looking back up at Luciano, who studied me with hawk-like eyes. "If you have any issues with any of it, then by all means, let me know." He invited me with a wave of his hand and a warm smile.

"Well, I don't want the bodyguard, but it's for my safety... So, I'll learn to live with them hanging around." I grumbled with a relenting sigh. "Anything else?"

Nodding his head, Luciano fished around in his pocket and pulled out a small pouch. "Just one last thing." From the bag, he pulled out a necklace with a pendant of a pair of bat-like wings with two horns and a pointed tail in the shape of the letter 'L' on it. "Well, this one might not be much of a request, more of a... Demand, I guess."

"I'm guessing you want me to wear it and never take it off?" I asked with an unsure voice and expression while I studied the thing closely. "It's not really my style..."

"But it is for your safety." He added in a firm voice. "I won't always be around for people to know you are under my protection. This is my symbol within the mafia, so everyone will know who you belong to while you have it on your body."

Involuntarily, I shivered at his words. He probably didn't mean anything to them, and hearing him say I belonged to him broke open a dam of heat within me. Strangely, I felt happy at the words, and it made me feel safe knowing I belonged somewhere. It was stupid of me to feel and think too much about it, though, because he probably didn't mean it like *that* or anything close.

Bunching my hair up, I slowly turned around and peered back at Luciano with an eager smile. "Put it on me, please?"

The way Luciano's eyes darkened with his widening smile sent another rush of heat down my body where it settled in areas I never thought I'd feel for a long time. I thought I'd be fearful of getting such a hungry gaze from a man, but for some reason, I felt a need to run into Luciano's arms and press my body right up against his rather than the adrenaline rush to run far away.

It felt so wrong, yet so right. I shouldn't be eager to get close to a man after what I went through. Well, in a way, I wasn't. The thought of being within arm's reach of any male made me want to hurl and curl away in a corner until I became nothing. I was disgusted with myself at how much I craved Luciano; it was a constant tug-of-war within me.

Unable to help it, I shuddered at the feeling of his rough fingers brushing against my collarbone and neck as he looped the delicate chain around and secured it. The weight of the pendant sank into my upper chest like a weight, or at least it felt like it. Turning around, I looked up at Luciano intensely with wanton eyes and heavy breaths.

The air between us thickened with unadulterated heat with our locked gazes. Inhaling deeply, I watched Luciano's jaw tense before he swept a hand across his stubbled jaw with the faintest of growls. Then, slowly, his hand reached out and settled around my neck, his thumb brushing against my thrumming carotid as I offered more of my neck to him.

Then, nothing. Confusion and disappointment crashed into me like a freezing tsunami when he dropped his hand from my neck and stepped away from me. "Don't take it off, and have a good day at school, Juliet."

Disappointment sank into me more when he used my name instead of *principessa*, something he had been calling me quite a bit recently.

Swallowing the lump in my throat, I smiled flatly at him and nodded. "I'll try. Thank you for the necklace."

Feeling rejected, I quickly made my way out of his office with my head down.

Asshole.

I should have listened to Luciano.

"Juliet." The usual calming voice of Gale, paired with his touch, nearly gave me a damn heart attack when I jumped away from him as if he were a monster.

Holding his hands up, he looked at me with a worried frown. "Juliet, you need to go home before you faint." Slowly, he approached me with caution. Hesitantly, he reached out and hugged my stiff body tightly. "What's wrong? What happened? You go silent over the whole break, then you come back a whole different person and refuse to tell any of us anything."

Sighing heavily, I softly pushed Gale away. "I-I can't... It's too much for me to bring up again right now." The notion of it seemed simple enough, but I already had a trip to Hell and back when I had to tell my therapist everything.

Luciano's home, where I felt remotely safe, was the only place I would accept having a breakdown. "Maybe later... Not here, though." I mean, Luciano did say I was free to bring whoever over, that it was now as much my place as it was his.

Exhaling heavily, Gale's frown deepened as his hands twitched at his side. "Alright, but you still need to go home, Juliet." He strained out flatly.

I wanted to shake my head and argue with him, but I was too tired to. It took so much energy to make it to lunch without going into a panic attack or jumping at every person who approached me. The fight in me was nearly nonexistent now.

"Do you need me to call your par—"

"No!" Not even the full mention of my parents got my anxiety spiking again to where my heart raced and tightened in my suffocating chest.

Frantically, my hand scratched at my chest until Luciano's pendant dug into my palm from gripping it so hard. It was the only thing that has kept me rooted in reality so far.

Luciano. I needed to get back to Luciano.

Chapter 13
Luciano

WHAT IS WRONG WITH me?

Okay, that was a fucking loaded question. So, correction: what was wrong with me when it came to Juliet.

I needed to distance myself from her, but that proved rather difficult with how she sought me out for comfort. I could have been heartless and denied her, but seeing her frown and cry pulled out the little humanity I had within me.

I tried to ignore her a few times, but the moment her small body pressed up against mine, and those acid-like tears burned my skin, any resolve I had disappeared within seconds. Somehow, I always ended up with my arms tightly around her with my hands doing some idle comforting, and my mouth moved on its own accord with my uncontrolled thoughts to spew sugar coated words. Well, more like sugar coated reality.

Even though I comforted her and wanted to lift her spirits, I always kept things straight with her. The last thing I wanted to do was give her false hopes and promises because like hell I want to deal with the fallout if shit hits the fan. Also, I wasn't good at this comforting business—I found it all a waste of time.

Honestly, I was rather surprised at myself at how I hadn't told Juliet to suck it the fuck up and move on. As harsh as it was, I would have told that to most people. Well, maybe not if they were in her exact situation because that really would be fucked up of me.

Yes, I was a fucked-up person, but not *that* fucked up. I had loose morals. I knew right and wrong. I just chose to operate in the darker gray zone for the most part.

Speaking of operating... I needed to ensure things for the next fight were going smoothly. I would probably go ballistic if it weren't for these underground fights. It had been too long since the last one was held because I had to shut it down at the last minute due to a leak. So, I have been pent up for months on end.

Actually, maybe that was my problem. Maybe I was more than just pent up regarding my aggression and murderous needs; I was probably pent up sexually, too. Thinking about it, I couldn't recall the last time I had a good fuck because business kept getting in the way. I was probably hung over Juliet because of my stupid raging hormones from not getting laid—not because I couldn't.

A man like me had no issues getting a good woman for a good fucking—I just didn't put the effort into contacting the escort company to send someone. For the most part, dealing with things myself in the shower curbed the edge enough to keep my mind on track, but everyone has a breaking point—even me. Guess I finally reached it again.

It probably didn't help my urges to have a beauty like Juliet hanging on me nearly every day. No matter how much I kicked my stupid brain, apparently, it didn't get the gist that she was off limits. She was much too young for me, and she had so much to live for still for me to damn her to a life with me.

Her life is gonna be damned to you at the end of the year.

Then there was the dumb reminder of my spur of the moment fuck up. I really needed to fix the stupid sham marriage contract shit before it got blown out of proportion.

Fucking hell. So much shit to fix. Fuck me.

Juliet *will not* be my wife. She couldn't. It wasn't that I didn't want her; it was the sheer difference in our lives. I mean, physically, she was a thing of perfect beauty. Then, if her brattiness was any indication of her personality blooming, then fuck me; I was beyond screwed.

She was still a ball of anxiety and traumatic outbursts, but the periods of reprieve between the attacks were amusing to me. To me, it seemed as if she started to recover pretty well and let her true self come out during those moments, even if she was hesitant and would pull back most of the time; it was heartwarming to see her bloom again.

Then the fact she only let herself come out around me gave me an ego boost I didn't need because it was already too fucking big for me to handle. Of course, then my dick became too hard to handle when she acted up and got all up in my face being a defiant little brat; the dominant side of me wanted nothing more than to grab her by the neck or her hair and bend her over my knee for a spanking, or over the table so I could fuck the attitude out of her.

Fuck, then this morning. The necklace really was an innocent gift for her to wear so that others would know who she belonged to. Yet, it went completely off the rails in my mind when I slipped it around her precious neck. I wanted to rip the flimsy chain off and replace it with a leather collar. Or I could be more insane and brand her with it, really mark her as mine for life.

If I didn't have an ounce of control, I would have given into her fuck me eyes. Juliet would have been pinned to the desk by her neck with my cock buried deep in her tight cunt, fucking her until she couldn't even remember her own name.

Fucking stop it!

Letting out a frustrated growl, I kicked the side of my desk as I shoved my boiling desires away. If only my dick got the damn message and went down, then that would be much appreciated.

Gritting my teeth in a hard scowl, I ran a hand through my ebony hair and gripped at the top of it, hoping the pain would draw my thoughts away from Juliet. "Escort," I muttered to myself through my lustful haze.

Snatching my phone off the desk, I quickly messaged the Madam of the escort company I often used. Just as the message was sent and the phone clattered on the desk from me tossing it, the door to my office opened without an announcement.

"I am sorry for barging in without knocking, but miss Juliet—"

Holding my hand out, I stopped my man mid-sentence. "Where is she?" Any anger I felt was gone when Juliet's name was brought up. It had to be dire for any of my men to barge into my office and risk my wrath.

The faint sobs from Juliet became more prominent the closer my long strides carried me toward the living area. Hit after hit, the louder her heart-wrenching sobs became, the more my body ached. It felt like someone was kidney punching me in the ring, with each step being another blow until it felt endless to where my stomach threatened to empty its contents.

I hated Juliet crying, not because it was annoying, but because it hurt me. Never have I wanted to take someone's suffering away so badly until her. I have ended people's suffering before—with a bullet—just so I could be done with the annoyance. With Juliet, though, I wanted to take it all away to the pits of Hell and lock it away so she could live an unburdened life with me right beside her.

"Juliet, you have to breathe. You're okay."

Well, that didn't sound like any of my men.

Rounding the corner, my eyes instantly landed on a somewhat familiar-looking boy from Juliet's pictures sitting on the couch with Juliet. What was his name? Gage? Gavin? Well, whatever it was, it didn't matter to me through my rising anger at how close he was to Juliet. If Juliet weren't in such distress, I would pick a bloody fight with him—or shove a gun into his gut—but she came first.

Rushing over, I shoved the boy away and pulled Juliet tightly into my arms. "*Principessa*, shh, you are safe." I spoke deeply into her ear as I stroked the back of her head with one hand. "Focus on my voice," I commanded with a tightening hand around the nape of her neck. "That's it. *Brava ragazza*." I praised her when her hyperventilating steadied out to even breaths. "*Sono così fiero di te. Hai fatto benissimo*."

Resting my chin atop her head, I resisted the urge to kiss her forehead—it would have been very inappropriate of me.

"Juliet, what's going on?" Her male friend asked in a very wary voice as he leaned away from me, looking like a scared dog ready to bolt.

"What happened?" I asked no one in particular, my eyes bouncing from Juliet's bodyguards to the boy, then back to Juliet, who was a sniffling mess in my arms.

"She called for me to take her home because she wasn't feeling well and wanted her friend to come along too. She was fine for most of the ride but went into an episode shortly before we came home." The guard reported to me.

"What's going on with Juliet?" At least I could appreciate her friend's genuine concern for her.

Ignoring the boy's question, I momentarily glanced down at Juliet. "Did any of you say or do something to trigger her?" I questioned with a pointed look at the guard and Juliet's friend.

"No, I did nothing but drive and keep quiet." The guard answered calmly and politely.

Her friend was quick to shake his head in denial. "No, I didn't say or do anything. I kept quiet and let her hold and play with my hands while she looked out the window. Literally, she was fine one minute, then she became inconsolable the next."

Keeping Juliet safely pressed against me, I rubbed her upper arm as she trembled against me. "Hilly, go get some water and snacks for Juliet from the kitchen," I ordered her bodyguard with a quick, stern look.

Without a word, she nodded and slipped away, leaving me alone with two anxious adult teens.

Not looking directly at the boy, I merely peered at him out of the corners of my eyes. "How was she at school?" I doubted I would get a straight answer—or any—from Juliet right now.

"Not herself." *Well, no fucking shit Sherlock.* "She's been really anxious all day long and just..." Frowning, the boy clenched his fists by his sides. "Is she going to be okay? What's wrong with her? She won't tell me anything, but I know something must have happened over spring break for her to end up like this."

Juliet's scratchy voice came out muffled as she had her face against my chest. "Gale, I'll be okay..." Slowly, she turned her face to look at her friend with a weak smile.

"Juliet, if you weren't in the arms of a gangster, then I'd be more inclined to believe that." Gale sighed with a wary look at me.

Scoffing with a sneer, I turned my head to fully face him with a displeased scowl. "I'm one of the heads of The Syndicate; don't make me sound like a street rat with a gun that has one functioning brain cell amped on drugs." I couldn't help but chuckle a little out of amusement when Gale flinched a bit from my snappiness.

"Luciano, be nice to him. He's my best friend." Juliet softly snapped at me with a pout after she pushed apart from me.

Softly, Juliet hit my chest. "Quit looking at him like that, too. You're gonna scare him, and if you do, I'll make you regret it." Okay, it was impossible not to laugh a little at her cute little—empty—threat. "I'm serious." She growled softly with a flurry of smacks against me.

Grabbing her wrists, I held both in one hand and petted her head. "Do you want me to leave you with your friend? Seems like you two have a lot to talk about." Did I want to? No. The only thing I wanted right now was to literally grab Gale and chuck him out the door to have Juliet give me her undivided attention.

Okay, maybe the last bit would be a bad idea since I wanted to distance myself from her. Actually, I probably should leave her and Gale alone, but I hated the thought of that. Thinking about Juliet being alone with anyone of the opposite gender rubbed me the wrong way, which was ridiculous and selfish of me.

Fuck, maybe I need to get my head set straight again.

Sighing softly, I settled her fully against the couch and did a quick once-over to make sure she wasn't injured in any way. "Do you want to talk about what triggered you? Or do you want to talk about it later?"

Surely, something had to have set her off. Juliet hasn't had any random panic attacks recently without a trigger. The first two to three days were a little rough because of her nightmares and constant relapse into her trauma, but she faired better in the coming days after the therapist.

"Later, please." She replied in a small voice, averting her eyes from me to pick at her painted nails.

Cupping her face, I gently wiped her tears away with my thumbs before stroking her cheek slowly. "When Hilly gets back with water and food, I expect you to take it. You need to replenish yourself, alright?" My eyes searched for

Juliet's, making her look at my firm gaze directly. "If I hear otherwise from Hilly later, then you don't want to know what I have in store for you."

Lord, I hope she won't disobey me because I did not want to come up with a punishment that didn't involve her baring her juicy ass for me to turn red with my hands. How the hell was I even supposed to punish her? I shouldn't have let my mouth run on instinct and habit.

Juliet wasn't my sub—far from it. So, I needed to stop, even if her bratty ass needed a good lesson or two. But hell, I shouldn't be thinking about that kind of stuff with her. After what she had been through, I wouldn't be surprised if she chose to remain celibate for the rest of her life.

Chewing her bottom lip softly, she nodded her head with a defeated sigh. "Yes, sir."

Fuck. Me.

Chapter 14

Juliet

"JULIET, WHY ARE YOU in a mobster's home?" Gale asked frantically in a hushed voice, waving his hand around the area.

Curling my legs up to my chest, I hugged them tightly and picked at the seams of my sweatpants. "It's my home now too..." I admitted almost shamefully.

Hesitantly, Gale scooted closer to me with his arms open as if he were ready to hug me. "Juliet, what do you mean? What's going on? I mean, do you know who *he* is?" Gale continued to worry with a deepening frown.

How do I even begin to tell Gale about all that happened? It's so much.

Sighing heavily, I let my knees go to grab a throw pillow to hug instead. Gripping and tugging at the tassels of the pillow, I nearly ripped them off in my little anxious fit as I lined my story up in my mind. "When break started, like that night, my parents sold me off to a brothel. I was auctioned off days later, and..." The words caught in my aching throat as I fought my emotions from spilling over. "A-and..."

Gale's gentle hand on my shoulder made me flinch in my heightened state. Immediately, Gale pulled me into a tight hug. "You don't have to force yourself to tell me if you're not ready." He said in an understanding voice.

"Luciano saved me and gave me a new life here with him. He's been good to me, I swear." Except for the occasional cold shoulder the past few days.

"That doesn't change the fact that he's a syndicate head, a cold-hearted killer." Gale sighed and pulled away from me with a worried frown. "Isn't there someone else you can stay with?"

Smiling sadly, I shook my head, "No, not with how messy my situation is. It's a lot more complicated than it sounds like. I'm not safe without Luciano's protection." The fact of being tied to him for the rest of my life didn't bother me as much as I thought. Granted, he didn't really restrict me, so maybe that was why I didn't mind him being in charge.

"I promise, Gale, I am fine with Luciano," I assured my friend with a confident smile. "He may be bad to others, but he's good to me." And shouldn't that be all that mattered at the end of the day?

"I still don't like it," Gale grumbled with a defeated sigh. "I just have an icky feeling about this. He seems like he's hiding something from you." Before I could question Gale, he held a hand up to stop me, "I don't know what it is. It was just a feeling when I saw him interact with you. I mean, I can see that he genuinely cares for your well-being, but there's something else behind his eyes."

I couldn't help but silently agree with Gale because I sensed it, too. There was something behind Luciano's kind smile, and I was afraid to dig to uncover what it was. Unfortunately, my hands were tied. It was either grit it out with Luciano or face my chances with the sharks out in the open waters with slabs of meat chained to my body.

Better to lay with the devil you know than the one you don't, or whatever that saying was. Maybe I needed to remind myself of that more often than not. At the end of the day, Luciano was The Devil, and the Devil always had ulterior motives up his sleeves. Nothing ever came free of stipulations, and I might best be wary of that.

"I'll be fine... I have to..." I tried to put on a confident smile for Gale, but I could feel the corners of my lips falter when Gale tilted his head at me with a pointed look. "Well, even if there is something wrong, I can't do anything about it," I remarked with a roll of my eyes.

"What if he's planning on killing you?" Gale threw out the ridiculous idea in an unsure voice.

I couldn't help but laugh a bit at his words because they were so absurd. "Luciano isn't going to kill me. There is literally no reason for him to, and if he was, wouldn't he have done it by now?" To me, it would make no sense to keep me around and ensure my safety and comfort only to put a bullet through me later.

"Maybe he's some sicko who gets off on some weird shit." Gale rebutted with an unsure voice.

The sounds of footsteps, along with the sight of a dark figure out of the corner of my eye, made me turn my head towards Luciano, who was walking towards the front door. "Hey, Luciano," I called out for him, making him stop and turn his head at me. "You're not going to kill me, are you?"

Lowering his phone, Luciano chuckled amusingly as he studied me closely with his gem-like amber eyes. "I wouldn't have saved you that night if that is my intention, nor would you still be alive if I wanted you dead any time after. What brought on the asinine question, my Juliet?"

My Juliet.

Damn my heart for fluttering at those two words.

"Just a random thought," I replied dismissively with a cheeky grin.

"Well, don't get too many random thoughts then." Luciano chuckled with a shake of his head. "You two don't make a mess of the house now. I have to head out until late."

My face quickly furrowed with suspicion, "Where you going?" Luciano seemed a little too peppy with his steps for a usual business run. He was usually pretty grumpy and scowly when he had to go out the past few days.

"Business like usual." He answered bluntly while averting his eyes from me. "I won't be home for dinner, so let Gina know whenever you are hungry." Luciano rushed out the door before I could say bye to him properly, which peeved me a little.

"Juliet, why are you still up? It's way past midnight." Luciano's dragging sigh made me smile at him sheepishly as I peered around my computer screen.

"I just wanted to finish setting up to pass the time while I waited for you to get home... And I couldn't sleep without you here." The last part barely came out as a whisper, as I didn't want to sound desperate and clingy to him.

Disapprovingly, he shook his head and sighed as he entered my room and approached my desk. "Juliet, it's not healthy for you to stay up late like this." His face softened with concern as he reached out and turned my monitor off.

"Hey, I was in the middle of a bank break." I joked with a pout. It was a simulated one, but practice was practice. Also, these simulations by my cousin and his friend were no joke.

"Well, you can steal more monopoly money tomorrow *after* you've gotten a good night's sleep." He retorted with an amused smirk. "It's not like you're stealing money for real."

Rolling my eyes, I smack his hand away from my monitor. "I will be one day." I shot back at him in a determined voice.

Well, that seemed to have pushed the wrong button in him because his face grew hard and stern as he leaned over the desk and settled his palms on its surface. "No, you will not."

Gritting my teeth, I scowled at him softly as I leaned up and got in his face. "Says who?" I shouldn't be challenging him, but fuck I wanted to see how far I could push him to see him tick.

Dangerously, his face loomed over mine with barely an inch between us. "Says me." He replied in a low, gravelly voice as his jaw tensed and twitched.

Swallowing my nerves, I gripped the armrests of my chair. "Last I checked, you aren't in charge of me. You said I was free to do whatever I want living with you." I shot back with a cocky smirk.

"Juliet." It was a warning with how grave my name came out. "Do not play this game with me. It won't end well for you, and the last thing I want to do is hurt you. So, drop it." His fingers slowly clawed at the edge of my desk and gripped it, making it creak under him.

"Make. Me."

Chapter 15
Luciano

~3 weeks later~

"Juliet."
Slam!
Okay, still pissed at me.

I had to give her credit where it was due; I didn't expect her to hold a grudge for this long.

It had been a little over three weeks since our little tiff argument in her room, where I abruptly walked out on her after she told me to make her because if I hadn't removed myself that very instant, then I would have wrapped my hand around her neck and made her obey. She didn't need that from me, and I didn't need to possibly traumatize her further.

The cold treatment from her shouldn't bother me this much, though. After all, I wanted some distance between us to drown any kind of budding heat between us. The less interaction we had with each other, the better.

If only her determination to shut me out extended to her need for my comfort. Juliet still sought me out during her drops and attacks, which gave me a twisted sense of relief. Despite everything, she still needed me at the end of the day. It was fucked up of me to be so possessive of her when I didn't want her close, but the thought of her being with anyone else or getting her happiness from anyone besides me still made the red beast inside of me spring to life.

Leah's soft voice broke through my thoughts. "Luciano."

"What?" I winced internally when I heard how harshly I snapped at her. "Sorry." I quickly apologized with averted eyes and turned my body towards my good doctor friend.

"What is going on with you and Juliet? You two are acting like bipolar cats and dogs with this stupid silent anger and back-n-forth sweetness." Looking at me pointedly, she crossed her arms and leaned on a leg. "Frankly, it's getting annoying, and it's affecting Juliet from what her therapist has told me."

Just fucking great.

Groaning, I ran a hand down my face as I leaned back against my desk. "What the fuck am I supposed to do, Leah? If I reject her, then that can send her spiraling—"

Leah quickly interrupted me with a questioning raise of her brow and a smirk. "Do you want to reject her? Do you really not want her as much as she wants you?"

Throwing my hands up in defeat, I let my head fall back to take some interest in my ceiling for a moment to collect my thoughts before looking back at my waiting friend. "It doesn't matter if she wants me as badly as I want her. We cannot work." Holding up a hand, I started listing things off. "For one, I am twice her fucking age. Two, she is just misplacing everything and being infatuated with me because I saved her from a shitty situation and gave her a better life. Three, we are from two completely different worlds, and I don't want to ruin her with all the bloodshed that I create."

Sighing heavily, I frowned sadly to myself. "I can't have her. I have already ruined so many lives, but hers is one I refuse to taint." Pushing off my desk,

I stuffed my hands into my pants pockets. "She will get over me. She's still so young and still has a world to explore."

Leah's sudden advance and attack caught me off guard. "You. Stupid. Dense. Fucking. Idiot." Each word was punctuated by a whack to my cowering form from her hard bag.

"Would you stop hitting me?" I grunted out between the hits as I kept my arms up to defend myself.

"Are you going to quit being an idiot?" Leah gritted through her teeth, holding her bag in the air with the threat of more to come.

"How am I being a stu—ow! Quit it!" I went back to cowering and covering myself from her onslaught while she spat out more things at me. "I swear, I will throttle you." I threatened half-heartedly after the hits became annoying.

"And I will make sure you never have kids if you do." She threatened back with an angry huff before hitting me one last time and then pulling back. "Seriously, you're hurting her more by not giving both her and you a chance."

Plopping down in the armchair across from my desk, Leah scowled and glared at me scoldingly. "Who gives a flying shit about your stupid age gap? People date others who are older and younger than them by decades all the time in this day and age. I mean, for fuck's sake, look at Aidan. He is literally dating someone his daughter's age!" She pointed out, jabbing a finger at my side. "So, that reason of yours is utterly pointless and moot."

"Second of all, have you ever sat down and talked to her about her feelings for you and tried to work it out based on her answer? Honestly, how else are you supposed to know whether her infatuation with you is because you saved her or if she is actually developing feelings for you because she likes you." Leah pointed out with another angry jab at me, making me wince at the feeling of her sharp nail digging into me.

"Because there is nothing about me to like." I hissed back, waving Leah's hand away from my body. "She's barely been with me a month and a half, and she has not even scratched the surface of me."

Scoffing, I ran a hand through my hair and gripped at it. "I haven't exactly shown her any part of the real me, just the mushy and somewhat cold side when I try to distance her." Going full mafia boss around Juliet was definitely not in the plans at all.

Groaning exasperatedly, Leah threw her hands up and ran them down her face. "Then fucking sit down and talk to her, let her in, show her your true self and the world you live in, and then let her decide for herself whether or not she wants to remain in it after you've gone through all the risks with her." Rolling her eyes at me, she kicked her leg out and caught my shin with the tip of her shoe.

Then, a devious smile crept its way onto Leah's face, sending a wary shiver down my spine. "Take her to your fight tonight." It wasn't so much a suggestion as it was a command.

Groaning tiredly, I rubbed at my temples with my thumb and forefinger. "You can't be fucking serious, Leah." Of all the ideas of easing Juliet into my hectic life, taking her to one of my fights right off the bat like that would be the worst idea. "If there's one way to scare her off for good, then my fight tonight with no preparation would be it."

"Or it's a good way. I mean, it might be a bit of a shock to her, but if she saw the bloody and violent part of your life, then for sure, she'll know what she'll get into." Leah remarked with a shrug of her shoulders. "She can handle it. Trust me. I'm a doctor."

"Isn't that like the last famous words before something tragic happens?" I joked with a dry chuckle and shook my head.

Standing up, Leah placed a hand on my shoulder and softly squeezed it. "Show her The Devil and let her decide whether she wants to continue her feelings with you." Then, she gave me a somewhat sad smile. "Either she will run into your arms or away, but she can't make that decision until she sees you for who you truly are."

That's what I was afraid of. She probably would run for the hills if she saw my ugly side. Granted, that would solve my issue with wanting her away from me, but my heart hated that idea.

I didn't want Juliet to run anywhere but right into my bloody arms after tonight.

Question is: is she ready to meet The Devil in all his gory glory?

Chapter 16

Juliet

"Get out of my room!"

Luciano barely gave me a warning before barging in, which pissed me off. Needless to say, I was more than fed up with Luciano for cowardly dipping that night I challenged him about a month ago. It was bold of me and probably insane, but I wanted to egg him into action. I wanted him to lay his hands on me, take me, and release the fire burning in his eyes until his very essence was seared into me.

God, I hated how I felt this way. It felt so wrong to desire someone so strongly after what I went through. I shouldn't want anyone, and I don't, kind of. I didn't want anyone physically or intimately. Well, anyone but Luciano because somehow, he lit a fire in me that somehow turned into a raging inferno.

When I brought up the concerns of my fixation and feelings towards Luciano to my therapist, she assured me it wasn't something completely abnormal. The fact I wasn't hypersexual towards him or completely inebriated by him was a good sign, according to the therapist.

She assured me that it was fine and somewhat typical for me to develop feelings for the person whom I defined as my safe space, err person. It could be interpreted as a typical trauma response, clinging to my savior and all, and I kind of took it as that for a little while until it was clear my feelings for him weren't a result of that.

Well, trauma response was a huge information dump onto me after a few sessions, and I still barely grasped and accepted it myself.

Apparently, trauma response went beyond being an anxious mess and shutting everyone out like how it was portrayed most of the time. There was nothing typical when it came to trauma—yeah, that was still a hard pill for me to digest. I still felt disgusted and confused about my feelings towards everyone around me—for the most part.

Some people I used to be fine around now set me on edge, even after a month of hanging around them. Hell, I was barely adjusting to some normalcy with some, but I still kept them at a distance all the same.

I was paranoid of nearly everyone, hesitant to try anything or go anywhere new even though I had the urge to explore.

It also felt wrong to recover and be 'fine' while others in similar situations weren't.

Why should I be better before others? Why should I even get better in the first place?

Well, my guilt about it all was being slowly chipped away at by the therapist to where I didn't beat myself up over it.

Besides my guilt being a hindrance in my road to recovery, there was my anger in knowing the people who did this to me—and probably others—were still free out there. How and why should I be 'fine' knowing my assailants were still out there? It also wasn't fair that I had to suffer and learn how to be myself again, to piece my broken soul back together while they continued on with their merry lives as if they did nothing wrong.

It was utter bullshit!

Taking a few deep breaths, I slowly counted in my head to ease my storming rage. "Luciano, please... Get out of my room. I can't deal with you today. I just want to be alone." My tired voice dragged out of my defeated body.

I expected to hear a sigh and retreating footsteps, so imagine my fucking surprise when he bluntly said, "No." Then, he rounded the desk to pull me away by my chair. "We are going out tonight. There is an important event that requires your presence."

Annoyed, I rolled my eyes and scoffed at him as I reached out and grabbed the edge of my desk to pull myself back, only to be kept in place by his firm hand on the back of my chair. "There are nicer ways to ask me out on a date." I snarked in mock playfulness.

"But no thanks. Pretty sure the Barbie of the week would be better arm candy and company." Yeah, I wasn't amused by any means about him seeing other women. But hey, what right or say did I have in that matter? I was only a broken whore he picked up off the streets and kept out of pity.

I heard a heavy sigh from Luciano right before my body was lifted from the chair by a pair of muscular arms that should be fucking illegal for a man to have. "You can be pissy later, but we are not playing that game right now." He replied as he took me over to my bed and set me down at the foot of it.

My mouth opened to snark back at him, but my words hitched with my breath when Luciano leaned down and caged me between his arms. The air around us instantly heated up as a tiny distance separated our hot breaths.

"You are going to quit being a brat and listen to me tonight. His deep voice sent shivers down my spine as I let my eyes take in every inch of his immaculate face. From his somewhat deeply set amber eyes to his tall nose and kissable lips framed by a sharp, chiseled jawline covered in dark stubble—practically a short beard at this point.

A rough fingertip slowly ran up the side of my neck before the warmth of his calloused hand cupped my face with such tender gentleness. "I am going to get an outfit for you, and you will wear what I pick out without any complaints. If I hear a peep out of you that sounds like any kind of backtalk, I will punish you when we return after the event." His hard eyes darkened to where they turned deep brown with lust. "Am I understood?"

Shuddering, I gave a shaky nod of my head. God, it felt so wrong to be turned on right now and have such impure thoughts about him ravaging me. I shouldn't want him this badly, but I *needed* him so badly. I hated how he had become my only solace. I thought the need for him would go away once I got my friends—Gale especially—back in my life, but no. I craved Luciano like never before, which sucked the past few weeks because of us being cold with each other.

Thankfully, even with the strange tension of him walking out on me, he didn't shut his door to me. He was always there for me during my moments of crisis and drops without a single ounce of hesitation. No matter what, if I needed him and his comfort, he was there despite our stale anger.

Shivering in response to his thumb brushing across my bottom lip, I let my eyes close a bit in bliss as I kept my gaze on his. "Words, *principessa*." His dominating voice made me shudder as I swept the tip of my tongue across my lips. "Don't do that. It makes you too fucking tempting." He growled lowly, making me smile unconsciously from the jolt of prideful joy washing over me.

Daringly, I reached my hands out and placed them on his chest with a bated breath. Slowly, I exhaled with him after he puffed his chest out and leaned into my touch, letting me feel his hard pectorals under his thin dress shirt. Timidly, I glided my eyes quickly down his body before snapping them back to his intense amber orbs.

Slowly, I inched my hands down his body, letting my delicate fingers follow the covered grooves of his muscles until I reached his pants. Carefully, I hooked my fingers around his belt and softened my eyes wantonly as I pulled him towards me. "Do you want me?" Then, I couldn't stop the bad thought from slipping with my saddening eyes. "Even though I am broken and ruined?"

Luciano's face softened momentarily before his pupils sharpened with a lustful edge again. Dropping his hand from my face, he slid his hands down to my thighs, gripping the back of them with a firm squeeze as he parted my legs enough to pull me flush against him. My body jerked with a gasp as my hands instantly gripped the front of his shirt, my hips bucking at the hard bulge pressing into my aching core instinctively.

"Does it feel like I care about *that*?" His fierce gaze made me shudder and shrink under him as I struggled to keep my full attention on him. "What happened wasn't your fault. You didn't ask or want for any of it to happen. You are *not* broken and ruined. You are a survivor, a warrior, and you are resilient and strong."

"So, I don't ever," a hard roll of his hips pulled a soft, gasping moan from me as a shock of pleasure zapped my body, "Want to hear you say anything like that about yourself, ever again."

Slowly, one of his hands snakes up my trembling body while the other remains firmly planted against the back of my thigh to keep me locked against him. A familiar warmth enveloped my neck as his fingers wrapped themselves against my slender neck until I had a nice hand collar from Luciano. His hot words fanned my face as his deep voice trembled at his chest against my body. "If I ever hear you talk bad about yourself or even get the feeling that you are thinking ill of yourself because of your trauma, I will not hesitate to bend you over my knee that very moment, no matter where we are, to spank you. Or, depending on how bad of a punishment you need, I might just bend you over and fuck the thoughts out of your head, or at least fuck you stupid enough to where you can't form a single thought."

Oh. My. God.

I nearly came right then and there from his words alone and the images that flashed through my mind.

But holy shit, what was happening?!

"L-Luciano," I pleaded with my eyes, "Please, don't fuck with my fragile heart and soul like that. Don't say things you don't mean." I couldn't help but whimper out a small sob as tears stung my eyes from the false hope.

Ghosting his lips against mine, he breathed in deeply and hesitated. "I told you before, Juliet, I am a man of my word." Pulling his head away so that a mere inch hung between us, he looked at me with controlled eyes. "If you were mine, then that would all happen." He sounded almost sad at the fact with how his eyes fell a little. "But I cannot be the one to decide who you choose to trust your heart with."

Breathing heavily, he looked deeply into my eyes as his thumb brushed against the side of my neck. "You do not have to make a decision right now," he quickly held his hand up when I opened my mouth to say something, "And I do not want you to, not when you haven't seen my true self. You have only seen the side of me that no one else has, the one I have catered to you for your sake."

Licking his lips, he leaned his forehead against mine. "You haven't seen the other side of me yet, the ugly and bloody side of the mafia world that I run, and just how I truly am." His eyes slowly closed for a few seconds as he paced his breaths and leaned back to look at me fully. "I don't want you making any kind of decision about me until you see for yourself just who I am."

Coldness washed over me as he removed himself from me completely, and I couldn't help but frown and pout while I watched him disappear into my closet for a bit.

As much as I wanted to argue with him, he was right. Even if I wanted him, I only knew this crafted side of him that gave me comfort. I knew he was a ruthless mafia boss because of rumors about his reputation, but I had never witnessed that side of him this whole time. Yeah, I appreciated him shielding me away from such ugly work, but then I became blind to a huge part of him.

It made me feel a little silly and stupid, honestly. How could I think about a serious relationship with him when I didn't truly know him? What if I couldn't handle his mafia business? I couldn't stay oblivious to it forever if I did get intimately involved with him.

Swallowing the lump in my throat, I followed Luciano with my eyes when he emerged from my closet with a short, blood-red dress on his arms and a pair of white, heeled ankle boots in his hand. "Change into these. I have another thing for you to wear, but it's in my room." He told me after setting the clothes down on the bed next to me—shoes on the ground.

"Yes, sir," I muttered, hopping off the bed.

"Juliet." He growled lowly with a look of warning in his darkened eyes. "Don't play with me unless you are prepared to step in the ring with me."

Gulping, I nodded my head in response before turning my back to him to change after he left my room. The sweetheart neckline of the silky strapless dress framed my small breasts perfectly to where it made my measly A-cups look like something. Then, the subtle curves that have been filling out—thanks to Luciano giving me no diet restrictions—were nicely highlighted by how the dress hugged my pear-shaped body. Oh, and my bubbly round ass looked very delectable in this dress.

Unfortunately, admiring myself didn't last long because of the bad thoughts coming in like a trainwreck.

I didn't want to go out like this.

I couldn't.

Chapter 17
Luciano

Concern weighed the corners of my lips down when I saw Juliet's shoulders drop with her smile as she cowered her body before the mirror.

I couldn't find it in me to stop her from admiring herself. The way she smiled so brightly as she twirled a bit in her spot and the way her appreciative eyes drank in her own image, it was too happy of a moment for me to shatter. So, I hung back at the doorway, leaning against the frame with a small smile of my own as I enjoyed the little moment myself.

Well, it was nice until the switch in her. I immediately sprang into action at the sight of her shutting down. The robe I had in hand was thrown onto the bed as I took big strides to her and embraced her in my arms. "Hey, don't," I commanded sternly, forcing her attention up to me with a face grab. "What is going on in that mind of yours, *principessa?*"

"I don't want to go out like this. I don't like it. Everyone is going to look, and everyone is going to think I'm a whore for dressing like this, and if anything happens, it's because I was asking for it." Her whimpering words rambled on as her eyes grew distant and her breaths picked up in pace.

Shifting my hand from her cheek to her neck, I gently applied some pressure as I tightened my other arm around her to keep her firmly pressed against my body. "Stop." I bit out sternly. "Pay attention to my voice. Don't let your thoughts race because they aren't true. Don't listen to the demons in your mind and the lies they spew."

Slowly, her eyes came back into focus. "That's it, good girl, come back to me. Just breathe, in through your nose, out through the mouth." I praised and instructed her with a proud smile.

"I swear to you, as long as I am alive, no harm will ever come to you. If anyone dares to look at you wrong or say such things to you, I will rip their tongue out, break their jaw, then use their own jaw to beat them to death." I promised her with a serious gaze and voice. "And don't you ever think like that. It doesn't matter how you dress or act. That is *not* an invitation or consent. And if anyone tries to tell you otherwise or convince you, you let me know or clock them in the face and deliver a blow to their balls. Is that clear?"

Letting out a deep, shaky breath, Juliet nodded her head before leaning into my hand. "Yes, understood." Her reply came out airy as she let her eyes flutter closed.

"Good girl," I whispered against her forehead with a smile before kissing it softly. "We will leave when you are ready." Time crunch or not, Juliet's safety and comfort took precedence. I would have to cut my warmup a little short, but that did not matter to me. Thankfully, Juliet didn't take long to recover.

Once she was back to baseline, I released her to go pick up the black robe I had brought in for her to wear. Standing before her again, I helped her slip my black robe on, carefully tied it around her, and fashioned it into a makeshift off-the-shoulder dress with a satisfied smile on my face. She couldn't see it, but my symbol was in red on the back. It was my robe for the ring, which kind of swallowed her up and almost looked like a long dress.

"There, now everyone there will know that you are mine for tonight." I couldn't help the possessiveness from coming out as I admired her delicate body wrapped in the dark material.

"What happened to me deciding?" She remarked with a hesitant smirk.

Chuckling, I reached out and pinched her cheek softly. "There's my spunky brat."

"We should be mindful of our words to each other until I do decide after tonight." She said with a saddening smile.

Humming softly, I nodded my head in agreement. "You are right. I am sorry." I shouldn't be calling her mine when she wasn't.

But by God, I hope she will be mine.

Reaching out, I took her hand and dragged her out of the house to my car. "I will have to leave you with some people at the event towards the end, but you will be more than safe with Leah and Aidan," I told her as we were on the road.

"Aidan? As in Aidan The Vulture?" She sounded wary at the possibility of being left with another person in the syndicate, not that I blamed her.

Nodding my head, I focused on the road as I spoke, "Yes. You will be more than safe, and he knows a bit of your situation and how you came into my care." Out of the corner of my eyes, I could see her frown faintly in the dimly lit cabin of the car. "I would take you with me if I could, but I can't for that part."

Well, I probably could take her to the back with me while I warmed up and prepped myself for the ring, but I would need a moment alone to fully set myself straight. Also, I would be too distracted with her beauty if she were around.

Movement in my peripheral made my eyes flicker to her to see her fidgeting hands. "I think I'll be fine with Leah around." She tried to sound confident, but I could hear the slight tremble in her voice.

Taking a hand off the wheel, I rest it on her thigh and stroke it comfortingly. "You can do it, Juliet, but if it gets too much, just let them know, and they can take you somewhere to decompress." I wanted to push Juliet with this event, too. "Plus, I think Aidan is bringing his girlfriend this time, so maybe you can make a new friend. She's a few years older than you but a delight. I think you two can get along pretty well."

The other reason why Aidan was bringing his girlfriend along was because of Juliet. Much like Juliet, Aidan's girlfriend had a really sheltered life and only recently broke out into the world on her own after a run-in with Aidan's boisterous daughter. So, Aidan was more than eager to get more people in her life, and he was the one who suggested having our women meet up to get them acquainted. Juliet didn't need to know all of that, though.

"So, what exactly is this event?" Juliet asked as she wrapped her arms around my outstretched arm and hugged it tightly.

"It's an underground fight," I replied bluntly. There was no sugarcoating the event, nor did I want to. "I run them every three to four months as a way for lesser-known names to make their way to fame, entertainment to those who can afford it, so business venture in a sense, and I take care of other syndicate business there which you will see later."

"So, an illegal underground fight ring?" Juliet asked timidly while poking the back of my hand with her fingers.

Amused, I chuckled and squeezed her thigh softly, causing her to gasp softly. "Underground fight already means that it's illegal."

"Oh shut up, I don't know all the technical terms and shit of the shady world." Sometimes, her innocence was adorable and refreshing, and that part of her made me not want to drag her into Hell with me.

Smiling sadly, I moved my hand up her body to her nape, rubbing it with my fingers. "I hope your light continues to grow and never dims, no matter what choice you make." I couldn't ruin her, and I would do my best to preserve what goodness she had in her heart and soul if she were to join my side.

Scoffing and chuckling dryly, I felt her head shake. "I think it's a little late for that."

If I wasn't driving, then I would've taken her face into my hands and said some stern words or pulled her over my knee. But for now, I had to settle with choking her softly by slipping my hand around the column of her neck from the back. "Juliet, do not make me pull this car over to teach you a lesson already and make us late," I warned her with a subtle squeeze. "I hate being late."

The subtle vibrations of her words tickled my hand. "Luciano, is it wrong that I like you choking me?" I could feel the subtle bob of her throat when she swallowed hard. "It always feels so calming to me and gets me turned on sometimes. And I feel like it should feel wrong after everything, but I like it when you're close. I crave for you to touch and guide me."

Loosening my hold, I stroked her neck gently with my fingers. "No, nothing wrong with kinks and preferences, especially for a little bratty submissive like you." It was a loaded conversation; one this car ride wouldn't even begin to cover. "We can talk about that tomorrow or sometime after tonight. It's a lot to cover, and how we go about things depends on your decision about us after you witness everything tonight."

"You make me sound like a child saying I'm a brat, and saying I'm submissive makes it sound like I'm weak." She remarked with a 'hmph' at the end.

"Depending on context, it could very well mean that, but that's not the case here. A brat and a submissive are roles in a BDSM dynamic, and nothing about them makes you feel weak. Just because you are submissive does not indicate a lack of power. If anything, the submissive in any dynamic is the strongest because of the total control they have." I needed to put a lid on it before I overloaded her before the night even began. "But that's something we can talk in-depth about later or something you can explore on your own and ask me about."

Sighing reluctantly, I suggested to her, "You can also ask Aidan since he's more knowledgeable and can probably teach you about it in a way that's more understandable than me." Did I want her to talk to my friend about sex and BDSM? No, not particularly, but I knew for a damn fact Aidan would be able to navigate it a lot better than me because of his lifestyle.

Humming softly, I felt her head shake. "It's okay. I can wait to talk to you about it after researching." I couldn't help but let out a sigh of relief at her response.

Thank fucking God.

Then, after a brief silence, I asked the dreaded question. "Juliet, do you like me because I saved you, and is it that aspect that you love and grew your emotions on? Or is it something else?" I wanted to see if she was on the right road to begin with.

Sighing heavily, Juliet chuckled dryly. "I actually spoke to my therapist about that quite a bit over the past few weeks. I thought about my gravitation towards you and my feelings towards you. I thought I was displacing my emotions and clinging onto you because you saved me and whatnot, but after I got over my gratitude for you, I still found myself fascinated with you and wanting to know more about you. Your presence alone is enough to calm me and keep me more than content. I can relax around you, feel safe, and stuff." Her words trailed out into a strangle of incomprehensible mumbles before she recollected herself. "Sorry, my mind rushed ahead of me." Her body shook softly with her sheepish chuckle.

Letting out a long sigh, she leaned against my arm. "I thought the feelings would simmer once I reconnected with my friends, especially Gale, who I always found comfort in as much as I do with you. Yet, I felt nothing close to the warmth and bliss I always feel with you." The soft pads of her fingers danced along the back of my fingers, making me shiver softly at the contrast between our bodies.

Her delicate fingers pried at my stiff ones until I released her neck. Then, she held my hand in her lap before continuing, "Although, I guess I've only fallen for a part of you, and if I am being honest, I am more afraid of losing what I have developed for you after seeing your true self tonight. I mean, I know that's the point, for me to know what kind of man you are to see if I can feel for all of you..."

"But you are afraid of the other possibilities." I finished in a somber but understanding voice. "Just know that no matter what you decide tonight or after, I will still be there for you in whatever way you need. Whether it be a friend or a lover, I won't abandon you based on your decision." It would be very shitty of me to completely shun her if she rejected me or chose to keep me at a certain distance.

At least, if she decided to keep me in the friend zone, that would make my life a lot easier with moving on from her. I wouldn't have to worry about hurting her feelings or think about ways to let her down easily.

Unfortunately, the idea of her as a friend irked me. An ache threatened to pull the corners of my lips down into a deep scowl when I thought about not being able to have her intimately. Which was fucking confusing and stupid because wasn't that my goal? To not have her as a lover?

This weird situation between us confused me more than I liked to admit because I really shouldn't have her—I didn't deserve her. Yet, the selfish part of me challenged all of that. Because why not? Why couldn't I have her? I was Luciano fucking Agosti, and I could have whatever the fuck I desired in this damn world. I could very well force the lie of the marriage onto Juliet and turn it into a truth, and she won't be able to do anything about it. And I won't lie; I have entertained the idea more than I should've throughout the past month, especially when I felt myself grow a little fed up about Juliet's little stubborn stint.

If she weren't a traumatized woman who needed a careful hand, then I very well might have kicked her door down, thrown her over my shoulder, and forced her down the aisle.

Yeah, very fucked up of me to even think about that, but something about Juliet made my desires go haywire.

On the other hand, whenever my sense of whatever sanity I had was intact and functioning, I instantly backtracked.

It was a constant tug-of-war in me when it came to Juliet, and I hated it. Not as much as I hated the thought of not having her as mine, though.

God, how the hell did Juliet throw my stable life into such turmoil?

Okay, maybe my life wasn't stable to start with, but it was livable. I had my routines, thoughts, and emotions as straight as possible. Then Juliet came along like a tornado and fucked it all up, making me feel like some incompetent teenage boy crushing for the first time. It was ridiculous because I was a grown fucking man! I shouldn't feel this lack of control over myself because of someone like Juliet.

Yeah, in theory, letting her go if she didn't feel the same way should be easy. I mean, I never had any issues in my past relationships if things didn't work out. However, I have never felt such intense lust for someone until Juliet. No matter how many relationships I've been in, I have never loved any of them. None of them made my breath hitch with a racing heart or invoke such eagerness from me.

As much as I wanted to shove Juliet out of my life, I always found myself rounding back to her at the end of the day, whether it be physically or mentally.

Juliet had a fucking chokehold on me.

And I didn't want to escape.

Chapter 18
Juliet

No matter how much I psyched myself up and told myself to stay strong, I couldn't keep the momentum up when we entered the crowded underground area filled with hundreds of people dressed in formal wear.

I hated how my chest tightened; my own body suffocated me as I hid behind Luciano like a scared child. "I'm sorry." I could see people pointing their crooked, blinged-out fingers at us as we walked down the aisle towards the VIP section.

Wrapping an arm around my waist, Luciano pulled me next to him and kept me tucked against him. Bending his head down, he brushed his lips against my ear with a chuckle, making me shiver. "Ignore them. They are jealous and wish it was them around my arms instead of a beauty like you." He told me in a low voice before continuing to walk unbothered.

Right at the entrance of the VIP area, where I could see Leah, was where we stopped. "Mister Agosti, so glad you made it. It's a full house tonight, and your stage is set like always." A man in black slacks and a matching polo with a familiar symbol of bat wings, a pointed tail, and an L on the back greeted Luciano with a polite smile.

"Gregory," Luciano greeted the man back with a small smile and nod. "Everyone all set?"

"Yes, sir, all the contestants are warmed up and ready. Refreshments and other accommodations for the guest have also been well underway." I had to quickly scan around the area when Gregory said something.

Only then did I notice the scantily clad servers with trays of drinks and... Holy shit!

Looking up at Luciano, I tugged on his sleeve to get him to bend to my level. "Is that drugs on the trays?"

No, it's fucking sugar, Juliet.

I mentally slapped myself for asking such a stupid question, and I honestly have no idea why I even asked, given the kind of event this was—and who ran the event.

Amused, Luciano chuckled and raised an eyebrow at me with a smirk. "Whatever you think it is, it probably is." It wasn't much of a confirmation or denial, but I could surmise easily based on the devious tone of his voice.

Gently, he curled a finger under my chin and grasped it with his thumb, tilting my head around slowly. "This isn't just some run-of-the-mill underground fight, *principessa*. This is the highest-end event there is. Only the richest and dirtiest come here to spend their money to watch potential fights to the death." Then, he set my gaze on the bench of fighters right outside the caged ring. "Those who participate are doing it for a chance at fame or wealth, and only the best get filtered through to these final event fights where many big-name scouts are looking for their next champion."

"W-what if this place gets raided?" I mean, it happens all the time in TV shows and movies, and knowing my bad luck, that would probably happen tonight.

Luciano chuckled amusingly and shook his head. "I am much too careful for that to happen. Besides, it's not like I let just anyone into this place. Everyone here has something grave to lose. If one person snitches, then everyone goes down, so they're all more than mindful about keeping these events a secret and keeping others accountable." That seemed rather risky, in my opinion, but

I was sure Luciano went about things more complicated than he played it out to me. "Also, I have contingencies for the other syndicate members and me if things go belly up, so don't worry your pretty little head about it."

Exhaling deeply, I nodded my head in response to him and dropped the subject. "Can we sit by Leah?" I asked as Luciano led us behind the roped-off area.

"Of course, but we are also sitting there anyway. I have a special VIP area for me and the syndicate members." He replied with a brief smile before nodding at the guards standing before another set of ropes.

The moment we crossed over, Leah instantly shot up from her seat and came to us, greeting Luciano with a hug and grin. "Finally, I thought you were going to chicken out or not bring Juliet with you." Then, her attention locked onto me, making me smile shyly at her.

Shoving Luciano aside, she wrapped her arm around mine. "Come on, let me introduce you to Aidan and his girlfriend." She gave me little choice in the matter with how she dragged me away toward the couple she sat next to.

"Leah, stop it, you're going to scare her." Luciano scolded with a worried sigh as he took his place next to me, pulling me away from Leah with a jealous glare.

Rolling her eyes, Leah waved a dismissive hand at Luciano. "You have her all to yourself all the damn time with her cooped up at your place. Let us have her for a bit. It's not like we're going to eat her alive." Leah teased with a snicker as she leaned back into me and hugged my arm.

Sighing heavily, Luciano shook his head before running a hand down his face. "How much has she had to drink?" It was hard to determine who the question was shot at because his eyes didn't land on someone until a few seconds after the words left his mouth.

The red-haired man who sat in the chair next to Leah with his arms thrown around an Asian woman's shoulders shrugged and laughed softly. "She was already a little too friendly when I got here not long before you. So, take your guess." It was a little hard to pick up at a distance, but he had a slight Scottish accent.

With a friendly smile etched on his face, he turned his head to me. Tilting his head, he quickly ran his curious eyes over me before holding a hand out.

"Aidan Knox. It's finally a pleasure to meet the person who's been getting under Luciano's skin." He chuckled warmly.

Awkwardly, I smiled back as I took his hand in a quick shake. "Juliet." I couldn't bring myself to say my last name.

In all honesty, I wanted to be rid of it. I wanted nothing to do with my dead life the day I packed my stuff up and left my despicable parents' property.

Movement from the female next to Aidan made my eyes snap to her. I watched as she looked at Aidan pleadingly as if she were asking permission without verbalizing it. Aidan chuckled and leaned in close to the woman, whispering something in her ear that made her lips widen in a smile as her eyes lit up. Fully grinning, she kissed Aidan on the cheek before getting up and standing before me with the brightest face I have ever seen from someone in my life.

"Hey, I'm Eve, but I like to go by Evie. It's nice to have another girl in the group finally." She sounded so cheerful and excited that it was a little daunting to me. "It gets so boring with just me, Leah, and Natty. Well, it's just Leah and me most of the time since Natty doesn't like to partake much in the shady side of her father's business."

"You look familiar..." I couldn't help but ponder out loud as I studied her closely.

She seemed to be around my height, but that was hard to tell, considering how we were both wearing heels. Her long, baby-pink ombre hair came down to her lower back in soft curls, evening out her oval-shaped face. Then, her petite box-shaped body was nicely displayed in the long black dress she wore, especially her leg that peaked through the slit of the dress.

Clearly, I had never met her before, but there was something about her I couldn't quite put my finger on. She really did look familiar, but why?

"Hmm, have you heard of Nebula? Or listen to any of their music?" Evie asked with a tilt of her head and a cheeky grin.

That's when it hit me fully.

"Wait, are you Star?" I was taken aback by my own question because the woman before me didn't exactly match the image of the famous pop star I frequently listened to before she retired from her pop star career recently.

Humming cheerfully, she nodded her head with a grin and giggle. "Was, but yep."

Yeah, the woman before me did not look too much like the pop star I grew familiar with—in a good way. She looked pretty on stage and in music videos and such, but she looked so much happier and healthier standing before me currently. Evie actually looked genuinely happy, too. Even though she always had a smile on her face with her group, her eyes never truly reflected it if one were to pay attention enough.

Reaching out, she took my hand and dragged me over to the seats, but Luciano swooped in before I could sit in her seat.

Wrapping an arm around my waist, he pulled me into his lap as he sat next to Aidan. "Can you let me have you like this for a moment?" His deep words tingled my spine and made my nipples harden under my bra.

"Usually, people ask before pulling people into their laps," I remarked with a scoffing chuckle and roll of my eyes. "But I guess I'll give you a free pass this time." I mean, his lap was pretty comfortable and lovely. Well, it was a little hard for a seat, but no doubt that was all his muscles under there.

"Don't be giving out any more free passes to anyone, even me, alright, *principessa*?" Luciano mused with a chuckle and kissed my temple before settling his arms comfortably around my waist.

Giggling, Evie leaned in and whispered to me, "That was so cute. He's like never all smiley and mushy like that with anyone. I honestly didn't think he could smile in a not crazy way."

That last bit had me tilting my head and furrowing my eyebrows at Evie. "What do you mean?"

Pulling back, she kept herself in my space to talk to me while Aidan and Luciano leaned back in their own conversation. "Have you seen Luciano in action before?" She looked at me, a little shocked and worried, and quickly glanced at Luciano.

Slowly, I shook my head back and forth with a small frown. "I haven't known about Luciano until about two months ago, give or take. This is actually the first time I've gone anywhere like this with him." The sinking feeling from before came back tenfold and winded me.

Am I going to regret this night?

Swallowing nervously, I shifted a bit in Luciano's lap and picked at the sleeve of his suit jacket. A part of me knew better, the naïve side who wanted to keep Luciano in a good light and live in lala land.

Unfortunately, the jaded side of me, who was in touch with reality, knew better and pushed me into this situation tonight. No matter how much I argued with myself, I always ended up back here. I had to see this event through, see exactly who Luciano was. Even if I could end up hurt in the end, at least it would be better to know now than later after I become completely enamored with him.

Evie's lips flattened into a sympathetic smile as she grabbed my hands and squeezed them. "Well, you're definitely going to be in for an interesting night. Although I will warn you now, things *will* get bloody and very gory once Luciano's turn is up."

Opening my mouth, I was about to ask her for more information but was unable to because of the announcer coming on the big screens that hung at the center of the room. I didn't want to be rude and tear anyone's attention away as the event started. On the other hand, I couldn't really bring myself to pay much attention to the stage because of everyone else in the area.

Every single spot in the place was taken; the whole place was literally packed with—

Holy shit, is that Judge Ger?!

Okay, after another quick sweep, I felt rather appalled at how many of these people I recognized—people of high standing in society. I didn't want to study the room again to see if I could pick out more people. Also, I didn't want to run the chance of possibly seeing those people snort coke off a person's ass or tits. I'm pretty sure I saw that some of them were getting serviced, too, while the fight continued.

The sound of the bell going off, along with the cascading cheers, forced me to pay attention to the ring, where the referee stood with a rather blood-soaked fighter with their arms in the air. For a winner, he looked rather beat up. Like, yeah, no fucking duh since this was a fight, but he looked so much worse than what I would see on TV fights. God, I shouldn't even look at the other guy, but my curiosity got the best of me—and nearly my stomach.

Looking back at Luciano with disbelief, I darted my head quickly at the fallen man. "Oh my... Is he even still alive?" I asked Luciano with a shocked and worried frown.

Unbothered, Luciano gave a shrug of his shoulders. "Who knows, the doctors will let me know of the casualties after the event has ended." He stated nonchalantly. "Besides, they all knew the risks when they signed up, and they have up until they die to pull out. Even in the middle of the fight, they can throw in the towel if they wish to have their lives intact."

It still didn't sit quite right with me, but if they knew, then not much could be done... Right? I hated how my mind spiraled down the endless pit of 'what ifs' and all, but I quickly shoved it out of my mind when two guards came up on stage to drag the unconscious man off to let the cleaning crew jump into action.

Within a minute, the stage was spotless for the next match.

I was about to let my eyes wander again to avoid seeing a bloody fight, but a glimpse of the fighters had me suckered in. Because hot smoking damn did they look—

Quickly, I turned to Evie and slapped her arm to get her full attention. "Girl, does that dude seriously have a tattoo of an arrow pointing down there that says bang bang stick?" Okay, stupid tattoos were a thing, but come on, there was no way that was actually real, right?

"Girl, you'll be surprised at the dumb shit that some people get." Evie laughed amusingly in response. "But check out the other dude." Her smile turned mischievous as she wagged her eyebrows at me.

Just as my mouth opened to make a comment, a low growl in my ear made me shudder and gasp. "I would be careful with your next words, *principessa*." His warning sent a wave of heat down to my nether regions, making me throb and ache as I looked back into Luciano's dark and possessive eyes.

Guess Evie didn't get let off the hook either because Aidan hooked his finger around her black leather collar and yanked her back against him before wrapping his hand around her neck. Then, he leaned in close to her ear and said something to her that made her body shiver and melt into him as her eyes softened with pure submission. There was a quick moment where her lips grew into a cheeky smile before a quick jerk from Aidan wiped it away.

Nervously, I chewed my lip as I looked back at Luciano, who studied me with such calculating eyes that made me feel naked. "H-he looks like he's a good fighter and might win." I stammered while averting my eyes. "Y-your body looks a lot better and hotter anyways," I muttered under my breath with a blushing pout.

I haven't seen Luciano completely naked or anything, but I might or might not have occasionally watched him work out and train in the home gym. It wasn't like I stalked him; I just happened to be passing by when he worked out sometimes and got a nice eyeful of his glorious muscles. Seriously, those arms and legs were so perfect. And don't even get me started on his ass because that—mhmm!

"You better not be getting turned on because of him, or I will have to add another name to my list tonight." I couldn't tell if Luciano was being playful or not with the unreadable smirk on his face.

"It's not him, I swear," I said in a shaky breath as I leaned back into Luciano.

"Then who are you thinking about?" Okay, now he was being a cheeky bastard with that question in such a playfully smug tone.

I stuttered as heat flooded my face. "Y-you." I wouldn't be surprised if the cameras panned onto us, and I found myself looking like a damn tomato up on the big screens.

My nipples tightened almost painfully as my stomach knotted with arousal with his reply. "Good girl. I should only ever be the only man in your damn mind."

Fucking hell, that needs to be illegal. Actually, he needs to be illegal because he is a hazard to panties.

Because I was pretty sure they were completely soaked from that growl of his.

"Maybe you should show me why it should be you and only you."
Big fucking mistake.

Chapter 19
Luciano

Fuck me.

I didn't give a fuck about the damn fight, not when she says things like that. The only thing on my mind was getting my hands and lips on Juliet's lovely body to mark it all up with love bites and bruises in the shape of my hands.

"Luc—ah!" Her cry cut out with her choking gasp the moment my hand ended up around her neck and squeezed.

"I am one shred away from lifting your dress and shoving myself into you and fucking you for everyone in this place to see who you belong to," I growled deeply against her ear with a hard thrust of my hips for her to feel the raging hard-on her words gave me.

Taking in a deep breath of her intoxicating scent of citrus and berries, I calmed myself a little. "The only thing stopping me from doing that or pulling you back into the locker rooms to hike this dress of yours up to fuck and fill your cunt with my cum is the fact that you aren't ready." Even in my lustful haze, her well-being remained a priority.

The last thing I wanted to do was add to her trauma or, God forbid, become her next trigger.

Whimpering, she softly pressed herself back against me hesitantly. "What if I am?" Her voice was a little hoarse from how tightly I held her neck.

Easing my grip, I softly shook my head at her. "You are not, even if it feels like you are right now." Damn me for having a conscience when it came to Juliet; I blue-balled myself for fuck's sake. "I won't touch you until we have a long talk about boundaries and limits and set a safe-word."

Pouting, Juliet reached down and slipped a hand between our pressed bodies to palm my hard bulge. "Can I at least have a taste, please? I just need to touch you and feel you somehow, please." Damn vixen wrapped me around her fingers with such sweet words.

And fuck me for giving in.

In one swift movement, I stood up, grabbed Juliet's hand tightly, and dragged us to the private locker area. "Out. Now." I demanded the few fighters in the area with a fiery glare, making them scurry out without a peep of protest.

Pulling her over to a bench, I pulled her down into my lap again after setting my own ass down. Only this time, I made her straddle my lap and face me. With one hand splayed against her lower back, I reach my other hand up and hold her face to bring it to mine. My forehead settled against hers with a deep breath, keeping our lips a thread apart. "You are in control, Juliet. I won't touch you or do anything unless you ask, say, or guide me otherwise." She had the reins now, even if it went against every dominant bone in my body, and this was how things had to go for now.

Granted, I wasn't bothered by it much because any true dominant knew that the one truly in control is the submissive. As contradictory as it sounded, that was how the dynamic worked. The submissive set the foundation for the dominant to build upon; without rules and boundaries from the sub, there was nothing.

"Kiss me." She demanded with a breathy smile, her soft hands cupping my face eagerly.

The hand on her face immediately slipped into the back of her hair and gripped it to smash her lips against mine in a hungry kiss filled with red-hot lust. Shivers ran down my spine at the feeling of her soft tongue tracing the seams of my lips for entrance. Groaning with a smile, I parted my lips to let her in for a few seconds before forcing her tongue into her mouth with my own.

My own chest rumbled with a deep groaning growl when her hands slipped around my neck and gripped it before she moved her hands across my shoulders, pushing my jacket off. Goosebumps erupted over my body at the feeling of her nails through the thin material of my dress shirt as she raked them down my body. Her tiny fists bunched the end of my shirt up, pulling it out of my pants before her nimble fingers made quick work of my buttons.

"Juliet." I groaned softly against her lips before taking them again in a heated kiss.

Breaking the kiss, Juliet rested her head against mine to catch her breath as her hands traveled along the grooves of my muscles. Nervously, she licked her lips as she looked at me with unsure eyes. "I..." She started with a shaky breath. "I want to taste you, but I'm scared."

Smiling softly, I let go of her hair to take her hand, bringing it up to kiss the back of it before sliding it down my body with a deep exhale and making her palm me through my pants. "Do not force yourself. It will only do more harm than good. If touching me like this is all you can manage, then that is great progress on your part, and I won't be complaining one bit."

Frowning, Juliet's eyes softened with sadness as she moved her hand to the waistband of my pants, hooking her fingers around it. "But I want to make you feel good. It doesn't feel fair."

"Oh, Juliet, *principessa*, no." I spoke in a hushed tone as I pulled her hand out to hold. "Sex isn't some exchange, and don't you ever let anyone make you feel that way. You give and take what you are comfortable with, end of discussion. Don't let anyone guilt trip you, nor do you guilt trip yourself into going way out of your comfort zone like that. If they are a decent person, then they will understand and accept your decision."

Looking deeply into her eyes with my tender gaze, I stroked the back of her hand. "I can handle my own boner if you can't go any further, and I won't hold anything against you if you choose not to do anything beyond what we have done. And honestly, I don't care if you 'created a problem' for me, and shit, that doesn't mean you have an obligation to 'take care' of it. That should go beyond me, as well." Pausing to chuckle, I shook my head playfully, "I mean, lord, have mercy on your partner because they'll have to face my wrath, especially if they mistreat you." The playfulness in my voice dulled out to a stern edge. "Point is, don't let anyone make you think you have to take care of their own dicks or cunts." Pressing my lips against her forehead, I let my kiss linger momentarily as I collected my thoughts. "Yeah, it sucks, but that shouldn't be put above your own comfort and consent."

Leaning back to a smile, I curled a finger under her chin to tilt her head up. "Am I understood?"

I wasn't about to go cry to the world about not getting my dick sucked or wet in a pussy. Honestly, the men who complained about that shit were boys, not men, in my books.

With a hesitant smile, Juliet nodded her head in response.

"Words, *principessa*." I demanded in a soft but firm voice, making her eyes widen slightly as her cheeks flushed up.

"Yes, sir, understood." Her response had shivers of pleasure tingling down my spine.

God, she would make the perfect sub.

Her eyes deviated from mine to roam my body along with her fingers. Then, once she got down to my waist, her eyes widened momentarily before narrowing with cheeky curiosity as she looked up at me with a smile that she tried to hold back. "Do you seriously have a tattoo pointing to your crotch?" I could hear the strain in her voice as she tried to hold back her chuckle or laugh.

Rolling my eyes, I pushed my open shirt aside to expose my abdomen to her fully. "It wasn't on purpose. The tail just kind of ended up where it did." I mused with a chuckle as I leaned back so the lights of the room could hit my exposed body.

Okay, maybe having the pointed tail of my tattoo wrapped around my waist to my front side and pointing downward to my nether regions was done a little on purpose. But hey, I was only a stupid sixteen-year-old teenager who honestly thought it was funny at the time. If someone wanted to chase my tail, then they could follow it and get fucked.

Juliet didn't need to know that, though; no one did. This would be a secret I would take to the grave with me.

Sitting up straight, she traced the tattoo's outline with the tip of her finger before following the dip of my V-line. "Can I see the full tattoo?" She asked with a voice and face full of curiosity.

As tempting as it was to shed my shirt fully, I reluctantly shook my head at her. "Later, I have to go get ready soon, and I'm afraid that if I get more undressed for you, I will get too distracted and cut into my warmup." I apologized with a smile before leaning in and kissing her forehead.

"What do you have to warm up for?" She questioned with a tilt of her head as she settled her hands on the waistband of my pants again.

"My match," I answered kind of bluntly.

Juliet's eyes widened slightly in shock, and she looked at me in a way that silently asked if I was serious or not. When I didn't say anything in return and only offered a smirk and shrug of my shoulders, she huffed and frowned at me worriedly. "You're going to fight? Why? What if you get hurt or killed?"

I didn't mean to laugh at her, but she was just too cute, fretting over me and all. "Juliet, I've been fighting since I was in high school, and I am still standing strong." Reassuring her with a smile, I draped my arms around her waist and pulled her back in for a quick kiss. "And I'm not being a cocky bastard saying I'm unbeatable. It's a damn fact."

I haven't lost a business match yet, nor do I ever plan to.

Not like the people I fought and punished weren't fighters by any means, so I wasn't worried about getting beat. Even if they were fighters, I had over three decades of training and conditioning that I still kept going on a daily.

Juliet's throat bobbed with her swallow as her eyes grew nervous. My mouth opened to ask her about her mind, but I quickly shut it when her hands started to undo my belt and pants. "Juliet, you don't—"

"Shh." Her boldness took me aback when she pressed a finger against my lips. "Let me, please." She begged softly as she played with the waistband of my boxers. "I want to give you a little luck."

Fuck.

Shuddering, I relaxed my hips into her as I leaned back a little on the bench to give her some room to work.

A sharp, flabbergasted gasp followed the sharp slap of my cock against my stomach the moment Juliet peeled my boxers back, and my rock-hard cock sprung out. I had to hold my tongue to keep myself from laughing at how shocked and amazed Juliet's wide eyes stared at my twitching monstrosity.

"Luc... That thing's a weapon!" She squeaked out with a red face, squirming a bit in my lap as she kept reaching a hand out but pulling it back at the last second toward my member. "You've fucked people with this? And they lived?" She looked up at me in disbelief, cracking my self-control.

Letting out a hearty chuckle, I moved a hand down and stroked my girthy length lazily. "There are so many things I could say that are so dirty and crude." Yeah, she didn't need to know how arrogantly filthy I could be... yet.

Biting her bottom lip, Juliet took in some nervous breaths before knocking my hand away with her own trembling one to take me into her small hand. I couldn't help but groan at the feeling of her soft, warm hands gripping my throbbing length. Then, the sight of her fingers barely touching once she fully wrapped her hand around me made my chest swell with some pride. Granted, she did have small hands, but hey, can't blame a guy for feeling a little arrogant.

Slowly and awkwardly, she started to stroke me unevenly. After a few strokes, she stopped and looked up at me in defeat with a pout. "I need help." She mumbled, all embarrassed.

Chuckling softly, I placed my hand around hers and tightened her hold to where it felt right to me as I guided her to stroke my full length from tip to base. "Get used to touching and having me in your hand before you try to handle me," I told her softly with a breathy groan.

Our lustful eyes locked onto each other, intensifying the heat of passion around us as I picked up the pace and forced her to tighten her grip on me. "J-just up and down? Like this?" Her words came out breathy and shaky as she tried to take over, only to falter the rhythm I had set us into.

Straining out a chuckle, I tightened our hold and got her back into a good pace. "It's so much more than that, *principessa.*" In theory, yes, it was a simple motion, but there was a right and wrong way to go about it. "Long strokes, baby," I tell her hotly while guiding her until she gets the idea. "All the way, that's it, good girl." I groaned with an unconsciously happy smile on my face.

Slowly, I release her hand and hover mine around hers. "You are doing great, baby." I praised her with a groan. "Keep your hand wrapped nice and tight." Involuntarily, I sucked in a sharp breath when the pleasure of her grip tightening hit me. "Oh fuck, just like that."

Leaning back on one hand, I made some room to watch her work my cock while occasionally looking back up into her determined eyes.

Something about this felt so hot. I mean, never in my life did I ever think I would get such a rush from a handjob, from someone I had to teach, nonetheless. Watching her like this, I couldn't help but feel a rush of excitement at the thought of her lips wrapped around me while she was on her knees.

Fuck, I would be willing to bet that her mouth feels like heaven, and her throat—fuck. I might not last long if I forced myself down her tight throat and made her gag and choke on me.

Thinking about all of that got my blood pumping right down into my cock, making it throb in her hand as she jacked me off. "Fuck, that's it. You are doing amazing." I could feel the edge come closer and closer with every jerk of her hand. "Get it wet, baby. Lean over and spit on my cock to get it wet. Then get rougher."

Unsure, she looked at me with her softened brown eyes. "I don't want to hurt you."

I couldn't help but chuckle at her unnecessary worry. "I like it rough, baby. I can handle it." I assured her with a confident smile before thrusting my hips at her. "Now, show me how good of a girl you are with what I just taught and told you."

Her eyes darkened with determination and desire at my words, and she was quick to lean over and let her saliva slip from between her lovely lips and onto my engorged tip that glistened with precum.

Juliet gave me one last look—earning a nod from me—before working me harder and faster with the new slickness from her spit. "*Merda!*" I gasped at the sudden feeling of her hand squeezing my tip harder with the added motion of her twisting as she came upwards.

Fuck. I wanted this moment to last just in case it would be the only time I ever got anything from her after tonight. But fuck me, with how rough she kept jerking the swollen head of my cock, and the feeling of her hand gliding smoothly along everything, I couldn't last.

"Fuck, I'm coming." I strained through gritted teeth before letting out a guttural groan as my release took hold of me.

"*Cazzo, sei così meraviglioso, principessa.*"

Chapter 20

Juliet

THE MOMENT LUCIANO'S BODY tensed up with his release, I panicked and leaned back as I continued jerking off his spurting cock. Amazed, I watched the thick ropes of his cum spray out of his throbbing cock and painted his delicious abs.

My heart raced with excitement and pride as I imprinted the image of Luciano being in a state of breathless bliss in the afterglow of the orgasm that I gave him. This rush was indescribable. The fact I could bring a strong man like him to such a vulnerable state with just my hand was riveting.

I felt proud of myself, shockingly. Initially, touching him felt dirty to me, even just through his pants. Hell, sitting in his lap earlier felt wrong. It felt too bold and lewd of me when I exposed him. Then, I straight up felt filthy when I directly touched his hard shaft. I was about ready to throw in the towel and die of embarrassment when I asked him for help giving him a handjob. Well, I still wanted to give in after he assisted me because of how ashamed I felt.

But something in me just flipped when he started encouraging and praising me. Was it a little strange to be praised for doing something dirty? Yeah, but something about how wrong it was felt right and arousing.

Shoving my worries away, I bit my lip seductively with a smirk as I slid off his lap and leaned down to his stomach. Looking up at him, I carefully swiped my finger through his cum as his lustful eyes looked at me in wonder. Hesitantly, I brought my finger to my mouth, suppressing the nausea that churned up my body at the horrid memory of the men at the brothel.

The men there violated me in so many ways, and forcing their nasty pricks into my mouth was one of those ways, unfortunately. What was even more fucked up was the fact I couldn't escape the rotting taste. Even now, when I felt a little eager to taste Luciano because I truly wanted to, the sight and scent pulled those traumatic memories to the forefront of my mind. I didn't want to feel disgusted with Luciano, but those men ruined it for me.

"Juliet, you don't have to." Luciano's eyes softened with concern as he grabbed my wrist when my finger was shy of my parted lips.

Swallowing nervously, I pulled myself from his grip. "I want to... I want to get rid of their bad taste and replace it with yours so I can try to make new and better memories." I said with a stubborn determination, popping my finger into my mouth quickly before my mind could be changed.

Tension scrunched my face up when the salty, tangy taste of his cum bathed my tongue. Involuntarily, my body jerked with a gag as the memories bombarded me, pulling me back to that night. Unable to help it, I let out a small cry as some tears escaped my eyes.

I needed to escape, get out of my own head.

And the solution to that problem: lean back in and lick up Luciano's cum.

His unique taste pulled me back and kept me rooted in reality. He didn't taste like the other men. He wasn't the other men. Luciano, that's whose cum I swallowed, whose taste I found myself craving more of with each lick.

Luciano's hand slipped against my cheek, his fingers threading through my hair and gripping at it lightly to keep my head still. "Juliet, don't force yourself." His thumb softly stroked my cheek, wiping my tears away. "What is wrong?"

Going against his force, I leaned back down to lick up another line of his cum. "Please, I need this. I need you. You are the only thing that keeps the bad men away." I pleaded softly against him before looking up at him with my teary eyes.

It didn't take long for me to get lost in his amber orbs, my nerves melting away with his relaxing pupil. "You taste good." I let the thought slip my tongue as I savored his lingering taste in my mouth.

Chuckling and smiling smugly, he ran and pressed his thumb against my lips, slipping it into my mouth and sucking a breath in between his teeth when I sucked and licked it. "Then be a good girl and lick it all up." He told me with a cocky grin, pulling his finger from my mouth and grabbing the back of my head to shove my face into his abdomen.

I should feel a little offended by him shoving me around like that, but fuck, it turned me on too much to resist. With a hand on his hip to steady myself, I eagerly lapped up every last drop of his cum before using my other hand to milk out the last of him from his semi-hard cock.

"I can't believe you're still hard," I mumbled my thoughts out loud as I watched beads of his cum squeeze out from the slit of his mushroom tip and pool on his tip. Once no more came out, I leaned down and gave him a long lick with my full tongue and a soft moan.

With a tender smile, he pulled me up by my arms and settled me back fully in his lap before grabbing my face gently to bring me into a heart-stopping kiss. "How are you feeling?" He murmured against my lips while looking at me tenderly.

"Pretty okay... I guess." I answered truthfully in an unsure voice as I played with the edges of his shirt.

Tilting my gaze to his, he looked at me with serious concern. "Do you regret any of it? I need you to be completely honest with me." He demanded with a worried tremble in his voice.

There wasn't an ounce of hesitation with my answer. "No." It was probably the most confident I have been with anything so far in my life after what happened. "I do not regret any second of it. It's just a lot for me to process right now because it feels dirty and wrong but also right and freeing."

Humming softly and nodding in understanding, he pressed a soft kiss against my forehead before sliding me off his lap to stand. "Don't think too much about it, *principessa*. Don't let the actions of the men in your past jade you because they are nothing but scum." He told me as he buttoned his shirt back up. "If it feels right to you, then it is right. Who gives a shit what other people's outdated or simple-minded thoughts about things are."

Giggling softly, I nodded in response and straightened my outfit back out. "Easier said than done, but I'm trying."

Once he was put back together, he took my hand and led me back out to our seats. The moment we came within sight of the others—Leah, Aidan, and Evie—they all shot the two of us a knowing smirk that made me hide behind Luciano a little before he forced me to sit down in his seat from before.

Confused, I looked up at Luciano with raised brows when he didn't make any indications to take a seat.

Flashing a smile, he leaned down and kissed the top of my head. "I have some business to attend to." He replied, his smile flattening. "Stay with Aidan and Leah."

As if there was somewhere else I would run off to without him. "Yeah, yeah," I grumbled, rolling my eyes and waving my hand dismissively, earning a look of warning from Luciano. "Don't worry, I'll be fine here." I flashed him a quick smile to assure him. "I promise, I'm not going anywhere," I deadpanned playfully with a huff.

Luciano's eyes went over to his two friends, who reassured my safety and waved him off.

After Luciano had been gone for a while, I looked over at Leah and Aidan. "Where does Luciano disappear to?" I couldn't help but worry a little about his missing presence.

"Probably to warm up. Don't worry. He's safe wherever he is." Aidan reassured me with a rather cheeky smile.

A small tug at my sleeve forced my attention to Evie, who leaned toward me. "You're about to see just how much of a beast your man is." She snickered with an excited grin.

And that's what I was afraid of.

What if I didn't like the beast that comes out?

We just had a nice and special moment back there in the locker room, and I didn't want it to be the only one. Nor did I want it to be ruined. I wanted to keep *my* version of Luciano intact for my own selfish sake.

Honestly, he might not be 'my man' after his match, and that terrified me to death.

Swallowing the nervous lump in my throat, I picked at the hem of my outfit as I zoned everything around me out.

Numbingly, I sat there in a white space until a loud shout of excitement from the emcee jolted me back to reality when my heart clenched in fear.

The emcee's voice boomed and echoed through the speakers with pure excitement that matched his almost crazed look. "The one person all you folks ever come to see at these events! The highlight of the event! Please, welcome!" It seemed like everyone in the place stirred at his words, even Aidan, Evie, and Leah—though they weren't screaming their lungs out.

"*Il Diavolo!*"

All the spotlights darted over and focused on a hallway, locking onto a hooded figure as they made their way to the cage. A hooded figure wearing something very similar—as in the exact same thing—to my outfit, particularly what Luciano wrapped and fashioned into a dress around me.

Right before they ascended the steps, someone from the side approached them and peeled the robe off to reveal a shirtless Luciano in all his muscular glory. And hot fucking damn, was he fine as fuck! Especially that full back tattoo of his bat wings and the letter L fashioned in a little pointed tail that curved around his waist to his front side. Other tattoos scattered his body, especially his arms, but his back was the main stage.

"Girl," Evie's voice broke through my dreamy daze as she nudged me, "Close your mouth, you're gonna drool." She teased with a soft, snickering laugh.

Instantly, I shut my mouth, which apparently had been hanging open. What made it even more embarrassing was when I caught Luciano's cocky little smirk and wink at me—yes, he looked directly at me and did that. Breathlessly, I smiled unconsciously as I spoke, "If he's the Devil, then he can take me to Hell whenever he wants." Hell, I would go with him willingly.

Damn hormones.

The cage door slammed shut behind Luciano before the other side opened, and three ruffled men in disheveled casual business clothes were shoved through. "Luciano, please, let's be reasonable." One of them began to grin nervously as he begged on his knees.

Like a tiger stalking its prey, Luciano slowly circled around the men, causing them to all cower together at the center of the ring. "I was more than reasonable with you all. I was even generous and gave you all a chance that you fucked up." Luciano's foot kicked out, catching one man's back, which sent him forward to his front side.

Pausing, Luciano let out a long sigh with a fake look of pity. "Not only do you steal from me, but you try to work with the old mafia to get me overthrown." Luciano's voice hardened with anger towards the end as he trudged up to the men, grabbing one of them by the shoulders and hauling them up into a chokehold.

As the man struggled feebly in Luciano's arms, whacking and flailing his arms and legs, Luciano ignored him to look at the other two men. "But, since I am a reasonable man and love a good fight, I will give you all a chance to fight for your forgiveness and freedom." He proposed with a twisted grin.

"If the three of you can knock me out or pin me for ten seconds, then I will consider your slate clean and let you go about your useless, mundane lives." Chuckling darkly, he released the man in his arms and threw him back to the others. "I'll even let all three of you work together."

The fact Luciano was so relaxed and nonchalant about his wager set me on edge. Sure, he seemed like a capable fighter, and I didn't doubt the abilities he boasted about. But three against one? The three men weren't some scrawny or sickly-looking men either. Granted, they weren't buff or muscular, but they were pretty averagely built, so surely they could pack a bit of a punch or kick.

Turning to Aidan, I tugged at his sleeve to get his attention. "That can't be fair. It's three against one." I voiced my concern to him with a worried look.

Chuckling, Aidan smiled at me confidently. "Those three are going to be nothing but a warm-up to Luciano." Placing a hand on my shoulder, he squeezed and rubbed it. "Trust Luciano. He never bites off more than he can chew."

Maybe I should take some comfort in the fact that Leah and Aidan were so calm about this, but my concern for Luciano came almost instinctively. What if this time was the odd one out? What if they managed to gang up on him and beat him to a bloody pulp?

Or worse, to death.

Chapter 21
Luciano

One last glance at Juliet's worried face, and I focused my full attention on the fearful men who slowly stood up on their shaking legs.

Haphazardly, the three of them all charged me at once with their arms cocked back. Then, like a stupid assembly line, they took their turns swinging—and missing—at me when they came within range. It felt like they weren't even trying with how easily I sidestepped their punches. Sure, there were lots of hands coming at me, but there wasn't really much of an order to their strikes.

All I had to do was carefully keep track of them and act accordingly. For the sake of my entertainment, I hoped they would get it together sooner rather than later.

I was known to be rather destructive when bored.

Thankfully, they put their three brain cells together and started working together. The three of them rushed me together in an attempt to dogpile me, and I managed to dodge two of them successfully, but the third reached out just far enough to snag my shorts and throw me off balance. Throwing his body down, he took us both down to the ground.

Before the other two could jump me, I rolled over and kicked the knees out of the man standing closest to me, knocking him down. Rolling up onto my feet, I went after the only standing man and threw a screw jab at him to break his guard before kidney-punching him repeatedly until I caught movement out of the corner of my eye.

With my guard up, I pivoted around and right-hooked the unfortunate fool right behind me. The force of my punch made his jaw give away, and I couldn't help but grin madly with twisted joy at the feeling of his lower face giving into my fist.

Down the man went in a screaming mess, his hands clutching his deformed face as he wailed in pain.

Whipping back around, I closed the distance between me and my earlier punching bag, and Roundhouse kicked him, sending him to the ground in a bloody mess as he coughed his insides up. Wheezing and coughing heavily, he barely had enough in him to pull himself away from me using his forearms. I probably broke a rib or a few with my blows and punctured his lungs.

"Oof!" The cage's metal bars rattled with the impact of my grunting body.

At least the last man was gutsy enough to charge me like that. Too bad he didn't lock around me tight enough or correctly to do much.

I easily slipped an arm between us, broke his hold on me, and kicked him off. Then, slowly, I stalked up to him, only to have my ankle grabbed and bit by the man who had a waterfall of blood coming out his mouth.

Turning my full attention to the ankle biter, I cocked my elbow and dropped myself down onto him, winding him and literally crushing the life out of him. The sounds of his ribs cracking as they gave away under my weight when I landed on him full force spiked my adrenaline up from the excitement rushing throughout my body.

Getting up, I was quick to disregard the dying man on his last breaths for the trembling man a few feet from me. "Aww, come on, what happened to the fight from before? Did I scare it from ya just now?" A dark chuckle shook out from my sweaty and bloody body as I approached the man with a bloodthirsty grin. "You've seen more than one of my fights. You should be used to it by now."

Lunging at him, I grabbed him by the front of his shirt and pulled him into my knee, digging it deeply into his gut until I heard his ragged breath drag out. "Come on," I growled, shoving him against the cage violently, "Fight back you pussy." Gritting out a grunt, I threw a jab right at his face, making him groan as blood streamed down his face from his nose.

"Luciano, please, I'm sorry." The man's muffled, nasally plea was nothing to me. No matter how much he begged for mercy on his knees, I didn't give a single fuck because he was only sorry after I caught him forging his profits to pay the old mafia people to try and get on their payroll to leave The Syndicate.

In this line of work, seldom are people truly remorseful for their actions; they are only ever apologetic if they get caught or exposed. If they were truly sorry, then they never would have done it in the first place or stopped the process at the very least.

Reaching down, I hauled the man by the back of his shirt to the center of the ring again and forced him to stand.

"EVERYONE LISTEN UP!" The crowd instantly went silent from my furious shouting, filling the area with a very heavy tension. "You might recognize some of the men tonight as a colleague or friend of yours! Let it be known that just because you work for The Syndicate or me that you are not spared from consequences! These men here tonight thought it was wise to forge their records to me, skim from my profits, and try to sell me out to another retired mafia!"

Hushed chatter and murmurs filled the area as everyone paid close attention to us. "Let this be the only warning to all of you out there! If you are thinking about betraying The Syndicate or any of its members, then fucking don't!" Reaching down, I grabbed the man's hand and broke each of his fingers, filling the area with his screams of pain.

Once all ten fingers were broken, I proceeded to break and dislocate his arms before laying him on his back. Above him, I stood, grinning like the most unhinged, feral man ever—the sane man who snapped.

"Have fun in Hell."

The sounds of his ribs cracking filled the air with his winded scream after I dropped my knee down onto his chest. For something that was supposed to protect the vital organs of our bodies, they were rather shitty at it. Ribs were so fragile, and one single injury could be fatal if it punctured a lung or even the heart itself.

Standing back up, I wiped the sweat off my face with the back of my wrapped hands and walked over to the man with the broken jaw. One last apathetic look, and I stomped down on the back of his neck.

Then, looking up, I slowly looked at everyone in the place before zoning my attention onto Juliet, who stood there in a stupor. Her mouth hung open slightly with her parted lips, and her eyes stared at me with a mixture of fear and amazement.

"Juliet," I called out for her in a gentle voice, holding my hand out in her direction. "Come up here, *principessa.*"

Her slender throat bobbed with a nervous swallow before she followed the guard to me inside the cage. She was careful of her steps as she approached me, her hesitant steps avoiding the blood and bodily fluids on the ground as best as possible.

"You have nothing to be afraid of from me," I assured her with a warm smile as I took her hands in my bloodied ones, making her flinch and grimace when the wet bandage wrappings came in contact with her.

Relaxing my expression, I brushed her hair out of her face before turning serious. "Do you know why they call me The Devil?"

Taking in a trembling breath, she looked at the carnage around her, then rounded back to me with a different edge to her eyes. "It's because you are vicious and ruthless, isn't it?" She should be running for the hills. So, why wasn't she? Her warm eyes were practically melting every second they remained on me.

Smirking a little, I began to undo the makeshift robe dress as I spoke. "Yes, but there is so much more than that." Letting the sash and robe fall open, I slipped my hands under to her smooth shoulders. "It is because I bring hell to the wicked. Anyone who dares cross me or The Syndicate and ends up in my ring to face me is met with nothing but pain and suffering until they can no longer take it or their body gives out. Even then, I still punish them until nothing remains but an example to others."

Leaning into me, she gently shrugged the robe off her shoulders fully. "Are you going to punish me then?" The playfully wanton smirk on her face told me she knew fully well what she insinuated.

Then, very shockingly, I went against my need for her. Leaning my forehead against hers, I smiled almost apologetically.

"Not until you are ready to dance with The Devil for all of eternity in my ring of fire."

Chapter 22

Juliet

~1 month later~

THAT SON OF A bitch!

Frustrated, I shut my laptop with an angry sigh while crossing my arms and leaning back in my seat.

"What? Your program didn't work?" Gale teased with a cheeky smirk.

Grumbling to myself, I scowled and spun my chair around a few times before huffing loudly. "Luciano's going out on a date with some bimbo," I whined with a pout.

Gale rolled his eyes and chucked a throw pillow at me from his position on my lounger. "You're the one who rejected him." He reminded me with a deadpan expression. "Also, you're being a little dramatic."

"I did not reject him." I corrected Gale with a soft glare after whacking the pillow away. "I just told him I needed more time." Which, I mean, could be seen along the lines of rejection, I guess. "And I am not being dramatic...!"

"Basically a rejection," Gale shrugged his shoulders softly with a pitying stretch of his lips. "And I hate to break it to ya, but he's a man with needs. He's not going to wait around forever for you, but you're also blowing this out of proportion. He's doing nothing wrong with going on a dinner with some woman for business purposes."

I wanted to argue with Gale, but he was right. Luciano and I weren't an exclusive item, nor did we make any promises to wait for each other... And maybe I was exaggerating things a bit... It was stupid but true.

"He doesn't even like that woman, so why even do business with her..." I continued to grumble with a scowl. "He just told Aidan the other day that she's annoying."

And, of course, Luciano just shrugged me off whenever I brought up the topic of women and relationships with him.

It was probably pathetic of me to run away from Luciano with my tail tucked between my legs that night at the event, but I couldn't find it within myself to agree to a full relationship with him, no matter how hard I tried. It wasn't because I was scared of him after seeing the bloodbath he made, either.

Honestly, I found it rather exciting and amazing that he could do all that with his bare hands. And something about watching him get all worked up and feral in the ring got my blood pumping and passion burning until I ached with need between my legs. I wanted to jump him in the ring that night, and I would have if my reservations weren't intact.

The only thing that held me back from fully falling into Luciano was me. What kind of person would I be if I was with a man like him? Why the fuck was I fine with the thought of being with him? He was a mafia boss, a very violent and ruthless one. I really should be sprinting for the hills, terrified as hell, but my instincts told me to stay. Luciano was my safe space, my comfort person.

Even after seeing him all bloody and sweaty that night, I gladly let him hold me while the blood of others painted his skin. It took me a minute or two, but I got over my disgust for the blood. Then, the fact I had been so fine with it all terrified me. It wasn't normal to be fine with any of that.

Like, how insane must I be to find comfort in the arms of a killer? To want to seek happiness in them?

I hesitated for my sake and sanity, and I still did now. I hated the thought of him being with any other woman; it always got my blood rushing until the heat of anger ached my body. Yet, I still couldn't bring myself to be his woman.

Did I even deserve to be his woman, though? Would that even be fair to him?

Crazy mafia boss or not, he was a good man underneath—in my humble opinion. He deserved more than a broken girl like me. Someone who could actually take care of him and his needs.

As much as I lusted for Luciano, sometimes it wasn't enough to keep the monsters at bay. Luciano deserved a woman who could serve his every need and whim without hesitation and someone who was experienced. I couldn't guarantee any of that to him because what if I randomly got triggered in the middle? I didn't want his pleasure to be ruined because of my trauma. Or if he wanted something and I couldn't give it to him because I didn't know how. Or if I just couldn't because of the trauma.

I didn't know when I would fully recover from everything either because everyone processed things differently at their own unique pace. Sometimes, great strides would be made; others would be baby steps.

It wouldn't be fair of me to make Luciano suffer my recovery with me.

Then again, was anything in life fair?

"Juliet?" Gale's concerned voice became distant as the bad thoughts flooded my mind.

Down and down I went, spiraling until I went under with no way up. But that was fine; there was nothing up on the surface for me. Luciano wouldn't be there forever. Gale would eventually leave me for college. My other friends couldn't care less about me.

Trash.

Broken.

Useless.

Dirty.

Tainted.

A whore.

That's all I am.

Oh God, they're touching me again.
I don't like it! Make it stop!
I can't breathe. Can't catch my breath.
Everything is hurting. Everything is numb.
God, it's so hard to breathe.

Unconsciously and instinctively, my body shot off my chair and rushed through the house in a frantic frenzy of sobs and tears. I knew in the back of my mind I shouldn't bother him, but my need to seek for him felt so primal. I couldn't control myself. I needed to see him, hear him, feel him—him.

Bang!

"Ju—"

I barreled myself into him just as he stood up from his desk, making him grunt softly. "Make them go away...!" I begged between my sharp gasps.

My hands mindlessly searched for one of his, practically yanking it up and throwing it around my neck. "Luciano. Please, help me. I can't—I don't—please, make it stop...!" I struggled to strain my words out because of my hyperventilating.

Pressure tightened around my neck, making my own pulse thrum in my ears as everything slowly turned into a white noise. Then, it eased slightly, making me breathe in deeply. "Shh, you are safe." I knew he was right there, a few inches from me, but he sounded so muffled and distant.

Something hard snakes around my lower back, and my body is pressed against a hard wall of warmth. "Focus on my voice." He sounded clearer through the haze, but not enough to fully pull me through as I felt some kind of weight threaten to drag me back down. "Breathe for me. In through the nose, out through the mouth." His hot breath washed across my cheek and ear, sending a warm and calm wave down my body. "No one will touch you here. No one will dare come close to you with me around."

Luciano's soothing voice, paired with the feeling of his thumb brushing against my carotid, was enough to make the voices in my head become muffled to the point where I could start pulling myself out. "That's it. Good girl. Relax. Breathe. You can do it." He encouraged and praised me with a smile in his voice as he rocked us back and forth softly. "The bad men can't hurt you anymore. It's not their hands on your body. It is mine. It is my hand around your neck. It is me touching you, and I am safe."

Something soft and warm pressed against my forehead before Luciano uttered a string of incoherent Italian. "You are always safe with me, Juliet."

Safe. I am safe.

Breathing in his words, I let my nerves slowly settle with my breaths. I was almost there; I just needed a little more to take the edge off completely. "Luciano," I whispered through a choked sob, "Tighter, please. I need to feel you." More. I needed more. "Please."

"Juliet." His unsure eyes searched mine as his grip remained unchanged.

"Please. I'll tap you if it gets too much. I just need you to take control, please." I assured him with a desperate frown.

Hesitation cleared his darkened eyes momentarily, but it fled when he pulled me closer until our bodies were pressed hard against each other.

The sudden increase in pressure around my neck made me choke out a strangled gasp as I felt my mind buzz and numb out from the lack of oxygen. Fear gripped me as my instinct for survival caused my adrenaline to surge. The sound of my heart pounding against my ribcage echoed all the way into my muffled ears.

A part of me wanted to fight him out of fear of suffocating to death, but the part of me that trusted him kept my heavy breaths even in rhythm and depth while my heart steadied out in my chest with renewed excitement.

Unable to control my bliss, I let it show through my spreading lips and softening eyes. "Luca... Thank you." I gasped out happily as I stroked the back of his hand with my thumb.

"You're never going to stop calling me that, are you?" He mused with a rather happy smirk as he eased his grip a little to let the blood rush back to my head. "You are lucky that I like it coming from you."

Yeah, he made his displeasure about nicknames known when someone tried to be friendly with him and called him Luci. I don't know what happened to the man, because I ran off when one of the guards caught me snooping around Luciano's office when I shouldn't have.

I don't really know fully how Luca became a thing with him and me, but I chalked it up to my mumbling and stuttering and moments of shortening my speech. Then I kept it up because he would get this annoyed twitch of his eyebrow whenever I called him it. It lost its irritating effect on him after a while, but I liked how his eyes lit up at the sound of his nickname. When it no longer got a rouse out of him, I debated stopping until Gale told me the meaning behind the name.

Bringer of light. Fucking ironic, given his moniker of The Devil and being a mafia boss.

Although, I might be fucking insane for my thought process behind keeping his nickname. No matter how much violence and bloodshed he brought to the world, he could never taint mine. To me, he was a ray of light in my darkness. No one brightened up my life as much as he has. He was both the sun and the moon to me.

Honestly, I had no idea why my therapist hadn't tried to have me committed for how insanely stupid and pathetic I was when it came to Luciano. He may be The Devil, but even The Devil is an angel—or once was.

I might have once hoped for an angel to save me, but now I could see that what I needed was a devil.

An angel would save the world and leave me to burn.

A devil would burn the world for me.

And Luciano had the kerosene and lighter ready.

Chapter 23
Juliet

Juliet.

Unlock my car.

Now.

Are you going on that date still?

It's not a date. It's a business meeting.

Now, unlock the fucking car door.

Now!

Business meetings aren't you and one other person of the opposite gender over a fancy meal.

That is a date, and since it sounds like you are still going to go.

So... N.O. :)

You're lucky I don't have time to deal with your bratty ass right now.

Ooooooh, I'm sooooo scared XP

"CHEATER," I MUTTERED TO myself with a flat, unamused expression as I watched Luciano get into one of the bodyguard's SUVs through the security camera.

Apparently, cuddling on the couch with ice cream after my panic attack wasn't enough to convince him to ditch his date tonight.

Fine.

Enjoy your stupid date.

Just don't expect to come back to me tonight after leaving me.

Let's see... What to do...

I pondered in silence, twirling in my desk chair like some stupid cartoon villain. With my head thrown back, I lazily looked around my room, trying to see if I could spot something amiss.

Then, a wicked smile curled at my lips after staring at my computer desk for a while.

Booting my computer back up, I pulled out Luciano's credit card from one of my drawers and plopped it onto the desk with a satisfied face.

Tab after tab, I opened up as many shopping websites as I could think of and started filling up the virtual carts. It didn't even matter if I *needed* the item; if I liked how it looked or sounded, then into the cart it went. I doubt this hissy fit of a shopping spree would hurt his wallet. His funds were basically unlimited with his legal and illegal businesses.

Of course, my phone occasionally went off the whole time with texts from Luciano—all of which I ignored.

I only bothered touching my phone when I was completely done, and that was only to send him a picture of my feet kicked up on the desk with my screen showing the brand new, customized Lamborghini Huracán Evo Spyder proudly displayed. After reading through his storm of messages.

> Juliet.

> Juliet. I know what you are doing, and it is childish.

> Juliet, if you think this will get me to leave my business meeting…

> Why the fuck do you need 4000 dollars worth of lingerie!?

> When are you even going to use it?

> Who are you wearing it for?

> Juliet, stop this stupid nonsense spending.

My phone lit up with a call from Luciano, one I purposely ignored with a smug smirk on my face.

Juliet, answer your damn phone you brat.

Don't think I am going to forgive you for this.

Humming happily to myself, I hit send on the picture and watched it load fully with a devious grin.

Can't wait for my new baby :)

That better be a fucking joke you brat.

You don't even know how to fucking drive!

You better prepare yourself for when I get home tonight, brat.

Ooooooh that sounded like a threat :P

What are you gonna do? Spank me?

You're going to wish that's all I do the moment I walk through that front door later.

I have no idea what came over me to cause me to become so bold, but I ended up sending him a photo of me perched on my chair with my slip bunched around my waist and my ass sticking out.

You better not have been wearing that thong for that stupid boy.

What if I was?

Juliet.

Snickering to myself, I tossed my phone back onto the desk and leaned back in my chair with my arms crossed behind my head.

I would probably get my ass handed to me later, but that was a problem for later. On the other hand, I wasn't too worried because it was Luciano. He was more of a barker than a biter with me. Honestly, sometimes I wondered if he could deliver his threats with me. He liked to make a lot of them, but I have never seen any follow-through.

Oh well.

Also, not like he would be able to get to me tonight.

Not with how I hacked his security system, changed all the codes for the locks, and jammed the locks. Yeah, he wasn't getting in tonight. Serves him right, in my opinion. Man, his reaction later was going to be priceless.

The only hard part now was waiting for him to get home. Well, nothing a quick episode of anime wouldn't fix.

Honestly, besides our little awkward moments, life was great. I have never been this happy or satisfied in my life. I had everything I could ever want, and whatever I did want, I got. It felt so amazing to actually be in control of my own life, to do whatever I wanted whenever I wanted. I even got to eat freely without any kind of dietary restriction! Yeah, that freedom over my food kind of made me put on a little—a lot of—weight, but I was happy.

Initially, when I was brought here, I was around a hundred and fifteen pounds, if I remembered the physical with Leah correctly. According to the scale now, I was around a hundred and forty-five pounds, which was on the overweight end for a five-foot-three female.

Thud! Thud! Thud!

"Damn it, Juliet, open the door!" I heard Luciano shout through the monitor.

Taking my sweet time, I got out of bed and went back over to my desk, where I had the front cameras pulled up on my screen. Luciano and some of his men were at the front door, jiggling and tugging at the handle with growing frustration as each and every single one of their attempts at putting in the code was met with a big error buzz.

I couldn't help but laugh at their attempts while one of the guards was on the phone with the security company.

Yeah, good luck with that, buddy.

It would probably take them the whole night to unscramble the mess I made. I fucked up A LOT of the coding when I installed my own shit. I copied and pasted the original in a document on my computer. They could try to hack my computer and dig it up, but they would probably have better luck hacking the government with how fortified my system was after my cousin and his friend got done helping me with it.

Tapping a key on my keyboard, I activated the microphone to the front door camera. "I told you not to expect to return home tonight if you go on that date. Did you think I was kidding?" The smugness and anger in my dry chuckle almost hurt my throat, and I was surprised such a sound could even come from me. "It's a good thing the gardeners do a good job. Those rose beds look nice and fluffy. Hope you enjoy your bed of roses, and I hope the thorns get you. Good night, Luca." I dragged out the 'a' in his name before cutting the microphone off.

Now, foolish of me for thinking that would be the end of it all and crawling into bed with a false sense of safety. I bundled myself up in my sheets with a satisfied smile on my face and lulled myself to sleep.

Unfortunately, none of that bliss lasted. The shattering sound of glass cut through the air, and the banging and slamming of my balcony doors flying open startled my body upright in my bed.

"Oh fuck." I let out a frightened gasp under my breath when I saw Luciano standing there with his eyes narrowed at me, jaw clenched so tightly that his neck muscles became stiff and prominent, and nostrils flaring with each heaving breath.

He only looked more menacing with how the moonlight shadowed him and gave him a hard glow. Then, the destruction around his feet didn't help that aggressive edge.

Glass crunched under his weight as he stalked up to me with a tense glare full of...

Oh fuck.

Chuckling nervously with a sheepish, apologetic smile, I slowly backed away until I was at the edge of my bed. "Listen, Luca, I'm sorry, okay?" I felt like a lamb cornered by a feral wolf with how he overshadowed me with his suffocating presence.

"Off the bed." He wasn't asking, not with how hard and stern his dominating voice carried to my shuddering body.

Not wanting to be in any more trouble tonight, I obeyed. Slowly, I slipped my legs off the edge until I stood with my nervous hands clutched to my chest.

His hulking figure moved around the bed in calculated steps, and my wide eyes remained locked onto his moving figure.

Shivers pricked at my body with each wave of heat that washed over my body from my budding arousal. God, I didn't know why I found this so exciting when I should be terrified of what was to come. Although, to be fair, I deserved all he had in store for me, given my actions.

But that was what I hoped for, wasn't it? Spending his money on my every whim, buying a whole-ass car when he told me no, then locking him out of the house and taunting him. I had an inkling of an idea of what would happen, yet I still did it to get a rise out of him.

This was what I wanted... Right? For him to snap and show me he meant business.

Well, wish fucking granted. Only problem was, I wasn't feeling so sure now that it was happening.

Sucking a trembling breath, I cowered slightly when he came to a stop right next to me. Gulping, I looked at him out of the corner of my eye for a second, taking in his still-hardened face and darkened eyes. His pupils were so dilated that they nearly blacked out all of his glassy amber eyes. I couldn't help but let myself be pulled into his lustful amber pools.

Then, against my better judgment, I crawled back onto the bed to put some distance between us. "Luca," I started nervously with an unconfident smile. "Shit. I'm sorry. I—ah!"

His hand shot out faster than a blink of an eye and grabbed my neck, hauling me towards him and off the bed until he was seething inches from my face. Then, I made my next mistake of looking directly into his eyes again, letting myself melt under his heated gaze. As anger hardened as his face was, there was a twisted spark in his lustful eyes.

The tension in his neck muscles relaxed with his crazy smile, and that's when I really felt screwed. "We are way past apologies, you little brat." The rumble in his deep voice shook my body with each syllable, and damn me for getting so turned on by it.

What nearly got me coming in my thong were his next words after he pulled me in so close that I thought he would kiss me. "Now, get on your fucking knees." The dominance in his command made my knees want to buckle that instant.

"W-what? Why?" Okay, stupid question, because why else would a man like him in this moment want me to get on my knees? Doubt it was to beg.

The moment his smile turned into a feral, lustful grin, I wanted to be slumped at his feet—forget being on my knees!

"Because I am giving you one chance to show me how sorry you are." His voice came out soft but was saturated with intense passion. "You are going to show me how sorry you are by putting that mouth of yours to use."

He didn't give me a moment to think as he released my neck to fist the back of my head and shove me down to my knees, tilting my head up to look at him. "Until tears are running down your face while you are happily choking on my cock, I won't consider any forgiveness for tonight."

A worried ache sank my facial features as I continued to look up at him. "I want to, I do, but what if..." A disgusted shudder racked my body at the sudden memory, which caused my stomach to churn with nausea.

Luciano's face softened with an understanding smile as his hand moved to cup my face and stroke my cheek. "If at any point it becomes too much for you or you have any reservations, you tell me to stop, or if you can't speak, then tap me wherever you can." Pressing his thumb against my lips, I instinctively took the digit into my mouth. "It's not ideal, but we will talk about it more tomorrow and work out an actual safe-word, alright?"

I quickly nodded in response with an eager smile before my hands grabbed at his pants to undo it along with his belt in a fluster. A wide smile broke out on my face the moment I pulled his throbbing cock out of its confines, and my heart fluttered with excitement as I wrapped my hand around his girthy length.

Recalling our little locker room fun, I started to stroke him as he taught me to get comfortable handling him again.

"Need me to guide you, *principessa*?" I didn't need to look up to see the smirk on his face. The amusement that laced his voice was evidence enough for me.

"No." I bit my response out more curtly than I would've liked, but I felt a little peeved at how he made me feel stupid. "I know how to suck a dick." I quickly uttered, deflating a bit with a soft pout.

"Oh? And how do you know how to do that, hm?" Now he sounded a little too amused and a little pissed from the edge of his uplifted voice.

A soft gasp crept out of my throat when he wrenched my head back by my hair to look up at him fully. And oh boy, he was pissed, judging by how his jaw was clenched tight in a scowl. "Is Gale about to find himself in a bind?" His darkened eyes narrowed sharply with his words, making me shiver and shake my head.

Averting my eyes, I swallowed my nerves. "I've only been watching porn and looking around on the internet," I confessed with an embarrassed tremble in my voice.

Clicking his tongue in a scolding manner, he tilted his head at me with a lightening expression. "So, instead of coming to me to learn and get experience, you go look at someone else's cock to learn?" A mocking anger was amid his amusement as his chest rumbled with a dry chuckle.

Pressure at the back of my head caused me to gasp and whimper as Luciano pressed my face right up against his cock. "If I ever catch you looking at another man's cock or hear about it, I will send you to your knees where you stand and make you take me that instant." My neck craned back at an awkward angle from how much he pulled my hair downwards. "The only cock you are ever allowed to see, touch, and get pleasure from is mine, understood?"

My body trembled with the growl in his voice as he looked down at me sternly. Instinctively, my eyes softened with a smile just as I placed a kiss on his hard length. "Yes, sir." I felt my nerves relax and melt completely to him without any hesitation.

His grip on me slackened slightly as he thrust his hip against my face, rubbing his throbbing member against my lips. "Good girl, now show me what you've learned." The smug smirk on his face lit a competitive fire within me, making me want to show off to him.

Steeling my nerves, I mentally hyped myself up in hopes of keeping my demons at bay so I could make it through one fucking blowjob without embarrassing myself or throwing in the towel.

As confident as possible, I looked up at him with eyes filled with determination as I licked him from base to tip with the full length of my hot tongue. Seeing his jaw twitch with his hitched breath and shudder gave my budding confidence the exact boost it needed.

All reservations aside, I swirled my tongue around the crown of his tip and along his slit to pick up the hint of his precum before taking him into my mouth with a soft groan. I honestly couldn't believe he fit. It was a tight fit with how tightly my lips stretched and wrapped around him, but I got him in, which made me feel proud.

Slowly, I bobbed my head, working him in inch by little inch until I felt him hit the back of my throat, causing my gag reflex to kick in and jerk my body. But, before I could reel back, Luciano grabbed the back of my head with both his hands and held me there with a low groan. "Relax." He commanded, rolling his hips softly at me.

With every thrust, his tip rubbed the back of my throat, causing my body to jerk with a gag. And him telling me to relax wasn't much help because everything was reflexive. No matter how much I calmed myself down, the moment his tip assaulted my throat, my nerves flared back up tenfold.

"Juliet, if you keep gagging like that..." He hissed under his breath, his grip on my head tightening as he shoved himself deeper into my throat. "Fuck."

Panicking, I gripped his hips, digging my nails into him as I struggled to breathe with his fat dick down my throat. The fucked up part of it all was how much Luciano seemed to be enjoying the fact I choked and struggled on his cock. What was more shocking was my own reaction to it all.

I was dripping wet.

The panic that gripped my body paved the way to a twisted arousal that tightened my nipples and made my clit ache with a need to be touched. A part of me felt ashamed to be turned on by this. It was dirty and wrong. I shouldn't be letting a man treat me like this.

But this wasn't any man. This was Luciano, and that made it all okay. Luciano was safe.

Easing my grip on his hips, I let my eyes trail up his body to his sculpted face before settling my eyes into his warm amber pools with needy eyes of my own.

Luciano's body trembled as his own eyes softened with pure desire and want. "Oh, Juliet, *amorina*, don't look at me like that unless you are ready." His grip on me eased fully, letting me pull off of him with a deep gasp of breath before I went into a coughing fit.

Calming myself, I leaned back in and trailed kisses along his length with a happy smile. Then, slowly, I looked back up at him with sure eyes as I let my body submit to him fully.

"I am all yours, Luciano. I trust you, so do what you will with me, sir."

Chapter 24

Luciano

THE SINGLE THREAD OF control I had left within my body snapped and burned to ashes with her sweet submission.

I was ready to grab her and throw her on the bed when she looked up at me earlier with her softening eyes. I could feel her soul melting into me when she fully yielded her control to me with that confident, trusting look. Then, to hear her verbalize it. Fuck. That really did me in, bad.

"I'll tell you to stop or tap you repeatedly with an open hand if it becomes too much for tonight, promise." She assured me when I looked at her questioningly.

Relenting with a deep breath, I nodded in response before cupping the back of her head with one hand and her face with the other. "Promise me, not just for tonight but from here on out, that you will communicate to me whenever you feel any discomfort. You will use your safe-word once we discuss one tomorrow, and you will verbally tell me what is wrong. This is not a negotiation. Either you agree to this term and condition of mine, and we continue, or you disagree, and everything, this potential relationship included, comes to a stop until we work something solid out."

I wanted to grab her face and fuck it until tears and spit streamed down her pretty face, but not at the expense of possibly losing her forever. No matter how much pain I wanted to inflict upon her body, the thought of her being uncomfortable with any of it was enough to repulse me.

I needed her to want it, crave it, and beg me for it.

Juliet's bright face lit up with confidence as her head nodded without hesitation. "Yes, sir, promise." Her cheeky little smile made my eyes roll with my chuckle.

"Sarai la fine per me, lo giuro." I muttered under my breath as I fisted the back of her head tightly. "No hard feelings about this, but I still have to punish you for tonight." I couldn't help the wicked grin spreading on my face as a surge of lust hardened my desire to ruin her at this very moment.

Without warning, I forced her mouth open and thrust myself in until she fought against me too much by pressing against my hips and tried to reel her head back despite me holding her firm. "Shh, relax." How fucking ironic of me to try and calm her so I could make her choke on my cock.

Gritting my teeth, I sucked in a sharp breath before forcing more of myself into her hot mouth and down her tight throat. "Breathe through your nose, Juliet," I strained out a groan as I struggled a bit to adjust to the tightness of her throat constricting around me with her struggle.

Juliet's sarcastic eyes looked up at me and rolled, earning a hard thrust of my hips as a reprimand. The small glare she threw back after she gagged violently made my shoulders shake with amusement and steeled my grip on her to force her to take more. "You should be grateful that I am even letting you have the pleasure of having my cock in your mouth, you little brat." I sneered down arrogantly at her as I began to fuck her mouth despite her protests.

"Hands behind your back, *amorina.*" Her little fists pounding against my abdomen became rather annoying after they became persistent. "Don't make me take my belt off to tie them." I threatened with a low growl when her eyes narrowed at me defiantly.

At least the threat seemed to be enough because she immediately dropped her hands and crossed them behind her lower back. The sight of her obedience brought a proud warmth to my swelling chest.

I didn't mind taming a brat, but I didn't want an absolute one who wouldn't know when to quit. So, I was glad to see that Juliet had at least one completely submissive bone in her body. Or at least she knew when enough was enough.

"Good girl." I praised her with a warm and proud smile, wiping her tears away with my thumb of the hand that held her face. "I am going to fuck this lovely mouth of yours and fill it with my cum, and you are going to swallow every last drop of it, understood?" I asked, my pace picking up to chase my release.

Juliet moaned in response and nodded her head to the best of her abilities. Then, she surprised me with her eagerness, pulling a deep groan from me when I felt her suck and swallow me.

The dirty words hung on my tongue, but I bit it back. I didn't want to scare her off by calling her a cum slut or a desperate whore for me. I didn't know what her limits were yet, and I was sure I pushed them greatly by face fucking her right now. It went against my rules and better judgment to engage with someone without establishing clear lines of boundaries and their soft and hard limits, especially engaging in a scene without a set safe-word.

But fuck me and my damn rules when it came to Juliet. I wanted to give her time and space, but obviously, that wasn't helping. She needed a firm hand, one I was too afraid to give. If I let her continue her little power trip, then it would bite me in the ass.

Better to ask for forgiveness than permission, I suppose.

Choking out a sharp breath, I pulled back just in the nick of time as my release washed over me. "Fuck." I strained out a groan as I felt my release tighten my balls.

With just my tip in Juliet's mouth, I held her head still as I emptied myself completely into her needy mouth that sucked and licked at me with every spurt and throb.

Greedy slut.

I wanted to say but bit my tongue and smirked back as I focused on riding out my orgasm. She wasn't ready for it—I had to constantly remind myself to keep myself in check.

Letting out a satisfied exhale, I pulled her off completely as I looked down at her with a proud smile full of bliss. "You did such an amazing job, Juliet." I praised her as I released her hair.

Holding her face still with my other hand, I stroked her wet cheek with my thumb as I tilted her head up high. "Open that pretty mouth of yours, baby. Show me that you got every last drop." I commanded in a soft voice, encouraging her with a downward nudge of her bottom lip with my thumb.

My smile widened at the sight of her opening her mouth and sticking her tongue out proudly. "Such a good girl. I am so proud of you." I truly was because this was a big step for Juliet.

I won't lie; I thought she would tap out halfway through. So, the fact she let me get as rough with her as I did and finish in her mouth was much more credit than I gave her.

Fully letting go of her, I quickly tucked myself back in and fixed my pants before reaching down and picking Juliet up into my arms. "You are so perfect," I said breathlessly with an appreciative smile.

Leaning down, I pressed a deep kiss against her slightly swollen lips, groaning softly when I invaded her mouth and quickly claimed it with my tongue. "I really am so proud of you. And thank you." Smiling against her lips, I chuckle deeply and let my eyes fall into hers. "Thank you for allowing me this privilege." I could feel my heart ache as I poured every ounce of my happiness and gratitude into my words and eyes while I looked down at her with the biggest smile ever.

"It feels weird for you to thank me for all of that." Juliet's words hummed against my chest after she buried her face into it.

"Well, get used to it." I playfully bit back with a hearty chuckle as I carried her to my room. "If you don't allow anything to happen, then it doesn't happen. Anything you permit me to do is a privilege on its own. You really have no idea how much it means to me for you to let me do that to you just now."

Placing a kiss on her forehead, I set her down on my bed and took a step back to fully admire the beauty of her fucked out face because, well, I could.

Also, I might have wanted an ego boost. Seeing her flushed and tear-stained cheeks with her lips pouted slightly because they were a little swollen made my pride puff at my chest.

She *allowed* me to do that despite what she had been through.

I was the only man to have such an honor.

Her face scrunched up softly as her hands gently wandered her cute face. "Do I have something on my face?" Her soft voice worried.

"No, but now I am wishing I came all over it instead of having you swallow." The thought slipped off my tongue before I could control it. I just hope it wasn't too much for her right now.

Honestly, I didn't mean for my thought to voice itself when the image of her sweet face painted with my cum burned itself into my dirty mind. Well, hopefully, tonight will be the start of something new for us, and I will get the opportunity to make that vision come true sooner rather than later.

"You want to do that to me?" Shit. I didn't like how wary she sounded with her shying body.

Easing off, I held my hands up in the air as I shrunk my shoulders to make myself seem smaller. "Only if you allow me to. If not, then I will get rid of the idea immediately." I promised her with a serious look as I slowly sat down on the edge of the bed. "We won't do anything you are not comfortable with. You will set the pace of our relationship and what we will and won't do. Whatever rules you set forth will be what I operate within." I assured her in all seriousness, slowly crawling over to her with each word because she had scooted back into the center of the bed.

Sighing softly with concern, I remained on all fours as I reached a hand out and cupped her face. "What is on your mind, *principessa*?" As open as Juliet was with me, she still had a habit of clamming up when push came to shove. The only time she let me have it was when she was really upset.

Juliet's face twisted softly along with her fidgeting hands, and it didn't take long for her shoulders to tense up with her growing anxiety. "I..." Her mouth shut as it opened, her nervous tongue darting out for a split second before her bottom lip tucked between her teeth.

"Juliet." My soft voice grew stern as I tightened my grip on her face. "Look at me."

Gasping sharply, she let her shaky eyes find mine. "Sorry... It's just... When you said that, the image of it ran through my mind, and I was scared at how turned on I got from it. I mean, it's so dirty and wrong, and I know what we just did probably wasn't any better, but it just feels weird for me to want and like that."

"Oh, *amorina*, come here." Scooting up in the bed, I pulled her up by her arms and settled her in my lap after I swapped spots with her. "That is perfectly fine, and don't let anyone else tell you otherwise." Sneering dryly, I flashed her a confident grin. "Besides, who gives a shit what others think and say. It is fine as long as you are happy and it's not self-destructive."

Cradling the back of her head, I held her close and tight and pressed a tender kiss to the top of her head. "I know it is going to be a long and hard road for you still, and it will be for a while, but that won't deter me from you. I have already accepted the fact you will be more hesitant when it comes to anything sexual or physical contact-related." Stroking her hair, I showered her face with soft and caring kisses. "Given everything, I still want to be with you, or at least try to give a relationship between us a chance. You will need a lot of time and patience, all of which I am more than willing to give you, no matter how long it takes."

Softly, she pushed against me to lean back and look up at me with a saddened curve of her lips and teary eyes. "What if I am never ready? It's not fair to you. What if I am never ready to go all the way again? What if you never have sex again?" She worried, her frown deepening with every question that flew out of her mouth.

I felt bad for chuckling in response, but I found her fretting too amusing. "I am not some horny teenage boy who is going to throw a fit because I can't get my dick wet." I teased her in hopes of lightening her mood up. "I can handle no sex until you are ready. Worse comes to worse, I got my own hand and the shower. I don't *need* sex to function and live." I assured her with a warm yet firm smile. "I have faith in you, and I know that with time and help, you will get there. And I will be there with you every step of the way."

Gently, I grabbed her face and brought her into a deep kiss. "We will talk more about this in the morning after breakfast. For now, relax while I get ready for bed." I murmured against her lips before settling her under the covers and kissing her forehead. "Drink some water, too, while I'm gone," I told her as I got off the bed, picking up the water bottle I always kept at the bedside and setting it next to her. "If I don't see some of it gone, then I'll pull you out of bed when I'm back and make you drink." I threatened her in a playful voice before leaving to go through my nightly routine.

Once I was done, I slipped next to her in bed and secured her lovely body right against mine by wrapping my arms tightly around her waist. "Good girl," I spoke into her hair when I saw the water bottle on the nightstand across from us with a large volume missing.

Her body tensed against mine briefly as she peered up at me. "Wait, are you having me sleep here with you?" Her eyes were bright with hope but distant with fear.

"Well, I'm certainly not having you sleep in your room with the balcony busted like that," I remarked sarcastically with a snort, earning a smack in the chest from her.

"And whose fault is that?" She retorted with a chuckling snort and roll of her eyes.

"Well, if someone had let me into my own home," I chided playfully with a smirk and raised brow.

Grabbing her sides, I dug my fingers into her, making her giggle and laugh. "Are you going to lock me out again?" I asked with a playful growl and laugh of my own as I continued to tickle her.

"You're such a jerk!" She laughed while whacking my hands with hers. "And it's your fault, I warned you." She retorted through her fits of laughter. "Take me seriously next time, and I won't." Her uncontrollable laughter grew in volume. "I promise." Gasping and snorting through her laughter, she continued to struggle. "Please, no more tickling." She begged through strained laughter while struggling to breathe.

Ceasing the attack on her sides, I tightened my arms around her waist again and pulled her flush against me. "I won't go on any more dates, business-related or not, unless you are with me or it's with you, promise." At least it wasn't too important of a date tonight. Otherwise, Juliet really would have had her ass handed to her.

"Now," kissing her forehead, I ran a hand up her back to her nape, holding it firmly, "Sleep. We have a lot to do tomorrow."

"Keep me safe all night?" Her small voice was muffled by my chest.

Chuckling softly, I kissed the top of her head.
"Always, *amorina*."
Safe in the arms of The Devil, how ironic.

Chapter 25
Luciano

It felt amazing to wake up to Juliet in my arms like this, and I hoped this wouldn't be the last.

We've slept together before, but not in an intimate sense. She would often come to me in the middle of the night whenever she had a nightmare and couldn't calm down, or I would go to her if I heard her screaming in the middle of the night.

No feelings were attached before, just two friends who sought and gave comfort. At the very least, I never felt intimate waking up to her after a bad night; it also felt wrong to feel anything but sympathy during those moments. If anything, I only ever wished I could take away her pain and suffering in those times.

The irony of her worrying about our relationship being unfair because I wouldn't be able to have sex with her made me want to laugh out loud. It was all unfair to her, in my opinion. She was the one who had to continue suffering because of what was done to her, and I couldn't do anything about it to help her take any of it away. I could easily take care of my own problems with my arousal, a luxury she doesn't have unless she could be rid of those memories permanently.

It wasn't fair that her love life got torn to shreds before it even began. Her joys of a good relationship were ruined because of those bastards; even if she wanted to enjoy things, she couldn't. I could only give her so much and hope it all goes well. I would always be right behind her, picking up the pieces and helping her patch herself back together, but ultimately, it was up to her to make things stay.

Afraid this dream would fade, I held her slumbering form against me tightly. "*Lo giuro, non conoscerai mai la sofferenza per mano di qualcun altro con me.*" I vowed to the both of us then and there.

Not a moment later, Juliet stirred in my arms and peered her sleepy face up at me. "Luca?" She struggled to blink her squinting eyes as the morning sunlight shone on her face. "Too early... Sleep more." She whined, pulling the covers over her head and shimmying into bed.

"Tell your buddy to go back to sleep." Her muffled voice came from under the covers, making me laugh softly. "I don't wanna see him yet. My throat still hurts." She whined with a light smack against my stomach.

"Well, remember that next time you think about trying something with me," I remarked with a deep laugh before yanking the covers off of her protestant body. "Come on, time to get up, *principessa*." I urged her with a pat on her bubbly ass. "We have breakfast and a lot to talk about."

That only made her groan and pout while sinking into the bed more. "It's too early. Go work out, then come get me." She bargained with a sleepy glare. "And go fix my balcony."

"I already have some men on it," I assured her with a roll of my eyes before climbing out of bed. "You aren't going to hide behind the corner and watch me work out today?" I teased her with a knowing smirk.

The way her face blushed up with embarrassment before she hid under the sheets again was too adorable not to chuckle at. "You aren't exactly sneaky." At least, I didn't count hiding behind the corner and peeking her head around sneaky. "I don't mind it. It's kind of adorable." From her, it was; it made me feel desired by her in a strange way.

After pulling the sheets off to kiss her on the forehead, I tucked her back in and continued my morning routine, leaving her to stew until it was time for breakfast. Juliet wasn't too thrilled about me dragging her out of bed and throwing her over my shoulder to take her to the dining room. At least she didn't fight me about actually eating breakfast, as in I didn't have to load her plate up and make her eat what she needed. I wasn't trying to fatten her up, just making sure she ate a healthy amount; otherwise, she'd eat so frugally that it concerned me. Granted, she has gotten better about eating, but it was a bad habit from her parents, and we haven't fully broken it yet.

"Don't run off anywhere, Juliet. We still have to talk." I probably didn't have to tell her because there weren't many places she could run to avoid our talk, but seeing her try to shuffle away out of the corner of my eyes had the words coming out before I realized it.

"I won't. I'm just grabbing my blanket, and then I'll be on the couch." She replied in a defeated voice before the sounds of her soft footsteps disappeared down the hallway.

True to her word, I found her bundled up on the couch in her fluffy pink blanket, watching something about coding on the TV. I almost didn't want to disturb her, but it was better to rip the bandage off sooner rather than later. "Pause it or turn it off, Juliet," I told her in a firm voice as I sat beside her and pulled her into my lap, blanket and all.

Carefully, I positioned her to straddle and face me, wrapping her blanket around her shoulders and securing it before looking straight into her eyes. Then, the dreaded question, "Do you want to give a relationship a try with me? Given everything you have seen and know about me." Brushing her hair out of her face, I continued, "If you have any hesitation or reluctance, then I do not want you to engage with me for your sake." Looking at her seriously, I told her, "If we are going to give a relationship a try and make it work, you need to be in it a hundred percent."

Juliet's tension eased from her shoulders as her chest deflated with her exhale and bright smile. "Yes, I want to, and I shouldn't have hesitated that night of the fight, but I am more than sure now after thinking about it." A shaky breath rose at her chest, and her throat bobbed with her nervous swallow before a small smile worked its way to her lips. "I'm not going to lie. I am scared, but I trust you." Her confident words and sure smile brought a happy smile to my face when I felt my clenched heart relax.

Hugging her tightly, I kissed her forehead. "You have no idea how much it means to me to hear that from you and see how much you mean it. I swear, I will never abuse the privilege you have granted me." I promised her with a passionate kiss, letting her steal my breath and soul away with our connected lips.

"Have you done any kind of research, or god forbid, asked Aidan about anything?" Best friend or not, I still didn't like the thought of him discussing anything sexual or BDSM related with Juliet when I could easily have that conversation with her.

Giggling softly, she nodded in response, "I Googled a lot of things, and I talked to Evie and Leah about whatever questions I had. If they didn't know the answer, then they asked Aidan for me to save me some embarrassment and awkwardness."

"Well, what did you learn then? Did you discover anything about yourself?" I was genuinely curious and wanted to see if I could gauge her confidence and where she could possibly land on the scale of BDSM relationships.

Humming softly, she nodded before averting her eyes down to her twirling fingers. "It's kind of weird for me to process still, and it feels kind of weird to talk about it and to be *into* the lifestyle." She struggled awkwardly with her words, but I was proud of her for getting it out instead of withholding her thoughts and feelings.

Curling a finger under her chin, I tilted her head up to fix her gaze back onto me. "Is it something that you see yourself fitting into or rejecting? I know the lifestyle isn't for everyone, and it is still somewhat taboo even today." It definitely wasn't something that was everyone's cup of tea.

Even if someone were interested or involved in BDSM, it all varied so much. Some lived it twenty-four seven while others a scene here and there. Then, there were others who only liked certain aspects of it all and wanted certain things out of dynamics.

"With you? Yeah... If we're compatible." She sounded wary and almost sad even though we hadn't even started. I guess she still saw the glass as half empty rather than full.

"Well, tell me what kind of relationship you see yourself engaging in, what kind of dynamic, what you want out of a dominant and submissive relationship, just everything that you can think of. I want you to dump it all on me so I can gauge where you stand." I encouraged her with a warm smile and stroke of her jaw.

Taking a few deep breaths, Juliet shifted around nervously in my lap, and I let her have the moment to settle herself because pushing her would do no good right now. "Well, I guess I am kind of a brat... It's weird to think about it and accept it, but I kind of fit the general description of liking to push your buttons and challenge you to get a rise out of you. I also do it because I want you to snap, to punish me for being uppity, which is weird because I shouldn't even like the thought of punishment, yet I get so turned on thinking about you grabbing me by my neck or hair to bend me over and spank me or to keep me on edge and never let me come." Her words came out like a whirlwind and so small that I almost missed them.

Chuckling, I grabbed her face in my hands and squished her cheeks together. "Slow down. Don't be embarrassed or ashamed about any of it. I am never going to judge you for your kinks and fetishes. Trust me, I would be the last person on earth to do that." Unless she was into something very taboo, like wanting to cannibalize someone and have sex with their corpse, then I might question her sanity a little.

"It's just weird to digest and process given how I was taught things growing up, but I mean, at this point, I'm not even going to try and fully process it and just let it play out how it does and enjoy it as it comes." She sounded a little hesitant towards the end, but at least she admitted it out loud.

Pushing my hands away, she held them in my lap, playing with my fingers for a few seconds before looking up at me timidly. "Besides being a brat and all, I guess I like the thought of you being in control because it makes me feel a little less anxious. I mean, I still don't really know what to do with my life, so I hate feeling lost, and you telling me what to do, taking charge, all of that makes me feel at ease knowing I don't have to stress about thinking what's next."

"Do you want to relinquish all control to me? Or?" I prodded further, hoping to get her to open up more about her feelings, wants, and needs.

Juliet quickly shook her head in denial and looked at me with a soft frown. "Total power exchange didn't really strike my fancy. As much as I want you to direct and guide me, I don't necessarily want you to dictate every aspect of my life. I'm not really keen on being a slave. I want you to take care of me, give me a firm hand when I need it or ask for it, guide me, and be the strong person for me if any of that makes any sense."

Scrunching her face up, she puffed her cheeks out momentarily before huffing, "It's kind of confusing because I kind of want something that's kind of like a caregiver relationship, but I'm not really digging the whole Daddy aspect of it. I want it to continue for the duration of our relationship, but again, not in the whole master/slave sense." Sighing frustratedly, she pouted and flailed her hands a bit. "I'm sorry if I'm making no sense."

Amused at her flustered state, I rested my hands on her hips and rubbed small circles with my thumbs. "*Amorina*, we don't have to put labels on our dynamic. Maybe it will become one or another as time passes, or we simply engage in a Dom/sub relationship. There isn't a rule that says we have to fit into one category or another." Her trying to slot us into a category was rather adorable, though.

"That is the joy of the BDSM community. Nearly everything and everyone is welcome. No need for labels and fitting into any specific mold. We just do what we enjoy within three vital aspects: safe, sane, and consensual. It does not matter what you like or choose to participate in. As long as you keep to those three pillars, then you are golden." I assured her with a smile. "Is that clear?"

Cracking a smile of her own, she nodded and pulled one of my hands up to kiss the back of it. "Yes, sir, it is."

Holding my palm against her face, she pressed into it with a happy hum and smiled as she rocked back and forth a little bit. "You smell good." She spoke against my palm with an embarrassed smile. "It always calms me and makes me feel safe."

Fully cupping her face, I smiled tenderly at her and stroked her cheek with my thumb. "I am glad you feel that way with me." It beats being bat-shit scared of me.

"If I'm being honest, I don't really want things to change much between us, like routine-wise, and maybe a bit of our dynamic. I mean, yeah, I want to be your girlfriend, so that has to change, but other than that, the rules you set for me so far are kind of what I want anyway." She admitted after a moment of peaceful silence. "Well, and maybe I want you to be a little stricter, but that's about it."

Pulling her in close to my smirking face, I slipped my hand from her face down to her neck, gripping it softly. "Oh, don't worry about that. Things are going to be much different now that we are together." The twisted joy in my voice was hard to hide as the dirty thoughts of Juliet at my mercy crashed through my mind.

Unable to help myself, I kissed her deeply with a hungry groan as I pulled her hips right into me. I wanted her so badly. It would be so easy to pin her down to the couch right now and take her until she couldn't go anymore. The idea was tempting, but I knew I couldn't act on it.

Releasing her, I breathed deeply while resting my forehead against hers. I needed to calm down before I scared her off. "Did you get as far as figuring out what your limits are? Or have an idea of them?" Talking about her limits would get me back in the right headspace; I needed to know her comfort zone and where I could operate within.

Juliet's safety and comfort. That was my anchor to reality. She trusted me with herself, and I can't ruin that.

"A bit. There's a lot, but I think I have a good idea of my soft and hard limits." Juliet answered between her soft pants.

It was tedious to go through it all, but it had to be done. Of course, once she was done, we had to move on to mine because even Doms had their limits.

After our discussion, I was glad to see we were both on the same page. However, there was quite a bit on her soft list that we needed to test out, which frightened me a little because I didn't like the thought of pushing Juliet to her breaking point. Unfortunately, the only way for us to find out was to test out the limit. It won't be fun for either of us—it would definitely be painful. I just hoped that she could handle it for her sake.

"And have you decided on a safe-word?" The air around us grew heavy with my question as I looked at her with bated breath, only releasing it when she nodded her head.

"Tap out."

Chapter 26
Juliet

THE REST OF THE day was spent without Luciano because he had business to take care of—hopefully, that didn't mean killing someone.

However, it wasn't the fact of him possibly killing someone out there that tripped me up. It was the fact I was fine with it. I shouldn't be fine with a life being taken so easily like that, but at the same time, why did it matter? If Luciano went after someone, they probably deserved it in some sense.

If I was being honest, with every passing day, I have become more jaded with life while finding some kind of joy in it. The world sucked, more so the people in it. I knew not everyone had a good heart and soul, but the meager amount astounded me. Our streets were filled with more black than white or gray—it made me sick.

Even if I had top-end bodyguards with me whenever I left the house, I never stopped feeling paranoid. Granted, my paranoia was brought on by my own devices.

I knew better than to dig and shove my nose into places I shouldn't, but after seeing all those people at the fight, I grew an itch to snoop. Skeleton after skeleton, I pulled so many dark secrets from people's closets to where I could fill up a few graveyards.

The mountains of dirt I had sat safely in some hard drives for another time. When? I had no idea. Honestly, I only dug because I was curious and wanted to test my hacking capabilities.

People really need to have better cyber security.

It was almost comical how easily I unraveled someone's life completely by grasping a single thread.

Now, I could be a good person and turn all this into the police, but that meant shutting down The Syndicate's business and Luciano's in passing.

Okay, I did turn one person into the police, but it wasn't out of the goodness of my heart. I wasn't a hundred percent sure, maybe about ninety-eight percent sure, but one of the people I happened upon in my little hacking spree was one of the men who raped me.

I didn't want to bug Luciano about one stupid man, so I decided to save him some trouble and take care of my own problem myself. Whatever fucked up shit I dug up on Marley Goth got packaged neatly into a flash drive and mailed first-class to the NYPD. As a second safe measure, I emailed everyone in the whole department from an untraceable email account. That single mail could get lost in transit or while it sat at the department. An email to *everyone* in the whole NYPD? Yeah, at least one person was bound to see it and bring it to someone's attention.

That was probably two days... I should probably snoop around to see if a case got opened up.

Did the police even work that fast, though? I assumed they would, but hey, there were more things of precedent than some serial child rapist (note the fucking sarcasm). Honestly, not gonna lie, I briefly debated putting the horrible man on blast all over the internet in hopes he would get jumped in the streets. I still wasn't against the idea, but I figured going the 'legal' route would be best.

I might be living with a crime boss, but that didn't mean I should let myself become one. On the other hand, my brand-new boyfriend was a mafia boss who could get away with almost anything...

The fact we were officially together now still tripped me out. Yeah, it has only been what? A few hours technically since we made it official, but we lived together for a while, so it shouldn't be *that* weird. However, we lived together more like friends or roommates before this, so I guess putting an actual label on our relationship slightly shifted things.

Also, it was more of a personal problem than anything. I mean, never in my life did I ever think I would be dating someone twice my age or a criminal. Okay, maybe that last part was a bit offensive because he wasn't necessarily some street thug or someone despicable.

At least he was a handsome criminal. Luciano Agosti was sin on legs, a live and breathing work of art.

And he was all mine now.

Call me a greedy and selfish bitch, but I wanted Luciano all to myself for now and ever. Yeah, maybe I had slowly become a little obsessed and addicted to him over time, but I fell into a safety net with him. I never wanted to let him go now that he let me sink my claws into him. And don't even get me started on the jealous rage that stormed within me at the thought of him being with anyone else who wasn't me.

The sheer need and desire for Luciano burned at every nerve ending in my body—it always had. My issue was not acknowledging my body's and mind's need for him because of my fear. Fear that held me back from taking the full leap with Luciano, which I hated.

I wanted to give myself to him, I really did, but I was so fucking terrified of it breaking us before we even got started. What if I couldn't get over the pain? He wasn't exactly small or average in size, and the men before hurt so much being less endowed than Luciano. And what if the memories came back with sex? I didn't want to ruin a special moment between us and make a fool of myself. What if, after one time, he decided I wasn't worth it? He said I was worth it, but what if he changed his mind after experiencing the fact I wouldn't be able to have sex with him for a long while, or possibly forever?

My cowering body jarred with a sudden shake, snapping me out of my own drowning thoughts. "Juliet, what's wrong?" Luciano's face appeared right before me after a few blinks, startling me with how close his concerned face hung from mine. "*Principessa*, what's the matter? You wouldn't answer when I called out for you, and you started to slip."

Sitting on the couch, he took my laptop from me and set it aside to pull me onto his lap and tuck me tightly against him. "What's going on in that mind of yours, *amorina*." His deep voice rumbled against my ear as he nuzzled the side of my head.

"Are you really sure about me?" I worried with a frown, not daring to lift my head up to face him out of fear of seeing regret or disappointment crossing his features.

Sighing deeply, he pressed a kiss against my temple before turning my head up to face his worried smile. "Shouldn't that be a question for a few months from now?" He joked with a dry chuckle. "Even if you do ask months from now, my answer will still be the same as it is now."

Sliding me off his lap, he sat me properly on the couch and got down onto the floor on his knees before me. "And you better tattoo my answer into your brain because it will never change." His voice held so much conviction with his deepening eyes that I couldn't help but shiver from the force of it. "I will never regret taking a chance with you. I will always, without a doubt or ounce of hesitation, be infinitely sure about you."

Leaning down, he kissed my knee before looking back up at me with the most heart-melting smile ever. "You know why I started to call you *amorina* along with *principessa*?" His voice lightened with a happy warmth as the corners of his lips twitched excitedly.

Shaking my head softly, I reached a hand down and threaded it through his fluffy hair. "No... But I also don't really know why you call me *principessa* either because I'm the furthest thing away from a princess." I had no idea what *amorina* meant, but guessing from the sound of it, I would assume it had to do something with love. Unless I really flubbed up *that* badly in Spanish class.

"Well, you are my little princess, precious and to be treasured and spoiled. You also act like a petulant princess when you act up, so it is fitting." He mused with a chuckle as he leaned into my touch. "*Amorina* means little love, a cuter way of saying *amore mio*, which means my love."

Reaching up, he gently wrapped his hand around my wrist to bring my hand to his lips, where he kissed the back of it. "You are my piece of bliss in this world, my light, my beauty, my breath. You are the reason why I am capable of feeling love. You are my little love in this world, and I wouldn't have it any other way. I do not want anyone else to have that title in my life either, nor will I let anyone else besides you."

Leaning up, he grabbed my face and brought me down into a breathtaking kiss. Shivers trickled down my spine at the feeling of the walls around my heart crumbling with each press of his lips and each wave of his hot breath washing over me. "Please, do not ever doubt my feelings for you nor the lengths I will go for you. Even if it means waiting an eternity for you to be ready, I will gladly do it." He whispered against my lips.

"What if I don't like sex? What if we try, and it really hurts, and I don't like it? What if you—"

My worrying was promptly cut off by his lips pressing against mine. "Stop." He prompted me sternly. "Do not think about that. I do not care about how soon we can fuck, so do not put a time frame on when we have to get into bed naked with each other." He sounded a little upset, but it didn't feel directly towards me with how his eyes averted. "And I am sorry if I give off the impression that sex is all I want from you or is what I am looking forward to in our relationship because it is not. Yes, I am a man with needs, but as I said before, I have my damn hand and the shower."

Sitting back on his haunches, he took my hands in his and rested them in my lap. "If we end up trying and you don't like it, then that is that. We just won't have sex." He made that ridiculous statement sound so normal and decisive. "And don't you dare argue with me on that. If you are not comfortable with sex after or if we try it, then so be it. As long as you are comfortable and happy in our relationship, that is all that matters."

Letting out a frustrated sigh, I leaned my head against his. "I want to try, but I am just so fucking terrified. It feels wrong, too, because I can fantasize about us fucking if I'm in a mood, but then other times, it chills me to my very soul. I mean, just the thought of being naked in front of you scares me sometimes. What if you don't like how I look? What if I'm not enough?"

Luciano's body shook against me with his amused chuckle. "Baby, you are perfection to me. I'm not some shallow bastard who cares about their woman having nice tits or a huge ass. You are always going to look nothing shy of beautiful and perfect to me, I swear. Though I'm not gonna lie, I love how you are slowly filling out from your sticky figure before." He admitted with a cheeky grin.

"Is that why you keep shoveling food onto my plate? I'm around a hundred and forty-five pounds, you jerk." I playfully hit his shoulder with a weak chuckle. "But you're just saying all of that for the sake of it."

"My goal is to get you nice and plump. Sue me." He playfully remarked with a short laugh when my fists came at his chest. "You look good with a little meat on you." He admitted with a grin.

"Well, don't expect me to get much more than this. I like where I'm at, but I'm starting to muffin top a little and go up in pant sizes a little too much for my liking." I admitted with a lopsided smile, looking down and pinching at the little bit hanging over the waistband of my shorts.

Luciano's hand lightly pushed mine away, and his head leaned in to kiss my stomach. "You are perfect, so don't start on that negative train." He spoke against my tummy, making me giggle from the ticklish feeling.

Laying his head in my lap, he loosely hugged my waist and stayed like that for a peaceful moment before looking up at me with curious eyes. "I want to try something with you." The corners of his soft smile turned hopeful as he leaned back fully on the back of his legs again. "I want to see what your comfort level is with me touching you and undressing you."

Thinking about it for a moment, I slowly agreed with a nod of my head. "Okay... But how are you going to do that exactly?"

"Slowly." He started with a chuckle. "I am going to touch every inch of your body, starting from the least private to the most. Every time I move to a new area, you let me know how comfortable you feel with me touching you there, and the moment I get to an area that you don't like or feel hesitant about, you use the safe-word. Understood?"

"Okay, I can do that, sir." Sounded simple and painless enough.

"What is the safe-word? And what will you do if you cannot speak?" It should be illegal how mindful and caring Luciano was.

"Tap out, and if I can't speak, then tap you repeatedly," I replied with a confident smile before asking him a quick question. "Clothes stay on? Or?" He did say something about undressing me just earlier.

Nodding softly, he assured me with a comforting smile, "For now, yes. After we establish your comfort with me appreciating your body, we can move on to stripping you if you are still up for it." Small steps; we were taking small steps.

I can do it.

Scooting to the edge of the couch, I widened my legs so Luciano sat between them, and then I grabbed his face to bring him into a nervous kiss. Not long after our lips connected, his hand was on my feet. "Fine," I whispered before closing the distance between us. "But tickle me, and I will kick your balls." I threatened playfully with a gasp of a snicker.

"No tickling, promise." He chuckled softly against my lips before deepening the kiss as he inched his hands up my legs. "I am going to touch your thighs." He told me after breaking the kiss.

Keeping a distance between our panting lips, he kept his eyes focused on me as he let his big hands roam my almost bare thighs. Starting from the outside, he slowly curved his hands inwards until I could feel the rough pads of his fingers and the callouses of his palm rubbing against the sensitive skin of my inner thighs.

Reaching out, I carefully ran my hands up his arms and gripped his shoulders as a trembling gasp of pleasure escaped my parted lips. "S-slow, please." I whimpered as I felt my body tense up from the surge of adrenaline rushing it. "I... It feels weird, but in a good way." I hated being in the gray zone, but the tingling feeling between my legs and in my stomach made me feel funny.

It felt strange to be getting aroused from such a simple touch, and it made me feel dirty because I shouldn't be this sensitive and easy, right? But a part of me was fine with it all because this reaction came from Luciano's touch, not someone else's.

"Do you want me to continue?" He asked in a soft voice filled with some concern as he observed me closely with his falcon-like eyes.

Chewing my bottom lip, I shook my head. "Not yet. I just need a minute... D-don't move your hand." I strained out a shaky exhale as I slowly counted in my head to calm myself. "I don't want to stop yet, but I just need a moment to breathe."

It's okay. It's okay. I am safe. I'm not back there. They're not touching me. It's not them. It's Luciano. It's Luciano's hands on me, and he is safe.

Leaning over Luciano, I hugged his head and breathed his rich scent in deeply to soothe my nerves completely. "Luca." I hummed happily into his hair. "Your hands feel so good... It scares me how easily turned on some simple touches from you gets me." I admitted almost shamefully.

"Don't fight it, sweetheart. Let your body feel and react how it wants to me, and learn to accept that feeling." His words rumbled against my chest with his chuckle. "There is nothing wrong as long as you want it." Forcefully, he pulled his head back to look up at me. "Do you want this? Me touching you?" His hands tensed on my thighs as if he wanted to pull them away.

Quickly, I placed my hands over his and pressed them against my inner thighs some more. "Yes. Please, don't stop this right now. It's just... It feels good, but I'm just getting into my own head." Honest to God, I didn't want this test of ours to end because I could feel my body adjusting to the feeling of warmth his hands brought to me.

A sudden shot of boldness kicked my ass into gear, causing me to move one of his hands further up to right between my legs and making him cup my covered sex. "C-can you touch me a bit here?" It felt so embarrassing to ask that of him, but the aching need became impossible to ignore—and his hand was right there.

Luciano's eyes narrowed slightly with wariness as he pressed one of my legs open more to get more access. "Safe-word?" His eyes desperately searched mine as he kept his hands stiff in their positions.

Giving him a reassuring smile, I stroked his cheek with the back of my fingers while I answered him, "Tap out."

Inhaling deeply, he pressed his hand harder against my aching core, making me gasp out a soft moan at the feeling of his palm rubbing against my throbbing clit. "That feels good." I let out a breathy moan as I slowly bucked my hips at his hand rather stiffly because it felt a little strange, and I kept trying to match his pacing and rhythm.

"*Amorina*, slow down." He chuckled softly, moving his other hand to grip my hip and help me move smoothly and correctly. "Slow, just like that. Don't rush it, baby. Just let the feeling grow and build until it comes back down." He sounded so damn sexy, guiding me like this. It's so weird but hot.

Leaning up, he buried his face into the junction of my neck and shoulder, kissing and nipping all along the length of my neck to the edge of my shoulder softly. "Still feeling okay, *amorina*?" His husky voice tickled my neck with his beard, making me giggle softly as I replied with a nod of my head and a soft 'yes' as he picked up the pace and force of his hand against my sex.

Shudders violently shook my body at the feeling of him kissing up to my ear and breathing hotly against it. "Take your shirt off, baby, I want to see your lovely tits."

Oh God. That is so dirty and demanding, but fuck, it's so hot.

Not wanting my own mind to psyche me out of it, I quickly grabbed my shirt and pulled it off my body, not thinking about the fact that I completely exposed my upper half to him because I wasn't wearing a bra. "Sorry, they're kinda small." I felt so stupid for apologizing about something out of my control—not my fault I had the flat-chested Asian genes.

Luciano's dark and hungry eyes looked up at me almost menacingly as a low growl rumbled from his throat. "They are fucking perfect, so don't you ever say otherwise. Just like how all of your precious body is perfect, slight chub or not, it is fucking perfect and sexy to me." Leaning down, he pressed a long and hard kiss against the area where my heart was. "If I ever hear you talk bad about yourself or your body from here on out, I will start tallying for punishments."

It sounded like this would be my one and only warning from him with how serious he sounded. "Y-yes, sir," I replied, exhaling shakily as I watched him kiss across and down my chest to my left breast.

Carefully watching my face, he kissed around my breast until he got to my hardened nipple. My eyes zoned in on his lips when I caught the tip of his tongue slipping out between those lovable lips of his. Following him, I watched him press his full tongue against my nipple, licking it with the whole length of his tongue, making my breath hitch with a sharp gasp at the soft and hot feeling of his tongue against my sensitive nipple.

Grabbing the back of his head with both hands, I clung to him for dear life. "Luca!" I gasped with a soft squeal when he took me into his mouth after two more long licks. "Oh, that feels amazing." I whimpered with a hot face.

My body shivers in response to him sucking and licking my hard bud. Then, just as I felt myself come close to the edge, he pulled off, making me whimper in protest and shove his head back to my breast. "So close, please," I begged needily, bucking my hips at his hand some more to get more pleasure.

"Will you be fine with me sliding my hands into your panties to touch you?" His lips hovered right over mine with his question, making my desire for him soar to new heights from wanting a kiss along with my orgasm.

"Yes, just please, touch me more, I'm so close." The sheer desperation made me sound almost pathetic, but I didn't care—for a moment, at least. "B-but I didn't shave." Was I coming up with excuses to avoid my shame and in hopes he would forgo the matter? Maybe a little.

Fed up with my shit, he rolled his eyes at me and slipped his hand right into my panties, cupping my soaked pussy with his bare, hot hand. "Baby, I don't give a shit if it's a bush or a jungle down there. I will always love seeing it, touching, and tasting it when you give me the pleasure of using my mouth on you." Holy shit. Here, I thought falling harder for him would be impossible. "Fuck you're so wet."

His fingers parted me and dipped down deep until they brushed along the entrance of my vagina, causing me to suck in a sharp breath and tense up. "Shh," he quickly soothed me with a deep kiss, "I won't enter you, not today, not until you are ready." He assured me with a warm and firm voice. "Just getting a good feel of you and getting your juices to rub your clit better."

Breathing shakily, I nodded and relaxed against him after letting my arms fall around his neck. "I promise, one day, I will let you fill me full of your cock and cum." Though terrifying, the thought sent a bolt of pleasure straight down to my aching clit.

Groaning, Luciano looked up at me with a sad but sweet smile. "You don't have to promise me that, *amorina.*"

"But I want to. I know I want you, all of you, someday in the future and for the rest of our lives... I can't let my fears and past stop me... I... I just have to get to that point first..." Somehow, I would make it there. I was determined to, not for Luciano but for me.

A new step into my new life.

"Luciano!" I squealed out a moan as I felt the knot in my stomach tighten from his fingers stroking and rubbing my sensitive clit. "Close." I whimpered, bucking my hips at him. "Gonna come. Gonna cum on your hand." This was so dirty, but fuck me.

"That's it, sweetheart, that's it. Ride my hand until you cream all over it for me to lick it all up. Come on my hand, baby, you can do it. Be my good girl and come for me." He encouraged me hotly with needy kisses as he picked up his pace. "Can't wait to taste you on my fingers."

His other hand suddenly slid up my body and grabbed my breast, squeezing it a little roughly, which caused me to suck in a sharp breath. I opened my mouth to tell him to ease up but found myself unable to utter the words as the ache dulled out to pleasure. "Luca, pinch my nipple." I was surprised by my bold words when they left my mouth, and Luciano looked even more surprised.

"Are you sure?" He asked, a little wary as he softly pinched my nipple between his fingers, not applying any pressure or tugging at it while he waited for me to answer.

"Yes, I am sure." My confidence in my voice became a little shaky because of the rush of excitement washing over my body.

Rolling my hard nipple between his fingers, his gaze still unsure as he slowly applied pressure.

But it wasn't enough for me.

"Harder," I demanded, almost snapping at him.

His Adam's apple bobbed with his hard swallow as he gave into my demand, increasing the pressure with his rough fingers.

Yet, it still wasn't enough.

"More, please. Make me scream." Yeah, my own words horrified me a bit, but the fear of him inflicting such sweet pain on me knocked any sense I had out the window. "Quit looking at me like an idiot and do it." I snapped at him when all he did was look at me dumbfounded.

Taking in a deep breath, I watched his inhibitions fade from his darkening eyes. A twisted smile broke on my face when the monster I knew came back up to the surface. Then, a pained moan ripped from my arching body when his fingers clamped down hard on my bud.

"Oh fuck!" There was so much pain, but the rush from the constant sting made it more than worth it.

"Luciano!" I nearly screamed his name in pleasure at the sudden snap in my stomach.

"Fuckfuckfuck." I muttered and groaned as the intense waves of pleasure consumed my trembling body like a tidal wave.

Fuck!

White hot pleasure blanketed my vision as I let myself become lost in this new sensation.

Luciano's voice sounded so far in my haze. "Juliet, come back to me, baby." I was slipping back to reality, but I didn't want to.

I want more.

I need more.

Mindlessly, I bucked my hips in hopes of rubbing myself against his hand, only to find my panties empty of the familiar warmth.

"No, more, please, more." I don't know what came over me to have this newfound lust, and I didn't have the necessary mental capacity to dwell on it.

"*Amorina.*" His voice remained stern but inviting as I felt something tighten around me, enveloping me in a familiar, comforting warmth as something pecks at my face and neck. "Come back to me. I know it's not fun and that you don't want to, but you need to, baby." His damn accented voice, so rich and deep like chocolate, was impossible to resist.

"But feels good." I pouted, scrambling around for his hand with my own to try and grab it to stuff it down my pants.

Unfortunately, he wouldn't budge an inch no matter how much I pulled his hand and begged him.

Then, just as the euphoria came, it went—too fast, in my opinion—leaving me to feel empty and anxious. The tear works came out of nowhere as I clung to Luciano, who held me tightly and showered me with kisses and sweet nothings while he rocked me back and forth.

"W-why am I like this? Why do I feel so empty?" I asked between my sobs and hiccups.

"You went into subspace, something that happens when a person experiences a rush of endorphins with their adrenaline during sex and other stimulating activities. It's different for everyone, and not everyone can get into a subspace because it depends on their own threshold." He explained to me in a soft voice as he stroked my back. "And, of course, with every high comes the crash, the sub-drop, which is what you are experiencing now. And again, everyone's drop is different."

Releasing me for a moment, he picked my shirt up and slipped it back on me, fixed my shorts, and set me down on the couch.

The feeling of his warmth disappearing made me pout and whimper in protest as I held my arms out to him. Hope brightened my beating heart when he leaned in, only to crash when he kissed my forehead and leaned away. "Don't frown, *principessa*. I am not leaving you, but I need to get you some water and food. Otherwise, this drop won't be fun for either of us. I will be quick, I promise."

Flashing a sorry smile, he sped off, leaving me alone for what felt like an eternity—it was only a minute at most—before returning with everything he said he'd be getting in his hands and arms, along with a bottle of lotion.

Sitting back beside me, he pulled me back onto his lap and bundled me up in my blanket before holding a water bottle to my lips. "Drink, and don't fight me, or I will force-feed it to you."

"Well, isn't that just fucking caring and loving of you," I remarked sarcastically with a roll of my eyes.

Before I could tilt my head to get a sip of water, Luciano pulled it away from me and took a big swig of it. "Hey! Jer—mhmphf!" Cold water rushed by the feeling of his warm lips against mine, filling my mouth full instantly.

I was practically forced to swallow the water unless I wanted to sputter it all out and make a mess. I drank it all in a single gulp before shoving Luciano away to cough and gasp. "You jerk." I playfully slapped his chest with a forced pout, trying—and failing—to be angry at him.

"Don't sass me next time, and you get the easy way." He retorted with a shit-eating grin and chuckle.

Grumbling to myself, I crossed my arms and pulled my blanket tighter around myself while snuggling into Luciano's muscular body.

In a somewhat peaceful moment, we sat there in each other's presence with the TV on some fight show. I didn't really pay too much attention because I was too busy eating and drinking everything Luciano shoved in my face. Then, I couldn't focus when he started to lotion and massage my legs; I nodded before he got past my knees.

"Rest, *amorina*, I got you. You are safe."

That was the last thing I heard before I drifted off completely with a goofy smile on my face.

Chapter 27
Luciano

~2 weeks later~

CRASH!

Immediately, I bolted out of my office to the source of the loud sound, drawing my gun out when I heard Juliet's distressed cry.

Fear of the worst ran through my mind as I ran to the living area as fast as possible. Our home was safe with top-of-the-line security systems in place—although I question that often after how easily Juliet hacked through it—and too many bodyguards stationed around the place, but no place was ever truly impenetrable.

I had never had anyone break in and make an attempt on my life at this home yet, but the first was always bound to happen—a matter of when, not if. I just didn't want that first to be directed towards Juliet. I don't know what I would do if something happened to her because of me. I already felt guilty about pulling her into my life because of the passive danger she would be in from being associated with me, and the guilt piled on the moment I decided to make her my lover due to the increased risk and danger of everything.

All my worries about finding Juliet in a bind, beaten and bloodied, or—worse—dead disappeared the moment I saw her unharmed body curled up on the couch. "*Amorina*," I quickly held my tongue from scolding her about screaming like that because she nearly gave me a heart attack, but seeing how upset she was made me change my mind.

Pushing my annoyance away, I disengaged my gun and set it down on the coffee table when I rounded the couch to kneel down before her. "Sweetheart, what is wrong? What made you scream like that? Are you hurt anywhere?" Visibly, I couldn't see anything wrong, but maybe it was something internal.

Looking around, nearly everything seemed in order. The only odd thing besides my distressed lover was a laptop destroyed a little ways from the couch, probably the crash I heard.

My concern rose at the sight of it because Juliet wasn't one to mistreat her things, especially her electronics—her 'babies' as she liked to call them. Yeah, call me stupid and pathetic for being jealous of inanimate technology, but she gave more attention to those damn screens than me a lot of the time.

"*Amorina*." I urged in a heavily concerned voice, placing my hands on her shaking shoulders and rubbing them soothingly. "Talk to me, please. You are worrying me."

Juliet opened her mouth to reply, but all that came out were more sobs and hiccups. "Hey, shh," every sob and sharp hiccup felt like a stab to my aching heart as I sat on the couch and pulled her shaking body into my lap to hold her tightly.

I hated how useless I was to her right now. Whatever went on wasn't something I could rid her of, most likely. What was the point of having all this power and resources and being her protector when I couldn't do anything for her in this state?

When it was obvious Juliet wouldn't calm down for a while, I looked over to her bodyguard. "What happened?" I didn't mean to sound accusatory towards the bodyguard, but my anger seeped out.

"I am not sure, sir. She was scrolling on her laptop and pulled something up, and everything about her just changed. She instantly got emotional and distressed and threw her laptop, and that's when you came out here." The guard quickly answered me in a polite tone, making me feel slightly bad about snapping a little at them.

"Did you see what she was looking at?" The only time I really hoped they looked more than they should, but if I knew what set her off, maybe I could be useful.

"It was some kind of case about some rich guy getting exonerated. I can try to find the article—"

"It's fucking bullshit!" Juliet shouted suddenly. "That shouldn't have happened! There was more than enough to get him put away forever! It's fucking bullshit and rigged! The fucking system is broken and rigged!"

"Give us a moment." I nodded at the guard for them to leave, waiting for them to disappear around the corner before giving Juliet my full attention. "Juliet, talk to me, sweetheart." Because I sure as hell didn't have a clue about what was happening.

Going silent, Juliet stewed for a bit, and I let her have her moment. "I am going to get you some water and snacks, and when I am back, we will talk, alright?" I asked her while wiping her tears away and pushing her hair out of her face.

Sniffling, she nodded her head in response before crawling out of my lap and curling up on the couch with her knees to her chest. "Can you get me some jerky?" She asked in a small voice while poking at her toes.

Chuckling softly with a smile, I nodded my head in response and kissed her forehead before leaving her for a moment, hoping the small moment of space would be enough for her to get into a better headspace.

Thankfully, that was the case when I returned and saw her sitting comfortably on the couch. She was still silent and broody, but she wasn't utterly upset, at least.

Sitting beside her, I made her drink and eat a little before pressing her again on the matter.

Juliet sighed deeply before letting me in. "I got the idea of sending evidence to the police about one of the men who raped me to get them prosecuted after I came across his profile when I was digging around into the lives of the people who were at the fight. I sent the whole NYPD *everything* I found, which was way more than enough to get his rotten ass a few life sentences."

Tightening her jaw, she scowled and seethed silently with balled-up fists by her side. "I thought the next time I saw anything about him would be that he was incarcerated, and I meant to check up on things a while back but forgot." Gritting her teeth, she took a few deep breaths, "Then today, some stupid article came up when I was scrolling through Facebook, and I just... Ugh!"

Her feet stomped angrily against the floor as she cursed under her breath and worked herself up again until she cried. "It's not fair! How fucked up is our system that a man like him can go free after all the evidence against him?!"

It was no secret that our system was fucked up; I knew firsthand because I was involved with pulling the strings to keep things weighted in our favor. I just never cared much about it all until now. Seeing how much it affected Juliet made me wonder just how many victims were fucked over out there in the world.

I thought I rigged the system pretty well to ensure the smallest amount slipped through the cracks. Guess not if Juliet slipped through the cracks.

"Who is the bastard?" I didn't give a shit if it was the damn president themselves who harmed Juliet. I would still beat them to death and make an example and warning out of them to others.

Frowning deeply with disgust, Juliet visibly shook and gagged as she struggled to tell me the name. "Marely Goth."

Now, I felt disgusted with myself.

I knew the man a little too well because I did quite a bit of business with him. He ran many of the warehouses along the coastline that The Syndicate used as storage and drop-off points.

This was going to get fucking messy, but shit needed to be done.

Without a word, I stood up and pulled my phone out to send a text to others in a group chat before looking at Juliet with an expressionless face to hide the darkness brewing within me.

"Luca? What's a matter?" Her scared voice made my walls rise up more.

"I have a meeting to attend to."

Chapter 28

Juliet

THE NEXT THREE DAYS were tense...

Okay, that might be an understatement.

Things haven't been well around the house or with anything ever since Luciano upped and left me in the air for his evening meeting. I tried to question him about it that night when he came to bed, but he shrugged me off and kept changing the subject whenever I would return to it.

My annoyance only grew the next day when he kept telling me not to worry about it and that it wasn't any of my business to get involved with. Then, he placed a wall between us with everything and practically locked himself in his office for the past two days. He only ever came out during meal times and when it was time for bed, but even then, he came to bed pretty late both nights.

I hated how stressed out he became and how he refused to let me in to help. I wasn't useless, and I wanted to help. But his grumpy ass has been like, 'No, it's Syndicate business,' and blah blah blah.

Ugh!

Clatter!

Making a mess out of frustration probably wasn't wise because I would have to clean it up later, but my arm lashed out across my desk before I could control myself.

Deciding I've had enough, I let out a frustrated groaning shout and trudged my ass down to Luciano's office, not giving a damn about his stupid rule. I was even bold enough in my emotional state that I glared and flipped the guards off when they tried to stop me from entering his office.

"Touch me, and I will scream bloody murder and drain your bank accounts later tonight and order glitter bomb mail to your places." I threatened them when they reached out to restrain me physically.

Holding their hands up in surrender, they backed away from me, giving me full access to the closed office door.

Letting my adrenaline guide me, I grabbed the doorknob and kicked the door open, causing it to slam against the wall. "We are talking."

Luciano's dead eyes didn't soften up one bit at the sight of me. If anything, he only seemed more peeved that I barged in. "Juliet. Now is not the time. Leave." Luciano was very much *not* amused by my sudden appearance with his somewhat hostile tone.

"No." I stood my ground with my head held high.

Shutting the door, I crossed my arms and mustered up as much confidence as possible while I walked up to Luciano's glaring figure. Closer and closer, his huge figure grew bigger than I remembered with each step I took toward him. Standing before him, he felt like a mountain giant even though he remained sitting in his chair after he turned it around to face me.

"I am done with this stupid macho man act of yours." I don't know what spurred my hand forward to jab him in the chest, but no taking it back now. "I am done being in the fucking dark about shit that is clearly about me. You didn't get all silent and moody until I told you that person's name, so it has something to do with me to an extent."

Seething breaths heaved at my chest as I struggled to gather myself together enough to form coherent thoughts with my rising anger. "I don't give a damn if it is mafia business or not, if you are involved, then so am I. You are mine, so, therefore, your problems are mine, too. That is how a fucking relationship works. At least a good and functioning relationship works like that last time I checked." Okay, that didn't come out as I planned, and it also sounded a lot better in my head.

Taking a deep, calming breath, I stepped forward and fell into his lap, straddling him and wrapping my arms around his neck. "I refuse to be in those pointless relationships where the guy keeps the girl out of things because he thinks it's best for her. I knew what I was getting into the moment I made up my mind about you and stepped into your world. I know it's a shit show filled with violence, guns, blood, and crime galore, and I accepted all of that before I accepted you."

Sliding a hand down to his cheek, I rested my forehead against his while my thumb stroked his cheek. "I know you want what is best for me and want to protect me, but I am not a child. I am your woman, so let me step into that role. I might not be able to shoot a gun or knock someone out with a single punch to the face. Hell, I don't think I can throw a proper punch without breaking my hand, but that's not the point right now." Okay, maybe I did sound a little useless compared to him and a lot of other people now that I thought about it.

"Just let me in and let me help, please. I want to ease your burdens and help you with them. We are in this together now, whether you like it or not. If you had no intentions of letting me be involved in this part of your life, then please, do us both a favor and end this relationship before it ends itself down the line." It didn't feel fair for Luciano to keep me shut out of his whole life. "I do not want this to be some cliche book or movie where the mob boss keeps his wife ignorant and out of his business. We are in the twenty-first fucking century, so I am going to be just as involved as you."

"Are you done?" Luciano asked bluntly with a twitch of his eyebrow.

"No, because you asked, so no, I am not." Did I have anything further to say? Fuck no, but I didn't want to shut up because he wanted me to. "I will be done when I want. You are not the boss of me."

Eek!

THAT WAS THE WRONG FUCKING THING TO SAY!

My words flipped a switch in Luciano, and his hand wrapped around my neck in a nanosecond. "I'm sorry, I didn't quite catch that, *principessa*. Care to repeat that?" His eyes grew dangerous with a wave of excited anger as he leaned off the chair and pressed me lower than him.

Gulping, I shrunk under his intense gaze. Not out of fear, no, it was out of submission.

"I-I said you're not the boss of me." I squeaked, barely recognizing my nervous voice as I shivered in his hold.

Ghosting his smirking lips across mine, he let out a chuckle so deep and feral that I nearly came in my panties right then and there. A trail of burning pleasure followed in the wake of his lips as he moved across my cheek to my ear. "We'll see about that." His words rumbled in my ear, making me shiver with a delightful excitement. "Let's see how many spanks it will take for you to change your tone with me."

"What?"

Did I hear him right?

"W-wait, you're not serious, are you? You're going to spank me? Here? Now?" Aaaand there went all the confidence out the window.

"Yes." Shoving me off his lap, he dragged me over his knees and shifted the hand around my neck to my lower back. "We're going to see what your limit is."

"Luciano, this is—"

Smack!

A sharp gasp left me as I flinched in response to the sudden snap against my backside. "Luca! You did not—"

Smack!

"Ah!" Leaning down, I gripped the leg of his pants. "We are having a conversation! This is not the time to be testing my limits out!" I protested with my words but was more than compliant with my body.

"We can talk while you are being tested." He replied nonchalantly as his large hand groped my ass.

"You know, I'm not gonna lie, you coming in like that and being all demanding and confident was really hot." He remarked with a proudness to his voice.

Lifting my head up, I craned it back to look at him, smiling at the sight of his warm and prideful smile as he looked at me with such adoring and appreciative eyes. "Y-you're not mad about that?"

Chuckling wholeheartedly, he shook his head. "No, I would never be mad at you for standing up and speaking out for yourself, even if it is against me. I know I can be a stubborn asshole, and I am sorry for upsetting you as much as I have the past few days." Reaching down with the hand that was on my back, he cups my face and runs a tender finger across my lips. "And I keep forgetting that you are just as formidable as me, and I am sorry for that."

His eyes softened with nostalgia as he continued to smile down at me. "Sometimes, when I look at you, I make the mistake of thinking you were the broken girl that my car hit." It was so easy to lose myself in the shine of his proud eyes. "But you have grown into such a beautiful and strong woman in such a short amount of time that sometimes I find it hard to believe that you two are the same person. That the woman I have the privilege of calling mine was that girl a few months ago."

Supporting my neck, he pulls me into a deep, electrifying kiss. "I will always want to protect you and shield you from this world, *amorina*. It is a natural thing for me when it comes to you. Even though you have been wronged so much, I want to make you forget it and live a good life free of all your demons." Keeping our foreheads together, he chastely kissed my lips with a heavy breath. "I know it is not fair of me to try and control your life like that, as I haven't even tried much ever since it became clear to me that you are your own spunky brat of a person." Chuckling dryly, an apology flashed through his eyes. "But I still try unconsciously to do so because I want you to have the best life."

With a sad but happy smile of my own, I reached up and ran a hand through his hair. "Luciano, I have the best life with you, Syndicate and all. I can't trick myself into thinking the world is full of sunshine and superheroes when really it's cloudy with villains. I have to learn to live in the ugly world as it is, and as long as I have the devil by my side, I have nothing to fear." Gripping the back of his head, I press him into another kiss.

"I will apologize better for my behavior and treatment of you tomorrow and in the days to come, I promise." He whispered against my lips with a shudder. "And I will let you in on it all tomorrow." He said with a voice full of sincerity.

His lips tensed against mine as they pulled back in a snarl. "But I don't want to deal, think, or talk anymore about it tonight. I am way too fucking stressed and done with it right now." Pulling back, all I could see was my dominating Luciano with his powerful and playful eyes.

"What's the safe-word?" He asked once he sat up fully and looked down at me.

"Tap out." I breathed out excitedly with a nervous smile. "And if I can't talk, tap you repeatedly."

"Good girl." Was all I got along with a glimpse of his devilish smirk before he pushed my front side down and settled his hand back on my lower back to keep me anchored.

"Since we are just testing the waters out, you let me know if something is too much or if you can take more, alright?" He asked while palming the globe of my ass.

"Yes, sir," I replied with a nervous gulp, gripping his leg to brace myself.

Thankfully, Luciano started out light, almost playfully so that they felt more like taps than actual spanks, but then, as time went on, the force behind his hand grew until it actually stung a little.

Smack!

"Ouch! That hurt!" I cried out a yelp from the sting of the impact on my covered bottom.

"A good hurt or bad hurt?" Luciano asked while palming my stinging ass cheek. "Remember, we are seeing what your pain threshold is, and yes, a lot of it is going to hurt to some extent, but there is a fine line between pain and pleasure." He reminded me with a hard squeeze of my round globe, making me suck in a deep breath.

"Well, it doesn't really hurt now..." I murmured, squirming in his lap so his leg didn't dig into my stomach too much. "C-can you do it again?"

The warmth of Luciano's hand left my yoga short-clad ass briefly before it came back down with the same force as before. My body flinched and yelped reflexively with the impact, my eyes stinging a little with tears from the ache. "Again?" Despite the pain, an underlying pleasure bloomed from the ache and sting.

"I am going to go a little harder, alright?" The hand that rested on my lower back rubbed at it soothingly while he waited for my answer.

"Okay, Luca." I let out a shaky breath and clung onto his pants with trembling fists.

"Breathe." His hand on my back pressed firmly against me. "Relax."

Easier said than done, he wasn't the one getting his ass smacked by someone twice his size.

Yeah, it sucked this had to be done, but better establish a baseline rather than find out during the moment if he went too far by accident.

Smack!

"Oh fuck!" I gasped sharply with a loud cry. "Nghn fuck!" I whimpered with a shudder.

His firm voice wavered with concern as he rested his hand on my butt. "Too much?" No doubt if I looked back, then the corners of his lips would be frowning a little.

"No." Yeah, my answer surprised me, too. "I-it hurt, but it felt good... Better than the other." The rush of pleasure that chased the pain was so good.

Luciano's hand pulled back, and another pair of smacks landed on each of my ass cheeks, making me cry out in pain and pleasure. "Luca, more, please," I begged with a soft moan.

I could feel the tremors of Luciano's amused chuckle as he palmed my ass again. "Think we might have found your sweet spot, or at least getting very close to it." He commented before pulling his hand back and delivering another spank to my bubbly ass. "Think you can go harder than this?" He asked after giving me another spank.

"No." I immediately shook my head and looked back at him. "Think this is my limit." The thought of him going harder threatened to erode my arousal.

"Think you can orgasm if I keep going? Or do you want to try and see if you can come from being spanked?"

Intrigued, I pondered it for a second before giving him an unsure look. "That's actually possible? I could do that?" The thought of orgasming from non-direct sexual contact seemed a little absurd but interesting.

"Of course, but it's a tedious thing. You would have to hold out until the pain reaches a certain point where everything turns to pleasure. We don't have to try it if you aren't comfortable. It's not exactly a beginner thing either." His face remained in a patient and understanding smile as he rubbed my butt.

I didn't hesitate to give him a reply. "I want to try."

Oh well, it didn't hurt to try. Okay, it would hurt to try in this sense, but hey, either I get an orgasm or find out my limit with how many spanks I could take.

His face softened with concern as his eyes searched my face for any signs of hesitation. "Are you sure, *amorina*?"

"Yes, I am sure," I answered him confidently, giving him a reassuring smile.

His lips slowly curved into a soft smirk. "What's the safe-word again? Or if you can't use your words, then what's the gesture?" His hand playfully smacked my bottom as his eyes gained a wild look to them.

Gripping his pants, I shuddered at the look in his eyes. He looked a little too excited to have a go at me, and for some reason, that made my heart race with eagerness. With a confident smile, I replied in a single, shaky breath.

The hand on my back slid up and fisted the back of my hair, making me gasp and whimper from the tingling pain. With my upper body level with his legs, he slipped my legs under him and used one of his to pin the back of my thighs. "I can't wait until you let me spank your bare ass. Fuck, the thought of watching them turn red with the imprints of my hands or the belt drives me wild." He said through a feral grin.

A part of me wanted to pull my pants down this very instant to appease him, but the thought of exposing myself like that to him frightened me a little. "I'm sorry I can't give that to you right now." I still felt bad about how much I held out with Luciano because of my trauma.

No matter how much he reassured me whenever I brought up how unfair it was, it didn't really make me feel less guilty.

"I am more than happy with what you are willing to give me, *amorina*. Please, don't fret over it, as I have told you many times." How he could look so content with this restraint ate at me, knowing what kind of life he had before me. "If you keep it up, I will add it to your punishment list. You know I hate it when you put yourself down or feel sad about something out of your control."

"What? You can't punish me for that... Can you?" My list of punishable things wasn't too long... Hopefully...

Amused, he let out a dark chuckle and looked at me in such a way that made me want to kneel at his feet. "Oh baby, I can punish you for anything I want and deem necessary. So, keep that in mind as you continue to be a brat with me." The pressure at the back of my head tightened with his grip, making me gasp. "And since spanking will be on the table now. Well, for the sake of being able to sit and walk, I hope you think twice before being one."

Luciano didn't give me a chance to snap back as his hand started to deliver spank after spank to my ass. Whatever words wanted to come out of my mouth quickly caught in my throat as I was too busy yelping and moaning. Pain and pleasure ravaged my body with each spank. The burning always followed the sting of the impact, but then immediately with the burn came the surge of indescribable pleasure that had my pussy aching and clenching around nothing as I chased after my building orgasm.

It hurt so good. I wanted to scream at him to stop, but fuck, this red-hot pleasure was something else. Who gave a shit if I couldn't sit for hours after this, it would be worth it.

"Lu-ca... Close, please." I whimpered as I felt myself creeping close to the edge of utmost pleasure.

Luciano chuckled deeply with a growl. "You can do it, baby, come for me. Be my good girl and come from your spanking." He encouraged me in a voice laced heavily with lust and excitement.

The force of the impacts picked up slightly, just enough to send me over the edge fully. My body shook with pleasure from the knot in my stomach snapping, sending—what felt like—endless waves of pleasure throughout me.

Slowly, the spanks came to a stop as my body shook from the aftershocks of my orgasm.

"Luciano." I whimpered needily, reaching back and grabbing at him just as he released me fully.

My crash was coming; I could feel it.

"Shh, shh, I got you." Luciano soothed me after he pulled me up fully into his arms.

Holding my trembling body tightly, he showered my face in kisses while whispering sweet nothings in Italian for a good moment before switching back to English. "You did so amazing, *amorina*. I am so proud. Just breathe. You are okay. I am here. You are safe."

Chapter 29
Luciano

"My ass hurts."

Peering up from my phone, I looked at Juliet with an amused and satisfied smirk. "Well, I wonder whose fault that is," I remarked sarcastically with a hidden chuckle bubbling in my chest.

Unable to reply, Juliet narrowed her eyes at me and stuck her tongue out while flipping me the middle finger. "Asshole." She pouted at me before bundling herself back up in her blanket and turning her body away from me on the couch.

No, her ass didn't hurt from testing her limits. She was fine this morning when we woke. The reason for her perky little behind hurting right now was that she decided to throw a little fit after breakfast when I told her to be patient about the matter last night. I had every intention of keeping my word to her last night about filling her in on everything, just not right after breakfast because I had meetings to attend.

So, here we were in my office, her grumbling away on my office couch while I busied myself with work behind my desk. "Juliet, please leave. I have a video meeting."

"No." She bit back defiantly with a pouting glare.

"Juliet, this is an important meeting, so please—"

God damn it!

The ringing of the call and the popup on the computer screen prevented me from furthering my persistence with Juliet to leave.

"Don't think you're going to get away with this. You better be prepared to cry tonight while you apologize over my knee." I growled at her before straightening myself out and picking up the group call.

"Hey everyone, Leah's gonna be a few moments late. She's wrapping up a patient right now." My friend and fellow Syndicate member said after popping into the group call with everyone else.

"That's fine. She's a busy woman. She already has to put up with enough shit as it is with her work as a doctor and us, so give her a break. We can handle the rest of the nitty gritty shit." Ares, another friend and member, spoke up with a dismissive wave of his hand.

"Hate how we even have to have these meetings in the first place because of stupid people." Aidan groaned in complaint, sighing heavily at the end.

"It's unfortunate, but we all knew times like these were bound to happen when we took over and stomped over the old cockroaches." Ares brought up the silent problem that had been stewing in the pot for way too long. "It's also unfortunate that it has gone on this far because of our own comfort and trust in the old farts. We should have been more diligent and vigilant. If we had, then Luciano's girl probably never would have ended up in that deplorable place, and other victims like her wouldn't have had to suffer because their assailants went on free as a bird."

Sighing heavily, I ran a hand through my hair and leaned back in my chair. "I hate to agree with Ares, but we have gotten a little too comfortable with our power. And I am afraid we are not being taken as seriously as we should be. How we operate things works for us in this day and age, but a lot of people are starting to mistake that as a weakness."

"What's wrong with agreeing with me?" Ares retorted in an offended but playful voice.

"Because you're not the brightest of the bunch," Aidan remarked with a laugh, causing the rest of us to join him. "I swear, they should call you The Hippo instead of The Shark as you are just a mindless idiot with too much rage at the world, and you're the biggest out of the five of us." He added with a snicker and shit-eating grin.

"Excuse you! What I got is pure love and buff muscles. I am a fucking tank, not a cushion. How dare you compare me to such a homicidal beast." Ares argued with a soft scoff. "And as if you're one to talk about size, you walking stick bug. Honestly, how do you pull girls with a dick the size of a twig." He shot back at Aidan, who rolled his eyes in return.

"Because I ain't built like a stick down there." Aidan guffawed. "Ask Evie, she'll be happy to tell—" A pillow flew at Aidan's face, hitting him with a rather loud *thwump*.

"DO NOT BRING OUR SEX LIFE TO YOUR FRIENDS!" Evie's voice shouted somewhere off-screen.

Chuckling, Sebastian lightly slapped his table to regain control of our rowdy group. "We can bust out the measuring tape after the meeting, even though we already know who would win that contest by a mile."

Of course, Leah would pop in in the midst of it. "Whose measuring whose dick? I thought we already established that all of you are inadequate in that area." She chimed in the moment she fully connected. "And no, Aidan, your dumb piercings don't count for anything."

"Well, we all know he only got some extra help in the pleasure department because he had to make up for other areas that lacked." Ares snickered and snorted.

"At least I can make a woman come and know where the clit is, ya blubbering one-second wonder." Aidan's growing irritation showed through his thickening Scottish accent, making us all roll our eyes and chuckle.

"Alright boys, that's enough dick talk." Leah chuckled with a shake of her head. "What's the update? Have we decided on anything or have inklings of a plan?" Leave it to Leah to round us up like a mother done with her children.

"I say we need to remind everyone of who we are because they are starting to get a little cocky and resistant towards us." Ares threw in his two cents. "Sebastian and I will take a trip up north to help smoke out and rid the rats that have been festering for too long."

"I'd rather handle things not so violently, but it is obvious our more hands-off approaches won't cut it. So, Ares is right. We must reinstate ourselves and remind everyone who The Syndicate is and what we are all capable of." Sebastian agreed begrudgingly with a long sigh, running a hand down his face.

"I say the first on our list would be the old mafia we booted off the throne. We have been too lenient with them, and I am tired of trying to play nice to them." Screw respecting them and keeping in the little good graces they had. "It's not much, and I still have my men digging into things, but there has been talking of a revolt against us for them to reclaim their stake of New York."

"Some of my spies have been telling me the same thing, and apparently, it has been going on for a while without any indication of action, though. Which is why I have been holding my hand back." Aidan commented with an irritated sigh. "We need to nip it before it grows out of control."

"Alright, so it seems we are all on the same page about what needs to be done. Are we all in agreement to plan and act on ridding New York of the old mafia and running the streets red?" Ares seemed a little too excited with the storming bloodlust in his bright green eyes, and his crooked grin did nothing to help the growing edge.

Sebastian's shoulders rose and fell with a heavy breath before his voice filled out the speakers. "Those who are in agreement, raise their hand."

Simultaneously, the five of us raised our hands into the air, causing Ares to let out an excited shout of joy. "Finally! You have any idea how bored I've been getting over here in Miami?"

Chuckling, I opened my mouth to speak, but no words came out as my eyes locked with Juliet, who slipped off the couch onto her hands and knees. Clenching my jaw shut, I gave her a look of warning as she crawled over to me with a devious smirk and eyes full of mischief brattiness.

Not wanting to give anything away to the others, I kept my head pointed at the screen while I followed Juliet's sultry figure. I couldn't tear my eyes away from her plump ass swaying with each movement of her crawl as she came closer and closer, rounding the desk and looking up at me with such a determined coquettish smile. And damn my aching cock for twitching and straining to be freed from my pants at the sight of my lovely little vixen.

"Luciano!" Leah's voice snapped my attention away from my stunning lover, making me frown internally. "The hell was that?"

Straightening in my seat, I cleared my throat and quickly lied, "Sorry, I got distracted with coming up with a list of troublemakers I would love to throw into the ring."

"Luciano, you aren't seriously thinking about beating each and every single one of those people to death in a fight match, are you?" Leah asked with a concerned raise of her eyebrows. "But also, you are lying. Your eyes were watching something." And leave it to Leah to call us out on everything being the observant little shit she is.

"I—" I cut myself off by flinching and looking down between my legs with a tense expression.

Quickly, I hit the mute button and harshened my gaze at Juliet, who continued to palm the tent in my pants oh so casually. "Juliet," I growled lowly in warning, reaching a hand down to shove her away.

I didn't get a chance to do so because Sebastian was calling out to me. "Luciano, what's going on over there?"

With a seething, growling sigh, I looked back up at the monitor and forced a smile on my face as I unmuted myself. "Sorry, thought I saw something scamper by. Though maybe it was the runaway squirrel Juliet accidentally let in yesterday." I lied through gritted teeth.

Don't know how much of that they bought because it sounded stupid as fuck. "Just... Let's move on. We have a lot to plan." I changed the subject back onto the matter at hand, sucking in a breath when I felt Juliet's hand wrap itself around my engorged length. I don't even know when she unzipped me and got me out, but I couldn't do anything about it now without seeming weird to the others.

Fucking brat. I swear, I'm gonna take a belt to her ass after this.

As the conversation went underway, I tried my best to focus on it and contribute as much as possible because it was half my territory that was involved, but God fucking damn it, I couldn't. All my energy went to holding myself together, and my attention kept flickering to Juliet, who happily sucked my soul out from my cock.

No matter how inconvenient her timing was, I enjoyed it with such a guilty pleasure. If the others knew I was getting a blowjob in the middle of the damn meeting... Fuck they would never let me live it down. I couldn't bring myself to stop Juliet, though, even though it would be easy to grab her head and shove her off. Not only did her mouth and throat feel too damn good, but it was her boldness and confidence that did me in. I didn't want to crush her by rejecting her when I knew damn well this must have taken so much for her to get over her fears to do this without any kind of prompting or urging from me.

Leaning over onto my desk, I propped my arm up on an elbow and buried my face in my hands. Pretending to nurse a headache, I kept my fingers at my temples as I hung my head to look down at Juliet while my other hand tangled itself into the back of her hair.

Fuck she looked so perfect with her lips tightly wrapped around me while my cock was buried all the way down to the base. Then her tight throat swallowing me as she kept her struggling quiet pressed me right up against the wall of pure ecstasy.

Of course, one look into her big, brown, tear eyes filled with needy delight and cheekiness meant she knew what she was doing and its effects on me.

Little brat.

I was close, so close. Shallow breaths ached at my chest as I tried my best to keep control of my reactions in front of the others. Unfortunately, there was no helping the small groan from escaping when I felt my balls tighten and my release surge out of me into her eagerly waiting mouth.

"Luciano... You alright over there, man?" Aidan asked in a concerned voice, making me let out another groan, this one from the embarrassment spilling over.

Faking a pained smile because it was fucking painful to keep myself straight enough to lie to my friends while Juliet's sweet mouth milked me for all I had, I looked back at the camera with heavy breaths. "Bad migraine came out of nowhere." And unfortunately, it was going to stay because Juliet was going to be a damn headache and a half for the rest of our relationship, no doubt about it.

"Do you want me to come over and give you some meds?" Leah offered with a soft frown of worry.

"No, that's okay. I still have some from the last time you gave me some." I lied smoothly through a shudder. "I think I'll regroup with you guys later. I can't think straight right now. Just text me the details once you guys are done, and I'll add in my thoughts and shit." After I was through with Juliet for this little stunt.

"Alright, man, go relax with your girl, have her give you a massage and shit, unwind ya bit." Aidan chuckled softly, making me roll my eyes internally.

With a smile plastered, I bid everyone farewell and hung up the call. Immediately after hanging up, I fully slumped in my seat with a drawn-out groan, letting the aftershock of my release ride out with Juliet's soft suckling and giggles.

Lazily, I looked down at her proud expression. "You are in so much trouble." I strained out between my heavy breaths.

Seeing how happy and proud she was broke my hard exterior, causing me to crack an uncontrollable smile as I looked down at her adoringly.

Come on, I couldn't stay upset at such a cute face.

Granted, that didn't mean she would be getting away scot-free.

Giggling, she flicked her tongue against the underside of my half-hard dick. "Do you think you can give me another mouthful?"

"*Sono così dannatamente fregato.*"

Chapter 30

Juliet

~1 week later~

"Juliet Hong Agosti."

I wanted to duck my head and run away into a dark corner to hide from the confused looks my whole graduating class gave me as I walked up the stage to get my diploma. The cheering from Luciano, Aidan, Leah, Sebastian, Ares, Evie, and some of the bodyguards from the bleachers didn't do much to ease my shame and embarrassment either. Anyone who saw them standing up and cheering instantly snapped their gazes to me right afterward, looking at me almost pityingly and all concerned and shit.

Yeah, probably not the best to have a whole mafia mob cheer you on at your high school graduation and have your association with them be made rather public.

Even after all this time with everyone, it was still kind of strange to have people figure out my connection to Luciano and The Syndicate—as in me living with Luciano and being associated passively. I wasn't necessarily fully ashamed of the fact; it just felt weird still. Also, whenever people find out about it, they put me at a distance, and that sucked, especially with how I was trying to resume a mostly normal life. Having people distance me before they even knew me or spoke to me was a bit of a barrier.

Not everyone was that way, though. Those who were in good standing with The Syndicate were more than welcoming of me—I fucking wonder why (note the fucking sarcasm). On the opposite end of the spectrum, I have noticed more hostility toward me from those who weren't on good terms with The Syndicate or Luciano.

It wasn't nice or appreciated, but this was the life I chose to step into when I took Luciano's hand. So, I had to learn to live with it.

At least it wasn't too bad with all the bodyguards around me, and Luciano was feared enough that so far, no one dared to try anything with me. Hopefully, that won't be the case for long, though. I didn't want to rely on Luciano's name and The Syndicate to keep people at bay. I wanted to make a name for myself, one people would fear as much as Luciano.

No, I had no intention of joining the bloody crusade The Syndicate was planning. Just because I was fine with the violence and bloodshed didn't mean I would partake in it. As much as I loved seeing people's lives crumble to dust, I wanted to remain hands-off—physically. I haven't put my theories to the test yet, but from what I've gathered from my cousin and his friends, what I cooked up in my mind would be just as effective and deadly as Luciano in the ring.

Oh, rounding back to The Syndicate and their plans of purging New York: Luciano still hasn't told me jack shit despite promising me that day in the office. To be fair, though, I did distract and drain him pretty well that day, and we were both busy the past week. I was busy wrapping things up with school while Luciano was occupied with making arrangements with Aidan for the rest of the members and their men.

We were so busy that we barely had time to crawl into bed with each other at night to get eight hours of sleep. Yeah, unfortunately, there was no sexy business throughout the past week because of our schedules and exhaustion by the end of the day.

But that would change tonight.

"Juliet, do not—"

The way Luciano's face grew red and irritated at me blatantly defying him by downing the shot of alcohol and flipping him off made me want to laugh. For the sake of my ass later tonight, I held it back.

"Gutsy one you got there, Luciano." Ares laughed mirthfully. "I like her, and I haven't even fully met her." The Greek man with dashing green eyes winked and grinned at me before looking over to Luciano, who glared jealous daggers at him. "You better keep her, or I will kick your ass for letting someone who is an actual match for you go." He playfully threatened his friend.

"I am violent, not stupid." Luciano snarked with a sneer. "Too bad the same can't be said about you."

Ares cursed at Luciano in Greek before nursing his bottle of booze in a sulking manner.

Grinning cheekily at Luciano, I picked up another filled shot glass from the coffee table. "Juliet, I swear, if you take another shot before you turn twenty-one, I will ground you until you are thirty." Luciano threatened with a tired groan while running his hand down his face.

"You're not my dad or the boss—"

Needless to say, I didn't dare finish that sentence because of the very pointed look of warning Luciano burned into me.

A chill washed over my body as I felt the color drain from my face when the corners of Luciano's lips twisted into a devious, taunting smirk. "I'm not what? I don't think I quite caught that, *principessa.*"

"You're not my dad... You're my boyfriend... Sir." I uttered with a pout as I hung my head slightly.

Smiling victoriously, he reached out, grabbed me by the waist, and pulled me into his lap so I was no longer standing in the space between the armchair and couch. "Good girl." He whispered with a soft chuckle in my ear.

"Sorry about that, just a little hiccup back home, but I got it figured out." Sebastian appeared in the area with an apologetic smile and sat down between Aidan and Ares.

Starting from Luciano's position at one of the armchairs, on the couch next to us were Aidan, Sebastian, and Ares, and on the other armchair across from Luciano and I sat Leah—oh, and Evie was present in Aidan's lap.

The whole area became quiet almost instantly with everyone present, and the air quickly grew tense and dire. "Thank you, everyone, for coming earlier than planned for Juliet's graduation," Luciano said after clearing his throat. "And I'm sorry it's taken this long for this introduction to happen, but everyone, this is my Juliet."

Heat instantly flushed my cheeks at all the attention on me when Luciano presented me on a platter to everyone. At least the tender smile and passionate look from Luciano's heart-melting eyes eased my nerves some. "H-hi, uhh I guess it's nice to meet you all and put faces to the voices finally." I smiled courteously with a small wave of my hand.

What happened next confused and intrigued me.

Ares exclaimed with glee and smacked Sebastian right in the middle of his chest with the back of his hand the moment I finished speaking. "Fucking knew it! You owe me that new bike now fucker." He laughed victoriously while Sebastian groaned and rolled his eyes.

"Better pay up to me as well motherfucker." Aidan chimed in with his own triumphant smirk at Sebastian before looking at Evie with a bright grin and whispering something to her that made her squeal with delight.

Perplexed, I turned my head to look at Luciano for an answer, only to be met with a lost look and shrug from him as he looked between his friends with bewildered eyes. "The fuck are you three going on about? What bet did I miss out on?" He questioned them after he gave up trying to figure out the mess.

A sighing groan from Leah and a shake of her head caught my attention. "Idiots. Men, all of them are idiots, I swear." He heard her grumble while rubbing her temples.

"Ares and Aidan called bullshit on your ridiculous 'I have a headache' excuse at that video chat meeting a week ago and said you were getting head from your girl under the desk, which is why you were acting funny," Sebastian explained with a scoff and shake of his head.

Throwing his hands over his face, Sebastian leaned back fully on the couch, throwing his head over the back of it and groaning into his hands. Sitting back up with a sigh, he looked at Luciano and me pleadingly. "Please don't tell me you were getting blown during the meeting, man. Please tell me these idiots are just dirty-minded fuckers." He sounded so desperate that I was tempted to lie and deny the truth just to save him and myself.

Running a hand down his face, Luciano remained quiet as he rested his hand across his jaw. His silence basically answered everything.

In response to the silent answer from Luciano, Evie snapped her head at me and shot me an overly interested look as she turned her body around to face me with a growing grin. "Girl, did you seriously blow him under the desk? Spill it. I need to know how much my little Juliet has grown into a kickass woman." She prodded me in Vietnamese, making me blush at the fact I'd been caught.

Of course, Leah jumped in as well. "Did you really?" She wasn't judgmental or disappointed, just rather interested, too, it seemed.

"Y-yeah, I was upset at him and wanted to mess with him. I mean, I thought I was sneaky and got away with it." I admitted with a cherry red face and embarrassed smile.

Giggling with a small wave of her hand, Leah replied, "Well, if it weren't for those two idiots being so dirty-minded, then you would have. I mean, I didn't know. I honestly thought he was having a bad headache. Don't ask me how those two came to the conclusion that you were under the desk. I don't want to know their reasoning myself for the sake of keeping my brain cells intact."

"Do you have any idea how happy I am for you right now? It's so good to see you getting more confident each and every time I see you. It really is amazing to see how much you've changed in a good direction since I met you that night at the fight." Evie's eyes started to tear up with her happy smile and cracking voice.

"We are all really happy for you with the progress you have made. It truly is stunning." Leah chimed in with her own happy and proud smile.

"You guys, you're going to make me cry." I could feel the emotions welling up in my eyes, ready to spill over if one more sappy thing came out of their mouths.

"What are you guys talking about? Did they upset you, *principessa*?" Luciano's concern made me let out a small sob as I shook my head in response. "Then what's wrong? You look like you're going to cry."

"Happy tears, don't worry," I assured him with a giggling grin.

"Alright, alright, everyone regroup. We can all chit-chat about other shit later after we get Juliet up to speed." Luciano's firm voice projected throughout the living area, commanding the place.

Tightening his arm around my waist, Luciano settled a kiss against my temple before smiling at me softly. "I am sorry for not filling you in on the whole situation before this, but things have been hectic." He whispered to me before looking at the others as he cleared his throat. "Juliet, this is everyone from The East Coast Syndicate. You have already met Aidan and Leah, but the other two blockheads are Sebastian Caro and Ares Drakos." He gestured toward the two men, who rolled their eyes at Luciano in response. "They are in charge of Florida, so they remain there for the most part."

Twisting my eyebrows together, I settled my eyes on Leah. "You're a part of The Syndicate?" Yeah, call me stupid for not putting two and two together, but I honestly thought she hung around because she was their good friend. She was their good friend, and she grew up together with them, so I just figured she stuck around out for the sake of their relationship.

"Cornelia Nguyen, but I go by Leah. I don't like to make myself known because of my practice and all. I also don't have a stationed place, so I bounce between New York and Florida, respectively." She replied with her usual warm and friendly smile.

Well, that was a little hard to imagine. Leah was one of the sweetest people I knew so far. So, seeing her as a hardened and feared mafia boss was a little difficult for me. However, maybe I shouldn't shove my foot into my mouth because even though she was an amazing doctor, I didn't know much about her life outside of her profession. We hung out, but she never really opened up much about her personal life.

Tossing the information into my endless file of Syndicate info, I centered my attention back on Luciano. "So, what's all going on?" I tried not to let my nervousness show through, but my words trembled on their own when they came out of my mouth.

Running a hand down his face, Luciano gave a stressed sigh before starting, "After you told me the name that day, I called an emergency meeting with everyone to reveal the fact to them. From that initial meeting, we decided that we have had enough with our hands-off approach with the city's people, particularly those of the old mafia who we overthrew."

"It has been an issue since we took over decades ago, but we have chosen not to actively do anything about it to keep things peaceful between us and the old mafia. It was also kind of a sign of respect." Aidan quickly picked up when Luciano paused, sighing a bit at the end as he rubbed the back of his head. "In hindsight, we were idiots to put too much faith in them and got too comfortable and sloppy."

"To be fair, they haven't done anything worth acting upon, just small jabs every now and then that would be stupid of us to retaliate against." Luciano sounded so exhausted and regretful of that decision now, though.

Luciano started up after a while, his eyes lingering on me as if I were his lifeline right now. "Either way, to make a long story short, when you told me the name, I realized how deeply involved he was with The Syndicate and everything. I called a meeting with everyone else to discuss all our partners and workers and basically everyone, especially those with the old mafia crew."

"So, the past week or so, we've all been working overtime with digging through everyone within our network and picking out the bad apples to dispose of." Sebastian spoke instead of Luciano this time. "We've come up with a pretty hefty list that will take us a very long while to get through because we have to figure out who to replace the rats once they are gone. If we went in now and went for the throat, we would be stabbing ourselves in the foot with the turmoil that would happen within our ranks about new leadership."

An ache gripped my hands as I rubbed them nearly raw with anxiety. "I... I didn't mean to create this much trouble..." I muttered under my breath, not liking that I was the first domino to fall and cause this chain reaction.

My hands were forced to come to a stop from Luciano's firm grip on them. "*Amorina*, no." Snaking a hand up my back and neck, he massaged my nape to calm me. "You didn't create anything for us. This has been an ongoing issue that all of us have ignored. If anything, you ripped the blindfold off of our eyes to the shit show we have let happen and grow."

"Luciano is right." Leah's calming voice rang through the air like a soothing bell. "We should be thanking you for kicking our asses into gear."

Forcing the lump in my throat down, I chewed at my bottom lip as I thought about my next decision. "I want to see the list." I had to force myself to remain stiff, so I wouldn't flinch at my own demanding voice.

"I'm not sure that would be wise, Juliet. It's very long and extensive." Aidan's voice wavered with his confused eyes. "Why do you want it?"

Steeling my nerves, I straightened myself in Luciano's arms and looked at everyone with as much confidence as I could manage. "I want to see how many 'good' people out there are terrors in disguise to make myself feel less guilty about ruining them for all they are worth."

Forcing myself to pause, I carefully sorted out my next train of words. "I know you all want to regain your footing in New York and in passing Florida once they catch wind of the carnage up north, but I don't want a quick death for the people on the list. I want to tear their lives apart, burn down the image they have worked so hard to build and maintain, make them be loathed by everyone who used to kiss their feet, make them more homeless than the transients on the streets, and only then do I want them dying a slow and painful death."

Wetting my lips, I breathed out and took in a shaky breath before continuing. "They have ruined too many lives to have the mercy of a quick death. Even if they are thrown in the ring with Luciano, that isn't enough suffering for what they have done."

I wanted blood and carnage but my way.

"I want that list. I am going to put their lives on blast on the whole internet and drain all their bank accounts. I want to put targets all over their bodies with flashing arrows pointing right at them." Well, maybe not *all* of them "I want to make the others squirm while they wait for their inevitable end. I just want the smaller fry to send a warning and message to the others." I had another idea in mind as well.

"You know how outrageous that sounds, Juliet? To hack people like them and do that kind of damage isn't exactly easy. There aren't many hackers within our ranks either who we can utilize for something like that at this time." Sebastian sounded wary and had a heavy gaze upon me. "That isn't something feasible."

"I said *I* am going to ruin them. Did I mention anyone else in that equation with me?" I almost regretted my bitchy sneer when everyone looked at me in surprise. Giving some attitude towards a mafia boss who wasn't my boyfriend was probably not the best idea.

At least Luciano found it funny with how he laughed softly and patted my thigh. "Give her the list and watch her work while we make and execute our plans fully," Luciano told the others with a wicked and confident smile. "She'll probably get through it all by the end of the month or sooner."

"Hacking them will be as easy as trigonometry." I boasted about myself with a brightening grin.

"Trig is not easy," Aidan remarked with a chuckle.

"It is for me... I mean, all math kind of is..." If I were with my group of friends or this wasn't such a serious situation, then I would be gutsy enough to make a somewhat stereotypical joke about Asians being good at math.

"So, you're going to single-handedly hack God knows how many highly guarded people, tear their lives apart on the web, and make them go broke by stealing from them after you hack their bank account? You do realize you're only 18, literally just graduated from high school today, and probably have half the skills our men do." Ares's mocking tone and dismissive look sparked a bad fuse within me.

Bubbling anger heated my body and drove me to get off Luciano's lap to trudge to my room.

If they all think they can underestimate and undermine me because I am young, then they have another thing coming to them.

I'll fucking show them.

Chapter 31
Luciano

"You shouldn't have pissed her off." Leah sighed chidingly at Ares with a disappointed smirk and amusement in her eyes.

Then, Leah's eyes sharpened harshly as they landed on me. "You should have defended her." The snap from her felt like a direct slap to the face. "She may be young, but she is more than skilled enough, and you, out of everyone, should know that or, at the very least, believe in that and back her up against Ares when he threw those nasty words at her. Not only that, but she is also your girlfriend. You should back her up even if it seems foolish."

"What was I supposed to say in that situation? She..." Well, great, now I couldn't even defend myself without looking and feeling like an asshole.

Scowling, I scoffed and hissed a curse under my breath in Italian. "She is young. Yes, she has formidable skills for someone her age, but compared to those we hire, she probably pales in comparison." My stomach churned at my doubting words about Juliet, even if they might be true. I felt disgusted about myself for doubting her, though.

I shouldn't be doubting her. Leah was right. At the end of the day, Juliet was my girlfriend. My unsolicited support should always be with her, even if she was unreasonable.

Ugh, I fucked up, didn't I?

Groaning frustratedly with a hand down my face, I leaned back in my seat. "I'll give her a moment to cool off." I also needed a bit to get something good sorted. Otherwise, I might just piss her off more and end up with all my accounts being locked... and being locked out of my own damn house—again.

Shaking my thoughts away, I ignored the dull ache in my head as I recollected myself. "We need to go after the small fry first, slowly pick off the weak to get our names crawling up the ranks, and it'll weaken the main body at the end of the day." A long sigh exhausted my chest as I thought about the uproar our actions would cause. "We need to make it bloody and violent." More so for our entertainment, but mangled bodies always did wonders to make a statement impactful.

"We will need to block off any escape routes. No point in doing all of this if our main targets scurry off to regroup elsewhere in safety." Sebastian mentioned with a frustrated sigh of his own.

"That's going to be the tricky part in all of this. It's fucking New York. Good luck cutting off one exit without two more popping up. It doesn't help that we somehow don't have our foothold with law enforcement as we thought. What happened with Juliet revealed to us that our hold on the police departments has slipped into the sewers. Which is another issue we have to fucking deal with on top of everything else." Aidan complained with an exasperated groan of his own.

More and more shit kept on hitting the fan the more we dug into everything to formulate our plans.

"It's going to be a big shit show, but we've handled worse." Leah's light voice encouraged us with a heavy smile. "If we don't regain full control and lose it all, everything we have done will be for nothing, and the whole state is going to end up in literal hell again."

The sound of leather creaking scratched at the air as Leah's body slowly rose from the chair. "We all know how bad it was growing up. We took over and changed things for the better for a fucking reason. I don't care if we end up martyrs, but like hell am I going to let New York go back to how it was before and damn the future generations to come." Strengthening her voice, she gave us the infamous look of murderous determination that always got anyone to crumple upon its gaze. "I refuse to fail our people, let them suffer more than they already have. I do not want another case like Juliet's to emerge. I want to stop it all before it can even have a spark to begin. So, we are going to see this through, even if our bodies join the mass grave we will create."

Surge after surge of anger burned my veins with each pump of my heart as I thought about Leah's words. It was an unavoidable shit show, but it had to be done. To think that situations like Juliet's currently happened while we sat here talking away made me crave a good skull to bash in with my fists.

And the thing was, there were worse things out there happening than what Juliet went through. Things that went unnoticed by us and continued to happen because of our ignorance and naivety. Things that shouldn't have gone as far as they are had we been more diligent.

If we had been doing our jobs as we should, then my Juliet wouldn't have had to suffer as she did.

But if that had been the case, then I wouldn't have Juliet to call as mine.

I hated that she went through the hell she did, but if she didn't, she never would have fallen into my arms.

To meet The Devil, she had to go into Hell.

I felt like a bastard thinking of all of that, and I wish I could say I wished things had been different—but I can't.

Resetting myself with a deep breath, I looked at everyone with a new-found energy and confidence. "Leah is right. We need to remember why we chose to conquer the old. We have to go back on our promise to make things right, to make this new empire fair and just." Maybe we have lost sight of ourselves with time, but now is better than ever to remember our sole reasons for taking the steps our parents didn't dare entertain. "We are better than those rats. We are the necessary evil the city needs, and it is time we reclaim it all."

"Back to our roots we go then." Sebastian agreed with a nostalgic smile. "Our ideals, not our fucking stupid selves getting wasted into alleyway fights for shits and giggles." He reminded us of our wild days with a hearty laugh.

"Those were the fun days, though." Ares's crazed grin probably rivaled as the two of us gave each other nostalgic looks.

"They were not fun," Leah grumbled with a scoffing sneer.

"Maybe not for you because you had to patch us up along with..." A silencing glare from Leah made Aidan shut his mouth before she-who-shall-not-be-named could be mentioned.

And that was one way to damper the whole room again with a heavy somber. All of us probably had the same thoughts going through our minds about the unfortunate situation years ago, but none of us dared speak up and risk Leah's wrath.

We liked our bodies intact and wanted the good doctor to stay good.

Slowly and awkwardly, I got up from my seat, fully intending to slip away to Juliet to avoid the very possible war path from Leah if one of the other idiots set her off.

"Oh fuck me, daddy! Yes! Daddy!"

Neither of us could keep a straight face the moment a phone went off with the most ridiculous ringtone we have ever heard. Nearly everyone burst out laughing in an instant as she watched a red-faced Ares fluster around to pull his phone out, cussing the whole time in Greek before snapping at the person on the other side after picking the call up. "What!? What do you mean all my money disappeared!? Billions don't just... No, I did not buy five new Bugattis! Why the fuck would I do that?!... I don't care, just fucking fix it!" I was surprised that Ares's teeth didn't shatter from how hard his jaw clenched as he growled at his phone menacingly after hanging up.

Clearing his throat in an attempt to cut his dying chuckle short, Sebastian popped the question bubbling between all of us. "What happened?" Poor Sebastian could barely keep a straight face as he curled his lips inward on each other, pressing them tightly together in a gummy smile.

"Interesting ringtone ya got there, bud. Didn't take ya for the Daddy Dom kind of fellow." Aidan's snickering turned into full-blown laughter that earned him a growling tackle from Ares after he shoved Sebastian aside.

"Ares, what is going on that's got you all fired up like that?" It didn't sound like a fun thing going off his brief phone call just now.

"Someone froze and drained all my bank accounts! And they think it's funny to fuck with my whole system that even our hackers can't get through them without tripping something new with whatever fix they patch in!" Ares seethed while choking out Aidan—playfully, of course.

"Who would..." Before I could finish my train of thought, a happy little Juliet humming to her heart's content as she came up to me with a smile that was much too innocent for her, distracting me.

"Can we go shopping?" Yeah, much too innocent for my Juliet.

Sighing, I rubbed my temples to ease the dull ache of my head before bending down to pick Juliet up and throw her over my shoulder. We needed to have a long talk away from everyone.

"Wha—hey! Luca, put me down!" Juliet's arms and legs flailed against me in protest as I took us to our room.

As gently as possible, I threw her down onto the bed and got on top of her with a knowing smirk as I trapped her between my arms and legs. "You know he's going to go after your throat when he figures out it was you." Trying to sound firm with Juliet failed because I felt much too amused at Ares's situation and proud of Juliet.

"I don't know what you're talking about." Juliet played innocent with an exaggerated smile and cheeky giggle. "I mean, after all, I am just a petulant and inexperienced teenage adult who doesn't know what she is doing." She mocked playfully with a few bats of her eyes.

Chuckling, I leaned down and kissed her deeply. "You didn't actually buy five Bugattis, did you?" Not like I would let her drive them. Also, if she did do that, then it meant I had to pay Ares back for the damage she did to his bank account.

Snickering, Juliet grinned up at me and shook her head. "Psh, no, it was just a fake statement and spam email I created for fun. I mean, one Bugatti, maybe, the idea was really tempting, but come on, five? That's a bit excessive, even if he could afford it."

"Did you actually drain his accounts?" Because that was a shit ton of money that would be a bitch to recover if she did do anything with it or didn't distribute it properly.

"No. I made carbon copy accounts, set those at zero balance, and swapped his real accounts with the copies. His real ones are still there but are locked, and only I have the key." Juliet grinned proudly at me, happily kicking her little feet under me.

Smiling proudly, I admired her momentarily before letting out an amused chuckle and kissing her softly. "You are such a troublesome brat." Taking her bottom lip between my teeth, I pulled at it with a soft growl. "I fucking love it." Or at least, I loved seeing the trouble she could cause as long as it wasn't me on the receiving end.

Sighing a soft, sad exhale, she smiled flatly while picking at the collar of my t-shirt. "You should probably head back there before Aidan loses his head." If she didn't sound so torn and sad, then I would listen, but an ache clawed under my chest at the thought of leaving her right now.

Rejecting her suggestion with a firm shake of my head, I leaned down and attacked her neck with some kisses. "What is wrong, *amorina*? Are you still upset about what Ares said out there?" Or was she upset at me for not being a better boyfriend to stand up for her?

Hesitantly, she strained out a small 'yes' with her nod as she tightened her arms around my neck. "It's stupid, though. I shouldn't let his words get to me so much like that, but it just... Ugh! He just reminded me how useless, broken, and pathetic I am. But I also hate how everyone underestimates me because I am so young. Yeah, I am still learning, but I'm learning from the best of the best. I mean, who better to learn from than another top mafia hacker?"

Slipping down next to her, I let her rant as I held her close, nodding and humming in agreeance with her as she vented about—what felt like—everything. I didn't utter a single word until she came to a full stop with an angry huff. "Juliet, sweetheart, you are not useless or broken or pathetic. You are young, yes, but there is nothing wrong with being passionate and excited about something. You have such a drive for what you want to do, and I really love that about you."

A wave of nostalgia warms my lips into a smile as I peered down at Juliet. "Reminds me of myself when I was younger, and it's a good reminder now for me to bring that side of me out to play again. I might be motivated, but I definitely am not as tenacious as I should be like you." Threading my fingers through her silk locks, I smiled appreciatively at her. "You are bringing back a lively side of me that I have locked away with this life of mine."

It was clear to me now, after seeing how much Juliet has impacted my life, that I haven't changed for the better. Yes, I garnered fear and respect, but I also became stagnant. Life was... good... on the best days. Mostly, I lived each day almost robotically on my set schedule, not really enjoying life as I should. The only thing I ever really found joy in was my fights, but even then, the spark in me was short-lived. Surging adrenaline only gave me a needed high for so long, and there were only so many people to beat bloody before even they became dull.

Resting my forehead against hers, I deeply breathed in her citrusy and berry-like scent, letting it clear up my system and mind. "Sometimes, I wonder who saved who in our relationship." I mused my thoughts aloud. "Thank you, Juliet, for being mine," I whispered against her lips as my hand held the back of her head delicately.

Applying the smallest amount of pressure possible, I guided her into a heartfelt kiss, letting my very soul shudder out of my body the deeper I pressed on. With a hand on the back of her head, I wrapped the other around her waist and pressed her into my feverish body with a soft groan.

My Juliet, the light to my hellish domain, the surface air, the fire to my soul, the reason I looked forward to the next day. Eagerness to gaze in awe upon the sheer perfection of her beauty compelled me to open my eyes each and every morning. Her beautiful eyes lit my path towards a greater—gray—good.

More importantly, the air my lungs craved with each breath, and she was the electricity that pulsed through my heart, keeping its rhythm steady and alive.

She had truly become my everything.

"I love you, Juliet."

Chapter 32
Juliet

I LOVE YOU, JULIET.

How could three simple little words make me smile like a fool and cry like a happy idiot? They were just three silly words—words I have heard and seen countless times throughout my short life thus far. I didn't smile or internally coo when Jack dumped his heart out to Rose in 'Titanic,' nor did I feel a single heartstring pluck at Noah and Allie in 'The Notebook.'

Yet, hearing Luciano just now tore my heart open—in a good way!

The storm of emotions that ravaged and consumed me was indescribable. To say I felt pure bliss or mind-maddening euphoria would be so much of an understatement that it felt illegal. No words in this world would ever be enough to describe the way my body wanted to implode from hearing his rich voice say those three words to me with such passion in his eyes.

God, the way his amber pools opened his soul to me with those words. It felt like I could search in the endless desire, adoration, bliss, and lust mixing in his eyes until I became drunk on his emotions alone.

Then, the way his eyes opened to me, I could probably reach out and touch his soul with my bare hands because he exposed himself to me like this.

Although, through all the good, I could see a tinge of fear strip at his wonder as the two of us looked at each other longingly in silence. A silence that had been warm and comforting until now.

I hadn't realized how dry my mouth and lips had become until I tried to reciprocate his raw emotions with my own. Even after wetting my lips and salivating like a fool, my mouth felt like a damn sandbox.

So, to cover up my embarrassment, I grabbed his face with both my hands and smushed our lips together in a sloppy but hot kiss. Yeah, apparently, I couldn't even fucking kiss him right because of my nerves. To be fair, he always made me nervous, and every ounce of control and feeling in my body, along with any thoughts in my mind, disappeared at the slightest touch of his lips on my body.

Whenever I was with Luciano, I felt wild deep down. Anything and everything I did in return was based on pure instinct and need for him.

Which was why he terrified me.

To feel like I was losing control to my own desires felt so wrong, yet so right when it came to Luciano. I shouldn't be feeling so eager to spread my legs for him, to want him to claim me after everything. But the fact he made me feel so safe that I would blindly trust him with all of me scared me the most. I wasn't even going to think about the other need I wanted from him.

"Make love to me."

Okay, those were not the words I wanted to say in return to him after breaking our heavy kissing, but it was what I wanted badly.

Pulling back, Luciano shook his head at me as his eyes softened with control. "Juliet, don't let my confession pressure—"

Frustrated, I let out a low groan and pulled him into another kiss to shut him up. "I want you, Luciano. I need you. I have for so long." I spoke between my soft pants against his lips. "I want you to make love to me, please."

Giving us some breathing space, I held his face tenderly in my hands and let my sincere eyes lock with his. "I love you, Luciano, and I trust you. I really am ready to take it all the way with you." My cheeks ached from my delirious smile, but I didn't care—also because I couldn't fucking control it.

As I traced his lips with my thumb, I could feel my eyes grow heavy with desire. "I love you, and I need to feel you." Burning lust dripped like venom out of my mouth with my last words as I threw a leg around his waist to thrust my hips at his covered member, giggling softly when I felt his hardness rub against my covered sex. "And I think you need me just as badly," I whispered hotly against his lips before sealing our lips in a consuming kiss.

"Juliet..." He hesitated against my lips, a hand already resting on my hip to push me away.

Dropping a hand from his face, I slapped it over his to keep him from shoving me away. "If it gets too much at any point, I will stop you, promise. Just... please, let me have my man in me." I assured him with a sweet smile, slowly grinding myself against him to try and convince him some.

Gritting out a groan of defeat, he relented, "Safe-word and action?" He was close with how his eyes darkened with lust—lust for me.

A big grin of victory stretched at my lips as I kissed him and swept my tongue along his lips playfully when I pulled away. "Tap out, and tap you repeatedly," I replied to him with a grinning giggle.

Rolling over top of me completely, he admired me for a long moment before biting my bottom lip and engaging me in a bruising kiss. Not waiting for permission for entrance into my mouth, he forces his tongue through until I feel him fill and claim every inch of my mouth as our tongues tangle with each other.

Keeping our lips sealed, his hands gripped the top of my strapless dress and ripped it apart from the seams in one rough, smooth motion, making me gasp at the sudden chilly air hitting my bare body. "You're so lucky that wasn't a favorite dress of mine." I joked with a muffled chuckle; my words barely came out clearly because my lips remained pressed against his.

"I'd buy you a hundred new favorites so that I can keep tearing it away from your body." He growled softly against my lips before forcing his tongue into my mouth again, distracting me just enough to rip my lacy panties away the same manner he did my dress.

Playfully offended, I broke the kiss and turned my head to prevent him from stealing my breath away again. "Okay, those were my favorite, you jerk.

And they were limited edition." But by God, was it fucking hot how he took it away from my body like a needy beast in heat.

"As if you don't have a dresser full of expensive underwear from your little shopping spree." He muttered with a roll of his eyes, making me snicker a little at the memory of my online shopping spree in retaliation.

A smartass quip hung in the air after I opened my mouth. His hand ending up around my throat and choking me softly made it hard to formulate my train of thought correctly.

Leaning close, his hot breath bathed my cheek as he licked a trail to my ear. "But not like you'll need any of those after tonight." A sharp zip of painful pleasure tightened my aroused body from him biting my ear. "Think I am going to make a new rule that you can't wear panties from here on out, just so I can have easy access to you whenever the fuck I want. Bend you over the counter, lift your dress up, and just slide right into you, and I will go right in because you're going to be constantly wet in anticipation of when I am going to fuck and fill your needy cunt up next."

I shuddered at the dirty scenes racing through my mind like a speeding train. "Holy fuck." Why did I want that so badly? Even if it was a little humiliating to be used as a fuck doll for his whims. Seriously, why did the thought of it push me closer to the edge of an orgasm?! He hasn't even touched me yet I was so depraved to the point where I might come from a mere thought of being used by him.

"Like that, *amorina*? Do you want to be used by me like that? To be my good girl and give me access whenever I damn well please?" He whispered hotly with a soul-shaking chuckle.

All I could manage in response to him was a furious nod of my head as I tried to get my stiff tongue to work with my frazzled mind. "Y-yes, sir, I do." I squeaked with a small gasp.

"That's my good girl." His words ghosted over my lips with his smirking ones as he moved down my body.

Pressure around my neck eased a little but not completely as he kept a reassuring hold on me as his hot tongue burned my skin with its travel down my chest to my tender nipple. My body shivered in response to his fingers digging into what little plushness my breast offered, and waves of delightful pleasure warmed my aroused body more. "Luca." I moaned softly with a gasp at the feeling of his hot mouth engulfing my nipple into his mouth.

"You're still dressed. It's not fair," I complained playfully with a breathless chuckle as my hands fumbled at his clothes.

Desperately, I pushed his shirt up to gawk and touch every inch of his sculpted body. No matter how many times I have seen this perfect chiseled body of his, it never ceased to amaze me. Also, I couldn't keep my hands off him, no matter how hard I tried. It always felt like the first time whenever the pads of my soft fingers would follow the lines and dips of his muscles as if I were an artist tracing something endlessly until I could sculpt him blind from muscle memory.

My mind spiraled slightly into panic when Luciano suddenly pulled away and grabbed me by my arms. I don't know what made me freak out for that split second when he moved me up in the bed so my head was on the pillows. He wouldn't ever hurt me, yet I got the sudden chill to crawl away from him.

Not wanting to ruin our growing moment, I briskly shoved the icky feeling into the back of my mind. No longer distracted by my own head, I lurched up to reach down enough to grab the waistband of his jeans.

Unfortunately, I barely managed to pop off the button before his hand stopped me, causing me to look up at him with scrunched-up eyes. "Patience, *principessa*." He playfully chided me with a chuckle, kissing my forehead and pushing me flat on the bed again as he sat back on his knees.

A snap of fearful excitement hit my body when I became caught in his lust-crazed gaze. I felt like a deer caught in the headlights as his hungry eyes devoured every inch of me. He was the predator, and I was his prey. A feeling of vulnerability washed over me as he continued to study me in great detail. Yeah, I was completely naked, but his eyes made me feel exposed as if he could see everything beneath the surface.

Then, his hot and heavy words after he took his shirt off in one smooth movement. "Spread your legs for me, *amorina*, I want to see my pretty pussy before I eat it." Fuck. I was doomed.

On their own accord, my legs parted while my head turned away in shame. Embarrassment chilled my body like a wave of cold water, making my legs go stiff and try to snap shut, only to be stopped by Luciano's hands. "There is nothing to be ashamed of, sweetheart." His words whispered against my inner thighs, making my body twitch in response. "So fucking beautiful, so perfect." He kissed his way down my thighs, muttering sweet nothings until he couldn't because he had to use his tongue to lick me.

The fullness of his soft and wet tongue pressed against my pussy, and slowly he licked me from the bottom of my entrance to my clit, where he latched on and suckled softly. "Fuck." I gasped with my head thrown back, my hands instantly grabbing at his head to push him into me.

This felt so dirty and wrong, so why did I like it? Besides the obvious fact of his tongue being magic—seriously, he felt too skilled for his own good. He licked the right areas in the most sinful ways, running the edge of it along my labia, then using the flat tip of it for my pulsating clit. God, I shouldn't like this, liking how lost in me Luciano looked as he feasted on my cunt like no tomorrow.

Did he actually like this? Or was it an act? The far-out look of addiction in his eyes and the eagerness of his actions were more than real enough. But what if he was just a good actor?

No, stop it.

I mentally slapped myself before my thoughts could spiral into something more ridiculous. Luciano loved me. The sincerity in his voice and eyes were more than enough to convey the seriousness of his confession. He was doing this because I asked him and because he wanted to.

He wants me as badly as I want him.

Letting my insecurities fade to black, I immerse myself in the never-ending bliss of Luciano's mouth. A whining whimper of frustration filled the air when he removed himself from me. My mouth opened to protest as I glared down at him, but his light chuckle kept my words on my tongue, "Easy, I'm not stopping there. Just wanted to tell you that I am going to finger you to stretch you for me."

Frustration quickly morphed into nervousness as the thought of his fingers penetrating me pulled at my nerves. I had no problems with him touching me; frankly, I quite loved it and begged for it, but I have never let him go as far as penetrating me with anything. Hell, I didn't even put my own fingers in myself if I masturbated because it stirred up too many painful memories.

"S-slowly, just one at a time." The fact that his fingers were big didn't help calm me any.

Reassuring me with a smile and nod, he dipped his head back down between my legs, eating me out in earnest until I felt myself being driven up the wall with the madness of pleasure. Shamelessly, I pressed against the back of his head to shove more of his face into me, not caring if I might suffocate him as I grind myself against his mouth. "Oh fuck, Luciano, I'm—ah!" Fear froze my body at the feeling of something intruding my entrance.

Stiff as a board, I pressed myself against Luciano as I processed the new feeling. It felt so weird to have something inside of me. Oh God, his finger was inside of me, and I could feel it. Every little twitch and curl of his digit in me set my nerves ablaze, but it also sent a little fear with the slight pain. His stimulation of my clit helped settle the budding fear before it became too much, though, so I was thankful for that.

My nervous eyes locked onto his intense ones as he trained his sights on me. He was gauging me, seeing my reactions as he moved his finger in and out of my tight walls, seeing if any specific movement or spot made me tick. Yet, the only thing I offered him in return was an edged stare as I felt myself fighting the demons that threatened to drag me under.

Stop, stop, stop. Stop it!

I scolded myself as I forced my hips to buck against him.

I'm safe. I'm not being hurt. Luciano is safe. He won't hurt me, and he doesn't want to hurt me. He is doing this for my pleasure, to get me used to feeling penetrated.

Tension melted from my body with each shaky breath I took, blowing out the stress with every exhale. "Faster, please." The needy desire for him from before swung back tenfold the more I relaxed into him again. "I'm so close." Thank God my building orgasm didn't run away when my fear reared its ugly head.

Focusing on the pleasure, I actively ignored the slight discomfort from the friction of his fingers against my sensitive walls. I needed to adjust to him, that was all. Wincing, I pulled my hips away from him slightly when he went a little too rough. "Ow, n-not so hard, please."

Immediately, he eased off and peered up at me apologetically. "Sorry, baby." His words vibrated against my sensitive clit, making me shudder with pleasure.

Breathing deeply, I relaxed fully against the bed, letting the pleasure from Luciano take over once more until I felt myself being pushed up the wall. "Coming." I gasped with a soft moan right as I felt the tension snap and tense at my arching body.

Something didn't feel quite right, but I summed it up to first-time experiences. This was my first time willingly engaging in anything so sexual with anything. I wasn't going to count the bastards at the brothel. What happened that night wasn't my first time—I refuse to accept it as my first sexual encounter and experience.

This right now with Luciano would be my first of my own volition.

First-time jitters were a thing... right? Honestly, no amount of porn or stupid sex 101 guides on the internet could ever prepare me for this moment. I needed to get out of my head and enjoy this supposedly magical moment.

The feeling of the bed dipping next to me and something hot on my lips jarred me back to reality with a gasp of surprise. If Luciano's dizzying kiss hadn't brought me out of my thoughts, then the feeling of his thick cock rubbing along the length of my sex would have done the trick.

Oh God, it's really happening.

"Juliet, breathe." Luciano's calming voice washed over me with his peppering kisses on my face. "Relax."

That did it.

That one fucking word at this moment, paired with the intense burn of his dick pressing into my resistant sex, broke open the dam, causing everything to flood and drown me.

"Tap out!"

Chapter 33

Luciano

"Tapout! Tapout! Tapout!"

I had already pulled out the first time she used her safe-word, but she had become inconsolable ever since. Even now, as I held her tightly in my arms, her tears burned my skin like acid when they splattered on me, and her pained sobs with her uncontrolled use of her safe-word felt like a dull knife slicing away at my very being.

It felt like an eternity as I sat there feeling like a useless sack of shit while Juliet suffered in my arms. I didn't know what to do to help her. Soothing her with my words and soft touches did nothing, and I was too afraid of triggering her more if I went with the typical method.

She was already breaking in my arms; I didn't want to shatter her completely.

"Juliet, *amorina*, please." My heart cracked with my voice as I muttered a string of silent apologies to her.

I needed to take control of her, and it was what she needed of me as her lover and as her Dom. She trusted me to bring her back to safety in these moments, no matter the method.

In all honesty, this would hurt me more than it would her.

Jerking her body, I threw her head back with a violent motion and wrapped a hand around her neck while my other arm remained tightly around her like a constrictor. "Juliet! Get out of your fucking head." I raised my voice initially in hopes of breaking through to her.

Squeezing the sides of her neck, I watched as her hyperventilating slowed because I forced her to pace her breathing. "You are not there, so get out of your own head. Whatever you are seeing and feeling is not real anymore. It's all in the past, so leave it there and come back to me." I spoke in a dominating yet gentle voice as I adjusted the pressure around her neck as necessary; I wanted to choke her enough to shock her mind back to reality, not to make her pass out.

"Juliet, listen to my voice, focus on it. Come back. I know you can. You are a strong girl, my strong girl, so you can do it. You are in control, sweetheart. Those demons are nothing to you. Shove them back, put them in their place." God, if only I could take away her suffering, I would do it without a second thought. "*Amorina*, come back to me, love."

Swallowing the lump in my throat, I rest my forehead against hers. "I am so sorry for not being better, for sending you into this state." I sensed her reluctance and hesitance, and I should have stopped then. I should have listened to my heart and put a stop to it, even if she said otherwise. "I swear, never again. I will never hurt you like this again."

"Luca..." Her breathy voice squeaked between her hiccupping.

Completely freeing her neck, I settled my hand on her collarbone as I tucked her into me. "I am here, sweetheart, I am here." I kissed every inch of her face as I muttered apology after apology under my breath.

I only stopped running my mouth when Juliet grabbed my face with both her hands and forced me to look her dead in the eyes. "Stop." She commanded in a tired and raspy voice. "Stop apologizing. It's not your fault. I pushed myself when I shouldn't have because I wanted to enjoy things with you. I was fine, really, but I don't know exactly why it all came crashing through as it did. I don't fully understand it myself quite yet, but it is not your fault." Her fingers stroked at my eyebrows and cheeks as she reassured me with a warm smile that broke me.

"Luciano, darling, look at me." I didn't realize my far-out gaze until she said something. "I'm sorry for not being able to—"

I quickly shut her up with a kiss. "No." Now, it was my turn to hold her face with care. "Don't you ever apologize for not being able to give me something, especially sex."

"But I asked you for it and never delivered." I hated how torn she was over this trivial matter.

"And what did I tell you about consent?" I asked, hoping to jog her memory of our talk on the subject a while back.

Looking down, she muttered, "It can be taken back no matter when or what. It doesn't matter if I agreed to something beforehand. If I change my mind, then I can take it back."

With a tilt of her head, I peered into her avoidant eyes. "And that applies where and to who?"

Sighing softly, she presses her face further into my hands. "Everywhere and everyone, and if they don't respect it, then I can stab them." Seeing the small smile crack with her flat joke at the end made my chest feel slightly lighter.

"There's my Juliet," I chuckled, kissing her forehead. "But I prefer if you had me or one of your bodyguards do the dirty work of spilling blood."

"Stabbing's not my thing anyway, so that's fine." She forced a chuckle out as she slid her hands down to my bare chest. "But you really aren't mad or disappointed with me?"

A sad smile ached my face as I shook my head in response to her. "*Principessa*, no, never for something like that. I will never get mad or upset at you for using your safe-word, ever, and that is how it should be. A safe-word is there for a reason, sweetheart, and I told you before, but I will tell you again, I never want you to ever hesitate to use your safe-word with me at the slightest discomfort."

Bringing her face up into a deep kiss, I held us together for a while until Juliet's hands slapped at my chest. Chuckling in response, I broke the kiss and breathed heavily while Juliet gasped for breath. "Jerk, my lungs aren't as big as yours." She pouted with a soft glare.

"Would you dare say I take your breath away?" I joked with a laugh.

That was too fucking cheesy, but it got Juliet to soften up and respond with her own laugh, so I felt no shame in being a cheesy fucker.

Pulling her down fully onto the bed, I pulled the sheets over us and cuddled her. "What do you need right now, *amorina*?"

Humming happily, Juliet buried her face into my chest. "Just hold me for a bit, then food." She mumbled against my chest. "Can we have pasta tonight? Alfredo? And salad?"

"Think the others have already ordered pizza knowing them, but if that is what my sweetheart wants, then that is what she shall get." Not like that would be a hard meal to throw together.

"Give me my money back, you brat," Ares demanded of my girl with a menacing glare after he stalked up to her.

Not bothering to look at the hulking mafia boss, she continued to tap away at her phone. "Wow, you need to learn some manners." Juliet snickered with an innocent smile on her face when she peered up at Ares from her position next to me on the couch. "But also, I don't know what you're talking about. I mean, how can an inexperienced child like me possibly manage to come close to your accounts?" Okay, now she was being a little shit—and I was living for it.

Ares's jaw tightened in a scowl as he growled at Juliet. "Why, you little..." Clenching his fists at his sides, he harshened his glare at Juliet, who smiled humbly. "You better undo what you did, or else."

Uh oh.

Juliet's whole demeanor straightened out defiantly as she stood and got up in Ares's personal space with her arms crossed. "Or else what? You gonna hit me? Sue me? Go ahead, I dare you to try something." She goaded him with a crazed grin. "I heard your car collection is a lot more extensive than Luciano's. It would be a shame if they all just drove off one night, never to be seen again. And seeing as you are broke as a joke, you can't replace them."

Maybe I should stop this before they actually rip into each other. I mean, Ares wouldn't hurt Juliet physically; he wasn't one to be violent towards females. But he had an arrogant mouth that often ran way before his brain, and the last thing I wanted was for him to say something hurtful or triggering to Juliet in a moment of anger.

"I mean, if you have such great techies on your payroll, then they should have no problem undoing whatever this hacker did to your accounts." With the smile still on her face, she gave a nonchalant shrug of her shoulders as she sat down in my lap. "Although, I would tell them to chop chop because who knows how long the money will just sit there before it gets blown on whatever whim the hacker has."

"Also, I don't know why you're accusing me. There's no way I would be capable of something like this, being eighteen and fresh. I don't have the skills, as one would say." Juliet's sarcastic voice continued to lay it onto Ares, whose face grew redder and redder by the second. "Maybe you should go find this hacker and maybe beg at their feet to undo their fuckery." She suggested with a cruel smirk.

"Luciano, your little girlfriend is just as much of a little shithead as you." Ares bit out with a frustrated shout.

Laughing in response, I merely smirked at him as I threw an arm around Juliet's waist. "Well, maybe next time you will think twice about insulting someone and undermining them because of their age." Maybe he would have thought twice about his earlier words if he had known about Juliet's antics against me, but then he wouldn't have gotten a lesson out of all this.

Sometimes Ares was much too prideful as he was aggressive for his own good, so he needed to get his ass humbled from time to time.

Being the arrogant little shithead he was, Ares refused to bow to Juliet and sulked off a little ways to get back on the phone with his men. Although, it was only a matter of time at this point until all of us got a memorable event of Ares apologizing for the books.

"Honestly, if he ends up with someone, I'm gonna keel over and die because who on this earth can put up with such an ass like him," Juliet grumbled with a slight roll of her eyes.

All of us grew quiet with somber smiles, making regret twist on Juliet's face. "Oh my God, please don't tell me I just spoke ill of the dead." Her face paled as she sunk into me to hide.

Sighing heavily, Sebastian took a swing of his beer before looking at Juliet and replying in a forlorn voice. "Ares... well, I was going to say he wasn't always like this, but that would be a lie. I guess the more correct thing to say would be that he hadn't always been this intense. He did have someone years ago, but we don't know much or anything about who the woman was. All he would tell us was that she was some simple girl who he wanted to keep out of our mafia mess and that she was murdered one night."

"Well, now I feel like a complete ass." Juliet groaned dejectedly.

After a small moment of awkward silence, we all managed to get back into better spirits by talking about the shit we did in the past and our plans for the future. It was nice until Ares rejoined with an unamused glare.

We all thought he would start up some shit with Juliet when he approached her, so we were shocked at the words that came out of his mouth. "Can you please give me my accounts back? I am sorry for being an asshole to you and saying you aren't capable." It wasn't loud, but it was enough to be heard. "I'll give you the damn list myself once we are done compiling it, just please undo whatever the fuck you did, please."

Holding up a hand to Ares, I quickly stopped him before he could speak again. "I will discuss the list issue with Juliet at a later time, so just go back to apologizing sincerely and begging." I couldn't help but smirk like a cheeky bastard with my last words as I proudly held my girl.

Turning her head back at me, Juliet narrowed her eyes dangerously. "There is nothing to discuss about it. I am going to take part in ruining these people's lives, and if you think you can talk me out of it, then you have another thing coming for you." She didn't even have to sound threatening for me to internally shrink away in fear.

Sighingly tiredly, I flick her forehead. "I never said anything about keeping you out of it or talking you out. If you want to take part, then I am not going to stop you because lord have mercy on my bank accounts if I try."

As much as I didn't want her to, there was no stopping her. Besides, she would be safe behind her screen. Not like she would be out in the streets with us where she'd be in real physical danger.

"We just need to lay out expectations and ground rules for you, that's all, along with who you can and can't go after because of circumstances," I told her with a pointed look. "So don't get your panties in a twist, sweetheart."

The rebellious tension fell away with her shoulders as she smiled sheepishly at me. "Sorry, thought you were going to pull a macho mafia boss bullshit card."

Rolling my eyes, I gave a short, breathy chuckle and kissed her forehead. "With you? Never." Because she would raise Hell against me if I did.

Hell hath no fury like Juliet scorned.

I might actually end up in a bed of thorns next time.

Chapter 34

Juliet

~1 month later~

"Luca!"

I gasped sharply from my orgasm shattering my sensitive body. It was way too early in the morning for this shit, but like hell was I going to stop him.

Luciano's bell-tolling chuckle warmed the room as he sat back on his knees and wiped the back of his hand across his jaw. "I am never going to get enough of having you for breakfast." And I would never get over how satisfied and amazed he always looked after having his face all up between my thighs nearly every morning.

Yeah, somehow, morning head from him became a regular thing in our morning routine after the first week of me flipping out during sex. It was weird to wake up to him asking me if he could eat me out, especially in my half-asleep state.

Honestly, I misheard him that first time; I thought he asked if I wanted to eat out for breakfast. At least, in my sleepy mind, that's what it translated to. So, imagine my fucking surprise when he pulled my pants off, spread my legs, and went down on me until I saw stars and trembled uncontrollably from the aftershocks of my orgasms.

Well, I wasn't going to complain or put a stop to it. He loved it, I loved it, it was a win-win for everyone.

Crawling back up the bed, he leaned down and kissed me softly, letting me taste a hint of myself on his lips. "There's a lot that I have to do today with the others to finalize plans, so try not to get into too much trouble, alright?" He chuckled softly against my cheek before kissing it.

Rolling my eyes, I gave his cheek a little pinch. "I promise I won't buy any cars while I'm out today with Evie." I joked with a soft laugh that grew into a full-blown cackle when Luciano's fingers dug into my sides.

"You are not allowed to buy any car, period. You're lucky I even let you keep that custom-ordered one." Luciano told me with a joking smile and a serious look in his eyes.

"Not even when I need an SUV for our kids?" I joked with a dry chuckle, instantly regretting it the moment my words came into existence.

An unpleasant silence weighed down the air around us as we looked at each other awkwardly and crestfallen. "Sorry, forget I said anything." I quickly tried to push the subject away, not wanting it to damper our mood.

The subject of our long-term relationship and the matter of kids and family haven't been touched yet, and for good reason. Luciano was busy with Syndicate business while I was young and had college left to worry about. Also, our relationship was still fairly new—we hadn't even been together for half a year!

Growing up, I always knew I wanted children of my own someday, but definitely not at eighteen or in my early twenties. The notion of children with Luciano at this moment felt pleasing enough, but that didn't mean I wanted to start right now.

No matter how blatantly clear his love was for me and how much I reciprocated that. There was no guarantee that we would be together a few years down the road from now. People and their feelings change with time, so what if we naturally drifted apart as the years went on? I was still young. What if I found someone new?

Okay, that is fucking ridiculous. Me? Finding someone new and better than Luciano?

Yeah, I wanted to laugh and slap myself in the face for even thinking about giving someone else my heart. I loved Luciano greatly and couldn't imagine my life without him. I wasn't worried about Luciano leaving me either because his pure devotion to me was more than evident. Luciano was also at a point in his life where he was mostly stable, or at the very least, he had his head on straight. He wasn't some immature teen or lost young adult who had no clue about what they wanted in life.

But just because I felt good about Luciano didn't mean kids were in the cards. What if he didn't want any? What if I changed my mind about them? Either way, it was way too soon to have such a conversation.

Forcing a smile, Luciano kissed my forehead and got off the bed. "We'll cross such a bridge when, or if, we come to it." At least he didn't dig at the subject, thank goodness.

Clearing his throat, he changed the subject. "Do you want to shower with me, or are you going to laze in bed a little more?" His eyes lingered on me as he went to the dresser to pull out a shirt and some boxers.

Humming in thought, I entertained both ideas for a hot minute. I mean, stay comfortable in bed or shower with my sexy man? How much did I want to see and touch his perfect ass? Seriously, this man had an ass to die for, and I could never get enough of touching it, especially whenever he wore his sweatpants or jeans around me. Lord, give me strength to resist the booty because I definitely had none of my own to call upon.

Letting out a frustrated groan, I pulled the sheets over my head and sank down into the bed. "I'll be in in a bit," I grumbled from under the sheets.

The need for the booty won.

"You really think he's going to like it?" My nervous excitement trembled my words as I gawked at the piece of jewelry with a wide smile.

Giggling, Evie threw her arms around my shoulders and hugged me tightly with a little shake. "Girl, he is going to be over the moon. I mean, it's a serious commitment." Reaching out, she shut the black box and took it from me, shoving it into my bag so it was out of sight, out of mind.

Toning her excitement down, "Come on, let's get some lunch before we hit the lingerie and accessory stores." She suggested with a calming smile, tugging my hand toward the escalators.

A round trip around the food court later, and we finally sat down to enjoy the food we bought. "Hey, can I ask you something?" I asked tentatively after we had a few bites of our food.

Setting her drink down, she zoned all her attention on me. "Yeah, shoot." At least her friendly smile calmed my nerves a bit.

"I've been thinking about something and was wondering if you wanted to help since you have personal experience, and you can totally disagree if it seems too much for you, but I kinda want to do something about the trafficking problem here in New York." It was a farfetched idea and definitely one that was not flushed out, but I wanted to see what Evie thought before pitching it to Luciano to see if he would help me any.

Leaning forward onto the table, Evie completely engrossed herself with interest in whatever whacked-up idea I had cooking in my head. "What did you have in mind?"

"I want to bait people and shut down networks." I flat-out told her about the grand idea before going into details. "I came across a lot of nasty things when I was digging through some of the people I saw at the fight, and a lot of them are involved in trafficking networks that I can backtrace to the source. But I also want to bait people who aren't involved in the ones I have found and find new ones to track down. I know I can't find and shut all of them down and save everyone, but I want to do as much damage as I can and create a safe space for those saved so they can get back on their feet again."

The fact there were people out there who had been in my situation and Evie's without a fighting chance upset me greatly. We had been fortunate enough to be saved from it all, but it was also sheer luck. If I hadn't pushed myself to break out of the lounge that night, or if Luciano didn't have the meeting he did, then I might be on the streets or back in the hell hole, broken.

Some people are fortunate enough to have someone looking for them and making sure they didn't go unnoticed, but there were way too many who had no one out there or shitty people who put them in that situation in the first place. There were people who wanted to escape but couldn't because they had nowhere to go, so it came down to which evil was less.

"I know it is a lot and crazy, and I have no idea where I would even start. But I mean, you could easily spread awareness about whatever program I start up if I do, and you know how to talk to the predators and know how to spot one. So, I was hoping that we could put together like a fake profile for you to bait people." Okay, saying it out loud made it sound more stupid and insane.

Especially when Evie remained silent and stared at me pensively, I wanted to take it all back and pretend nothing happened. "That is a big idea, and it's definitely going to take some time to build fully, but I am totally down for helping ya." The eager grin on her face had me releasing a held breath. "We should talk to the boys about it, though. They'll definitely have more ideas on how to get things off the ground. Also, we need their wallets."

"Oh please, I can have all their banks in our names with a few keystrokes." I joked with a snicker, making Evie laugh a little.

She picked a fry up and threw it at me as her laughter died down. "I still can't believe you did that to Ares, granted the jerk deserved it." Resetting herself with a deep breath, she looked at me with serious determination. "I'll talk to Aidan about it later when things aren't so hectic with Syndicate business."

"Good idea." They probably didn't need more shoved onto their overflowing plates.

Stressing Luciano with resetting his phone settings or fucking with his car's system was harmless fun, and the stress never lingered. I mean, was it fun to have him blow off some steam by spanking me for being a little shit? Eh, debatable, but I wasn't going to complain about it. As long as I took some of the edge off him, that was all that mattered to me.

Nudging my food tray closer, Evie encouraged me with a smile. "Come on, we still have a lot of money to blow through." Said the picky, frugal gal.

We were probably the worst shoppers ever because we were picky and money-conserving. Yeah, our men could handle our shopping sprees with plenty to spare, but we also just weren't ones to buy things in excess.

Actually, I take that back. Maybe we were just bad clothes shoppers because we were more than content with the ones in our closet—we also cycle between the same outfits every week despite having enough for an outfit a day for a whole year. Evie had an obsession with purses and bags, and she would gladly swipe her cards away. For me, any piece of tech was fair game. Evie had a room—yes, a whole ass room—filled with shelves of purses, like it looked like a damn store in that room. I had an electronics room filled with game systems, TVs, and nearly a whole side dedicated to various computer systems and screens.

"So, why are we going to the lingerie store again?" I definitely didn't need any, and Evie already bought a shit ton two weeks ago.

"Because Aidan ruined a bunch." Evie deadpanned with a grumble under her breath, cussing out her man in Vietnamese.

What was supposed to be a smooth trip took a turn for the worst when we turned the corner, and the wicked witch ran into us. "I'm disappointed I wasn't invited to the wedding, dear Juliet. After all, you and Luciano wouldn't have met if it weren't for me." Carol, as I came to learn Lady Heral's legal name, cooed in a sickly sweet voice filled with venom.

Evie glared at the older hag as she pulled my arm to try and step around her. "Go away, Carol. We have no business with you."

The smart thing to do would be to leave, but I found myself digging my feet into the ground as her words took root in my weak mind. Wrenching my arm from Evie, who protested and grabbed onto me again, I ignored her while I glared at Carol. "What is your senile brain prattling on about?" It was probably nothing, and I shouldn't engage to fuel whatever vendetta she had going on.

The curve of her snakish lips turned devilish, making me regret pushing her. "Your marriage to Luciano, the wedding? Unless you two haven't had the wedding ceremony but signed papers. I mean, why else would you have taken his last name already? Although, I have to say, pretty gutsy of you to take his last name and have it announced at graduation like that." I didn't like how uppity and prying she sounded, as if she knew something I didn't and was toying around with me.

Tension filled my face as my features twisted downward with a cautious tilt of my head. I wasn't even going to linger on the fact she said something about my graduation because I was too hung up on the other parts. "I took his last name because I don't want to be tied to my family, and it has nothing to do with this marriage you are talking about. You are sounding like a crazy hag with that shit, you know that?"

Her haughty laugh made my jaw tighten up into a scowl. Then, just as her laugh started, it stopped with a feigned look of pity, "Oh, you don't know? He hasn't told you? Well, if you did, then you wouldn't be calling me the crazy one."

This bad idea would bite me in the ass, but curiosity killed the cat—and I was the damn cat. "What are you talking about?" I probably shouldn't have believed a single word that came out of her mouth—or even entertained her with my attention in the first place—but here we were.

Yeah, the way her smirk turned sadistically dark should have been a warning for me to turn and run with my ears covered, but I was too stubborn and stupid to do so. "The only reason why you are not locked up at the lounge is because you are his wife or to be his wife after your parents sold you out to him to relieve some debt." Scoffing and rolling her eyes, Carol muttered something under her breath before addressing me again. "I don't like taking losses, no matter how small, but I am not stupid enough to go against a Syndicate boss and their family. The fact that you are betrothed to him saved you from a lifetime of servitude at my establishments." My hand itched with an ache to lash across her face when her lips turned wild. "But judging by your reactions and questions, he never told you about any of it."

Before I could snap back at her, Evie tersely stepped before me and pushed me behind her. "That is enough out of you. Leave, or we will have the guards drag you away." She threatened Carol with an aggressive growl to her voice.

Evie remarked with a sneer, "Go get your Botox injections. Your face is starting to melt." As Carol left with her head held so high that it was probably up in the skies.

Turning to me, Evie smiled concernedly at me as she rubbed my shoulders. "Hey, don't let her get to you. She's just trying to be a bitch and get under your skin, and Luciano's to get back at you for what happened."

Anger boiled in my blood at Evie's words because she sounded so nervous trying to convince me. Tearing myself away from her, I found my eyes narrowing into slits as I looked up at Evie. "How much of what she said was true though?" Would my friend dare lie to me?

At this moment, her hesitation and silence were as good of an answer as any because it was a confirmation of guilt to me, especially with how crestfallen she got. Then, the fact that she tried to make excuses as I stormed out of the mall didn't help her case or my turbulent emotions.

Whatever good I felt towards Luciano eroded away and flew out the window on the drive home. By the time I made it home, all I could feel toward Luciano was anger, hate, and betrayal.

I wanted to believe that all Carol said was a lie, but her eyes were firm and honest despite how malicious she sounded.

Yeah, the truth fucking hurt like a knife to the gut and chest. All the pain of everything intensified with every step I took toward Luciano's office, every step feeling like a punch to the gut.

By the time I stood before the office door, I felt winded, as if I had gone ten rounds in the ring with Luciano himself.

Not bothering to knock, I kicked the door. Bad fucking idea because the only thing I accomplished was hurting myself. Seriously, they made it look so easy in the movies, and Luciano and his men also made it look simple. Granted, Luciano was twice, maybe triple, my size and packed from head to toe in muscles galore.

Letting out a frustrated shout, I twisted the doorknob and peeped the door open like a normal person before kicking it fully open with my foot, causing it to slam against the wall.

I didn't care about the meeting happening; this matter took precedence—in my opinion. "Everyone out!" I demanded in a booming voice, pointing at the open door behind me without turning around.

"Juliet, where are your manners? We—"

Too furious to let Luciano finish, I snapped at him, cutting him off. "Need to talk about our fucking wedding, the one you failed to mention to me, by the way!"

Yeah, that seemed to get everyone to zip their mouths and leave quickly with their heads down. I'd pick my bones with them later; right now, Luciano would know my wrath.

Marching up to him behind his desk, I shoved at him with all my strength when he tried to stand up from his chair, making him land with a winded grunt. "When the fuck were you going to tell me, hm? Before I walked down the aisle, or after? Or were you going to just force my hand to sign the papers after I say my vows with a gun to my back and let you cuff me with a ring?"

I wanted to strangle him so badly that my fingers hurt from the restraint I exhibited on myself. Of course, strangling him to death should be the least of his worries if I got my hands on him right now. I wanted to grab the stupid pen off his desk and stab him with it repeatedly until he would hurt like me or at least feel a fraction of it. Or maybe I'd toy with him and choke him with the electrical cords and release when he was close, only to choke him again.

No, no. None of that would suffice. He needed to have everything crushed: mind, body, and soul.

"I fucking trusted you, let myself be vulnerable to you, gave you my heart, only to find out from the damn bitch who stole my life from me that you stooped to her level and basically bought me from my parents to relieve some debt they owed you apparently." The volume of my voice slowly died down with my words until it was slightly above a normal volume, but that didn't mean my anger simmered or subsided.

No, I was still furious and ready to blow again with the slightest trigger.

The hurt my heart suffered cracked through my angry voice as I continued to press into Luciano, with both my words and my finger to his chest. "Seriously, what the fuck were you thinking? And why didn't you tell me? Were you ever going to tell me anything? Any of it? Or were you going to play me until I broke, then discard me like trash?"

If only I could punch a hole in his chest and rip his heart out, make him watch as I squeezed the life out of it until he felt as dead as me right now. Or maybe throwing it into a vat of acid would be better; that way, he would feel the slow-burning pain of his heart disintegrating to nothing. Actually, that seemed like a grand idea the more I relished from it.

Luciano's mouth opened, but I didn't give him a chance to spew whatever bullshit he had stewing in his head. "You are despicable. You save me under the guise of some hero only to find out you have your own motives. You are no better than my fucking parents, who sold me to a damn brothel. You are no better than the bitch who auctioned me off like an object and let those men gang-rape me. You did exactly what they did. You bought me for a stupid motive. You really are a fucking devil." Angrily, I shoved at him, making him roll back a bit.

Heavily, his chest rose and fell a few times before his dumbass reply came out, cranking my fury past one hundred. "Well, at least you'll have a handsome devil of a husband."

The callousness in his voice did me in. Whatever hope I had about us sank to the bottom of the endless ocean, taking everything in me with it. "If you think I am going to marry you, then you're fucking delusional." The last of my seething anger faded with my next words. "I can't marry you. I don't love you." Surprisingly, my heart had something left of it to break with those words.

A tick of anger and sadness starkened Luciano's eyes before his hurtful words came coldly, "If that's the silly reason why you're against marrying me, then fine, get ready to be loved so hard that your heart won't have any other choice but to give in." He sounded so chilled and distant and unlike the man I have been with all this time. "I'll make you love me one way or another, even if it means confining you to this house. Hell, I'll lock you in the room, chain you to the bed, all until you melt under me and learn to love me."

Then again, did I really know him?

What he said next answered that question. "We are going to wed whether you like it or not. I saved you from that place under the pretense that you are my betrothed, but now people expect that end result from us now. So, unless you are wanting to go back to being a whore for everyone, I suggest you fix that attitude before I do it for you."

Oh yeah, that fucking did it.

Fully succumbing to my anger, I let it guide my actions.

Everything happened in a blur, and I barely registered the next few seconds into my memory bank.

The moment my hand shot out and snatched his glass of liquor off his desk, it felt like things happened in the blink of an eye.

I flung the liquid at his face, chucked the glass right into his chest, slapped him across the face, and punched him sometime right after the slap.

I almost wanted to deny my actions if it weren't for the reddened imprint of my hand on his cheek and the swelling on his other, paired with the dull ache in my hands.

"Fuck you." I seethed with anger so hot it felt like lava coming up my throat.

As a final 'fuck you' to him, I yanked the necklace he gave me in the beginning, his mark on me, and threw it at him.

"I hate you."

Chapter 35
Luciano

"I DON'T LOVE YOU."

"I hate you."

Her angry words cut themselves into my mind and engraved themselves into every groove of my brain. And what broke my barriers were her hurtful eyes. I wasn't even upset at her for the outburst of fury or the fact she laid her hands on me. No, none of that mattered when I saw how broken and hurt her beautiful eyes dulled out. I was a coward for looking away from her eyes, avoiding the penance for my sins.

I did the one thing I swore I would never do to her: I hurt her.

I hurt my Juliet.

No, I broke my Juliet.

I broke her, shattered her, then stomped all over the pieces.

"Cazzo!"

The pain in my foot from kicking my desk chair didn't faze me because of my numbing anger.

I'm such a fucking idiotic bastard!

Picking up the empty liquor glass, I threw it against the wall with a shout of anguish and anger.

Never before have I hated myself so much. This self-loathing felt disgusting but deserved. I should have never let my anger get the best of me, let alone said the things I did. I couldn't even comprehend the fact I said such words to Juliet, especially the part about her going back to the place and calling her a whore.

"You fucking idiot!" I cursed at myself as I slammed my head against the wall as a punishment.

Honestly, I didn't even know how such words came to my mind. Everything turned into a haze the moment she ripped into me and shoved at me.

Shouting angrily at the air, I punched the wall, putting a nice hole in it. I couldn't even bring myself to scream at the pain in my hand because I fucking deserved it.

Whatever pain and punishment came my way as a result of me being a shitty person was all deserved.

The only thing I didn't deserve right now was Juliet.

My sweet Juliet.

Sliding down the wall, I let myself drown in my despair while I mentally ripped myself apart like never before. I called myself every name in the book in both English and Italian, saying any and every hurtful thing I had ever heard or come up with in my life.

As the ocean of guilt swallowed me, something caught my eyes, causing the knife in my chest to sink deeper.

The necklace she had thrown at me lay discarded on the ground like my heart and mind because I damn well must have fucking lost it somewhere to say the shit I did to Juliet.

Hopelessly, I crawled over and picked up the necklace I had gifted her the day she went back to school. Back then, it really was meant as a symbol of my protection over her, but over time, it became my mark on her. As crude as it sounded, it was my way of marking her as my possession. My girl. Mine.

But the hurt I felt from her taking it off and chucking it at me was all my fault. I deluded myself into seeing the necklace as a collar on her, my collar that I had placed on her months ago when it was nowhere that close. Yet, the meaning to me became skewed over time.

So, when she threw it at me, it was the equivalent of her holding a loaded gun and putting a bullet into me. The thing felt like a bullet hitting me when it bounced off my chest. I had been too stunned at the moment from my heart shattering to pieces and numb from my sheer stupidity to grab it when it fell to the ground.

Why the hell did I even say the things I did?!

I never should have lost control and retaliated like that toward Juliet, no matter how much my fire was fed.

I didn't physically lay my hands on her, but the venomous words I spat were a million times worse than if I did put a hand on her. Physical wounds would heal, but the ones my words created might never.

Suffering in my never-ending cycle of anguish and guilt, the sound of the door opening and footsteps approaching me flew over my head by a mile. I didn't even realize my friends had surrounded me until someone nudged me with their foot.

"Wow, you look like shit." I didn't even have the energy to be mad at Ares and try to punch him for saying that.

"Damn, not even a glance." Sebastian sounded concerned, but I wasn't completely sure.

"Hey," another foot nudged me, Aidan's maybe, judging from the leaner leg. "Shit, how bad did you fuck up?"

A set of hands grabbed my arms, hauling my sorry ass up against the wall before a sharp sting bit my already aching cheek, making me hiss and wince. "God damn it, Luciano, get a fucking grip of yourself." Leah's harsh words scraped my ears like nails on a chalkboard. "Not to say I told you so, but I fucking told you so. You should have come clean with her from the start instead of trying to fix shit under her nose. It was only a matter of time, and unfortunately, that time just came and passed."

"What did you say to her? I mean, did she not understand when you explained yourself to her?" Aidan's question served as another slap to my face as the memories of my hurtful words hit my mind, making me physically wince at the pang to my chest.

"Oh my God, Luciano, what did you say?" Leah groaned tiredly with a shake of her head, her face falling in disappointment as if she already knew what my answer would be.

"Bad things that never should have been thought up in the first place," I admitted shamefully with a sharp inhale. "I just... I shouldn't have lost control... I hurt her so badly, and I'm afraid I've really pushed her off the deep end and lost her."

In no way, shape, or form did I deserve to have Juliet in my arms again or have the privilege to call her mine. But I would be straight-up lying if I said I was okay with that because there is no way in hell that the fact would sit well with me.

Grabbing the front of my shirt, Leah pulled me right up to her glaring face. "If you shoved her, then go jump after her and save her from your stupidity." A forceful shove back against the wall knocked a winded grunt out of me. "Get on your fucking knees and kiss her damn feet." Jabbing a finger right up to my face, she seethed at me, "If you don't make this remotely right, I will castrate you and make sure your dick can never be used again because you don't deserve it."

With a sympathetic pat to my chest, Sebastian let go of me and Ares, who had been on my other side. "Good luck, *compadre*." Sebastian sighed before stepping away and leaving with Leah.

Then, much to my surprise, something stupid didn't come out of Ares's mouth for once. "Don't make the same mistake I did. Go after her, fucking grovel like your life depends on it because it does. The last thing you want to do is to leave things tense between you two like this." His eyes looked out into the distance with a sad smile on his face. "In our line of work, each day could be our last. Don't leave this memory of yours to be the last she remembers, and you sure as hell don't want this to be the last memory of hers flashing through your mind before Death greets you."

For once in a long time, Ares sounded hurt and broken, more so than me with his heavy and forlorn voice. I couldn't help but wonder if that was the future I was looking at if I didn't make things right with Juliet.

A life of booze and parties didn't sound bad in hindsight, but it would all only be something to distract me from the truth and numb me to reality. I would be miserable living the life Ares was currently living. Hell, I was miserable with my life before Juliet came along and brightened it up with her sunny giggles and smiles.

"For both of your sakes, I really hope she forgives you at the very least... but I really hope you two can patch things up because love like that only comes once in a lifetime." Offering one last smile, he patted my shoulder and squeezed it. "Don't let her go. Fight for her until you cease to exist."

"Ares is right, for once." Aidan agreed with a dry chuckle and a sad smile. "You fucked up, but the damage isn't irreparable from the looks of it. Or, at least, you won't know until you've tried."

But if I tried and she still rejected me, or worse, refused to forgive me, I don't know if I could handle all of that without dying. The thought of Juliet being forever resentful of me or not having her as my girl physically ached my heart, and the more I thought about it, the more I could see myself becoming a shell of myself to pass by each day.

"Can you two do me a favor?"

"Depends on how illegal the favor is." Ares's madman grin stretched at his lips as his eyes set ablaze.

Crossing his arms, Aidan tilted his head slightly. "We're not helping you clean up your mess with Juliet, buddy." Aidan chuckled dryly with a shake of his head.

Forcing a smile to pinch on my face, I shook my head softly. "No, it has nothing to do with Juliet. So, are you in?"

"Fuck it, how bad can it be."

Maybe passing on alcohol was a bad idea.

Whatever courage I had in my body ran away like a cowardly dog now that I stood right outside Juliet's door. The debate to turn around to the kitchen for a few shots seemed tempting, but the faint sounds of Juliet's sobbing kept my heart anchored to my spot.

God damn it, quit being a pussy. Just man up, own up to your fuck ups, and fucking beg for her forgiveness and apologize.

It shouldn't be this much of a battle to apologize to Juliet, and it wasn't my stupid 'manly' pride getting in the way. I already chucked that aside during my wallowing of self-pity in the shower a few hours ago. At this point, I was fucking scared. The chance of things not working out for us was because of me terrified and ate at me. I didn't want to lose Juliet because of this, even if it was completely my fault.

Swallowing my nerves, I leaned my head against the door and knocked. "Juliet—"

"No! Go away! I don't want to talk to you! I don't want to see you! Ever again!"

The rawness of her voice felt like claws tearing at my heart. "Juliet, please!"

"No! I hate you! I fucking hate you! You are no better than everyone else in my life!"

Okay, fuck this.

I wasn't going to have another argument through a door.

Grabbing the handle, I tried to turn it but found it locked. The reasonable thing would be to find the key and unlock it like a normal person, but I wasn't being reasonable right now with my urgency to talk to Juliet. So, I kicked the door in.

"Luciano! What the fuck! Get out!" Juliet screamed at me with her raw throat, grabbing the nearest thing to her—a fucking lamp—and hurling it at me.

Ducking out of the way, I let the lamp shatter behind me as I shut the door as best as I could.

Juliet continued to chuck things at me as I approached her, from the little trinkets on her nightstands to the pillows on her bed. I easily dodged them as I made my way to Juliet, who fully stood at the edge of her bed with her hands clenched at her sides.

An ache in my knees caused my steps to falter when I came closer and saw her state. Her face was covered in tears with strands of her hair soaked and stuck to it, her eyes red and swollen, her stuffy nose was red and runny, and her poor lips were getting dry and chapped up. Then, her shoulders slumped, her chest spasmed with her hiccups, and how pained she looked hunched over twisted the dull knife into my stomach.

Fuck. I caused all of that. I did that to her.

"I am so sorry." I croaked out as my knees gave out from under me, sending me to her feet.

Throwing my arms around her waist, I pushed her back a little, forcing her to sit on the edge of the bed. "Juliet, I am so sorry." Everything started to crack with my voice as I hugged Juliet's legs.

"I am so fucking sorry." I couldn't bear to look at her. "Just please let me apologize and explain myself. All I ask is for you to listen. If you want me to leave when I am done, then I will."

I wasn't worthy to gaze upon her anymore.

"I know I can say sorry a million, billion, infinite times, and it won't undo the hurt I have dealt you with my words said in anger." My words strangled my tight throat as my tears started to burn my eyes. "I am sorry for not being a good man to you, the man I promised I would be. God, I am so sorry for hurting you like I did. I didn't physically raise my hand at you, but my words did worse than what a strike would have done, and I am so sorry from my very soul to the bottom of my heart."

Taking a second to breathe and recollect myself, I continued to speak while keeping my head bowed and pressed against her knees. "I had to do what I needed to protect you and keep you safe the day Carol came here for the meeting. The lie slipped my tongue before my mind could catch it. I had no intention of fulfilling it at all, I swear. It was empty-headed of me not to tell you about any of it, but I never thought I would have to cross the damn bridge. I had planned on taking Carol out of business and shutting other places down to put out the fire I had created with the lie. I mean, once I took care of everything, then I wouldn't have to face the music."

Pausing for another moment of silence, I cleared my fogging mind and stroked her calves with my thumbs. "I didn't buy you from your parents or anyone. The day we went to your parents, I tricked them into signing an NDA and gave them money to ensure their silence and cooperation in my lie and for them never to contact you ever again." I wasn't a monster, even if it seemed like it at times.

Swallowing nervously, I slowly tilted my head back to look up at Juliet with terrified but sincere eyes. "Everything about us, my feelings for you, my love for you, is all real. None of it was ever fake or under the guise of leading you into some sham of a marriage." Laughing at myself pathetically, I smiled forlornly at her. "I tried to push you away and keep you at a distance for so long because you kept clouding my mind and judgment, but I couldn't help my heart from bleeding out for you."

My fingers twitched with a need to hold Juliet's precious face and wipe those tears away with kisses. "I cannot imagine my life without you in it. There is no life for me without you, Juliet." A sudden ache in my heart caused me to wince. "I swear, I will get on my knees every second of every day and grovel before you, do whatever you say and ask of me, anything and everything, and you can say and do whatever the fuck you want to me as long as it helps you move towards forgiving me. I will take it all, but..."

The memory of those four words choked my breath and spilled my tears down my face. "But please, please don't ever say that you don't love me, ever again. You can say you hate me all you want, be mad at me, punch me, slap me, kick me, burn me, I don't care. Just don't burn me with those four words, please."

Choking out a pathetic sob because my damn emotions had a mind of their own, I bowed my head again to hide my face in her knees for a moment to straighten myself out as much as possible before looking up at her again with pained eyes. "I don't want that nightmare ever to come true. I don't want to wake up to our bed empty of you. To wake up to a life without you by my side."

My next words might mean nothing to her, but I had to get them out after putting all my heart and soul into them.

"I love you, Juliet, I truly do, and that will never change. You are my *principessa*, my *amorina*."

Chapter 36

Juliet

FUCKING BASTARD!

And fuck me for being so stupid and naïve! Seriously, how could I have been so, ugh!

The temptation to punch the wall or my computer monitor gnawed at my clenched fists as I paced around my room.

Everything inside of me felt like a mess. I was extremely hurt and sad, so much so that it felt like someone caved my chest in and squeezed at my heart. Then, my own idiocy made me feel like the damn teenager everyone claimed me to be. I really couldn't believe I got played like that.

I let him in, trusted him, gave him everything, only for him to play me. Then how I believed him, the lies he fed me... When he told me he loved me. It was all a fucking lie!

I had no one but myself to blame for all this hurt because I gave him the ammo to use against me. This damn heartache, me. These tears, me. My fucked-up life, me. I let myself grow comfortable around a damn mafia man. How fucking stupid of me. I really should have known better, especially after he warned me so blatantly. I shouldn't have listened and fallen for his empty promises.

I would be a sad, sobbing mess in bed right now if I hadn't let him in.

The whole fucked up part of all this was how hypocritical he was. He said he didn't traffic humans or partook in such activities, yet he fucking *bought* me from my parents. My parents were already on my shit list, but hearing about how they sold me out way before Carol put them higher on my shitlist.

Besides the fact he stooped as low as them, I was upset at how he toyed with my emotions despite knowing the shit I went through. I was even more furious at myself for loving him back.

God, and just when I was about to let him... I couldn't fucking believe it. I was ready to give myself fully to him, which was why I got that damn gift that still sat in my bag. I don't know what I would do with it now, maybe chuck it into the ocean or a volcano.

Letting out a frustrated cry, I rubbed at my sore and puffy eyes.

I hated how all I could do was cry about everything in bed like a sad sack of shit, but I couldn't find it in myself to muster up any kind of energy to do anything. Even the thought of marching my ass back down to the office to sock Luciano in the face again was losing its appeal. All I wanted to do was rest my tired eyes and sleep the rest of my life away.

Yeah, sleep sounded nice right now.

Unfortunately, that plan went out the window at the sound of knocking on my door. Whatever dying energy I had flared back up into full-blown madness at the sound of Luciano's voice from the other side of the door. And silly me for thinking Luciano would fucking leave. Damn bastard kicked my damn door in. Seriously, what was his problem with breaking his property? First, the balcony doors, now my room door.

I wasn't in the mood or in the right headspace to deal with him, though.

Whatever anger bottled up within me exploded upon the sight of Luciano, and I didn't bother trying to control it. Object after object, whatever I could get my hands on, was thrown at Luciano until he stopped before me and dropped to his knees.

I wanted to tell him to fuck off and shove him off, but my words refused to leave my mouth the moment he spilled everything. As he spoke, I found myself listening when I probably shouldn't. I mean, how could I believe what lies came out of his mouth now? They didn't feel or sound like lies, and I wanted to keep my walls up.

But damn those sad eyes of his.

The moment he looked up at me with his tear-strewn face and broken eyes filled with sincerity and genuineness, I felt everything crumble around me. I might regret this, but damn my heart for going back to him after he ripped it apart.

Slap!

The pain in my own hand from slapping him again was worth it.

"I hate that I can't not love you." My calm voice shook with my angry exhale as I looked down at him with a tense face. "But that doesn't mean I fully forgive you. You are going to have to earn everything back."

Hesitantly, I threaded my fingers through his hair, gripping the back of it to force him to crane his neck to look up at me. "I want proof. I want proof that what happened with my parents isn't true. I want you to prove every damn second of every fucking day that the feelings you claim for me are true. Prove to me with your actions and words that you cannot live without me."

Out of pure resentment, I tightened my grip on his hair until he visibly winced. Then, slowly, I leaned down until a mere inch separated us. "And if you want to put your ring on my finger, then you will spoil me with the blood of my enemies. Until all the bodies of the bastards who raped me are beaten and bloodied at my feet, where my face will be the last thing they see before Hell, don't even think about proposing to me until then."

"Consider it done. I will do anything." I shouldn't be finding any satisfaction in how desperate and miserable he sounded, but the fact that he slipped into such a state all for me made me feel powerful.

Sweeping my tongue across my lips, I let the devious smirk present itself on my face. "And I want Carol dead. I want her to suffer, and then I want her to burn down in the cursed lounge after I throw a match at it. I want my revenge, and I want it painful and bloody."

Bringing my other hand up to his face, I slowly trailed the tip of my finger down his cheek, across his jawline to his lips, and lightly traced the seam of them. "And after all of that, you will treat me like your fucking queen for the rest of your life."

"Yes, *amorina*." His airy reply came as he leaned into my touch.

The coarseness of his beard tickled my fingers and palms as I splayed my hand under his jaw, slowly pressing into him and holding his face for a moment to admire the image of this man melting before me. Until I remembered that I was pissed at him. My grip tightened out of nowhere, my nails digging into him as I jerked his face. "And you better not pull any more dominant shit with me. We are playing by my rules until I say."

I could feel his throat bob with his hard swallow as his eyes turned wary for a split second and softened back up with defeat. "Yes, *amorina*." His voice strained with reluctance, but he still gave in.

Okay, now what?

Do I kiss him? Slap him? Kick him in the nuts with this only chance?

The fact I could probably do literally anything to him right now without possible retaliation was a scary thought because I did not like having this much power.

Freaking out internally, I pulled back and let my body do whatever felt right, which was apparently all the above.

It was as if someone took a reflex hammer to my knee with how fast and hard my leg shot out and caught Luciano right between his legs, causing his face to twist with sheer agony and groans of pain to leave his mouth. Of course, that wasn't enough because down to the ground he went with a hard slap across his poor face. But I mean, I took some mercy on him with how I hauled him back up by the front of his shirt into a very hard and angry but passionate kiss.

I will admit I kind of got out of control for a second there.

Whoops.

Apparently, I could hold a bit of a grudge.

It took me three solid days of giving everyone the silent treatment before I accepted any of their apologies. Well, it was five days until I accepted Sebastian's and Ares's because they were off in Florida and didn't really know about me to really tell me anything. Leah, Aidan, and Evie, on the other hand, took another full week before I relented; the fact they saw me quite often and didn't think to mention any of it to me pissed off and hurt me greatly. Granted, it was Luciano's fault for telling them he'd take care of it, so they kind of thought he would tell me one way or another.

Luciano and I were by no means lovey-dovey again, nor were we back to normal. It was hard to think about returning to 'normal' with him after everything. Every time I thought about letting him back in, my walls would come right back up at the thought of how he deceived and hurt me. It wasn't fair to either of us, but I still questioned his feelings even if I could see them as plain as day in his eyes.

"Juliet baby, are you sure?" Luciano asked after looking through the four photos I handed to him.

I nearly snapped at him in response, but I shut the lid on the boiling pot. "Yes. I can't ever get rid of their ugly faces from my mind." I replied flatly with a scowl.

"I'm sorry. I don't mean to doubt you, and that question kind of came out wrong." Shaking his head, Luciano's eyes softened with an apology as he held up a picture. "This man, though. You sure?" It was as if he almost didn't want to believe it himself with the hardened edge of anger in his voice.

Without a word, I nodded my head firmly before my eyebrow rose in question. "Do you have a problem with that man?"

Muttering something under his breath, Luciano slapped the pictures onto the desk and ran a hand through his hair. "Now I do." He scowled deeply as he pulled his phone out and texted someone.

Moments of tense silence later, the door to his office opened, and someone was shoved in, followed by two guards behind him who proceeded to throw him face down on the ground. "Luciano, what is—" No words came out of the man's hung mouth when he looked up from his position on the floor.

Emotionlessly, I tilted my head and spoke up in an almost empty and eerie voice, "I think you just answered that question yourself."

"I-I am so sorry, please. I didn't know you belonged to Luciano. If you did, then I wouldn't have touched you or let any of the other men touch you." Empty apologies filled with nothing but desperation to live.

"You better shut up before I have Luciano rip your jaw off and beat you to death with it." Gruesome? Yeah, but I felt nothing for the scum. I don't think I could have if I had tried my hardest. He brought this upon himself, and who knows how many people he's assaulted over the years.

It was unfortunate to think about, but I was only one of many.

"You aren't sorry. You are only sorry that you are caught. It doesn't matter if I belonged to Luciano or not. You shouldn't have done it in the first place." I sounded like a pompous ass with too much arrogance speaking down to him like some mother belittling her child, but that was the least he deserved.

"Please, spare me." The man begged pathetically as he crawled and cowered at my feet.

Scowling in disgust, I kicked him away and rounded the desk to stand next to Luciano behind the desk. A wicked idea snaked a crazed smirk on my lips as I leaned down and wrapped my arms around Luciano's shoulders and neck. "It's been a while since I've seen you go at a punching bag. Why don't you remind me how hard you can hit, babe," I suggested—more like commanded—Luciano in a saccharine voice, tracing the tip of my finger along his shoulder. "But don't kill him. Just get a quick one in, then cut his pathetic dick and balls off and let him bleed to death."

Luciano whispered with a nervous chuckle to me. "Remind me to never piss you off again." His rough hands swallowed mine briefly to pry my arms off, and his lips pressed a quick kiss to the back of my hands before he returned them to me fully after he stood up.

As Luciano approached the man, the two guards in the room each took hold of the man's arms, holding him up upright and still for Luciano. No matter how much the man begged and struggled, no one paid him any attention, nor did either of the guards let their grip on him falter.

Luciano's casual voice slowly deepened with anger while he spoke and rolled his sleeves up his forearms. "I was going to take it easy on you and put a bullet through your head after I found out about you being a mole for Marley, but that train blew up the moment my girl here gave me your photo after she identified all her assaulters." Smiling to himself, Luciano shook his head in disbelief before throwing a fast punch at the man's face, filling the office with the sounds of his nasally screams. "Then the fact that you've been working for me this whole time knowing." Another punch hit the man's face, and Luciano switched gears.

Sitting pretty behind the desk, I propped my elbows up on the flat surface and watched the man's body jerk and twitch with each hit Luciano delivered. Throughout the next few minutes, the man continued to wail and plead futilely as Luciano turned his insides to mush.

"Darling, I changed my mind a little," I spoke up just as Luciano pulled his arm back to throw another punch. "After you cut his dick off, shove it in his mouth. See how he likes having a dick forced into his mouth while he's begging for everything to stop." Not gonna lie, this want for more scared me. "I wanna see him choke to death on his pathetic thing."

This wasn't me. It didn't feel like me. Never in my life would I ever want harm to someone, let alone ask someone to do it on my behalf.

Correction: this wasn't the old me.

The person sitting here relishing the sight of her mafia boss beau beating a man to death because she commanded it was who I had become after being burned by the fire.

They shoved me into The Devil's arms, so I will embrace him back.

I have fallen to Hell, so I shall raise it with Luciano.

Those who wronged me will be nothing but ashes by the time our crusade is over.

Chapter 37
Luciano

"Juliet."

My sigh of pleasure disappeared into the steam of the shower, along with my strangled groans, as I restrained myself from grabbing her head and fucking her face.

This wasn't fair. I couldn't touch her, but she could touch me. "Juliet, please," I begged with a deep groan at the feeling of her taking my cock in deeper into her throat. "Oh fuck, this is torture." I wanted to hold her face against me so badly right now, keep myself completely bottomed out in her.

In one swift movement, she pulled off me completely with a sharp gasp. "Why the fuck am I like this? You just beat a man bloody because I said so, cut his genitals off with a dull knife, and shoved it in his mouth. I should be horrified, not horny." I wish I had a good answer for why she was so torn.

"It's just how we are in this lifestyle. Also, it probably has to do with the fact you got a part of your revenge and watched your man take care of your problems while you remained safe." We were fucked up, but I wasn't about to tell her that right now when her emotions were strung high.

Letting out a groan of frustration, Juliet slapped the shower wall behind me and stood up, running a hand through her wet hair as the showerheads continued to rain water down on us. "I... Ugh!" Scowling, she stomped the tiled floor, splashing water on both of us. "I want to let you back in so badly, and I hate that my heart craves you like a drug addict craves their next high. But I don't want to get hurt again." Her hands gripped her arms tightly to where the flesh of her upper arms blanched.

Pushing off the shower wall, I wrapped my arms around her from behind, tucking her into my body. "And I will never stop killing myself every day for how I wronged you. I will never stop apologizing for the rest of our lives." It really did feel like getting shot in the chest every time I looked at her and saw the somber hurt in her eyes whenever they gazed at me.

"It hurts me to not have you, but I just... I don't know, Luca, I'm just so scared." Her body trembled against me as her sniffling started.

Fuck, I made her cry again.

"Juliet." All I could do was turn her around and hold her tightly as she broke down into full-blown sobs. "I really am so fucking sorry." My voice cracked along with the pattering of the water.

In almost an automatic action, my hand rubbed along the length of her back soothingly while the two of us stood there for a long while. I forced us to get out once the water started getting cold.

"Are you sure you want to see your parents today? If you aren't in the right—"

I didn't get to finish before Juliet tersely cut me off. "I do. I want them dealt with sooner rather than later. Besides, it's just to get everything off my chest. I already hacked their accounts and drained them into the negatives." She was firm in her decision, her soft eyes hard with determination.

Leaving the dresser, she came to a stop before me at the bed's edge, wedging herself between my parted legs. "And then we have to talk, too." Her wavering tone caused a wave of worry to churn my guts.

"A good talk? Or a bad talk?" I wanted clarification to better prepare myself emotionally and mentally.

Flashing a small smile, she reached out and pinched my cheek softly. "A good talk. I'm not breaking up with you for good or anything like that." She assured me in a soft yet firm voice.

Then, I swear, my heart skipped a beat when she leaned in and pressed her sweetly soft lips against mine in a trembling kiss.

Control burned up the moment her lips touched mine in forever. My arm wrapped itself around her waist like a constrictor would with prey while my other hand grabbed the back of her head to keep her intoxicating lips against mine. I didn't want this high to end, not after going this whole time without kissing her.

This was the first time since our blowout that we have kissed. I had respected Juliet's wishes and kept a certain distance between us, and I was mindful of physical contact with her. Unless she initiated it, I didn't attempt it.

Juliet said I was her drug, well she was mine. I meant what I said about not being able to live without her. She was the breath of life to me; every morning, whenever she kissed me, or I stole her breath from her, it felt like a hit of energy. Being around her or knowing she was around motivated me to go through my work to spend more time with her. And her touch, the feeling of her body, her kisses, *her*, was otherworldly euphoria that no drug could ever come close to mimicking.

A muffled cry of protest and the feeling of something tapping my shoulder snapped me back to my senses. Reluctantly, I broke away from Juliet with a sharp inhale of air. "Please, let me kiss you again." Call me a love-sick fool, whipped, desperate, I don't care. I'd stoop to any level as long as I could get another taste of her lip.

"Only one—" I didn't let her finish because of my eagerness. A muffled squeal and giggle vibrated against my mouth as I forced my way into Juliet's mouth, wanting to get every inch of her again on my tongue. "Luthca sthoph." She protested while trying to pull herself away.

Yielding to her request somewhat bitterly, I pulled away again, this time frowning a bit at her. I tried to go in for another kiss when she opened her mouth, but she was smarter and faster this time. Instead of her lips, I was met with the palm of her hand, causing my brows to furrow together as I pouted at her. "Luca, we can kiss all you want later after we have our talk. We won't leave the bed if we don't stop now."

"You make it sound like that's a bad thing." I mused against her lips before stealing another kiss, earning a smack on the shoulder and a pout from her in return.

"On any other day, maybe." Her smile seemed a little reluctant, and she sounded a little crestfallen.

Concern washed over me at her low demeanor. "Juliet, sweetheart." Taking her hands in mine, I rubbed the back of them with my thumbs. "What is wrong?" Had I done or said something without knowing? Was it my fault?

"I just... I'm trying not to get my hopes up with us right now." Her answer did nothing to soothe my growing worries. "But we'll talk about it later." I didn't like her brushing me off like this either—I didn't like being dismissed by anyone.

Juliet turned to leave, but I refused to let her walk away from this right now. It took some holding back to not violently jerk her back with my tug. "Why can't we talk about it now? It's obviously a bother to you. And what do you mean get your hopes up about us? You sound like you might put an end to our relationship." She couldn't even look me in the fucking eyes when she spoke earlier, and that really worried me.

"Because it's a lot, and I don't want to get into it before we deal with my parents." She still refused to meet my eyes as she spoke, her head turning to avoid me when I tried to maneuver my head to make eye contact. "Luca, please... It'll be the end of us if we find ourselves incompatible after tonight. I want to think and believe that you will be fine with later, but I don't want to be crushed if things go south." Sighing heavily, she wrestles her hands out of my vice grip, hugging them to her chest as she scurried away from me to the doorway.

Pressing her and arguing with her right now would do us no good. Annoyance and irritation clenched at my jaw as my lips pulled down into an aching scowl. Leaving it for later did not sit well with me, and I made my displeasure known with my brooding silence the whole trip to her parents' gaudy mansion. Seeing the damn place irked me more and pulled at the cork I had over my bottled violence.

A part of me wanted to set a bomb on the place and sit back and relax in a lawn chair right outside the gates to watch the chaos of the flames engulf the place to ashes. The other half wanted to charge in head first with my fists and beat every living being in the place six feet underground to run all this pent-up ire out before I exploded in an unhealthy way.

Once I pulled up to the front of the place, I threw the car into park and got out, rounding the vehicle to get Juliet's door for her. I was peeved at her, but that didn't mean I would treat her any less than perfect.

Taking my hand, Juliet let me help her out and take her to the front doors. "Kick the door down, I want a grand fucking entrance." With how she glared at the doors, I was surprised the thing didn't disintegrate into ashes.

This new side to Juliet unnerved me a little. Since our argument, she's changed so much, but definitely not for the better. I never thought I'd say it, but I wanted my sweet Juliet back—the one I killed with my words. This power-hungry, blood-lusting woman standing next to me right now might have been the kind of woman I imagined ruling with me, and it was the type of woman I wanted for the longest while until Juliet. She had been too soft and innocent for my world, but she was perfect in a way with how intelligent, cunning, and deadly she was in her own right.

Juliet might not be the type of person to knock a grown man down onto his ass or pull a gun out to put some bullets into him without a second thought, but she could wreck a different kind of havoc with her hacking and technical knack. She never made any kill shots with her drones, but she was willing to shoot at a person. Well, I don't know if she was a bad shot or wanted the person to live, but the few times I have seen her use her drones, the person always lived until me or my men swooped in. Of course, she told me it was on purpose, but the uptick and hesitation in her voice whenever she answered me made me a little suspicious.

I wanted *that* Juliet back. I wanted *my* Juliet back.

Sadly, I had no one to blame but myself.

Shoving my thoughts away, I let go of Juliet and pushed her behind me before kicking the doors in and throwing them open to make them slam against the wall.

"Mother! Father! I'm home!" Juliet's menacing shout echoed through the nearly empty mansion. "Don't you want to see your dear daughter!?"

A distressed voice cried from above the stairs, "You little! How dare you do this to us!? After all we have done!" Juliet's mother stumbled down the stairs hastily, looking worse than ever.

She already didn't look good before, but at least the twenty pounds of caked-on makeup and ridiculous hair updo made her less of an eyesore compared to now. To say she looked like an unhinged mess would be a gross understatement. Somehow, she looked like she'd lost quite a lot of body weight, gained more wrinkles, lost half her hair volume, and overall looked very shitty.

Mrs. Chau lashed out a hand to slap Juliet, but she quickly sidestepped it, pathetically letting the older woman fall to the ground. "I see you missed your botox and hair appointments." Juliet casually mentioned in a voice full of fake sympathy as she looked down at her mother. "Where's my sperm donor?"

A voice came around the corner of the hallway downstairs, following a frail-looking Arnold. "Juliet, oh sweetie, I knew you would come back around to us." I didn't know whether to laugh at how hopeful he sounded or puke at how fake he pretended to be.

When Mr. Chau showed no signs of stopping his path toward Juliet, I quickly placed myself between them and stopped him with a dead glare. "Juliet, please tell Mr. Agosti that I merely want to hug my dear daughter." Okay, maybe puking in his face and making him eat it sounded like a good plan, or maybe an elbow to the face to break it.

"Mr. Agosti? You mean my husband? Who you sold me to, like how you sold me to that damn brothel for your debts?" Juliet spat out with a snarling scowl, her words dripping with so much hatred that even I felt a little wary.

"J-Juliet, please, let us explain. That's not how it is. He's been lying to you." Mr. Chau tried to take a step forward, but a flinch from me stopped him dead and made his face pale with fear.

Scoffing and chuckling dryly, Juliet reached down, hauled Mrs. Chau up, and shoved her toward Mr. Chau, who didn't even bother reaching a hand out to catch his stumbling wife. "Oh? Then please entertain me with *your* lies." Juliet pressed Mr. Chau in a sardonic voice.

Like the spineless fool he was, Mr. Chau was quick to tell Juliet everything about my visit to them that day and how I made them sign the contract and lie. I wasn't phased by any of it; I had already told Juliet the full truth and showed her the contracts, both the adjusted and originals with that day's date.

"Huh." Juliet stammered out with some surprise as she looked at Mr. Chau amusingly. "I honestly thought you were gonna lie to me or some shit. Well, you still are going to feed me shit to try and get me on your good side, but that won't work." Juliet let out a whimsical sigh and smiled emptily at her parents.

Looking around the place, Juliet seemed to revel in its emptiness. "Either they were quick to repossess everything, or you had to sell off so much before that." She mused with a low chuckle as she looked back at the older couple. "You know, I want to feel sorry for you, considering you were my parents, but I just can't seem to muster anything up." She sounded a little crazed with her expressionless face.

Pathetically, Mr. Chau dropped to his knees and looked at Juliet pleadingly. "Juliet, please, just let us apologize. Give us one last chance, please." Darting his head over to his mess of a wife, he offered a shaky smile to Juliet. "Please, honey, look at your mother. Don't you feel bad about her withdrawals? Please, just give her something to help."

This poor acting started to bore me faster than I anticipated, and I almost wanted to put the man out of his misery by stomping his head in. Too bad that was a mercy he didn't deserve.

Letting out a sarcastic laugh, Juliet shook her head at Mr. Chau. "Like how you felt bad for me knowing the place you sent me to? Knowing what those disgusting pigs in there will do to me?" Calming herself down with a few deep breaths, she put on a stoic face again. "I am merely disregarding you as you did me. Whatever shit hole you find yourselves in from here on out is none of my concern. Besides, you blame me for draining your accounts and leaving you more broke than a hobo, but you had little to nothing by the time I got access to your accounts."

Sputtering in shock, "What about your brother? You're going to ruin him!" Mr. Chau argued.

Scoffing, she looked at Mr. Chau somewhat disgustingly. "What about him? He's not any better than you two. I mean, maybe if you had bothered to teach him how to be a semi-decent person, and if he was a decent person, then I would have spared him." Pulling out a phone from her pocket, she unlocked and opened up an album before sliding the phone to Mr. Chau.

"That's your 'precious golden boy' son right there, head deep in drugs and booze with girls who want his plastic credit card." With a mocking chuckle, she sighed disappointedly, "If he were a decent person, then he would be helping his poor, broke parents out in their time of need."

Breathing deeply, Juliet took my hand and squeezed it. "I have no more business here. I'm ready to burn my past to ashes."

The two of us didn't spare either of them a last look as we turned around and left through the busted doors. "Are you okay?" I asked in a low voice after I opened the car door for her.

"I don't know... Like, yes, but no..." She was exhausted, her words dragging a bit with her slumping shoulders.

Offering a sympathetic smile, I hugged her and kissed her forehead. "It is a huge step for you to completely erase the life you knew before, no matter how horrible, but you are doing it." Leaning back, I looked down at her with a proud and happy smile as I held her face with one hand. "And I am more than proud of you for becoming so strong."

It was somewhat of a sweet moment until my men interrupted, forcing me to begrudgingly remove myself from Juliet. "Mister Agosti, sir, the gas has been poured." One of them informed me.

Nodding at them, I dismissed them and turned my attention back to Juliet after pulling a lighter from my pocket. "Let's torch it and go home," I told her with an impatient smile.

"What? That eager to have me break up with you already?" Even though she was joking, I couldn't help but feel a little panicked. "Luca, I'm not gonna break up with you, so don't have a heart attack." She assured me with a laugh after she saw my face twist in fear.

A malicious grin played on her face as she took the lighter from me and lit it. Her eyes momentarily became mesmerized by the flame before she threw the lighter onto the gasoline stream, setting a fire trail that ran to the mansion and consumed it with a whoosh of heat.

Neither of us said a word while we stood there and watched for a moment and listened to the frantic screams of her ex-parents. Not a peep came from us either on the drive back, and I didn't dare speak up because I wanted Juliet to have her moment. This was a lot for her.

Whenever the subject would be brought up, she would claim to have no care about her parents. But her eyes could never lie. I always saw it, deep down, she had a small inkling left.

Well, it was gone now.

She really—quite literally—burned the bridges to her past life down.

However, I began to worry a little when we made it home, and she was still silent as she got ready for bed. I know it probably has been a long day for Juliet, from giving me the list of men who wronged her, watching me kill the man with my bare hands so cruelly and gruesomely up close like that, to the last confrontation with her ex-parents. It was more than a loaded day.

Unfortunately, a knock at my door pulled me away from my Juliet before I could bring the issue up. "Luciano, don't be going for a quickie. We leave in an hour." Sebastian's voice teased me with a chuckle from the other side of the door.

"Oh *stai zitto*. I'll be out there in a bit, just saying good night to Juliet real quick." I half shouted back at Sebastian before turning my complete attention to Juliet, who lingered by the window with a black velvet box in her hands.

"*Amorina*, I have to go out tonight." I didn't want to rush her, but whatever she wanted to tell me would either have to wait or be quick.

My eyes barely caught her hands clenching the long box tightly with her quickening breath. Standing there for a moment, it seemed as if she was deep in thought. I was about to leave her to get ready, but her sudden movement toward me kept my feet rooted.

Standing before me, she looked up at me as she licked her trembling lips. "I..." She stuttered and shut her mouth, clearing her throat. "This might be a lot to ask of you, and I thought about it for a while and tried to deny it. But... I would always round back to it, and it became clear to me after we tried to have our first night." Her fast words shook with her quickening breaths.

This started sounding a lot like a breakup, which did nothing to calm my racing heart in my tense chest. "Juliet, if you are going to end our relationship, then just save us both the torture and say it," I told her point blank, mentally scolding myself for the anger that slipped through.

Her eyes widened, and her head shook furiously. "No! I'm not breaking up with you." The resolution in her eyes assured me enough for some of my nerves to calm. "But you might break up with me." Her shoulders fell heavily as her hands reached for mine, placing the box in them.

Okay, now I was thoroughly confused. I only grew more perplexed upon opening the box. Wordlessly, I picked up the dainty leather collar with my symbol hanging off the center, and on either side of it were the words '*principessa*' and '*amorina*' etched in faint gold. "You think I am going to break up with you because of a collar?" Paint me stupid if I missed some huge point because no matter how much I racked my brain, I couldn't think of anything.

Needless to say, the next words out of her mouth made me feel like a deer in headlights, followed by the semi-truck crashing into me.

"I want you to rape me."

Chapter 38

Juliet

THE AGHAST EXPRESSION ON Luciano's face scared me, especially when he didn't respond to me calling out to him.

"Luciano." His body jerked away from my touch to his chest as if my hand was on fire.

"Juliet." Still bewildered, he let out a breathy chuckle of disbelief as he shook his head. "I am sorry, I must have misheard you. I thought you just said you wanted me to sexually assault you."

I didn't blame him for the denial and his response in general. After all, I had a hard time coming to terms with it myself until recently.

Keeping my face serious, I reached out and took the hand that held the collar. "You heard me right. It sounds so fucked up, but I want you to force yourself on me, pin me down, take me, let me fight against you all I can... It was a hard thing for me to accept until recently, but I need you to take that control away from me." Oh God, this was not going as well as I thought.

Whatever speech I had planned in my mind flew out the window at his shocked expression earlier. "I know rape fantasy isn't everyone's forte and whatnot, but I want to replace that night's memories with ones of you and me. So that whenever I think about being assaulted, all I can think about is how I wanted it, and it's with you." Frowning in discomfort, I squeezed his hand briefly. "I just want to take back that night and make it my own. I also just want to redo that night. I want to struggle, to fight like I wanted to."

Okay, maybe breaking up with Luciano didn't seem like a bad idea now, given how his face twisted with concern and uncertainty. "Juliet... are you of your sound mind and body right now? Maybe we should have this conversation tomorrow when you aren't riding on the high of what happened at your ex-parents."

"No!" I tightened my grip on him to prevent him from stepping away from me. "I thought about this long and hard, and trust me, it wasn't a decision that I came to on a whim," I assured him with a sure look.

Looking down at the collar in his palm, I lightly stroked the length of it. "On the day of our argument, I was going to give this to you and ask for what I am saying now, only maybe a little less blunt and less assaulty." I chuckled dryly with a sad smile.

"During the past weeks, being away from you gave me some time to think about our relationship fully. I really thought about what I needed and wanted to go forward with our relationship." Now, I felt like a selfish prick talking about what I needed and wanted. "I need this to fully give myself to you and be the woman you need."

Peering up at him tentatively, I smiled pleadingly. "I need you to free me by taking me for yourself. I need you to make me submit to you."

The past few weeks of freedom proved that I should not have complete control over my life, nor did I want to. Yeah, it was nice to run the show, but I got out of hand too much. Also, I didn't like not having a direction to go in and having to make a decision myself or making my own path.

Also, I hated being the authority. I liked challenging authority—well, I liked challenging Luciano. Yeah, I needed Luciano to take back control of my life, or at least as much as I was willing to give him.

"You don't have to give me an answer tonight or any time soon. I want you to have time to process and think about it all before giving me an answer.

I know it's not easy for me to get this out and ask it of you. I actually feel like a bitch for asking something like this from you." Offering him a sheepish smile, I pulled my hand back and curled his hand up around the collar. "When you have really thought about it, we can discuss it more. But for now, keep the collar. If you don't want to proceed with any of it, you can give it back to me or trash it. If not, keep it because I want you to lock it around my neck when you make me yours."

Gingerly, I grabbed the front of his shirt with trembling hands to pull him down a little so I could kiss his cheek. "I'll get your stuff ready for you." It felt a little awkward to stand around Luciano right now.

I felt so dirty and exposed from telling him all of that, but it also felt relieving with how light my chest felt now. Although, I couldn't help but worry about what Luciano thought of me. I mean, who in their right mind would ask someone to rape them?

It sounded so crude and fucked up, but it was valid—according to my therapist and the BDSM community. As long as it was done safely and correctly, rape fantasies were a good catharsis and a way for trauma victims to heal because of the aspect of control they regain with the scene.

Yes, I was asking something insane, but it didn't mean I wanted to be sexually assaulted by anyone. I wanted Luciano to force himself on me on my terms. He would do it because I wanted it. Me, it was all me.

I refuse to let those bastards ruin my first sexual experience. I know the memory and fact of it won't ever truly go away, but I *will* build something better over that pile of shit.

This is my life, and I am taking it back.

Breathing deeply, I shoved my thoughts aside and busied myself inside our closet to gather Luciano's tactical clothes. In the height of today's planned events, I had forgotten about his outing tonight.

Best girlfriend in the world, am I right?

It probably would have been best to leave our conversation for tomorrow so his mind would be clear for the mission, but I had to get it off my chest. I know it was selfish of me, but if I stewed on it any longer, then I might have exploded or locked it away and damaged my relationship with Luciano further—possibly to the point of no return.

Seeing Luciano how I left him made the guilt of laying it all on him deepen with each step I took toward him. "I'll leave you to get ready." I couldn't bring myself to look at him as I set the clothes on the dresser.

Then, like a beaten puppy, I dragged my feet towards the door, only to be stopped when my hand turned the doorknob. My body spun around in a dizzying movement, and strong arms crushed me in an embrace. "I promise we will talk about this first thing tomorrow morning." He promised with a kiss to my temple.

Unable to help it, I cracked a smile with my dry chuckle and hugged him back. "Come back to me alive and in one piece." It was the most I could demand of him out there. Telling him to stay safe and unharmed would be something impossible, given the nature of the activity. It wouldn't be fair of me to tell him to be safe and unharmed or demand that he stop doing what he needed to do.

"Always, *amorina*, always." His chest rumbled with his heartwarming chuckle. "Can't let any other man have a chance at you. Otherwise, I would have to disturb my peaceful rest to dig my way out of my own grave." He joked with a laugh, making me laugh as well.

"You are so possessive," I remarked with a roll of my eyes as I pulled away.

Before I could fully remove myself, Luciano grabbed my face, making me gasp when I caught sight of his burning eyes as they closed in on me. Words jumbled in my mouth, muffled by his lips and tongue invading my intimate space in a breathtaking kiss. "I am only possessive of you, *amorina*, because you are mine." He growled against my trembling lips. "And were you really going to leave without giving me my good luck kiss?"

My mouth opened, but no words came out because I was too busy melting under his possessive and dominating gaze and grin. No matter how much I tried to recollect myself to say something, I couldn't because my brain decided to remain in Luciano Land instead. So, all I could do was stare at him like a love-struck idiot.

Sucking in a sharp breath, he strained out a groan. "*Amorina*, stop looking at me like that." His lips lingered dangerously close to mine, letting his hot breath wash over me.

"L-like w-what?" I wasn't aware of my facial expressions right now. Did I look stupid?

Inhaling deeply, he slid his thumb across my jaw and pressed it against my bottom lip. "With those fuck me eyes."

Oh! Oh shit.

Shuddering and gasping softly, my hands desperately clung to the front of his shirt to keep myself up when my knees went weak. "I... I need to leave be—"

"No." He tersely cut me off, slipping his hand down around my neck and using the leverage to drag me to the end of the bed. "Strip." He commanded in an unwavering voice after sitting me on the edge of the bed.

"Y-yes, sir." I shouldn't encourage him by giving in to his whims, but fuck me because I was in too deep and didn't want to climb out.

Also, my hands started acting on their own accord to his words, so I already had my shirt off when my mind decided to listen. But as I reached behind to unclasp my bra, Luciano grabbed my wrist, making me look at him with a frown and scrunched eyes. "Safe-word?" And there was my gentleman.

The tension in my face eased with my smile. "Tap out, and if I can't talk, tap you repeatedly."

Upon hearing my answer, he nodded before releasing my wrist and letting me continue. Turning around, he lifted his gaze to my reflection in the dresser mirror across the room from us. "That's it, baby, spread those pretty legs for me, let me see that lovely cunt of mine." He spoke in between his own stripping, not turning to give me an ounce of attention as his eyes remained fixed on the mirror.

Pouting a frown, I glared at him softly as I kicked my panties off before bringing my feet up onto the edge of the bed, spreading myself wide for him with a flushed face. "It's not yours." I retorted as my head slowly turned away so I wasn't looking at my own lewd reflection.

"Yet." Unfortunately, his arrogant smile didn't go unnoticed by my eyes. "Now touch yourself, spread those lips for me, and show me how wet and needy you are." He commanded, his smile widening to where he almost grinned.

Defiantly, I turned my head completely off to the side to hide the blushing embarrassment on my face. "Hmp."

"*Principessa*," his voice deepened with a playful warning as the corners of his lips curled deviously, "If I have to get my hands dirty with spanking your cunt then you are going to be up until I return *hours* later." Flashing me with a cruel grin worthy of his moniker, he teased me with a dark voice full of playfulness. "The boys have been wanting to hang out. So, I think I might grab that drink with them after our success tonight, hit up the clubs, see how business is doing, and have some fun." Dragging out a mocking sigh, he tilted his head slightly. "All while my poor Juliet is waiting and wanting for some relief at home."

Fuming, I instantly turned my head back and glared at his back as if my eyes were lasers and holes would bore through him any second. "You so much as look at another girl, and I will lock you out of your whole property."

Forget a bed of roses. Have fun sleeping on the pavement, jerk.

Apparently, he thought I was funny by how he threw his head back with a soft laugh. "Then you won't like what happens when I have to break into my own house again." His body turned around in one smooth movement, striding towards me so effortlessly like some goddamn model on stage as he buckled his pants together.

His body towered over me as he stood between my open legs. Then, like a predator studying its prey, he looked over every inch of me with eyes so full of burning desire that I could feel my own body heat up in response.

In a flash, his hand shot out and grabbed my face, forcing me to lean up awkwardly because of my position. "I was nice to you before and held back for your sake. But now that I know your limits, you better watch out." He warned me with a dark smirk as he hovered inches above me. "Now, either you be a good girl and obey while I finish, or I will tie you up to the bed and strap a vibrator to you and leave it for however long I decide to be out."

Zipping my mouth shut, I averted my eyes from him and moved a hand down to spread my puffy lips for him to see my glistening slit. "Good girl." He purred, making me shiver with delight.

As much as I wanted to challenge him and make his life hard, I didn't want to be stuck to the damn bed for hours being stimulated. Knowing Luciano, he would purposely stay out a little extra to drag his point on.

Letting go, he went back to the dresser, keeping a watch on me with the mirror. "Get your juices on your fingers and slide two of them in." He didn't miss a beat with his smooth command, even as he was busy fixing the straps of his holster snug on his black-clad body.

God, this was so embarrassing. I barely touched myself in private, yet he made me do it for him to watch. Damn prick.

Chewing my bottom lip, I dragged things out by rubbing myself fully to spread my juices. I needed a moment to force my nerves down. Also, I hoped that maybe if I played stubborn and stupid, then he'd finish and leave.

Luciano's sweetened words melted my anxiety away completely. "Juliet, it's okay, sweetheart. You can do it for me like the good girl you are." A glimpse of his warm and proud smile was what really did me in, though.

Propping myself up on an elbow, I watched my own reflection and Luciano with shaky eyes as I penetrated myself with my ring and middle finger. The feeling of my tight walls being parted and stimulated with the movement of my fingers caused me to moan softly while my eyes closed on their own accord. "Eyes on me, sweetheart. I want you to watch me and yourself while you pleasure yourself." Luciano's dominating voice shook me to my core, his words taking hold of my body.

Like a puppet on strings, my body obeyed his words. I couldn't bring myself to look away from the mirror because the sight of myself masturbating was kind of mesmerizing, not gonna lie. I mean, it was weird to watch myself finger myself and the faces I made in response to the pleasure. But it was like bad porn where you couldn't stop watching because it was so bad, and you just had to see how it ended.

"That's it, *principessa*, get your fingers nice and deep, get your sweet spot, and come for me. Keep your eyes on me and the mirror. I want to see how wonderful you look when you hit that height of pleasure." I might have quipped back at him if I weren't so captivated with myself and the budding pleasure numbing my ears.

I mean, I did not look wonderful. I looked like I needed to sneeze or smelled something disgusting. Seriously, how did he find this hot? Luciano's made numerous comments about how fucking beautiful I looked when I orgasm, and I honestly don't understand it one bit now that I was seeing it for myself. But hey, beauty in the eye of the beholder...? Not like I could control my face when I orgasmed, so whether he liked it or not, he either had to get used to it or learn to look away.

"Eyes up." I didn't even realize my drifting gaze until my eyes recentered themselves on my reflection and Luciano's intense focus on me. "Good girl, are you close?" He asked with a smug little smirk.

"Yes." I could barely whisper out my response as I found my voice being lost in my moans.

Gripping the sheets, I pushed myself to reach the edge with a few hard thrusts, moaning deeply as the waves of pleasure filled my warm body. "Luciano." His name felt like a prayer leaving my lips so airily.

"That's it, baby, ride it out. Imagine it's my fingers stuffed inside of you." His rich voice sounded so distant but good. I kind of wanted to hear more, but I also wanted to float around a little more in my pool of pleasure.

I only came to when I felt something soft and wet press against my forehead before my fingers were forcefully removed from me, causing me to pout and whine. "Fuck." I shuddered at the sight and feeling of Luciano putting my fingers into his mouth. Those kissable lips of his wrapped so tightly around my digits as he sucked and licked them clean of my juices with a deep groan. His hot breath bathed the back of my hand as he exhaled and closed his eyes as if enjoying some delicious food.

Pulling my fingers from his mouth, he pressed my open hand against the side of his face, nuzzling it with a happy smile while his eyes looked at me adoringly. "If only I had time to dig into you." He mused with a soft chuckle, kissing the palm of my hand before releasing me to pick me up and settle me properly in our bed.

Luciano kissed the top of my head once he pulled the sheets over me. "I know you want to wait up for me, but if you get too tired, you need to sleep. I promise I will be next to you in the morning." The confidence in his promise was enough to ease my nerves.

Still, it was natural for me to worry about him, and I couldn't help it from showing through in my smile as I looked up at him. I wanted to tell him, but I couldn't bring myself to. So, I settled for kissing his hand and looking at him tenderly.

"I love you, too, *amorina*." I could see the tinge of sadness behind his smile and hear the soft disappointment cracking in his voice.

No matter how hard I tried, I could not bring myself to say those words to him since that day, even if I felt it strongly.

Chapter 39
Luciano

"YOU SHOULD HAVE BEEN more careful." Juliet chided me with a huff as she cleaned my shoulder wound. "This could have seriously hurt you. What if it hit a nerve or severed a tendon?" Usually, I found fretting annoying, but it was more than tolerable and cute coming from Juliet's worried lips.

Rolling my eyes, I reached back and grabbed her hand to stop her. "Sweetheart, it's just a shallow knife wound. I will be fine." I assured her with a strong smile.

A deep exhale dragged out of her glaring face as she stared back at me from her position at my side. "I still don't like you getting hurt." She grumbled with blushing cheeks.

Unable to help it, I pushed her against the bathroom counter and trapped her between my aching arms. Leaning down with a chuckling smirk, I trailed the tip of my nose across her cheek to her ear. "You sounding like you care makes me think you've forgiven me some."

This tense distance between us chipped at me with each passing day of the last two weeks. To see the dullness in her eyes when she would look at me, the apprehension, and what hurt the most was when I caught a glimpse of her love for me, only to have her put the walls up.

Sighing softly, Juliet lightly smacked my bare chest with the bloody rag in her hand. "Some, not fully." She remarked with a flat smile.

"I know, but some is better than none." With one hand on the counter's edge, I moved the other one to cup her face. "And with you, I will take anything." Anything to ease this distance and guilt within me—anything to move us to a better place.

Her fingers poked and prodded at my chest for a moment before she looked up at me with those round brown eyes of hers. "What would you have done if things didn't go your way? Would you have forced me to marry you? Or what would you have done?" Her breath picked up ever so slightly as her eyes grew unsure.

I opened my mouth to answer her, but nothing came out. I couldn't reply to her because I literally didn't have an answer. "I don't know." Groaning internally, I bury my face into the crook of her neck, inhaling her addictive scent to keep myself rooted. "I'll be honest, I didn't think that far because I don't plan for it to go that far. I mean, I kind of did, but it was a shaky idea at best. I thought of making up some excuse of you going to college and us reaching some other agreement."

Her back arched awkwardly as she leaned away from me and used her hands to push my head away. "Do you not want to marry me?" Now that was a loaded question, and the tone of her voice made me feel like I was fucked no matter the answer.

The nervous bob of my throat surely wouldn't have gone unnoticed by her eyes as I staled for a good answer. "W-well, uhh... It's not that simple. I mean, back then, you were still trying to figure everything out, and I had a lot I didn't want to put on you. Also, it wouldn't have been fair of me to possibly try to put something as a relationship onto you back then." And deeper and deeper my grave got—and I was digging it.

"Luciano." I snapped point blank with a glare. "Yes or no. Do you want to marry me?"

Without a millisecond of hesitation, I answered her from my heart, "Yes. I do not want to spend the rest of my life with anyone else besides you. You are the person I want to wake up to every morning and come back to every night. The only person I can ever imagine starting a family with. The only person I want to be the mother to my children." I don't know what came over me, but I couldn't stop. Words continued flowing out of my mouth like a broken dam as I held her face lovingly in my hands. "You make my life so perfect yet tear it all up at the same time. I want to be good to you, be the man you need and want, the one who won't smother you and put your flame out."

Leaning our foreheads together, I closed my eyes for a second. "But by God, I want to be a monster sometimes because you are too perfect to let go. I am so fucking obsessed with you now that if you tried to leave me, then I might just snap and lock you in the basement. I don't *ever* want to let you go."

I hated the two sides of me when it came to Juliet. The primal side that craved to dominate and consume her, and the sensible side that wanted to be good and steady. "It's such a storm inside of me whenever it comes to you. I want to hold you to keep you safe in my arms, feel your warmth against me, but at the same time, I want to tighten my arms around you and trap you against me forever." I strained against her lips with a scowl to myself.

"Oh, Luciano." The wicked yet adoring smile and glint in her eyes made my own furrow together in confusion. "Hearing how crazy I make you just... Mhmm fuck!" My groan, along with hers, echoed throughout the bathroom in response to her nails raking down my chest. "Who would have thought that the broken girl you hit with your car months ago would be your wife." She mused against my lips with a devious giggle.

"I love how crazy you are for me. I don't know how to explain the feeling, but I get such a rush when I feel wanted and desired by you. Hearing how much you need me, like how you need air, makes me feel important to you." The faint feeling of her lips ghosting over mine caused my eyes to flutter shut in anticipation. "I would have hated you so much if you did make me marry you back then or any time after, but I might have eventually gotten over it because it's not like you're a bad person, personality and look wise."

A wave of disappointment washed my eyes open from the lack of warmth bathing my face. With a frowning pout, I looked at Juliet, who had pulled away in confusion. "I hate how there is no sense or reason to all of this. I mean, yeah, how the truth came about was a nuclear bomb, but truthfully, there was no good way for any of this to come about." Her eyes dampened with a reluctant acceptance as she smiled sadly at me. "If it came out earlier, it probably would have sent me into a spiral. Now? Well, we went through the blowout. Later? Probably another petty argument."

Sighing longingly, she leaned into me, wrapping her arms around my torso and hugging me tightly. "And I also hate how I understand and agree with your decision to keep all of it from me. You shouldn't be keeping anything from me, but honestly, if things went your way, then I wouldn't know a single thing, and we'd be on our merry way." The seething in her tense words made me shiver with guilt because she was right.

Truly, I had no plans on telling her any of it and let it settle to dust once I took care of everything. It hurt me to think about it now and back then, but it would have been best for all of us if she knew nothing and remained ignorant. The unfortunate part of it all? If I had a chance to redo all of this, I would do nothing different except take care of the problem sooner to prevent Juliet from finding out.

Call me a shitty person, I didn't give a damn, but I only wanted to do what was best for Juliet, and that would have been the best.

"Well, it came out, we argued, and we've changed. We need to start moving forward." Regret at how blunted my words sounded made me wince because I didn't mean to sound like a pushy asshole.

Expecting some form of retaliation from Juliet, I braced myself for some harsh words or a slap to the face from her. Yet, nothing came but a pathetic chuckle from her. "I know we need to, and I guess I just don't want to because then that means forgiving you fully." Rubbing her face into my chest, she takes a few heavy breaths before looking up at me with a lopsided smile. "Don't think any of this means I'm not upset at you anymore because I still am. I still expect you to grovel every day for the rest of our lives."

Cracking a smile and chuckle, I leaned down and kissed the top of her head. "The rest of *our* lives? Don't say something you don't mean, sweetheart. I might just make you sign some papers and make you my wife before I take you."

Why does the thought of that get my blood pumping?

Juliet, my wife. It had a nice ring to it. I mean, Juliet Agosti sounded very nice, and maybe I played the way her name sounded during graduation too much in my mind. She really caught me off guard when she came up to me with the request to take my last name a week before her graduation. I couldn't deny her because her reasoning was pretty valid, and it wasn't as if she had any other name to take on. My agreeance wasn't out of some possessive nature to see her have my last name. It really was to grant Juliet's request of wanting to be completely cut off from her parents and old life, basically.

Now, though, after hearing it announced at her graduation and seeing the way her eyes darkened with wonder and lust just now at my words, I couldn't help but cling to it. "You would like that, wouldn't you, Mrs. Agosti?" I teased with a chuckle, running a hand through her hair.

The way her body shivered and leaned into me as her breath quickened. "S-stop that..." She squeaked after ducking her head from me. "It makes it harder to stay mad at you." She grumbled, making me laugh softly with a warm smile.

Confidence swelled up in my chest and down where it counts, something Juliet didn't let go unnoticed by how she gasped when I pressed myself into her soft thigh. "Would you still be mad at me if I made you my wife?" I teased smugly, leaning down and blowing a hot breath against her ear. "It wouldn't be nice of you to be upset at your husband right off the bat. I mean, you wouldn't want to start our marriage off on the wrong foot like that, would you?" My hands teased their way up the sides of her body to her breasts while my words worked at her psyche.

"Would you hate me if I shoved you over the desk and made you sign those papers with a gun to your back, make you accept your fate as my wife legally before I throw you onto the bed and force your legs open to consummate our marriage?" Wary eagerness filled my thumping heart from the images those playful words painted in my mind.

Anxious tension tightened my chest as I waited for her response, which surprised me when it came. With a seductive bite of her lip, she looked up at me with goading eyes full of lustful desire. "I heard angry and hate sex is the best kind, so maybe I will hate you and spite you so you can fuck me and mean it."

Holy shit.

I didn't think Juliet had this side of her, or at least, I didn't think it would come out this soon after everything. Hell, I expected and planned on things being more on the vanilla side for a long while. She had a long list of kinks, but most of it was in a gray landmine zone that we had to tiptoe through.

Swallowing the lump in my throat, I forced myself to take a step back from my alluring vixen. "Tomorrow, after a good night's sleep, we will discuss it all," I promised her with a smile and a quick kiss before picking up the discarded rag on the floor.

Having this conversation while I was still high on my adrenaline rush from my mission would do us no good. Usually, I wouldn't complain about getting a good fuck after a mission, but getting into it now with Juliet would be the worst thing for both of us.

I wanted to frown when Juliet's smiling face fell slightly after reading the room. "I'm sorry. I just... I missed you, and seeing you hurt kind of reminded me of the fact that you might not come home one night." She apologized with a half-hearted smile. "And I guess I'm just still a little confused with myself after today's events."

Pushing off the counter, she took the rag from me and went to the trash to throw it away. "I should have listened to you when you said it was too much, that I should slow things down today. I rode on the high, and now I realize everything as I'm crashing." A dry chuckle emitted from her trembling body. "You should have slapped me in the face and called me a crazy bitch. I was on such a power trip that I just..."

"Got ahead of yourself? Became some stranger to yourself?" I filled in the blanks for her with an understanding smile.

Juliet said nothing in return as she sighed and hung her head in shame.

"*Principessa*, come here." I waved her over with an open hand and a warm smile. She took a second but shuffled her way back over and snuggled into me. "We've all been there, and trust me when I tell you I've seen and experienced worse. At least you're humble enough to admit it sooner rather than later."

"Is it wrong for me to kind of like it? Being a boss ass bitch was kind of awesome." She tried so hard to hide her smile, but how her lips twitched in a struggle before giving up was amusing. "I mean, I still like it when you're in charge. Seeing you all macho mafia bossy is kinda hot." She added with a cheeky grin, her cheeks blushing up with her admission.

"I like seeing your confidence. It makes me proud to see that side of you bloom." I knew it was in there somewhere. I mean, would I have preferred if it came out in a more positive or constructive way? Yes, but nothing could be done about it now. "But maybe keep a level head and let me handle the bloody things. You stay behind the computer and wreak havoc that way."

"Deal." How fast she agreed took me by surprise. "As fun as it was to watch you tear that guy apart earlier while I sat there like a queen... I wanted to throw up so badly after the high died down." She admitted with a frown and gag, making me laugh a little.

"Don't worry, sweetheart, that's what I'm here for," I assured her with a cocky grin. "I'm already tainted, so more blood on my hands won't harm me. I will always be there to drench my hands for yours to stay clean." Such words should never exist so casually, but this was our normal now. "You want someone gone? Consider it done. All you have to do is tell me who, sit back, and relax."

Scoffing with a roll of her eyes, Juliet lightly smacked my chest and stepped away from me. "This is why you're so hard to stay mad at, you perfect jerk." She remarked, sticking her tongue out at me before picking up a clean rag from the little closet in the bathroom and chucking it at me. "Go finish up and come cuddle me."

"Whatever my *amorina* wants." I teased with a laugh, blocking another flying hand towel with my hand.

Chapter 40
Juliet

WELL, THIS IS AWKWARD.

It was simpler in my mind, but my mouth and tongue refused to work with me to get my words out. I kind of wish I had my confidence from last night, or at least the vibes we had going on. Maybe I should have pushed to talk last night when he decided for us.

"Can we not do this like some kind of business meeting?" I struggled out in a nervous voice, sliding down in my seat a bit.

His amused chuckle only aggravated me, and the temptation to snatch the stapler off his desk and throw it at him seemed fun to give in. "You didn't have to sit across from me like that." He mused, scooting back from his desk and patting his lap. "Come get comfortable." The shit-eating grin on his face made me glare at him.

Cheeky bastard.

Grumbling under my breath, I shove myself out of my seat and drag myself over to him, plopping myself down into his lap and crossing my arms. "I don't know how to start talking about this with you," I admitted begrudgingly.

Slinging an arm across my waist, he leaned back in his seat and propped an elbow up on the armrest of his chair, resting his chin on a closed fist. Pensively, he stared at me momentarily, making me more anxious about our conversation. "When you think about this fantasy, what do you usually imagine? How does the scene play out?" He was genuinely curious and serious with his question, not one bit ridiculing.

"Uhh..." Stalling, I took a profound interest in his forearm, poking and prodding at it with my fingers. "I... Well..." How did one go about telling their boyfriend how they imagined the ways he would sexually assault them? Without sounding crazy.

Gulping, I gripped his forearm to release some of the anxious energy from me. "I guess the common one that usually pops up is you getting fed up with me holding back and dragging me to our room kicking and screaming." My voice dragged out into an awkward pause as I recollected my scattered nerves. "Another would be us going to bed, and you want sex, but I don't want to, and you just take it anyway." Then, the one I dreaded somewhat. "The only other one that likes to pop up in my mind is you bringing me home one night after you've 'bought' me and take me because I'm your property now."

Okay, maybe I was a little fucked up in the head after hearing myself say all of that out loud, especially that last one. The only reason why the last fantasy appealed to me was the aspect of a do-over, as fucked up as that sounded. The others were whacked up in their own way, or at least the reasoning behind them was.

I wanted Luciano to take me and treat me like I was nothing to him. I wanted to please him by letting him use me as he saw fit and whenever he wanted. Yeah, very fucked up of me to think about, given everything I've been through. Although, the crazier part of it all was how I wanted to be independent and strong in my own right but wanted my man to force control over me. I mean, I understood the psychology and shit behind it after doing some research to see if I belonged in a mental ward, but it still felt weird.

"Do you see this being a one-off thing with us?" At least Luciano was being kind and thoughtful about this. I doubted he would ridicule me, but the fear naturally lingered.

Tapping my lip in thought, I bobbed my head around before looking at Luciano with unsure eyes. "Yes? I figured it'd be a one-and-done with us to get it out of my system and reset my psyche... But... I don't know..." The thought of doing something like this again felt so wrong yet so exciting. On the other hand, I don't even know how I'd take this first one.

Nodding with a soft hum, Luciano smiled softly at me as he moved his hand up to cup my face gently. "We'll take it one step at a time before we decide anything. Finish one scene before thinking about the next." He decided for us, much to my pleasure, because I sure as hell wasn't gonna make a decision.

"Anything absolutely off limits? Besides the list we've come up with already at the start of this relationship." His question was met with a small 'no' and a shake of my head. "And you know the scene doesn't stop unless one of us says the safe-word or gesture?"

A small 'yes' and nod of my head followed by a pensive silence before I broke it. "Are you going to be fine with me struggling against you? As in kicking, punching, slapping, biting, spitting, and scratching." I doubt I could actually hurt him unless I went for the family jewels.

Stifling a laugh, he pinched my face between his fingers and gave it a cute little shake. "You do realize I fight people my size and bigger, right?" He mused with a chuckle. "Don't worry, whatever you plan on throwing at me, go for it." He replied with a sure smile.

A calm silence fell upon us as we looked at each other thoughtfully. Then, something in Luciano's eyes changed, causing me to narrow my eyes at him. "What are you thinking of in that empty noggin of yours?" I did not like that mischievous glimmer in his eyes one bit.

"A suggestion, and you are more than free to say no to it." He started with a hopeful smile. "What do you say to a scene where I drag you out of bed, make you wear a lovely dress of my choosing, drag you down to one of the many clubs The Syndicate owns, make you sign our marriage papers before taking your ass back to our home where I will take you how I please?"

With my wary eyes still glaring softly at him, I thought about the presented scene, letting it play out in my mind. "The papers aren't real... Right? I know

I said I would marry you, but not this instant." I wanted to trust Luciano not to pull some dirty trick like that, but after what happened, I had a right to be wary.

"Yes, fake papers. Lord, you really think I'd pull one over your eyes like that? You deserve so much more than some sham like that. When we're both ready, I will get on my knees and make you cry from all the sappiness." He assured me with a chuckle and smile before pinching my cheek softly. "I have every intention of making you Mrs. Agosti officially someday, but not until you are ready."

"Then I guess I would be fine with that kind of scene." Worse comes to worse, I had our safe-word. "Well, I put it all out there, and we have added your little scene. So, whenever you are ready or want to do it, go for it." He should already know what days to avoid because of my menstrual cycle—all he had to do was go count my patches.

"I know it's on your gray area list, but just making sure, are you fine with me slapping you? I won't punch or kick you, just roughhouse you a lot and slap you a bit." He didn't sound too comfortable with the question, probably because it went against how he was as a person. Violent or not, he's never raised his hand against a woman from what he's told me—said his parents raised him better and would beat his ass if they ever found out.

Confidently, I assured him with a smile and firm nod. "Yes, I trust you to not truly harm me." He wasn't going to beat me or anything. There was a limit, and he knew it.

Shifting and turning around to straddle his lap, I reached up and nestled his face into my hands. "Are you fine with this, though? Your feelings and thoughts matter just as much as mine." It wasn't a take-and-take relationship, Dom and sub or not. The Dom's comfort and feelings should be taken into account just as much as the sub's from what I've learned.

"In theory, yes. When I think about acting it all out, I am fine with it, but performing it in real life can only be answered in the moment." Looks like we were in the same boat then—good.

Leaning up, I pressed my lips against him in a deep, breath-taking kiss. Then, when I broke the kiss, I locked my eyes with his.

"I love you, and I trust you."

Maybe I should have set a timeframe or given Luciano a list of dates because the anticipation was killing me.

Two fucking weeks and nothing.

Like, I get it; I wasn't supposed to see it coming and whatnot, but come on!

I guess I could cut him some slack, though. Luciano has been busy with the others, basically raiding the city nearly every other night. As much as I wanted him to throw me down and dick me down good, control over the city took precedence. After all, no city meant no business for The Syndicate, which meant the streets for Luciano and me. Well, maybe not the streets because Luciano had billions stashed away. If somehow he lost all his money, I could always hack some stupid sap and drain them for all they got.

Bored out of my mind, I marched myself over to the couch in my office slash gaming room and plopped down face-first with a grunt. Displeased and irritated, I grabbed a throw pillow, shoved my face into it, and let out a muffled groaning scream of sorts into it.

As I pondered what to do next to pass my boredom, my phone buzzed to life.

> Get dressed.

> I'm taking you out for dinner tonight.

> I set out some outfits in the closet, so pick one of them.

If you think about wearing something outside of what I set out without my permission, then you better be ready to cry tonight while I'm turning that sweet ass of yours cherry red.

I'll be home in about an hour, so you have til then.

And before you ask later, yes you have to wear EVERY-THING I set out.

The only thing you get to decide is which of the outfits I set out, but everything else is non-negotiable.

"Ugh." Tossing my phone onto the coffee table, I starfished on the couch for another few minutes before dragging my ass out of my little happy haven.

I wasn't complaining or being an ungrateful brat about Luciano taking me out; that wasn't the reason for my sluggishness. It was one of those moments where I was comfortable at home and didn't really want to leave. Motivation quickly filled me when I saw the outfits Luciano hung up in our closet.

The outfits ranged from dresses to pantsuits, all being really fancy. So, wherever he planned to take me was high class, like you need to be known and rich as fuck high class. Usually, fancy restaurants weren't my jam, but the occasional date at one where Luciano spoiled me was greatly appreciated. I liked being treated like a spoiled little princess by him.

After going through what he set out, I settled on a floor-length silk dress with a flowy skirt and slit up one side that was deep wine-red in color. I wasn't too thrilled about the skimpy thong he set out, but whatever.

As I finished with my makeup, Luciano walked in with a satisfied smile the second his eyes landed on my body. "Good girl, you listened." The proudness in his voice made me smile and blush in the mirror as I fixed the strapless, sweetheart neckline of the dress.

Turning around, I watched his approaching figure with eager eyes. "Welcome home, how was work?" I greeted him with a grin and kiss on the cheek.

"Surprisingly good. Clients have been more than compliant since we started our little crusade through the streets." Luciano replied, flashing me a quick smile and kissing the top of my head.

"Give me a moment to wash up and change, then we'll head out." Whatever excitement I had turned wary at the dip in his voice. Not even the smile on his face could settle my nerves because something about the hollowness of it threw me off.

And I should have listened to my gut when it told me to cancel dinner. If I had, then I wouldn't be here in an office at one of The Syndicate-owned clubs with a gun to my back.

Now, don't get me wrong, dinner was amazing, besides the fact I was anxious the whole time. The food was amazing, obviously, and Luciano was such a delightful gentleman. But that's where it all ended. The moment we left the restaurant, he shoved me into the car and dragged me here to the club. I wasn't thrilled to be in such a place, but he said he had some business to handle.

Unfortunately, the business was me. Particularly the wedding business.

"Luciano, you can't be serious. We talked about this already, and I'm not—" All I could get out was a sharp gasp from the feeling of his gun digging deeper into my lower back as he pressed himself closer to me.

"You are, and you will marry me tonight." His voice rasped against my ear, sending shivers down my spine. "Sign the papers, Juliet. Don't make this harder for yourself." His cruel voice pleaded with me as he slid the gun across my back, around to my front side, and right between my legs after sneaking it under the slit of my dress.

"Luciano, this isn't funny." I placed my hands against his chest after twisting my upper body back a little.

Shoving his big chest at me, my upper body jars forward over the desk while my hips bump into the edge of it. "Who said this was supposed to be funny?" There was no playfulness in his voice as he grabbed the pen and forced it into my hand before resting his hand on the desk again. "Sign, or my gun will have a new holster." As if to push his idea across, he pressed and rubbed the length of his gun against my aching slit, making me gasp and flinch.

"You wouldn't—" Once again, I was cut off by my own gasping when I felt the chilly barrel of the gun slide against my bare cunt after he slipped it under my thong.

"Or is that what you want because you're so desperate to have anything fill you right now?" His hot breath hitting my ear sent another hot wave of excitement crashing into my body. "Don't think I haven't noticed you over the past weeks. Always getting all up on me whenever I was around, rubbing yourself over me like some desperate whore."

I reacted to his words before my brain could stop me. Whirling around, I lashed my hand out to slap him across the face, but he grabbed my wrist right before impact. Before I could make a remark, Luciano forcefully turned me back around and pressed my upper body flat against the surface of the cold glass top of the desk. "You asshole! Let me go!" Kicking my feet back, I tried to get him, but he held firm for a second before slamming his body into mine to jerk me to a stop. "If you think I'm going to agree to be your wife after everything, then you're fucking delusional." I seethed, doing my best to glare back at him.

A strain pulled my neck from him yanking my head back by my hair. "Well, you have no choice in this matter. Either you sign it and make it easy for yourself, or I force your hand, and things will be really rough for you." He warned me in a deep voice while pressing the gun harder against me.

"Y-you wouldn't dare." I let out a trembling gasp at the feeling of pressure at my entrance. "That thing's not loaded, is it?" I mean, he wouldn't put a loaded gun against my vagina, would he?

Chuckling darkly, he bit my ear hard, making me whimper and flinch. "Sweetheart, why on earth would I carry an unloaded gun?" My attention barely went to his words because I was more focused on the pressure at my entrance.

Is he really going to fuck me with a gun?

My legs threatened to buckle under me when he pressed the end of the gun harder against me to where I feared the slightest movement would cause it to slip into me. "But, you wouldn't actually do it... Right?" Right!? I mean, we talked about how I would be fine with being fucked by objects and toys and such, within reason. A gun definitely didn't fall into the gray or white zone... I think.

"Do you really want to test that?" He challenged with a nudge and cruel chuckle.

Not wanting to risk having a gun shoved up my cunt, I frantically snatched the pen up and signed my life away. I feared the glass would shatter from how hard I slammed the pen down when I was done. "There. Happy? Now take the gun away and let me go—ah!" The sudden blood rushing to my head from having my body hauled over Luciano's shoulder quickly shut me up for a moment. "Asshole! Put me down!" My fists pounded against his back in protest while I flailed my legs to try and kick his front side.

The struggle didn't last long. I ceased the moment he delivered a few hard smacks to my ass and warned me to behave, or he'd have me between his legs on the car ride home. Things were good until I tried to make a run for freedom the moment we got home. Unfortunately, I didn't get far because Luciano was much faster than I anticipated.

With my hair bunched up in his fist, he dragged me into the house behind him. "Ow! Stop! Let me go! You're hurting me!" Okay, it wasn't *that* bad, but I wanted to complain.

Glaring back at me in warning, he pushed me onto my knees and dragged me before him. "Shut your mouth before I do it for you." His deep voice sounded so loud coming down on me, and he looked more menacing from down on the ground.

Letting out an angry outcry, I slammed my fist against his thigh repeatedly. "Then let me go, and I'll shut up. Better yet, let me go and go rip those papers up, you psycho." I seethed up at him with a heavy scowl.

His lips softened and curled into a sardonic smile as he leaned down close to my face. "No." He flatly replied, his smile widening to a grin as he stood up straight again.

"Fuck you!" Pulling my arm back, I aimed a punch at his abdomen, only to have Luciano easily block it.

Unhappy with my actions, evident by the annoyed scowl on his face, he reached behind him and pulled his gun back out. Somewhat firmly, he pressed the end into my cheek, making my breath hitch with panic. "Luciano, this isn't funny anymore." Were we still in a scene? He wouldn't be this brazen or crazy otherwise, right? Or did he finally snap?

"You will be fucking me in a bit." Pressing the flat side of the barrel against my cheek, he slid it across and held it up for me to see the typically glistening metal barrel dulled out by my dried-up juices. "You're going to coat my cock like you did this gun."

Instinct and adrenaline kicked in fully when I felt his hold on my hair slacken. Holding my breath, I knocked the gun away with a whack of my hand and threw myself at his knees, hooking my arms around the back of it to buckle them, causing his heavy body to topple over to the ground. The instant I heard his ass hit the ground, I scrambled to my feet, booking it for the front door, only to be stopped by a bullet embedding itself into the slab of wood a few feet from me.

Holy fucking shit! That thing was loaded!? Oh my God!

I hoped to dear God he pulled out a different gun to shoot with and not the one he almost jammed up my vagina!

Sharply turning on my heel, I flew up the stairs and down the hallway, filling the hollow air with the sounds of heels clicking and heavy pants. The tense air shattered with the booming of another gunshot, followed by my shriek at the splinting wood from the impact of the bullet just a few inches from my feet.

Okay, he had to be fucking around with me. I mean, there was no way he would miss such easy shots. Unless he was being a sadistic fuck and wanted to torment me before doing the worst to me, which was a high possibility.

Then, like a damn cheesy horror movie, my ankle twists, making me trip over myself. "Motherfucker!" I hissed in pain at the burning throb in my ankle as I forced myself back up to my feet.

Pushing myself to spur forward, I haphazardly kicked my heels off as I struggled down the hallway to one of the open rooms. Given my luck, the room I happened to duck into was our room. Yeah, smart move on my end.

My hands instinctively went for the door to slam it shut, but I was too late.

Slam!

"Aah!"

Chapter 41

Juliet

I SWEAR MY HEART stopped with my terrified shriek when Luciano's hand slammed against the door right before it fully shut.

A firm shove from his side sent the door open and me to the ground on my ass. "Luciano, please, don't." Maybe I could appease him and get him to stop, or at the very least, delay things enough to make another escape attempt.

"You really want to start off our marriage on such a wrong foot, sweetheart?" Oh God, the starkness and bite in his voice made my skin crawl at the term of endearment that usually had my heart purring with pleasure.

Kicking the door shut, Luciano kept his sharp eyes locked on me as he reached back and locked the door. Meanwhile, I was frantically scooting backward towards the balcony doors. I didn't get too far before stopping because of the sight of a gun barrel pointing right at me.

"I would really think twice about that plan, baby." He spoke in a calculated voice in tune with his slow and steady steps toward me.

Frozen in fear, all I could do was watch him with bated breath as he approached me, coming to a stop a mere inch from my terrified form. "On your knees." He commanded with a flick of his gun.

Not wanting to test his limits, I quickly fumbled onto my hands and knees before him. "Luciano, please, you're scaring me." I seriously wanted to piss and shit myself right now with him looming over me with his gun.

Uneven breaths tightened my anxious chest as I watched him carefully shed his suit jacket, discarding it randomly somewhere in the room—I was too focused on his damn gun to follow the jacket.

The sound of clicking caused me to flinch, and a small scream squeaked out of me at the feeling of him gripping the back of my hair. With some force, Luciano dragged me over to our bed, where he very unceremoniously grabbed and threw me up onto it.

"You know, I was really hoping you would pick that dress tonight." The sinister edge to his voice sent chills down my spine as I backed away on the bed. With bated breath, I watched his skillful fingers undo the buttons on his shirt in the blink of an eye before that was shrugged off effortlessly and discarded onto the floor. "It's like you knew red's my favorite color and how much I love it on your sexy little body. Pops against your skin so well, hugs your curves just right." Pausing, he looked at me and let out a feral groan.

Like lightning, his hand flashed forward and snatched my ankle, making me shriek out a sob as my body was yanked back to him. Out of sheer instinct from the rising panic, I kicked at him while my breathing picked back up. "Let me go!" The feeling of my foot catching his face sent a tidal wave of fear over me when he glared softly at me.

He was pissed, and I was royally fucked. Seeing his chest puff out should have been a clear sign for me to stop my struggle, but I was stupid. So, I kicked harder until he grabbed both my legs, spread them wide, and wedged himself between them, forcing me to keep them spread at a somewhat painful angle.

With a remark on my tongue, I opened my mouth to snap at him, but my words flew off my tongue from the sharp slap across my face. Stunned, all I could do was gasp for breath at the tightening feeling around my throat. "You better start behaving because as cute as your defiance is, it'll get real annoying, and I won't tolerate it, especially from my wife." His words pressed into the side of my face with his weight into my body.

"I don't want to be your wife! I never asked for it!" I struggled to get my airy words out while I clawed at his forearm, leaving trails of red streaks across inked-out skin.

"Yet you signed the papers." He remarked snidely with a curt laugh, catching my hand before it made contact with his face and pinning it to the mattress. "Don't make me tie you up." He threatened in a voice full of promise.

Swallowing hard, I did my best to glare at him through my teary eyes. "Because you had a gun shoved at my vagina, you bastard!" My scratchy voice squeaked out almost pathetically because of his hand choking me.

Sweet air filled my lungs the moment he released my throat, but my inhale cut short sharply from my head snapping to the side, a result of another slap from him. Shocked, my mouth hung open as I tried to formulate the words stuck in my throat. Nothing but my own gags came out because of Luciano's fingers forcing themselves down my throat.

"Don't make me shut you up with my cock." He said in a low growl as he gripped my open jaw. "The only place I want to shove myself tonight is inside that tight cunt of yours that you've been refusing me."

Taking my other wrist, he easily pinned both to the bed with one hand, leaving a free one to roam my squirming body. "No, Luciano, no, I don't... I can't. I'm not ready." Not gonna lie, the thought of him taking me scared me a little because of what happened last time.

A shocked, gasping whimper strained out of my tensing body at him shoving his hand against my throbbing core after he threw the skirt of my dress aside at the slit. "Liar, you're soaking wet." To press his point, he ripped my thong away and ran his fingers along my puffy lips a few times. "Look at this." I refused, closing my eyes when I caught movement out of my periphery.

His low voice rumbled above me as the tangy scent of my arousal hit my nostrils. "Open your eyes and look at your own mess, you slut, or I will shove my fingers into your mouth and make you taste yourself." The thought of choking on his fingers again with the added lewdness of my own juices made my eyes snap open.

Mockingly, he waved his fingers in front of my eyes. "You say you're not ready, yet look at this." Holding his fingers inches from my eyes, he let me see my glistening juices on his digits. Then, he slowly parted his fingers, making me watch the strings form between the gaps of his fingers, bridging them together. "I bet I'll slide right in no problem."

My eyes widened at his words, my head shaking in refusal as I began to struggle. "No, Luciano, can't we wait? Please? It's too late to be doing this." I pleaded desperately while trying to bring my leg up enough to push him off—to no avail, of course.

Grabbing my face, he pressed his thumb into my mouth and dragged it down my lips before kissing me hard and hungrily with a deep groan.

I don't know what came over me to do it, but I found myself biting his lip—hard. It was hard enough to where he reeled back and slapped me again as I swallowed the metallic taste in my mouth. Glancing at him, I watched as he wiped his smirking, bleeding lips with the back of his hand. "You little bitch." It was a little terrifying at how amber eyes glowed with angry excitement.

Another slap stunned me enough for his next act to go unnoticed until it was done. "I almost forgot to collar you like one." His words barely registered in my mind because I was too focused on the tight feeling around my throat. "Fuck, you look so beautiful, all collared with my mark."

"I'm not a dog! Take it off!" I wanted to rip the thing off in defiance, but my arms were bound tightly by his hand. His grip only seemed to tighten whenever I struggled to free my hands. If it weren't for the feeling of my hands going numb from my circulation cutting off, then I would have continued to struggle.

Chilly air hit my bare chest the next second, and it took me a hot minute to fully process that Luciano had pulled my dress down to expose my breasts. "Can't wait to cum all over these sweet tits of yours." The bottom of his lip tucked under his teeth with his sharp inhale as he eyed my chest eagerly.

Rough pads ghosted down my cheek and neck to my breasts, where he forcibly cupped one of them, squeezing until I whimpered out another sob. The pressure eased momentarily, and my heavy breaths filled the air for a quick second before it echoed with my short scream of pain in response to him clamping down on my nipple with his fingers. "Luciano, that hurts, please stop!" I begged between my sobs.

"If you say so." How his lips turned evil made me regret my plea, and oh boy did I regret it.

The moment he released my abused nipple, blood rushed back into it, causing even more pain that had me tearing up and nearly screaming. "Please, no more." My body ached so badly from the struggle and torment.

Soft rustles made me tear my eyes away from his face to his crotch, where his hand skillfully unbuckled his belt and undid his pants. "Luciano, please, don't!" I pleaded with fearful eyes.

No matter how much I tried to push away from him or push him away, I got nowhere with how he kept pressing himself into me while holding me firmly in place with his weight. He got annoyed enough to pull my arms down so he could lay them against my chest to press his forearm into me.

It was so hard to breathe through my panic from the weight, and I feared a full-blown attack was on the horizon until a pang of pain jarred me out of it. A scream filled my ears, and it took me a second to realize it was my own.

That painful feeling was him inside of me, filling me to the brim. It hurt so much; the burn and ache of his thick member forcing my tight walls to stretch and accommodate him was so unpleasant. "It hurts, it hurts, Luciano, please, it hurts, stop, pull out, please," I begged through my erratic breaths and tears.

Everything started to blur as the darkness threatened to pull me under. "Juliet, look at me." A faint voice demanded, forcing me to remain aware and follow the command. "Look at who is inside of you." Mindlessly, my eyes fell down to my parted legs where Luciano and I were connected so intimately.

That's right, Luciano. It's Luciano. My Luciano.

My thudding heart became calm as I breathed in the heavy scent of our bodies and his personal scent into my system. It's not those men back then, not the same dirty room. Safe, I was safe. I won't let them have this moment and ruin it like before. They weren't here to hurt me. They weren't the ones inside of me; Luciano was.

But fuck did it hurt so much.

I couldn't help the pained groan from coming out when Luciano started to move. "That's it, sweetheart, look at me. Look at your husband taking you for the first time." And fuck, he wasn't taking it easy on me either. "Feel me. Feel how good my cock is inside of you."

His body practically slammed into me with each thrust, his dick bullying its way deeper and deeper inside of my screaming body until his hips were flushed against me. "It's too much, stop, please." I felt like I'd break and split in half if he kept going. The ache of pain intensified with my orgasm that came out of nowhere when his tip hit a certain spot deep within me.

Tears spilled from the corners of my eyes as sweet rapture ravaged my body. It fucking hurt, but it hurt so good. The reason why I haven't screamed the safe-word was because there was a twisted pleasure always following closely behind the pain, making it much more bearable.

"You say stop, yet you cum all over my cock. What a little whore of a wife I've got." Luciano chuckled between his soft pants as he continued to pound into me. "So fucking tight. I'm never fucking you with a condom, ever. Never going to wear one because fucking you bare is the best feeling ever, and I get to fill your greedy cunt with my cum."

"No, don't come in me... Just stop this, please." This was all starting to feel so wrong but so right.

"No, if I stop now, then you're going to slip." Luciano's defiant words were sugarcoated in such warmth, and I caught how his eyes melted with concern for a split second before they hardened back up again with his increased pace. "I'm going to fuck you until those moments are erased from your mind. Whenever you get pulled under, you'll just be pulled to this moment."

Warm shivers washed over my body as I felt the knot in my stomach tighten back up at his words. He was right. I needed this moment to pave over the other. This was our moment—*my* moment. The shitty foundation that was laid by those bastards was demolished with each thrust from Luciano and every orgasm he brought me to.

I wanted none of them—abhorred them. Luciano was different; I wanted him to violate me and force me to my breaking point so I could break free. I never found any kind of pleasure from those animals, only pure agony and suffering. Yet, I found Heaven with Luciano despite the pain—the pain felt good and was wanted. Then, the orgasms, I gave those to Luciano; my body and heart knew before my mind did that I was safe, that I was with someone I trusted, and gave in.

Those evil men might have taken my innocence that night, but they never got my pleasure in return. This was all my choice right now: my choice of partner, and my choice of giving him everything because I trust and love him.

Through my teary eyes, I looked up at Luciano with a face filled with utmost gratitude and devotion.

No words needed to be exchanged between us as we looked deeply into each other's eyes in a mutual understanding. What got me the most was the way his eyes melted with such ardor and worship, as I was his life's purpose. God, I had this man whipped and chained on a leash, and I fucking loved it.

Luciano's hips slowed to long, sensual strokes as he leaned down and captured my lips in a hot, loving kiss. There was no rush now. Everything fell into place, so now it was time to enjoy it all.

Moaning softly, I let Luciano steal my soul away with the kiss. I was truly his now. I belonged to him because I *chose* to. I let him have me. I *allowed* him to act this way and allowed him access to me in such an intimate and vulnerable way.

Breaking the kiss, Luciano looked down at me with eyes so dark that they could almost be black. Consumed by lustful passion, he kissed me feverously, forcing his tongue into my mouth and abusing my lips with his own until they ached and swelled from all the sucking, biting, and pulling. "That's it, sweetheart, give in and let go. Show your husband how good of a whore you are for him and only him." Luciano groaned against my lips as he started to pound into me with no mercy, making the room fill up with the sounds of our bodies slapping against each other and my cries of pleasure.

"Luciano, please, it's too much, I can't... Please... Stop." Seriously, the tension in my body, especially my stomach, hurt so much. If I came this time, I would lose it completely. The thought of such a mind-shattering orgasm scared the shit out of me. Was I ready? Would I survive?

Taking his arm off my chest, he takes both my wrists in each hand and pins them above my head. "Not until I see your body break." I couldn't tell if he was serious or not with the playful but malicious edge to his eyes.

A shudder of fear moved its way down my body as I braced myself for the inevitable. As much as I wanted to hold out longer, a few more bruising thrusts from him were all it took to shatter my barriers like a wrecking ball to a glass castle.

White hot pleasure consumed my arching body, searing this otherworldly debauchery deep into my bones with every moan and scream that left my mouth from Luciano constantly throwing me off the edge whenever I climbed back up. One after another, orgasms ravaged my body until I fell into a familiar pool of pure bliss.

"Come back to me, *amorina*, come back." In a haze, I felt my head lull around until my dazed-out eyes met Luciano's face. "One more, sweetheart, give me one more."

"I'll give you all you want, Luca, anything and everything." I sounded and felt so high, which probably meant I needed to come back down to ease the crash, but I didn't want this moment to end.

"Fuck." I heard him groan, but it was hard to discern what brought it on with my head so high in the sky.

Thinking was really impossible with the hit of ecstasy that came from one final slam of Luciano's hips.

"Thank you." I barely heard myself as my vision became splotchy with spots.

The last thing I caught before I drifted off fully was Luciano's wonderful smile.

"I love you so much, Luciano."

Chapter 42

Luciano

I DIDN'T WANT TO end her high, but letting her linger in her sub-space too long wouldn't do her any good right now. It was too dangerous, not only for her but for me as well. She was too compliant for my comfort, and with her mind being higher than cloud nine, there was no way she could differentiate a limit if I accidentally hit one. I didn't want to keep a scene going if she couldn't use her safe-word.

Letting go of her wrists, I slowed my hips to a halt, keeping myself buried completely in her as I covered her face and neck in butterfly kisses. "Juliet, sweetheart, focus on my voice and come back to me." She didn't like that one bit. Her head shook with denial while her body pushed and struggled against mine.

This was going to be one hell of a crash for her, and all I could do was hold her and ease her through it all. I wish I could give her more relief than that, take away the mass anxiety I knew was coming. Juliet always became a sobbing, anxious, and clingy mess with her drops, and the severity of it depended on the high. Needless to say, she had never lost herself this much yet, so I braced myself for the worst.

The seconds dragged on to what felt like forever as I held her tightly in my arms, listening to her panting and whimpering slowly turn into hiccups and sobs. Her hands and arms that hit and pushed at me frantically grabbed and locked me in a vice grip as her crash took over.

"Hey, hey, it's okay, it's okay. I got you. I am right here, and I won't let you go." I assured her sweetly with back rubs and kisses to her face.

Carefully, with her clinging to me like a baby monkey, I got onto the bed and sat with my back against the headboard. We stayed like this for a long while, me comforting her while she went through her crash. I didn't care if I had to stay like this for a whole hour or more; as long as I provided Juliet with the safety she needed, then that was all I cared about.

When her shaking and sobbing calmed down a fair amount, I reluctantly released an arm from her to reach over to the nightstand and grab the supplies I always kept stashed there for these moments—her crashes. The top drawer of my nightstand was constantly stocked with water bottles and her favorite snacks.

"Small sips, *principessa*, small sips," I instructed her in a gentle voice as I tipped the bottle against her lips slightly. "There we go, that's it, slowly, good girl." Her head kept pressing forward for more, but I didn't want her to gulp down the water so fast and get sick from it. So, I carefully pulled away enough so she couldn't chug the thing down.

Setting the water down after she got a good amount in her, I rubbed her arms and shoulders. "You want your chocolate?" That question was met with a quick shake of her head. "One of your gummies?" Another quiet shake of her head before she buried herself into me more. "Trail mix?" A small hum of agreement followed the nodding of her head.

Digging through the drawer, I pulled out her bag of trail mix, mainly pieces of chocolates with cashews and yogurt-covered fruit bites. Like before, I slowly fed her until she turned her head away in refusal.

"I need to go to the bathroom to grab some washcloths. Will you be fine in the bed alone for a minute?" Sometimes, she liked me carrying her around, but sometimes, she was too tired to be bothered.

Dropping an arm from around my neck, she patted the bed and leaned away a bit from me. I felt bad for the way she winced when I shifted her under me and pulled out from her slowly. I was soft, but no doubt she was really sore after her first time with someone so big.

Moaning softly, Juliet pressed herself into the bed as she reached a hand down and cupped herself. "I know, I'm sorry, sweetheart." I apologized with a kiss on her forehead.

What she did next surprised me a little, and I couldn't help but sit there on my knees and marvel at the wonderful sight. I watched her slide her fingers along with her slit with bated breath, not daring to blink out of fear of missing something important. Picking up and covering her fingers with my cum that seeped out of her, she brought it up to her reddened lips and sucked them clean while keeping her sultry eyes zoned in on mine.

"Fuck." I gasped under my breath.

That was probably the hottest thing I have ever seen in my damn life.

If I weren't taking it easy on her, I would have dove right back this instant until she came undone around my cock again.

Recollecting myself with calculated breaths, I willed myself to leave my irresistible girl before I did something regretful. I felt bad for leaving her alone right now, even if it was for a few seconds. I didn't take long to dampen a few washcloths and return to Juliet, who laid there looking happier than ever with the widest smile ever. Seeing her in such a state of bliss made me want to snap a picture to keep this moment forever.

"Luciano, it's getting sticky." She whined with a pout.

Grinning like an idiot, I leaned down and kissed her softly. "I mean, I'm not complaining. The fact my cum is all inside of you and on your thighs is nice." Call me a feral idiot, but her being marked by my cum pulled at my primal heartstrings.

"Luca." She pleaded me with her eyes while pawing at my forearm weakly.

Chuckling, I relented and began to clean her up, taking my sweet time to enjoy her body. Also, I had to be careful and gentle not to hurt her any.

Done, I threw the washcloths over into the bathroom, intending to deal with it in the morning because all I wanted to do right now was hold Juliet and spoil her with affection, which was exactly what I did.

Pulling both of us under the sheets, I wrapped my arms tightly around her and held her tightly, pressing our bare bodies against each other. "I will never get enough of this plushy body of yours." I groaned happily into her hair, sliding a hand down the curve of her back to the round globe of her ass to grope it softly.

"It's your fault for making me eat." She groaned into my chest, snuggling into me more.

"This is how your body is naturally meant to be. I mean, you were a pile of big sticks for bones when I got you, and I did nothing but pad it with some meat." I remarked, kissing the top of her head.

Looking down at her, I smiled happily to myself as I stroked her hair with my other hand. "That aside, how are you? Was it too much? I didn't hurt you too much, did I?" Obviously, I held back a bit for both our sakes.

Juliet's head moved back and forth against my chest before her round almond eyes peered up at me with her giggly smile. "Perfect. I mean, you had me worried a bit with the gun and the shooting. But, the fake marriage certificate and papers were a nice touch."

"Who said they were fake?" I teased with a chuckle. "And, I mean, how else would I have gotten you to sign the papers?"

"Because it's just a scene. Besides, there's no way any of it could be legally binding, considering how you forced me to sign by shoving a gun up my vagina." She replied with a roll of her eyes, shifting to lean back and look at me fully. "And you could have just fucked me stupid then and there to get my compliance."

Twirling a lock of her hair around my finger, I looked at her with a cruel smirk. "I mean, I pay our lawyers enough to keep their mouths shut and ignore certain things."

"Luciano, I swear, you better have those papers shredded and burned to ashes." It was hard to tell if she was joking or not with the mixed glare in her eyes.

"Don't worry," I assured her with a kiss on the forehead. "Those papers will be shredded and burned to ashes."

Shame, it would have been nice to officially call her my wife.

Toning everything back to a calm and serious mood, I pressed her, "But tell me more. Let me know your thoughts and feelings about everything." It was important to debrief and decompress after such an intense scene, especially given that this was something huge for Juliet.

"I mean, I can't believe you had a loaded gun on me and that you shot at me." She grumbled, clearly displeased at the fact. "But I'm not gonna lie, the thrill and excitement of the adrenaline rush was unexpected and nice."

I didn't tell her, and I probably won't right now, but the gun was loaded with blanks.

Leaning up on her arms, Juliet pressed my arm against the bed flat open and laid her head on it like a pillow. "I liked it more than I thought, and it was so much more amazing than what I imagined." Seeing the uncontrolled smile spread on her face caused my own lips to curl happily. "I really can't explain it, this immense happiness and freedom. It's like having a breath of fresh air after being cooped up in a dank basement. And, it probably sounds weird, but I feel like I'm in control again, that my life is actually my own again."

Tears glistened in her eyes as she reached a hand out and placed it against my cheek. "You gave me a part of myself back, the part I thought died that day at the stupid *lounge*. Gave me back my firsts, let me have my firsts with someone I trust, someone I wanted." A few tears streaked down her cheeks with her blinking. "Thank you for doing this for me, for agreeing. I really can't put into words how grateful I am."

Words weren't needed with how stupid her kiss made me. The moment her lips touched and pressed harder into mine, my mind completely went blank. "I love you so much." She cried happily against me.

"Oh, *amorina*." I should be on my knees kissing her feet and thanking her for trusting and allowing me to help her act out the fantasy.

As I studied her closely, I couldn't help but frown when I noticed the slight bruising on her cheeks, hips, and inner thighs. I didn't get much of a chance to fret over her body fully; the feeling of her soft hand over mine to redirect it to her face stopped my roaming. "Darling, stop. I can see the gears turning in your head and the steam coming out of your ears." A strained chuckle left her teasing grin. "I am fine, promise. None of it hurts, not now, not then. If things got too much then I would have used the safe-word. I loved every second of what we did, and I loved everything you did to me."

My words became muffled by Juliet's mouth before they could be fully formed. "No more worrying about me. I am perfectly fine and happy." She assured me with a confident smile. "How about you? How are you feeling?" Now, it was her turn to look at me with worry.

"I don't like to admit it, but it was better than I thought. It took me a bit to get out of my own head, but once I got myself in the zone, I found myself enjoying it more than I thought I would." Yet, I couldn't help but feel a little guilty for indulging in the scene as much as I did.

Juliet looked at me with understanding eyes as she stroked the back of my hand with her thumb. "I know how you feel, and it's the same for me." She sympathized.

Peaceful silence washed over us like a calm wave as we lay there looking at each other adoring. Then, Juliet's demeanor changed with a bite of her lip as she leaned up over me, pushing me flat on the bed with a hand to my chest. "Did you enjoy it enough to possibly do it again?" She asked in a suggestive tone and seductive glimmer to her eyes.

Of all the things to come out of her mouth right now, that was probably the last thing on my list of possibilities for tonight. The curveball she threw me sent my mind for a spin, and it took me a minute to reset myself to reply to her after fully processing her question. "I might pull a knife on you next time." I half-joked with a smile of disbelief.

"Don't give me more ideas, dear husband." Juliet teased me back with a soft chuckle, pecking a kiss on my lips. "I might start to wonder if my brutish mafia husband might come back one night all bloody and high on bloodlust and demand some relief from his poor, helpless wife. And when I don't want to, maybe he gets a little forceful, the whole 'I take what I want when I want' bullshit, and cuts my clothes off with his knife, runs it against my body, holds it against me, maybe nick me a little to show he means business."

"Oh, I'm the one giving you ideas?" I shot back with a playful laugh, digging my fingers into her sides softly to tickle a few laughs out of her. "We are going to have to have another long talk about our limits again before we engage in any more role-playing and fantasies." It was obvious tonight tapped into a side neither of us was aware we had, so we had to reword our list with each other and establish new boundaries.

"That's a tomorrow problem. Right now, sleep." Juliet giggled, poking my nose.

"And maybe have your lawyer hold off on getting rid of those papers."

Chapter 43

Juliet

~2 weeks later~

"Please don't tell me you're pregnant or something." Gale half-joked with a worried chuckle.

Rolling my eyes, I scoffed and threw the wrapper of my straw at him. "No, what on earth makes you think that to be the news I'm cracking to you? I mean, I know I gained a few pounds, but come on." Unconsciously, I moved my arm over my pudgy little stomach.

It was still a little hard for me to love my curvy little body sometimes because I was so used to being skinny, and I was still self-conscious about it all. It was a strange love-and-hate relationship with my own body, right now. Yeah, I was 'average' and healthy now, filled out as I should have, and I did love the way I looked most of the time. I just didn't like the stares and whispers from people on the street or from my peers who were used to how I looked before.

"Hey, I didn't mean it like that, so don't go down that route. If I'm being honest, you look so much hotter a little curvy than you did skinny." At least I could always count on Gale and Luciano to pull me in the right direction.

"Don't let Luciano hear you say that now." I half-joked with a chuckle.

"Well, he's not here to hype you up and push away those icky thoughts of yours, so he can suck it." It was adorable how Gale tried to act a little tough with his unsure voice. "But uhh maybe don't let him know? Please?"

Laughing softly, I waved my hand at Gale. "Oh please, if he went after you, then I would divorce his ass so fast. Besides, he should know better than to mess with those close to me." The last time he was a jerk to Gale, he found his accounts locked for two days.

"Wait, so, are you two really married now? Like legally?" Gale knew about that night. Hell, he knew more about my life than he probably should, but we shared nearly everything with each other. I mean, I definitely knew way too much about his life behind closed doors than other people. I didn't get into full detail with him about the events of that night, but he got the Sparks Note version of it, basically.

"Eh? I mean, the papers are signed, but they're not filed or anything." Yeah, the papers from that one night still sat in limbo, but that's only because we were having a little too much fun with the whole husband and wife thing.

Lifting an eyebrow at me, Gale leaned back in his seat and sipped at his coffee. "Why don't you guys just file it then? I mean, you two are headed in that direction. Besides, you're not one for the grand wedding kind of shit. I mean, you barely want to throw your own birthday party every year." He had a good point.

"Well..." I started, dragging out my unsure voice and rubbing the back of my neck. "I mean, it just feels kind of rushed? Too soon? We haven't even been together for a year. Not that I plan on leaving him, but what if something happens down the line a few years from now?"

It really did feel too soon, even if things felt perfect right now. I mean, what if things fell apart after our honeymoon period? What if he got tired of me? What if he woke up one day three years down the line and decided I wasn't enough for him? Or that he was tired of me? Surely, a man like him wanted a woman, not some girl half his age who caused more trouble than good in his life.

"Hey." My body flinched at the feeling of something hitting my face. "Don't." Gale's firm voice warned me, along with his soft glare. "Don't start going down that rabbit hole. You two are perfect for each other, really." Gale assured me with a smile before balling up another piece of ripped napkin and throwing it at me. "I really hope I find someone who looks at me like how you two look at each other. The way your eyes light up at the slightest glance at each other, the uncontrollable smiles. If that's not true love, I don't know what is."

"You sound like a sappy movie." I jokingly remarked with a dry chuckle. "There's no way we look like that, especially Luciano."

"Juliet, that's what makes it true love. Men like him never show their hearts, keep a mask on, all that shit, but there's no hiding true love that comes through no matter what. That dude is wrapped around your finger, well, body in this case." Gale teased with a smirk, earning a middle finger from me. "You two are the epitome of love and relationships."

"Okay, quit sounding stupid and cheesy." I playfully scoffed with a roll of my eyes. "Let's just finish our coffee and spend some money."

"Seriously though, I say file those papers to make things official. I mean, you already took his last name." Gale commented before chugging down his drink. "And by the way, tell Luciano thank you."

My face instantly furrowed together in genuine confusion. "For?" I wasn't aware of anything, and Luciano definitely hadn't told me anything.

"The anonymous grant donation for me to attend Cornell," Gale replied with a breathy and confused chuckle of his own. "I mean, I don't want to take the hand-out, but I can't give up a chance at Cornell. So, tell him thanks."

Well, if this was true, then it would be the first time I had heard about it. "Sure, I'll tell him. But congrats, I'm really glad and happy for you. I know how much you wanted to go to Cornell and how bummed you were because of the cost, so I'm really happy for this opportunity for you. Even if it's coming from Luciano."

"He's not gonna, like, come after me in a few years and demand I work for him for helping me, is he?" Gale's nervous joke was strained out between his chuckles as he looked at me with an unsure but hopeful smile.

Smiling, I shook my head at Gale, waving my hand dismissively. "Luciano isn't like that. Contrary to what people say and what goes around the street, he is a good man. Unless you begged him for the money as a loan, he's not gonna go after you." I highly doubted this was the case because Gale wasn't the type of person to do something like that. "Besides, if he did do something like that, then he would have to go through me first, which he won't."

Honestly, Luciano was *that* bad of a man. However, he was only a bad man to bad people. Other than that, he was a good man—at least, as good as a mafia boss could be. "Oh, kinda unrelated, but what did he say to that idea about you starting up a little hacking and tracking business for pedos on the black market?"

"Surprisingly, he's cool about it and gonna help me, and Aidan is fine with Evie helping as well." Granted, there were a lot of stipulations, but they were ones I could live with. "We're still kinda setting things up, but the first stint should happen soon." One less creep out there in the world meant at least one person could sleep soundly.

"Are you fine with handling all of that, though? Not that I'm doubting you, but I just want to make sure you're fine mentally." And leave it to Gale to naturally worry about me when I couldn't find the time to do it myself. "And what about when school starts up? Are you sure you can handle a full schedule on top of that?"

"Yes, dad, I can," I replied sarcastically. "Most of it is a waiting game for someone to take the bait, unfortunately, and even after we get a bite, it still takes a little bit to trace shit. Besides, I'm not too worried about my classes this first term."

Sighing softly, Gale's eyes softened at me with concern as he looked at me for a few seconds. "Just take it easy, alright? Don't bite off more than you can chew."

Assuring him with a confident smile, I reached over and patted his forearm. "Don't worry, I will." Thankfully, I had a very good support system to help me through every step of the way now.

"Look at us two, future founder of the cure for cancer, world renown hacker who is gonna shut down the black market in New York and Florida. What a dashing pair of friends we are." I boosted with a grin and laugh.

Rolling his eyes, he sipped his drink before smiling at me half-heartedly. "Just because I'm going to be a geneticist doesn't mean finding the cure for cancer is in the cards for me. Like, it would be totally awesome if it was because that's ending a whole world of suffering." Gale was too humble sometimes, I swear.

"Gale, you got one hell of a brain up in that noggin of yours that needs to be used, and Cornell is going to pry all those juicy secrets out into the open." It was the honest truth, Gale was stupid smart, like nearly got full marks on his SATs and ACTs stupid smart. Hell, he got some stupid high mark on a mock MCAT he took a while back for shit and giggles on a bet from another person in our friend group.

"Okay, but the cure for cancer is a huge reach because it's more complex than people make it seem. I probably have a better chance of curing diabetes before cancer." Gale retorted with a soft chuckle. "But thank you for the faith in me. I promise I won't let you down, and if I get to name anything I discover or create, the first one is gonna be after you."

"As long as it's not some stupid bacteria that's annoying or some shit." I joked, flashing him a big grin.

"Oh please, you are above eukaryotes and prokaryotes." He remarked with a snort and playful chuckle. "Now, hush and finish. We got a whole mall to scour and a lot of time to burn through."

Finishing our drinks, the two of us took our time scouring every inch of the three-story mall for hours, filling every inch of our arms with bags from a majority of the stores—my bodyguards' arms were lined with bags, too. Then, after we dropped all our bags off at the car, we went for a fancy dinner because why not. It had been a while since Gale and I had a chance to hang out like this ever since the cleaning of New York went underway, so I figured I might as well enjoy it to the fullest.

"Thank you for this." Gale gave me a side hug as the two of us made our way to the car from the restaurant. "I'll make it up to you, promise."

Scoffing playfully, I playfully backhand his chest. "Hey, don't worry about it. You deserve to be spoiled. Besides, you put up with my shit, so consider this payment for that and all future occurrences." I don't know how Gale and Luciano put up with half my crap most days because I know how much of a pain in the ass I could be.

"The things we do for the people we love." There was a sadness in Gale's eyes, one that punched me in the gut.

Yeah, I held a special place in Gale's life, particularly his heart. Thankfully, he was smart enough not to try anything after I made my boundaries with him clear. Sometimes, I felt bad about being unable to reciprocate his feelings towards me, but at the end of the day, no chemistry meant no chemistry. I tried to feel something for him, but it was too forced and didn't feel right. Friendship and nothing beyond; it was unfortunate, but forcing something that wasn't there would do more harm than good.

Returning his sad smile with my own, I reached down and gave his hand a soft squeeze. "I love you, Gale, always have, always will." As a friend, a brother—the one I should have had with my own.

"I know, and I'm thankful for every day I still get to have you by my side, whether that be as a friend or something else. As long as you are in my life, that's all I ask for."

BANG!

Chapter 44

Luciano

"SHOTS WERE FIRED."

Three words I always dreaded hearing, and to hear them over the phone from one of the bodyguards assigned to Juliet almost broke me then and there. I already hated hearing it from my own men in the field, but regarding Juliet, the chill that nearly ripped my spine out was indescribable. The words following those three didn't matter to me one bit because my mind was too hung up on Juliet's well-being to take them into account.

I didn't care if Juliet wasn't the one shot. What if she got grazed or scratched and bruised up from the fall? What about her mental well-being? Seeing someone shot up close wasn't easy, especially someone close. Physically, she may be fine, but mentally? That's what I worried about.

But fuck, I don't know what I would have done if it was Juliet who had been hit. I don't think I'd be able to live with myself if Juliet got hurt because of me. She's already been through too much to be hurt now because of me. For fuck's sake, it hasn't even been a year since her ordeal at the brothel, so to add a traumatic attempt on her life on top of her healing wound wasn't something I wanted her to shoulder.

None of that should matter or bother me, though. Juliet wasn't the one hit. I just needed to worry about how to help her through this mentally.

As I barreled my way down to the private section of the hospital reserved for us, I could hear Juliet's shouting down the hallway. "No! Let me see him, please! Please! I just want to see him!" Judging by the distress in her voice, she wasn't well.

"Mrs. Agosti, please, it is very critical for the provider to operate on your friend, and they cannot do that with others in the room. We are doing the best for your friend, promise, so please, I need you to calm down so we can look you over." It wasn't a voice I recognized, but from the words being said, it was probably a nurse or some other medical worker.

As I approached the door, the guards parted to let me through to the chaos behind the closed doors. Chaos was definitely the right word to describe the scene.

Juliet was restrained by one of her bodyguards with a medical personnel in front of her with their hands held out in a supposedly calming manner—I don't know how effective it was given Juliet's escalated affect.

"Move," I commanded, politely shoving the person and bodyguard away.

Fretting over Juliet needed to wait until after I calmed her down. If she fought against me and the medical workers, then examining her would be almost impossible without some sedation—something I didn't want.

Settling a firm hand around her neck, I backed her into a corner and crowded her personal space to shut everything else around us out. "Juliet." I firmly snapped at her, making her breath hitch and her body go rigid under me. "Breathe," I commanded in a softer voice, stroking my thumb against her thrumming pulse. "You need to breathe and recollect yourself."

No words left her heaving body, the only sounds being her heavy breaths with the deep rises and falls of her chest. Giving her a moment, I stared deeply into her frantic eyes to pull her out of whatever shit show her mind was in. "I know you want to see Gale, but he is in surgery right now. The doctors can't operate if you go in there and interrupt them. There is nothing we can do right now besides wait." I wish I had more to offer her, but I didn't. I couldn't tell her Gale would be fine because I had no certainty about it, and to give her false hope would be beyond cruel.

Taking a deep breath, I leaned my head against hers. "You need to get checked out in the meantime." Sitting here biting her nails while her friend was in the operating room would do her no good.

"I'm fine." Juliet tersely spoke up with a shake of her head. "Only Gale was hit, he took the bullet, this blood isn't mine, it's his." Her words quickly became erratic with her breathing as she spoke in a single breath.

"Juliet." My hand tightened around her neck slightly. "Breathe." I waited for her breathing to even out before continuing, "We have to look you over still to make sure you don't have any other injuries or possibly got hit by some blowback or have any head injuries."

I hoped to all the high heavens that none of the blood on her came from inside her body. "We need to get you cleaned up and checked, *amorina*." It was hard to tell if she had anything with the dirt and blood on her. "I'm going to take you to the shower rooms, get you cleaned up, and a doctor will check you out." I wasn't asking for permission, merely informing her.

Thankfully, she didn't fight me when I began to drag her away, but she seemed a little out of it the whole time. Juliet didn't utter a single word or make the slightest peep of sounds as I moved her body around, undressed her, showered her, dressed her again in a hospital gown, and set her on an exam table in an exam room. As much as I didn't mind the cooperation, her zombie-like state worried me.

My concern grew with every clench of my heart as I watched the doctor examine Juliet and question her, only to receive a silent movement of her head or a shrug of her shoulders. It'd been a long while since she shut down to the point of being nonverbal, something we worked past weeks after her trauma.

"Juliet." My voice trembled with dread as I helped her out of the hospital gown and into one of the outfits she'd bought at the mall today. "Sweetheart, talk to me, please." Physically, she was in perfect health considering things, according to the doctor.

I didn't care about any of that, though. Physical wounds healed with time, but psychologically, she might never heal. "*Amorina*, please," I begged with a cracked voice as I held her face, making her look at me.

The emptiness dulling her normally bright eyes took me by surprise when her eyes slowly locked with mine. Correction: the way her empty eyes starkened with burning fury surprised me with her slow, deep, seething breaths. "Get me my laptop." She demanded in a voice as calm as a turbulent ocean.

"Juliet, that—"

Juliet pushing off the exam table caused my words to cut off with my step back. "Get. Me. My. Lap. Top." She demanded through gritted teeth, tilting her chin up at me with her scowl.

"No." I defied her with a step up to her. "You are not in the right headspace to do anything right now. I understand how you feel. Believe me, I have been there more than I can recount."

Reaching out, I gently wrapped a hand around her arm, only to have her jerk herself away. Too bad I refuse to have any of that. So, I reached out again, this time wrapping my arm around her waist, pulling her against me, and wrapping a hand around her neck again. "You are going to do something you regret later once your mind is set right. I won't let you do anything detrimental to yourself."

Nothing good would come from her ill-thought-out actions. If anything, they might make whatever the situation was worse. Or worse, Juliet might get into a dangerous situation because of her potential recklessness.

I understood her, and I truly did, which is why I refused to let her act. She wasn't experienced enough to handle things right now. Hell, even I had to force myself to step back a lot of the time when I got caught in similar situations that riled my emotions.

"If you don't get me my laptop, I swear—"

Now, it was my turn to cut her off. "No. You won't do anything because I won't give in to your demands. I am doing this for your own good, not because I am an ass." Refusing to let Juliet get a word in, I shut her up with a hard kiss before finishing my piece. "I am not saying you can't do anything, just not right now. Once you are in a better headspace where you can think straight, I will let you do what you want."

Lingering a kiss against her forehead, I shifted my hand from around her neck to the back of her head. "I have my men pulling up street cam footage and going through it to track down the car and the men who did this. So you don't have to worry about anything. I have it taken care of, promise." I informed her while stroking the back of her head. "They won't get away, and I swear, I will do whatever you want to them once we catch them."

"I want their lives gutted, their families ruined, and anyone else who is tied to them." Juliet's dark tone threatened to send shivers down my spine, especially after I caught a glance of her dead eyes.

"Let's save those decisions for after we catch the bastards who did this," I suggested strongly, bringing her into a kiss in hopes of clearing her mind a little.

Last thing I wanted was for her to be hit with a dump truck of regret after the fact. It might all sound good now because she was angry with a fire of vengeance, but Juliet wasn't a hardened criminal like me or the others. I knew for a fact she wouldn't be able to handle the consequences of her choices now if she made them.

Kissing her forehead, I scooped her into my arms and brought her back to the main area where Gale's parents had shown up. The older couple were obviously distraught as they held each other and cried. "Juliet, what happened? What happened to my baby?" Gale's mother barely held herself together as she gave Juliet a look of desperation.

"Someone shot at us from a car. A drive-by. We were heading back to the car after dinner, and the next thing I knew, I was on the ground with Gale on top of me after I heard a loud pop." Juliet hung her head in shame, shying behind me a little.

Guilt scribbled across Juliet's face as she slowly hid herself in me. "Hey, don't," I spoke softly to her with a shake of my head. "It's not your fault."

An unfortunate incident, yes, but in no way was Juliet at any fault. Gale's parents didn't seem to accuse Juliet too much, but there was no doubt that Juliet placed the blame on herself after seeing his parents. It was a typical reaction, one most of us have been guilty of in the past. This won't be an easy bump for Juliet to overcome, but she would have to.

"And before you come up with stupid excuses, just don't. What happened wasn't your fault. You didn't ask for a drive-by, nor did you ask to have Gale shot at. You were just out having a good time with your best friend, and something shitty happened." The only fault she had in this was being involved with me, but she didn't need any of that to slap her in the face right now.

After leading Juliet over to a chair and making her sit, I left briefly to gather some snacks and drinks for everyone, using the moment to remove myself from the suffocating room. Probably shitty of me to leave Juliet alone right now, even if it was for a second, but I needed to get myself straight to be of use to her.

Unfortunately, the eerie tension in the room did not improve upon my return. If anything, the air got thicker and heavier, as if we were in a humid bog. Everything turned deadly silent as we sat around waiting for news from anyone beyond the operating doors, but hours dragged onto days, it felt like.

I wasn't close to the kid but felt bad by proxy. Honestly, I could somewhat care less about the boy, but unfortunately, he meant something to Juliet. So, I had to care somewhat. Juliet would be devastated if something bad happened to him, which I didn't want—Juliet being devastated, of course.

Part of me wanted to tell her things would be alright, but my logical side knew better than to give false hope like that. So, all I could do was hold Juliet in silence while she bore holes into the double steel doors of the operating room with her worried eyes.

Hours dragged to days, it felt like, as we sat there baking in the growing tension. Relief was too brief when the double doors opened, and a crestfallen doctor walked through. "Doctor, my baby, please—"

"Let's go somewhere private." The doctor quickly cut off Gale's mother politely, gesturing to an empty exam room.

Dread and guilt sank into my chest like an anchor into an endless sea when I turned my attention to Juliet, who looked much too hopeful at the closed exam room. "Juliet, I am so sorry." I knew better after seeing this familiar scene one too many times.

I hated seeing all her faith shatter and detest fill her eyes as she looked at me like I was some villain. "What do you mean? The doctor hasn't said anything yet. He's still talking with Gale's parents." Juliet quickly threw up the wall of denial as she pulled herself away from me.

"Sweetheart, if Gale was fine, the doctor would have let us know the moment he stepped out, and he wouldn't have looked so down. He pulled Gale's parents aside to give them privacy and tell them their son is gone." I pointed the facts out to her bluntly with an apologetic smile.

Juliet's mouth dropped with her shoulders as she stared at me in disbelief. I could see her rebuttal twisting at her tongue and hardening her eyes, but nothing came out, no matter how much her mouth gasped like a suffocating fish. She really couldn't say anything after a wail came from the closed exam room.

"No... No...! No! Nonononono!" And there followed Juliet.

And once again, I was helpless to her. All I could do was hold her and offer her words of comfort and support, but I couldn't take away her pain and suffering.

Juliet seethed through her anguished sobs. "I'm gonna kill them. I'm going to fucking kill them when I get my hands on them." Deep, angry breaths heaved her body as she glared holes into the floor for a moment before looking up at me with demanding eyes. "You make them suffer as much as you plan on making my rapists suffer. Swear that to me." Her last demands were drilled into me along with her finger in my chest.

At least she didn't ask for something ridiculous, but even if she did, I'd still fulfill it. "I swear on my life, they will know Hell on earth and after death." Torture, I could definitely do it, no problem.

Slumping against me, Juliet hugged me tightly and sobbed into my chest for a good moment before recollecting herself just enough. "I want to go home after a moment with Gale." She sniffled, wiping her tears away with the back of her hands.

"Do you need me to go with you?" Honestly, I might go with her either way because the last thing I needed was to check her into the hospital for fainting or snapping.

Sad but grateful, she flashed me a smile and nod before getting up and dragging her feet over to the operating room. Staying right behind her, I watched her hesitate to open the doors the moment she settled her hands against them. For her sake, I had to let her go through with this plan of hers. Taking away her last moments with her best friend would not bode well for me unless I wanted to face Juliet's wrath.

Her slender throat clenched and bobbed with her hard swallow right before her trembling hands shoved the doors open. A gasping cry of horror stifled out of her the moment the room came into full view. "Oh my... Gale..."

Heavy steps and small sobs echoed through the chilly room as we approached the once lively boy. All the equipment had been removed from the body, and only a sheet pulled up to his pale neck remained. "Gale, I'm so sorry. You wouldn't be like this if we didn't go out today... You wouldn't be dead if you didn't know me." Her pained whispers tore at me like claws to my chest.

Lingering by the table side, she tenderly ran her hand through Gale's hair and down his cheek. "I love you, Gale, not how you might have wanted me to, but I love you." Her voice steeled with her calming breaths. "I swear, the people that did this will pay. You'll be able to watch them suffer down in Hell while you sit on your happy little cloud in Heaven." The last thing to fill the air was the faint sound of her kiss upon Gale's forehead before we silently left.

Was I happy about what transpired? No, not particularly, but to be jealous of a dead man would be a new low for me. The man was dead. No competition there. Besides, Juliet didn't love that boy in such a way; everything between them was only ever friendly or sibling-like at best.

My feelings were irrelevant to this situation because the person was dead, and secondly, it was closure for Juliet.

But that wasn't the main point; Juliet and her well-being were.

Fucking hell, what is wrong with me? Jealous of a dead teenager.

Grumbling to myself mentally, I kept a calm composure for Juliet as I led her to the car. "Do you want me to pick anything up for you on the way back?" I asked after opening the car door for Juliet.

Juliet gave me a flat smile and a shake of her head after she settled into the passenger seat. "I just want to go home and be with you, and I want you to make me forget about today."

"Whatever you want and need, *principessa*, I will provide."

Chapter 45

Juliet

HALF OF ME WANTED to continue being a sad potato in bed, and the other half wanted to get on my systems to wreak havoc to vent my turbulent emotions. The latter being somewhat productive and distracting, should be the better choice, but wallowing in the depths of shitty feelings while comfortable in bed right now felt fitting.

"*Amorina*." My heavy eyes barely managed to find Luciano's lingering figure at the foot of the bed. "Stop. I still see it written all over your face, and I know it's hard, but you need to accept that none of it is your fault." I wanted to snap at him to stop looking at me with his pitying eyes because they made me feel so frustrated.

Yes, none of it was technically my fault, but at the end of the day, if Gale hadn't been with me, then he wouldn't have been shot. Could it have been a chance drive-by? Maybe. However, I wasn't so inclined to believe that because of my connection to Luciano.

If I was supposed to be the intended victim and Gale died in my place—God, I don't know how I would live with that. The shitty fact is that bullet probably was for me. Again, I didn't want to believe in the accidental drive-by theory, given everything. Luciano was a top dog, and if people couldn't go after him, then I was the next best target to cripple him. So, the shooting made sense to me, and if I had been hit, then oh well, at least it would have been better me than Gale.

"Does it ever get any easier?" I asked Luciano numbingly, hugging the life out of the poor pillow I snatched earlier.

Somberly he sighed and shook his head as he rounded the bed and climbed in next to me. "No, and yes. It's never easy to lose someone close to you in this life because they're associated with you, but you learn to disassociate from it and grow numb to it after a while." He didn't sound too happy with the answer he gave me, but I guessed that's how it was. "I really wish I could give you a better answer, but that's how things usually are with mafia life."

Unfortunately, I couldn't help but see the truth of it all, and in the end, I had no one but myself to blame. I chose this life. Luciano didn't force me into it. Hell, he tried to steer me away from it, but I was too stubborn and in love to resist. Even now, the answer was crystal clear: leave. Yet, I couldn't because I love Luciano too much.

He may be wrapped and chained around me, but I was tightly wound around him as well—we might as well be attached to the hip by an unbreakable chain.

Sighing heavily, I replaced the pillow with Luciano, much preferring my human cuddle bear to a feather-stuffed object. "How do I get over this? I don't like feeling this icky." And wallowing around like a depressed sake of shit wouldn't do me any good, either.

"Tuck it in a box and throw it away after you finish grieving." Luciano's chest rumbled with his words, ticking my face a little because I had it pressed firmly against me. "Gale is your first loss, so take your time to let your grief run its course. But don't place any blame on yourself because, yes, again, what happened was very unfortunate, but bad shit happens in this life. If you take everything that happens upon yourself, then you'll end up dead sooner rather than later. Whether by your own hand from your own guilt or recklessness brought on by that same guilt."

Words eluded me as I lay there halfway on top of Luciano, letting his words sink into my mind. "Can we take care of Gale's funeral expenses?" It only felt fair to pay for his proceedings because of how things unfolded with his death. Also, I knew how poor his parents were, so a funeral would be a huge financial hit to them.

"Already taken care of, don't worry." He assured me with a kiss on the top of my head, his hands rubbing slow circles on my back.

"Any luck with tracking down the shooters?" I probably should have taken my mind off the situation instead of diving into it, but knowing myself, my mind wouldn't rest until my questions were answered.

Luciano's body tense with his long breath, and I could see his hesitation plastered across his face when I tilted my head up to look at him. "They'll be awaiting their execution by morning. We tracked them down, and some of the others are going with our men to smoke them out and capture them tonight."

"What if I want them skinned alive and thrown out to the ocean for the sharks to eat them alive?" I shouldn't sound so casual about the gory idea, but they deserved worse, in my opinion.

A satisfied humming chuckle warmed Luciano's body up. "Then I will make sure they stay alive and conscious throughout it all. Would be a nice date out, no? Just us out on the yacht, sipping on some wine and eating a nice lunch while we watch them scream and flail around as the sharks tear them apart and turn the water bloody." He sounded a little too fond of the idea for me to discern whether he was completely serious about making that idea a reality.

"But the smell of blood will ruin my appetite." I pouted up at him, making him laugh softly while pinching my cheek.

Now, I wondered if I was losing touch with reality because I sounded way too invested in this for my own liking.

"We'll be far enough from it all to not smell it. Besides, the scent of the ocean will drown out a lot of other scents, or we can be under the deck fucking while they're dying, drown out their screams with your moans and screams from all the orgasms I'll bring you to." His hand suggestively groped at my plush ass with his words as he looked at me wantonly.

"Luciano!" I gasped mockingly, slapping his chest softly. "What kind of lady do you take me for?" I asked in a voice full of sarcasm.

"My wife, that's who." He replied cheekily with a grin before kissing me with a chuckle.

"About that," I started after pulling away from the kiss, "I need to talk to you about that."

Luciano's eyes grew a little wary, but he covered it up well with his playfulness. "You want a divorce?" I could hear the dread trembling in his words.

Scoffing, I shook my head and chuckled. "What? No. I told you, you're stuck with me for life, so don't get your hopes up any time soon buddio." Smiling softly, I looked at him with serious eyes. "What if we filed those papers? Become legally married in the eyes of the state and have a ceremony later when I'm done with college and after you actually propose to me like the prince charming you are to me."

Shifting myself up onto him fully, I leaned up on his chest on my elbows. "I mean, I already have your last name. We live together already, sleep together, and love each other, and it's obvious neither of us will leave each other. It'll make life easier for us if we were legally married..." Seeing his blank expression made me backtrack just as fast. "We don't have to if you don't want to. I'll understand if you've changed your mind about me or don't want to jump into that boat with me."

A squeal of surprise preceded my giggle from Luciano's forceful jerk of my body upwards into his smiling lips. "You really think I'd pass up the chance to officially call you my wife?" A huge smile stretched at his lips, one I was sure he couldn't control if he wanted.

For a second, he remained quiet, marveling at me in wonder as he stroked my cheek with the back of his fingers. "I love you, now and forever. And nothing, not even time, will ever change that. The only thing that will change is how deeper my love will become for you with time. We can do whatever you want, *amorina*, legally marry now and ceremony later, ceremony now then papers later, do everything later, grand, small, just us, whatever the fuck you want. As long as you are happy with no regrets."

Yep. I am in fucking love. Complete love.

Smiling like a goof, I grabbed his face and kissed him like there was no tomorrow. "I want to officially be Missus Juliet Agosti." I giggled against his lips, grinning so happily that I thought my lips would rip.

Sitting up in the bed, Luciano shifted me in his lap, so I straddled him. "Not that I'm not happy because I'm over the fucking moon, but what brought this on all of a sudden? If you're making this decision because of something with Gale's death, then I might have to say no because I don't—"

Shutting him up with a finger to his lips, I smiled and shook my head at him. "No, it has nothing to do with Gale's death per se. I just... We were talking earlier when we got some coffee before pilfering the mall, and he mentioned something that got me thinking. And I was going to bring it up to you, though Gale's death might have sped things up a bit, but my answer hasn't changed."

Relaxing in his lap, I settled my hands against his bare chest because, of course, this hunk of mine slept shirtless. Randomly doodling on his chest with a finger, I lull myself into a warm comfort before speaking up again. "I've kind of gotten used to the thought of you being my husband. All our joking around kind of grew on me. And I like the idea of being your wife... And with Gale's death... If it were me on that operating table, I don't want to leave this world as your girlfriend or die knowing you weren't anything beyond a boyfriend." Okay, saying it all out loud made it all sound stupid, but it made sense to me, which is all that mattered... Right?

"I was going to bring it up to you before I had to submit my papers to college in a month or so... But I figured between now and then, timing doesn't really matter much in terms of making things legal or not." My voice trailed out with my little mumbling ramble as I got lost following the lines of the tattoos on his chest.

Everything came to a screeching halt when Luciano gripped my chin and tilted my head up to meet his eyes. "Would throwing the match to Champion's Lounge be a good wedding present for my lovely little bride?" He asked with a growing grin full of twisted excitement.

"Give me the present first, and then you can file it." I teased with a giggle.

Smiling, Luciano brought me into a heated kiss, sliding his hands down the sides of my body to grip at the globes of my ass, forcing me to press into his growing erection. "Isn't it a little too early to be celebrating, dear husband?" I teased, grinding down against him in slow and deliberate movements.

"It's never too early to make love to my soon-to-be official wife." Luciano gasped out between his chuckles, his hips bucking up against me.

"Touch me, please. Show me how much you love this body of mine." I whispered hotly against his lips, wrapping my arms around his neck and pulling myself right up against him. "I need to feel you, please." To sweeten my words, I pressed myself down harder against him with a soft moan. "Fill me."

"Safe-word?" He groaned softly against my lips, his eyes searching mine for any signs of hesitation.

In a confident voice and sure smile, I replied to him, "Tap out, and tap you repeatedly if I can't verbalize it."

An eager, animalistic grin took hold of his face, causing hot pools of excitement to pool at my tightening nipples and aching cunt. "Hope you aren't fond of this new outfit." His heated words washed over my face before he reached over the bed, fishing something possibly between the mattress.

Before I could ask him what he meant, I was shoved backward onto my back, making a winded grunt squeeze out of my body. Next thing I knew, the sounds of fabric ripping cut through the air along with my shudder in response to feeling something cold run against my sensitive skin. "I swear to God, Luciano, that better—holy shit!" I think I rather him have a gun than a fucking knife against me.

"Oh, don't act like this doesn't turn you on." He teased with a dark chuckle, trailing the tip of the blade up the inside of my leg right to my sex. "You're glistening wet right now." Dangerously, the knife hovered above my throbbing core.

Shaky breaths trembled at my chest as I remained deathly still, afraid the slightest movement would cause unnecessary damage to myself. "Do not—ah!" My body arched off the bed at the feeling of something penetrating me.

It wasn't the blade of the knife, thank fucking God, but the handle didn't feel all that pleasant either. "See how easily that slid in?" He teased, slowly moving the handle in and out.

In one sudden movement, he pulled it out and brought the covered handle to his lips, licking off my juices with a feral expression. Then, he leaned over me and trailed a long line from my thigh to my breast, making me shiver from the feeling of my skin being parted by the sharp blade and the sight of my nicked skin beading with spots of blood. "I should carve my name into you, mark you permanently for you and others to see who you belong to." He mused playfully while dragging the flat edge of the blade across my breast and over my nipple.

Shuddering, I looked up at him with trembling excitement as I gripped the tattered dress underneath me. "I'm at your mercy, sir." My body felt like I melted with my words of submission, making me feel vulnerable but happy.

"On your front side, sweetheart." He commanded, dipping the knife under my back and nudging me to move.

Smoothly, I flipped over onto my front side, crawling up to the foot of the bed with some convincing pressure from blade to my back. "Ass up, but keep yourself flat against the bed. I want you to look at us in the mirror, too." Shivers ran down my spine from the contrasting feeling of cold from his blade and hot from his tongue running up along my back.

"Oh fuck..." I gasped at the feeling of his tongue running along the stinging cut of his knife, shuddering when he stopped at my shoulder and assaulted the area and my neck with rough kisses and bites until it looked like I was mauled by an animal.

"I want you to watch yourself come apart on my cock. To see how much of a slut you turn into for me." His smug words were followed by a deep chuckle that caused a gasping moan of arousal to leave me involuntarily.

A sharp gasp and a flinch came from me in response to the sudden slap across my ass from his rough hand. "I said ass up." He growled softly before stabbing the knife down into the bed next to my head.

"It is!" I snarked with a pouting glare, earning a few slaps to my ass in return for my sass. "Jerk," I grumbled under my breath as I arched my back more until it felt uncomfortable.

"Keep up the attitude, and I won't let your ass go unpunished tonight." He warned with a daring look in his eyes, egging me to give him more reasons to punish me.

The smart thing would be not to give him what he wanted, but I wasn't always the brightest bulb in the shed. Also, not sassing him meant listening to him and giving him what he wanted, and I'd get no fun out of it.

So, naturally, I mocked him by repeating his words with some sass sprinkled on, promptly earning a very hard spank that nearly had me screaming. "That the best you can do? You know spanking me ain't gonna get you far."

Yeah, and there went my stupid mouth. "I've fallen harder on my ass than how you spank."

That really did it. Regret widened at my eyes when I saw the tick go off in him, turning that fire in his eyes into a blazing inferno. "You are going to regret those words sooner rather than later, you little brat." His excited words growled out of his chest as he grinned at me in the mirror.

"Fuck!" I had no warning before his fingers shoved themselves into my tight cunt, causing me to clench around his digits. "Fuck!" Whimpering, I gripped the edge of the bed as he pounded his fingers into me with no mercy.

A string of curses strained out of me from the blinding pleasure of my mind-numbing orgasm that hit me out of nowhere. The chance to bask in the glowing pleasure of it disappeared before I could consider it because of a sharp sting to my aching cunt. Squealing and gasping, I braced myself against the volley of smacks delivered to my cunt, my hips jerking instinctively to try and move away from Luciano's hand every time it came down on me. I only got a few attempts in before his hand pressed against my lower back, and one of his legs pressed down against the back of my thighs, pinning me down to the bed.

What happened next rendered me speechless. All I could do was hang my mouth open like a dying fish with my choppy gasp as Luciano's finger penetrated my—once—virgin asshole. "Would you look at that? I didn't even need to bring the lube out." He mocked me with a laugh as he slowly fucked my backdoor. "Once I'm done with that lovely cunt of yours tonight, I'm claiming this ass." There was no negotiating from the firmness in his voice, only a mere warning for me to brace myself for what was to come.

"Y-you won't fit!" I whimpered, truly afraid at the thought of his big cock going into my tight ass. "Ah!" Any stupid excuses I had floating around my brain jarred out from the sudden thrust of his cock into my cunt.

This felt so much more than that first night we fucked. For some reason, he felt deeper, almost, and bigger. Lewd sounds of his dick pumping in and out of me with our bodies slapping and the bed creaking from the force of his thrusts filled the room along with my moans. "You... There's no way you can—fuck!" I really should have shut my mouth before I dug my grave too deep. "You can't possibly go more than one round in a night." I managed to strain out between my moans.

It wasn't meant to be a challenge or an uppity statement, more of an exclamation of disbelief, but I didn't blame him for taking it as the former. "Watch me." He growled in my ear with an arrogant laugh before leaning back up and going harder at me.

Oh God, I'm fucked, literally and figuratively.

If I really wanted to egg him on, then I would have made a snide comment about him needing help from a little blue pill, which I was half tempted to do, not gonna lie, but I wasn't *that* stupid given the shock of everything.

A sob of pleasure gripped my throat as my body ached from the tension of another orgasm hitting me from his cock bullying my sensitive walls. "Luciano! Too much!" I whimpered in slight pain as my body shook from the aftershocks of my orgasm and from the overstimulation.

"You can take it." He stated, making the decision for me with his increasing pace. "You're my good little slut of a wife, so you can take it, and you will take it."

Fuck me.

But that's what I did, lay there and took it all like a greedy, depraved slut.

"That's it, good girl, keep your eyes on us." His praise cooed into my ears, forcing my wandering eyes to focus on our reflection. "Look at that beautiful face of yours. See how it twists with such pleasure from your husband's cock?"

I hated how much of an effect his words had on me. My body practically purred with delight in response to him as another orgasm slammed into me. "Only you though," I admitted in my lustful haze. "Don't want anyone but you."

Don't think I could be with anyone else if I wanted or tried. Pretty sure my damn body was conditioned to Luciano at this point after all we've been through. "God, I love you," I muttered with a dazed-out smile, moaning deeply as my stomach tightened with another orgasm. "Fuck." The room spun as my eyes rolled to the back of my head, my mouth hanging open in a silent scream of bliss as I felt my walls clamp around Luciano's pulsating cock to milk him for all he had to offer.

Pulling out with a groan, Luciano sat on his knees for a few seconds, breathing heavily along with me as I struggled to recollect my scattered mind. Everything came back like a speeding train at the feeling of pressure against my asshole from his finger removing itself. Then, a chill crept up my spine at the feeling and sound of him spitting onto my tight ring of muscles.

"Wait, Luc—ahh noooo." I nearly screamed out his name as it dragged out of me.

I barely got a few swipes of his half-mast cock before he shoved it all into me, only stopping when his hips pressed firmly against the back of my thighs and ass. I guessed the entry was softened by the fact he wasn't fully hard, but that quickly changed after a few slow thrusts because he grew to full size again. Him stretching me out while inside of me didn't feel all too pleasant, but surprisingly, I adjusted faster than I anticipated.

Also, I was surprised at how fast and much I enjoyed it. Yeah, it was an odd feeling to have something up my butt considering anatomy and whatnot, but it wasn't *that* bad after I somewhat got used to the feeling. And, well, his dirty words helped distract me enough, too.

"Fuck, your ass is so tight and good." At least I could give him a first of something from me. "So hot and soft. Fuck I'm going to fill it up good like your cunt. It's going to be so hot watching you leak my cum from both holes. Really makes you look like my filthy slut." He sounded so drunk and high as he fucked my ass, making me feel rather proud that I brought a mighty man like him down to nothing but a desperate beast in a rut.

Looping an arm under my hips, he kept my backside propped up as he practically laid down on top of me. Like some kind of animal, he rutted his hips into me impatiently with deep groans.

Judging how his face twisted with struggle, I was willing to bet his limit was soon. Granted, he lasted a lot longer than I credited him for. We've never gone for a round two right off the bat like this before. Hell, I didn't think it was possible for him to rebound that fast given his age—okay, thirty-six wasn't *that* old, but still.

"Coming, sweetheart? I can feel you twitching around me." His teasing words strained out with his labored breaths as he slammed into me harder.

"Yes, can't help it." I whimpered helplessly under him as I felt the claws of blissful rapture grip the edges of my mind, ready to pull me down into the depth of numbing lust.

The crazy part of it all was how I felt it everywhere, my ass and my cunt. I certainly didn't feel anything in my butt when my pussy got fucked, yet it was throbbing and clenching around nothing while my ass was being pounded into oblivion.

"I'll shove a toy in your other hole next time I fuck you." He promised with a weak chuckle before cutting himself off with a strained groan.

Sloppily, his hips jerked to a standstill against me, burying himself as deep as possible to fill my greedy hole with his cum while I hit my threshold and squeezed at his throbbing cock for dear life.

"Slipping." I whimpered with a soft sob as I felt myself falling into a familiar pit.

Kissing my temple, Luciano held me tightly. "It's okay, *amorina*, I got you. Let go, it's okay, I am right here."

His reassurance was all I needed to let my mind go blank for God knows how long. By the time I came back to reality, I was lying properly in the bed, securely in Luciano's arms.

"Thank you," I murmured, burying my face into his chest before he forced me away to shove a straw into my mouth so I could hydrate—I swear I'm gonna spit it back in his face one day.

"No, thank you for trusting me." He smiled against my lips before kissing me tenderly.

"*Ti amo.*" The way his face lit up at the two words could put a decked-out Christmas tree to shame when I said the two words.

"Judging by your reaction, I didn't fuck it up too badly." I joked with a giggle as he grinned at me like a goof in love.

"No, it was perfect, *amorina*." He whispered against my lips before crushing them in another sweet kiss. "*Anch'io ti amo.*"

Chapter 46

Luciano

~3 days later~

"*Principessa*, please don't tell me you just robbed a bank. Or at least, if you did, please tell me you covered your tracks."

Being bombarded with notifications from my accountant about Juliet's sudden surge in account balance was not fun, especially since I was in the middle of finalizing tonight's plans.

"Uhh... Well... I didn't rob like a national or federal bank... Do personal bank accounts count?" Juliet's sheepish voice came from the couch, her head refusing to meet mine as the speed of her fingers tapping against her keyboard increased.

"Juliet, what did you do?" I asked with a stressed sigh, rubbing my temples from the dull ache that quickly formed from her reaction.

"Nothing!" Yeah, that was a little too fast of an answer on her end in a very offended tone.

"Juliet, if I have to pry it out of you, you will not be walking or sitting for days," I warned her as I approached her, standing inches from her scrunched-up form on the couch. "And it won't be my hand this time."

Her head shot up at me, her wide eyes trembling a little at the sight of my looming face. "I only took the money from the people we're killing." Good to see I haven't lost my touch if she didn't fight me much. "I mean, they're not gonna miss it, and it's not like I'm going to use it for personal use. It's gonna go towards the business."

Okay, I couldn't argue much with her there because her points were rather valid. "Then open a separate account to funnel your business shit into before my account gives me an aneurysm with all these notifications of strange activity on your personal accounts," I told her with a roll of my eyes, releasing the tense breath that lingered in my chest.

"I will... I just kinda forgot...." Juliet mumbled while averting her head from me. "I got too caught up doing other stuff... Like tracking down the actual bad guy."

With an empty sigh, I shook my head at her with a small smile. "Juliet, you don't have to handle everything. You have a team put together for you to utilize. So, start delegating. Besides, you have other things to focus on, like university. I mean, you may be set for life being with me, but I still want you to get yourself set up with your own goals and dreams."

Pouting up at me, Juliet huffed and closed her laptop begrudgingly. "I know... But I don't want to be useless to you. I feel like I have to do stuff. Otherwise, I'm just a moocher." She admitted with a sigh.

"*Amorina*, you are not useless, never. Don't worry about me or syndicate business because that is not your battle to be fought. Yes, you're associated through me, but we don't expect you to fully immerse yourself in it or anything. All we want is for you to live the life you want and to be happy, especially me. You want the degree in computer sciences, analytics, or whatever else you said, so get it." I would never ask her to be involved if I could help it. It weighed on me enough that I pulled her into this life, so the last thing I wanted to do was put her in the direct line of fire.

Humming softly, Juliet nodded at me before getting up and hugging me tightly. "Are we still going out tonight? Everything in order?" She questioned after peering up at me with hopeful, eager eyes.

Chuckling, I leaned down and kissed the top of her head. "Yes, everything should be good to go, but I was in the middle of finalizing everything when my accountant rudely interrupted me. So, be good, and don't do anything for the next two hours while I prepare with the others." Or at least behave as much as my little brat could.

Squealing happily, she eagerly nodded her head while bouncing on the balls of her feet. "Yes, sir." Giggling giddily, she jumped back onto the couch and bundled herself up in her blanket with a wide grin. "I'll just take a nap until we're ready to go."

With that much energy bouncing at her? Doubtful, but if she said so, then who was I to argue? Giving out a soft, mocking chuckle, I reached down to cup her face, leaning down and kissing her softly. "Sleep tight then, *principessa*." Again, I was very doubtful of her actually napping, but there was no point in engaging in a pointless back-and-forth with her right now.

Turning on my heel, I looked at her bundled form on the couch with an admiring smile before returning to my office, where the others still remained. "False alarm, nothing to worry about," I informed them with a dismissive roll of my eyes. "So sorry about that, but where were we?"

"Remember—"

"I know, I know, I know," Juliet cut me off with an annoyed scoff. "You've only said it the whole damn ride here. If anything goes wrong, shoot and speed on out of here. Don't try to play hero and go after you, don't leave the car unless you or one of the other Syndicate members come get me personally, and do not leave the car under any circumstances unless a bomb gets thrown into it. Oh, and don't leave the car."

Little smart ass.

If I wasn't on the clock, then I'd bend her over the center console right now and spank her ass red for being mouthy with me. Well, I could always do it later when we got home—if we could even stay awake that long.

Tonight was going to be a long one, from the raid to the fight right after, and we were probably all going to be dead tired by the time we got home tonight. One step at a time, though.

First order of business: Champion's Lounge.

With one final look and kiss of Juliet, I slipped out of the car and slipped my earpiece in. "Everyone check-in," I commanded after checking in myself.

The next minute flew by with a slurry of names being a constant flow into my ear as I strapped myself down with my weapons. "Alright, everyone ready?" Once I got a positive response from everyone, I rounded the car, gave Juliet one last longing look, and blew her a kiss with a wink, making her giggle and smile like a lovesick teen.

"Everyone get into position and wait for my signal." This operation would be nothing shy of perfect. We've gone over the plan and scenario so many times over the past few months, accounted for strays, and planned for those, too.

I knew how important it was to see this place fall for Juliet, and I didn't want to disappoint her. This place falling tonight would also be a huge message to everyone in the old mafia that even they're not truly safe from us and that they are next on our list. We have rid the city of the smaller rats and bugs over the past months, a tactical decision on our end in hopes of shaking up the old. The plan did work somewhat because we had a few crawl out of their dark corners to grovel at our feet. They were promptly taken care of once we wrung them of their use. Now, it was time for stubborn ones to go, the damn cockroaches.

Caroline Heral was one of the bigger names in the old mafia, so her falling tonight would serve as a blaring message to the others that their time was up. I intend on making a spectacle of her death tonight. Which brought my attention to my bodycam to ensure it was running. This whole thing would be recorded and played at tonight's fight event for everyone to see.

Don't fuck with The Syndicate. Don't fuck with me, Luciano Agosti. And most importantly, don't fuck with my wife.

Time to get rid of this splinter.

"Alright, everyone is in position and clear on their roles and plans?" One last check before we stormed the place and decimated it.

Once I got a positive response from everyone, I gave them the go-ahead with an unhinged grin on my face when the sounds of chaos ensued from the doors being kicked in from all sides.

"Round them up! And remember, Caroline is mine." None of my attention went to the chaos around me as I stalked my way through the place, pulling the trigger on anyone who got in my way in a semi-threatening manner.

"Carol! Come out and face the music of your doing!" I shouted down the hallway with a crazed grin when I caught sight of her frantic figure running for her office.

The flimsy door—it felt flimsy to me—stood no chance against my loaded kick that nearly sent it off the hinges. Three gunshots from me went off in succession with each other the second I entered the room, sending the three guards to the ground dead before they even had a chance to aim at me. "You know Carol, if you weren't so much of a snake, I might have let you live. Too bad you burnt any bridges between you and The Syndicate when I happened upon Juliet." I mused in a sarcastic voice.

"Luciano, come on, let's be reasonable. Killing me would be detrimental to you all, and it'll be seen as a huge betrayal. You've already made a lot of enemies with what you have all done in the past few months. So, be reasonable here. Besides, I can provide so many resources to you all." Her yapping excuses droned on and on, and I couldn't care less for them.

Annoyed with her pointless excuses as to why I should spare her pathetic life, I raised my voice at her, making her flinch and shut her mouth. "If you weren't a trafficker, then maybe I might consider it, but you know the rules, Carol. Don't try to deny it either. I know the truth." Slowly, I approached her with dangerous and calculated steps, glaring her down as I approached her like a lion would an injured prey. "This is the end of the line for you."

Lunging at her, I tackled her to the ground in one smooth movement, zip-tying her wrists and ankles before dragging her down to the main floor where some others were bound and gathered in a small group on the center stage. "You're lucky I'm not one to lay my hands on women, even if they are absolute scum." Unless I wanted my parents to rise from the dead to beat my ass and drag it Hell, I refused to risk it.

I was a gentleman of a mafia boss and reasonable to an extent. At least, I liked to see myself as so.

"If anyone tries anything, shoot them, but don't kill them. I'm going to get Juliet." I gave the order to everyone before shoving Caroline into the group of people and turning around to leave momentarily.

As much as I wanted to execute everyone on the spot, maybe beat some to death with my fists, the only person who had the right to end them or command their end was Juliet.

Thankfully, Juliet was where I left her, safe and sound in my car. Although I was in a serious, killer mood, I couldn't help but let that exterior crack away at the sight of Juliet pressing her face against the window to purposedly smoosh her face. "*Principessa*, you're my wife, not my dog." I joked with a soft laugh after opening the door to her grinning face.

"But it made you smile." She retorted with a smug snicker before getting out of the car with my help.

Holding my hand tightly, she smiled nervously at the building for a second before letting me lead her in. "I really can't believe it's going to disappear after all this time." Her hands trembled in mine as we walked deeper into the place, only stopping once we were a few feet from the group of bound people.

"Doesn't feel good to be on the other end, does it?" Juliet spat spitefully at Caroline after approaching her with me right behind her. Her body lurched forward in the next second, and a hand shot out across Carol's face, leaving some lovely bloody slashes on the screaming woman's face. "At least you have the mercy of knowing how it ends for you."

"You little bitch!" That spat from Caroline earned her another slap from Juliet, which added a nice new set of nail marks across her face.

"Break their knees so they don't escape and gas the place," Juliet commanded everyone with her chest proud and head high. "I don't care if you kick them in or shoot them out. Just make sure it is done."

Slowly, Juliet backed away with me to watch our men carry out her orders from a safe-ish distance. Tucking herself into me, she leaned into me for support as she watched the scene unfold with a twisted, satisfied smile. "You know, I really thought the screams would get to me eventually, but I don't think I'll ever get enough of them." She commented with a soft sigh and giggle.

Drowning the pained screams and pleas out, I leaned down, kissed Juliet's cheek, and whispered into her ear. "My, my, what a twisted little thing my wife has become." This behavior shouldn't be encouraged normally, but we weren't anywhere near normal.

A quick minute or two passed, and the screams died down to pained whimpers and sobs once our men were done carrying out her orders. It didn't take long for the smell of gasoline to fill our nostrils and the sounds of sloshing in plastic canisters to our ears.

"If I was more fucked up, I'd find a way for you to be assaulted like I was before killing you slowly, but I'm not a total monster. So, count yourself lucky." Juliet feigned an apologetic sigh before slipping her hands into my pants pocket and fishing out the lighter. "You are going to be nothing but ashes along with this place, and once it's all gone to the ground, I'm going to build my business on top of it. I will be stepping and dancing all over your grave every single day while I rid the world of shitty people like you."

"Everyone, do one last sweep of the building to make sure it's clear, then clear the building yourself," I ordered everyone, looking around the room to ensure it was received and noted.

Countless footfalls filled the tense air as everyone swept the place one final time from the basement up to the rooftops. Then, a heavy, suffocating silence compressed the air once the place was cleared beside Juliet and me, along with the group of rats, to be executed.

"Y-you can't be serious. Please, be reasonable." Caroline begged with a nervous smile. "Please, I treated you well when you were here. Kept you fed, gave you a place to sleep."

The soft click of the lighter flipping open and the ignitor being pressed on silenced the older woman instantly. "And this is me being reasonable in return." Juliet retorted with an empty smile. "I'm not giving you the most horrible death I can think of. You get to rest for all of eternity after this. It might not be in peace, but that's a problem for you and the devil to discuss."

Tilting her head, she gave out a rather unhinged laugh. "Oh, wait, that conversation and judgment has already passed." Setting the lighter off, Juliet waved it in front of her face with a look of obsession and satisfaction. "Guess there are perks to being married to him. So, you're out of luck everywhere it seems."

The lighter clicked with each flick of Juliet's finger. "Hope you burn in Hell as much as you will here."
WHOOSH!

Chapter 47

Juliet

"Sweetheart, stop before I take you to the locker room and fuck you senseless."

Too bad his little warning or threat or whatever it'd be classified as didn't have the intended effect. If anything, it made my arousal worse, which in turn made me grind my hips against him more. "Don't threaten me with a good time, babe." I teased with a snicker. "But I can't help it, just... Fuck I feel so giddy and high."

Between setting the brothel ablaze and watching it burn to the ground with all those people in it, watching the underground fights, and knowing Luciano would be up soon to finish punishing those who wronged me, I really couldn't help but feel as high as a fucking kite. Lustful excitement drowned my whole body and mind now, and I didn't want to bother relieving any of it.

Being bad felt so good.

Unfortunately, I knew once the high died down, the guilt would set in, so I didn't want to let myself down from my little rush. I doubt the guilt would be *that* bad because I really wanted that place gone and those people dead, but I didn't want to risk that right now. I wanted to enjoy what I had going on and ride it until it was nothing but fumes.

"At this rate, we won't be getting any sleep tonight when we get home," Luciano remarked with a soft chuckle into my ear, making me giggle and squirm from the ticklish sensation.

Playfully pouting, I poked my finger into his cheek, shoving his head away slightly. "Don't make it sound like it's a bad thing." I joked with a laugh. "I mean, what better way to celebrate our official marriage than the first fuck as husband and wife, officially that is."

Yep, it was official as of today. Luciano and I were legally married in the eyes of the law.

"If I was ready, then I might even suggest starting to make little mini yous and mes tonight, but I am nowhere close to being ready to be a mom." Legally, I was an adult, but I sure as hell didn't feel like one.

I might have been forced to grow up fast these past months, but I was not mature enough to handle more. I still had much to learn and experience before I'd be remotely ready to procreate with Luciano. For a fact, I know I wanted kids with Luciano, and I also knew it to be in the future. I needed to be grown up for my children, not grow up with them.

Happily, Luciano smiled at me as if I made his day. "No rush, *amorina*, whenever you are fully ready." Giving me a sweet kiss, he held my face lovingly for a moment before kissing me again. "Now, behave. I have to go change." He gave me a knowing look that had my eyes rolling in response.

"Yes, sir, I will," I muttered begrudgingly, crossing my arms and sinking back into the seat after he removed me from his lap and stood up.

Rolling his eyes in return, he reached down and pinched my cheek. "Are you ready to make your debut as my wife?"

My body perked up at his proud smirk, a wide grin aching at my cheeks as my excitement overflowed my body. "More than ready." It's time for everyone to know I'm not one to be messed with.

Rather impatiently, I sat in my seat, clinging to Luciano's jacket for comfort as I waited for him to finish doing what he needed before taking the stage.

At least I was distracted by setting up the media to be played for the whole stadium, so I didn't die in a ball of impatience.

With everything set to roll, I tried my best to focus on the final fight, but the flurry of movements did nothing to calm my overstimulated nerves. I nearly jumped out of my skin when the bell went off, indicating the end of the match, and the shouting of everyone in the place grated at my hypersensitive nerves. My heart thudded against my ribcage like a rabid beast as the emcee calmed the whole place down and announced Luciano to the stage, making everyone hype up again as Luciano took his sweet time entering the caged arena.

"And tonight, his lovely new bride is joining him by the ringside. Please, everyone, welcome up the new, the one and only, Missus Juliet Agosti!" The spotlight blinked onto me with the emcee's gesture, and I couldn't help but feel a little nauseous with the sudden attention as I made my way to the cage, standing right outside the cage behind Luciano.

"Ladies and gentlemen, tonight's a special night. Not only are we celebrating and congratulating Mister Agosti on his new nuptials, but tonight is a new era for New York and The Syndicate. So, sit back and learn."

All the lights shut off instantly, and the big screens flashed momentarily and played the cued-up video of the raid and burning of Champion's Lounge. Everyone in the place, except those involved with the raid, watched the whole thing with horror-riddled expressions. Then, hysterical gasps and sobs chimed throughout the place when the lights came back on to reveal four bound men locked inside the cage with Luciano.

"We are done holding back and playing nice after all that's unfolded. The old mafia ends tonight. Those who engage in forbidden activities will face their consequences after tonight, and don't think you can escape if you have. We know who you are. It is a matter of time before we make our way to you." Luciano's projected voice silenced the stadium, causing the air to chill up with fear and soft, panicked whispers.

Menacingly, Luciano stalked up to the bound men, who cowered under his looming shadow. "Now, if you are thinking about running, I highly advise you think twice because if you run, and we have to chase your stupid ass down, you're going to end up in my cage like these fuck ups." Without warning, Luciano's leg shot out and kicked an expecting man in the face, toppling him over.

"Sweetheart, give me a knife," Luciano said with a hand held out towards me.

Oh yes, let me procure a knife out of thin air for you, babe.

A soft nudge to my side made my head dart to the source. "Thank you." I smiled gratefully at the emcee, taking the offered knife by the handle and passing it between the cage bars to Luciano.

Some quick snaps cut through the air from Luciano freeing the men, and then the knife was tossed back out of the cage.

"Don't kill them, babe. I want to tie their bodies to the cars and drag them through the streets. They'll make better sounds and decorations than cans to the back of our car." Call me a twisted bitch, but I didn't care, not when it came to those bastards begging me for mercy with their eyes.

From the sidelines in the VIP area, Aidan's warning rang through the air as clearly as if he spoke into a microphone. "I highly advise you cooperate and deal with us rather than Missus Agosti here! She's a twisted little thing who you don't want to be in charge of your demise!" Aidan's laughter rang through the area.

The pathetic, balding man of a person crawled up to me, clinging onto the bars of the cage while looking up at me with eyes full of panicked desperation. "Please, please, please, I'm sorry, please be reasonable. If I had known you belonged to The Devil, then I never would have touched you."

Looking down at him with mocking pity, I stared at him with empty eyes for a few seconds, acting as if I actually pondered his words. "You know, I'm getting real tired of hearing the same excuse from you bastards every time. I mean, if you were genuinely sorry, then maybe I'd consider something, but you aren't. You're only sorry that you got caught. The main point of it all is that it shouldn't matter who I belong to or not. You should have some kind of morals to know better than to rape anyone, let alone a minor."

Grabbing onto the bars for support, I pressed my heeled foot against his old face and shoved him back into the ring. "You had your chance and blew it when you bid for me." I spat out resentfully with a glare.

At least this fight proved more interesting than the last I saw with Luciano. The men actually tried to fight back despite the outcome. I mean, I wasn't too thrilled about watching Luciano eat a punch or few, but at least it was more entertaining to watch *some* action opposed to no action. A few small hits won't kill Luciano, so I wasn't too worried either. Granted, it didn't look like fun, especially when he got clocked in the jaw, but he rebounded and broke the person's nose in return.

Call me a psychopathic bitch, but I found myself enjoying the whole fight play out way too much. I even caught myself giggling and bouncing in my spot like a child opening their Christmas presents—yeah, that should have been a major red flag, but who cared.

When Luciano called it, I frowned in disappointment because I was so caught up in the excitement. Every punch, every swing, every kick sent a surge of adrenaline through my strung-out body. Needless to say, I didn't want any of it to end yet. It didn't matter to me if all four men were beaten bloody to the ground. If it weren't for the subtle rises of their chests and twitches of their body, then I would have thought them to be dead.

A soft whir hummed at my ears as the bars of the cage sank into the ground, removing the metal barrier between Luciano and me.

Seeing him all sweaty and bloody in all his glory made my heart race like an out-of-control race car on the tracks. I couldn't tear my eyes away from his form, which grew bigger and bigger with each step toward me. I was sure my heart would explode from the stimulation when Luciano stopped inches from me, his adrenaline-crazed face looking down at me like I was his next victim.

Remaining as still as a statue, I carefully followed his hands with my eyes as they reached out for my face. My breath hitched when I felt the scratchy feeling of the bandages cut across my cheek with his movement to cup my face. "Ready for our honeymoon, *amorina*?" He asked with an over-excited chuckle through his slightly busted lip.

Tension furrowed my face as I continued to look at him. We didn't discuss taking a trip anywhere, let alone a honeymoon, especially since Luciano and the others would still be busy with cleaning up New York. "Where we going?" Maybe this was all for show, but theatrics weren't Luciano's thing.

Luciano kept his voice low as he spoke, so much so that I barely caught his words. "I was thinking of a nice little trip to the Bahamas or Caribbeans, your choice, or we can go wherever you want. But for the next month, it'll be you and me on the yacht, out at sea, no mafia business or troubles, just thirty whole days of fun and bliss." His eyes were hopeful as he looked deeply at me. "What do you say?"

Unable to help it, I cracked a little laugh of amusement. "As if I'm going to say no to any of that," I remarked with a roll of my eyes. "Of course, you jerk. A hundred times yes." Honestly, the thought of escaping the busy streets of New York and the craziness of mafia life proved too tempting to resist.

Letting out a satisfied hum, his hold on my face tightened, and I was brought up into a rather bloody kiss. God, I really hoped it was his blood and not the others. That would just be gross.

Turning his head around, he looked at some of the guards approaching us. "String them to the back of my car, and make sure they're secure and won't fall off midway. I'm going to need a small team to follow me to the docks as well." He told them, earning nods and 'yes, sir' in response from them before the beaten men were dragged away.

"Well, folks, I hope you enjoyed tonight's events, and I hope to see some of your faces at the next event. If not, then, well, you probably deserved it." The emcee's twisted laugh blared at the speakers, sending worried murmurs over the crowd who remained rooted in their seats as Luciano and I took our leave along with the other Syndicate members.

And much to my slight surprise, the men were chained to the back of Luciano's car when we approached it. "Hey, since we're going on a honeymoon and like wedding presents and stuff, can I—"

Luciano tersely cut me off with a flat glare. "No, you cannot get another car."

"Wha!? Why? And I wasn't even going to ask for a car!" Okay, I totally was, but I didn't want to admit to him that he read me like an open book.

"*Principessa*, I've seen your browsing history, and you're not exactly secretive about keeping your computer screen covered. So, no car, no motorcycle." Luciano deadpanned as he opened the car door for me.

"Ugh." Rolling my eyes, I grumbled my displeasure under my breath with my arms crossed while plopping into the passenger seat.

"Keep rolling your eyes, and I'll really give you a reason to roll them tonight." He sneered with a soft glare, shutting the door right as I stuck my tongue out at him.

A whoosh of cold air filled the car with his door opening, and the car bounced slightly with his heavy body climbing in. "Keep acting like a little brat, and you won't be able to enjoy this honeymoon because you'll be too delirious in bed and unable to move from it because of how sore I'm gonna make you. And the only time you'll feel the sun and get some fresh air is when I tie you to the deck or railing to fuck and fill you before throwing you back in bed with a dildo shoved so far up your ass and cunt that you'll come from just being filled."

Oh shit.

A fantasy come true? Fuck yeah, but also kinda terrifying because, holy shit, I would be driven insane if he was remotely serious about any of what he said. Not gonna lie, a big part of me wanted to push his buttons to see how serious he'd go with his words, but the reasonable side of me knew better than to test him because he would probably end up doing much worse than what he threatened.

Without warning, his hand shot across to my side, grabbing me by my neck and making me flinch. "So, are you going to behave? Or am I going to have to unpack the ropes and cuffs first thing when we get on the boat?" His playfully narrowed eyes and smug smirk dared me to challenge him, and maybe if this were some other time, then I might've taken the bait. Too bad for him; I actually wanted to enjoy a little vacation time before university started.

Smirking in return, I reached out and patted his cheek mockingly. "Try harder next time, babe." I teased through gritted teeth before prying his hand off my neck with an exaggerated smile to goad him.

As I turned around to put my seat belt on, I squealed and laughed when I felt the back of my neck being grabbed and squeezed. A harsh jerk spun my body back around, and my lips crashed against Luciano's growling ones that sent heated waves of arousal throughout my body. "Oh, something is harder, alright." He muttered against my lips with a smirk.

"Luca!" I gasped in mock surprise, playfully slapping his chest. "We have people to kill, and the night's not young still. So, drive." I chuckled softly while turning the car on. "And drive fast."

"Whatever my wife wants."

In a hair of a second, the car roared to life the moment Luciano stomped down on the pedal. A squeal of excitement erupted from me as I slammed back against my seat from the car's sudden acceleration that sent it flying down the streets.

"Best husband ever!"

Chapter 48
Luciano

"Sweetheart, that's enough chum in the water."

We were also out of chum.

"It's a feeding frenzy already." I pointed out the violent waters to her as dorsal fins broke the churning surface. "The men are nicely skinned and ready to be shredded, too," I informed her, looking back at the huddled men who were bleeding from the skinned part of their bodies.

They looked crude, if I had to say so myself. The anatomical pictures in college textbooks were how they looked right now, the ones that would show all the muscles. Well, they didn't look *that* naked, but close enough. Pretty sure Juliet was a little disappointed that I couldn't make them look textbook perfect, but she got over it rather quickly once I handed her the chum bucket and told her to bring the sharks in.

Squealing with delight, she clapped her hands together. "I know, it's gonna be so fun!" Fear raced at my heart when she bounced around giddily.

I feared her slipping and somehow falling over the rails into the shark-infested water. "Throw them in already." She demanded, pulling impatiently at my arm.

Fairly amused by her enthusiasm, I wrapped my arms around her and trapped her energetic body against mine. "Patience, *principessa*, they're not going anywhere but the water in a second." The bastards could beg and plead all they wanted, but their fate wouldn't change.

Dragging her over to a chair, I forced her to sit down with me, holding her firm in my lap as I signaled for my men to start chucking the men overboard to their watery graves.

Shifting around in my lap, Juliet sat herself sideways on me with her arms around my neck. "Best marriage present ever." She giggled, grinning happily up at me. "Have I ever told you how much I love you?"

Cracking a mindless smile of my own, I leaned down and kissed her longingly. "You don't have to, sweetheart. I see it every time you look at me." Words would never fully express our love for each other either way.

I meant my words, though, Juliet never has to say anything because every time I looked into her eyes, I could see the depth of her immense affection for me. And she might say otherwise at times, but there's no hiding the truth from her eyes. I'd never tire of the way her eyes light up in my presence, the way they'd sparkle and shine with such amazement and adoration. Then, the goofy smile that always made its way to her face before she'd forcefully hide it once she caught herself. Everything about Juliet was a wonder and blessing to me.

"I know, but I love you a lot, like a lot, a lot." She admitted with a shy smile and blush to her cheeks.

Unable to help myself, I laughed softly as I held her dearly. "I love you a lot, too, my bratty wife," I whispered into her ear before moving my head up to kiss her head.

Peacefully, we sat there for a while, watching the sharks tear the screaming men apart until only the sounds of water splashing from the violent movements of the sharks could be heard. Honestly, it didn't feel any different than a movie date—all that was missing was some popcorn.

Mindlessly stroking her hair, I leaned my head against hers. "Have you decided where you want to go?" I asked her a while after the activity died down.

"Hmm," humming softly in thought, she turned herself around on my lap, straddling me. "Let's go to the Caribbeans. I wanna do a lot of diving and exploring." She answered with a little smile.

"Sounds good to me. I'll contact our people down there and arrange things for our stay there." Good thing we had vacation houses set up around the world for places we often frequent.

Grabbing my face, Juliet forced me to look at her momentarily before she graced me with her lips. "I can't believe we're actually going to have some personal time to ourselves." She sounded relieved and kind of tired, which I didn't blame her for.

I could barely believe it myself. Hell, I wondered if I lost some marbles when I planned this last-minute trip two nights ago because I became so fed up with running the city red. Taking a vacation now of all the times in the world probably wasn't the best call, but the others insisted I needed this along with Juliet to decompress and reset. For once, I relented without a fight, and thinking about it now and what's to happen next month—best decision ever.

"Just you and me and quality time." It was also about damn time we started this relationship off on the right foot.

"I know, it's just so hard to believe... And I don't know, after being so wound up all this time, it feels kind of weird just to relax finally." Juliet admitted with a sad smile. "And it's weird to think that it's finally all over in a sense. I mean, I know the city is going to take a lot of work and time, but such a big change happened so fast. It's unbelievable."

"I know what you mean, sweetheart. I can barely believe it myself, but we both deserve this." Easier said than done, but if we didn't step back, we would lose ourselves for the worse.

I hated it, but Juliet was a prime example. She was a completely different person from when I picked her up that night. Yes, trauma changes people, but she got her taste of blood and went into a frenzy with it. Hopefully, this little vacation will do well to reset her a little. I wanted to bring back the sweet side of her a little, not this power-hungry terror that would become a thorn in my ass if I didn't put a cap on things right now.

Yeah, I was happy for her newfound confidence and how she stepped into power, but by God, she needed to have a leash put on her before she went rabid and got herself into too deep of trouble that even I wouldn't be able to pull her out of.

Well, all of that was a worry for later. Right now, the only thing that mattered to me was returning Juliet's heated kiss with my own.

"I need you." Juliet's heated breath sent shudders down my body. "Right." **Rip**. "Now."

Holy shit.

I gripped her hips and suppressed my shiver from the chilly night air hitting me. Never would I have thought Juliet could be so forceful and passionate. She tore my shirt open like it was nothing to paw at my bare body with her frenzied hands. "I need to ride my husband's cock, now."

"Mhmm fuck." I hissed through gritted teeth from the feeling of her hips grinding down against me—hard. "Not yet. I need to taste my beautiful wife." I strained out a groan as I forced her away from me.

Then, with a grunt of effort, I flipped her upside down, causing her dress to pool down around her waist and upper body. "Fuck." My hand descended on her bare cunt before the thought crossed my mind. "You weren't wearing anything under this whole time?" Exciting but infuriating. The thought of someone possibly getting a peak at her if she accidentally bent over too much or somehow her skirt lifted really grated my nerves the wrong way.

Sinking two fingers into her, I curved them into her g-spot, pressing and rubbing hard against it as I kept my fingers hooked inside of her. "You risked another person getting a sight of my cunt? Did you want me to kill another bastard tonight for happening to glance upon something he shouldn't have?"

"Well?" I pressed her when all I got in response were some strangled moans. "What do you have to say for yourself?"

Her hips bucked away from me the more I drilled my fingers into her, but my arm around her lower back kept her anchored to me. "Nhnn... I... I wanted to fuck in the locker rooms, wanted less between us." She whimpered between her moans.

Throwing her legs over my shoulders, I nudged at them until she wrapped them around my head and neck. Then, I teasingly fingered her very slowly. "Have you been this soaking wet the whole time?" I asked her in a playfully accusatory tone. "All wet, needy, desperate, and ready while you waited like a bitch in heat for me to bend you over and fuck you?" The thought of her being ready to be taken by me at a second's notice was rather exciting, so much so that I felt my hardened member twitching in my pants.

A soft pressure tightened around my head with Juliet's tensing thighs as she moaned softly and shuddered. "Yes." She whimpered with a choked gasp, her soft walls throbbing around my fingers with the sound.

"Yes, to what, *principessa*?" It could be to both, for all I cared, but I wanted to toy with her some.

"Being a wet and needy slut for you this whole time and ready to be fucked." She quickly answered while bucking her hips at me. "Can't help it, you're so sexy."

Chuckling softly, I pulled my fingers out to stroke her from clit to ass, circling the tips of my coated fingers around her tight ring of muscles a few times before trailing back down to her clit. Lazily, I repeated this a few times as I ordered her around. "Take my cock out, baby." It barely felt like a second had passed before the cold air bit my aching member, following the sound of my zipper being undone. "Suck me off, sweetheart, put me in your mouth and choke on me while I feast on you."

"Yes, sir."

A strangled groan strained out of me when I felt her hot mouth take all of me in until she gagged. Her head started to reel back, but I didn't want the bliss to end. So, I reached a hand down to grab the back of her head and shove her down until her lips pressed against my pelvis. Leaning my head down, I sealed my mouth around her sex after I slid my fingers up to her ass and sank them into her to my knuckle. Keeping a firm hand on the back of her head, I forced her to struggle and choke on me as I lapped at her succulent cunt.

I don't know how long we sat there on the deck, locked with each other—I was too drunk on her addictive juices to care. All I knew was that I ate her out like a starved man. Even when she would squeal and try to buck away from me during her orgasms, I kept myself attached to her, riding her aftershocks and pushing her into orgasm after orgasm. I only stopped because of the tapping against my leg, which snapped me out of my lustful haze like a bull to the chest.

In a swift movement, I flipped her right side up, turning her to face me while I positioned her in my lap. "What's wrong? Was I too rough?" She looked winded and roughed up with her tousled hair, spit, tear-strewn face, and swelling red lips.

I kept a close eye on her the whole time, and yeah, I might have forced her to stay down on me longer than usual, but I let her come up for air when it looked like she desperately needed it. Also, when I felt her struggle too much, I let her up.

Worrying over her, I kept looking over every inch of her as I smoothed her hair out. She wasn't crying or sobbing, nor did she look at me all betrayed and hurt. So, why the taps?

"N-no, you weren't, but it was getting too much. I was gonna throw up, and the blood rush to my head was getting too much, too." She mumbled with a small sniffle and chuckled as she wiped her face with her hands.

Relieved, I let out a small sigh and kissed her forehead. "Want to take a little break?" I muttered against her forehead while using my own hands to wipe her mess away.

Juliet softly shook her head with a hum. "Just give me a few seconds, and I'll be good to go." I was about to question her, but her reassuring smile kept my worries at bay.

For a moment of solace, we sat there in each other's arms, listening to the calm waters while basking in the moonlight and heat from the heater—summer or not, it was still fucking cold at night this far north. I wouldn't mind it one bit if she decided to call it a night after her little moment; really, I wouldn't. I could always take care of my own problem or be patient with my fingers crossed for tomorrow.

Feeling some time pass, I was about to suggest we head down, but the thought escaped my mind when I felt a tight warmth blanket my length. Biting out a deep groan, I shut my eyes tightly as I gripped her bubbly ass cheeks with my full hands. "*Porca puttana, tesoro, mi ucciderai.*" At least I'd die happy if I went right now. "Relax, sweetheart, you're squeezing me so much." I let out a breathless chuckle as I struggled to hold myself together from her spasming walls.

"Can't help it. Feels too good." She whimpered with some jerky movements of her hips. "So big and full." She barely managed a few sloppy bounces before coming apart with another orgasm.

"Giving up already, *principessa*?" I teased with a cocky grin, slapping her ass to encourage her. "What happened to my eager little slutty wife?" Her body jerked with the next slap to her ass, spurring into action with slow rises and falls of her plush body. "My beautiful, curvy little sweetheart."

So fucking perfect.

I couldn't help my hands from wondering about her plump body, tracing over every little stretchmark, dip, curve, and roll of hers as I mapped out her body for the hundredth time. Every part of her was so beautiful and perfect. Nothing of hers was off-putting to me, even her little tummy jiggling with every bounce of her body. Hell, I loved how her body rippled under me with the impact of my thrusts or whenever I jerked her body when I fingered her. Just something about the little bounce to her body got me going.

Glaring at me softly, she dug her fingers into my shoulders, pulling a pained hiss from me when I felt the bite. Bracing herself with a renewed determination, she tightened her legs against me to steady herself before moving with more purpose.

"Shit." I hissed out a chuckle as I tightened my grip on her hips to help her bounce.

Guess she just needed a little convincing to kick her ass into gear.

Sliding an arm up her back, I bury my fingers into the back of her hair, fisting it to bring her head down into a tongue-tying kiss. Feeling her struggle awkwardly against me, I pulled my tongue back and broke the kiss briefly. "Keep your upper body still, and just move your hips," I instructed her, using my other hand to help guide her.

Thankfully, she was a quick learner because it only took a handful of stiff movements before she got down a smooth rhythm and pace that had both of us moaning and groaning while we made out feverishly. "I'm so close. Come with me, please." She panted against my lips, nipping and pulling at it while her nails dug into me more.

"*Amorina*, I'm going to come in you whether you like it or not if you keep it up." I was about to lose my damn mind with how much effort I'd put into holding myself back. My damn balls ached for a release so badly, but I wanted to hold out for her to get her share of pleasure.

If this were any other night, I wouldn't care because round two was on the table, but not tonight. After the raid and the fight, and now this, I would be beyond spent the moment I blew my load. Hell, if I weren't so pent up and desperate for Juliet's pussy, then I would have dragged her under the deck and into bed the moment the sharks were done with the bodies.

"Luciano." Call me vain, but I absolutely loved hearing my name from her sweet lips while her eyes were all on me. "Coming."

And that did. All my control out the window with how she moaned my name and kept on telling me that she was coming right up until she did. The moment her softness strangled my cock, I blew it.

"Fuck, Juliet." I groaned into her hair, holding her trembling body tightly against me as we rode out our orgasms together.

Peeling back from me, Juliet pressed her forehead against mine. With her eyes closed in bliss, she let her heavy breath wash over me as she came down from her high. And I swear, my soul left my body with her deep and tender kiss. I was left pretty breathless when she pulled away. "I love you, Luciano, so much. And thank you for giving me a new life and loving me." The ways her eyes sparkled with such love made me melt.

Giving her a loving kiss of my own, I held her precious face in my hands and smiled warmly at her. "No, I gave you what you deserved. I should be the only one thanking you for bringing life to my dullness. I love you, Juliet, now and forever. And as I've sworn before, I will spend the rest of our life proving it to you every day."

Epilogue: Juliet

~5 years later~

"Girl, you really are crazy as shit for having your wedding the day after your graduation," Evie remarked in her tipsy state.

Rolling my eyes, I snatched the shot glass from her before she could take another swig. "Well, I wanted it to be on the day Luciano saved me because, ya know, it was the first day I met him and the beginning of it all." Of course, with my luck, the day was literally the day after I graduated from graduate school.

I wasn't stressed about it, though. It wasn't a huge ceremony or anything, just a nice little beach wedding in our own backyard with our close friends, the bodyguards, and other syndicate members. A small, personal wedding, just like I wanted. The reception would also be held outback, and the tent area, heaters, and tables were all set up.

It was rather laid back for a wedding ceremony, and everything was planned to a tee. So, I wasn't worried one bit about the event tomorrow.

Especially since Luciano had so many people working on everything to ensure things went smoothly.

"I was a huge mess for my wedding, so I don't know how you're so chill about it all right now," Evie mentioned with a chuckle.

"You threw a whole ass party with like two hundred people. Of course, that's stressful as fuck. Honestly, how you didn't lose what marbles you had left in your head is a wonder of the world to me. Hell, how Aidan put up with you is the bigger question." I seriously couldn't fathom how Evie and Aidan managed to throw such a big wedding together and have it run smoothly.

Well, there was a small hiccup with some of the guests who decided to wear white, but nothing some red wine didn't fix. Besides the small group of haters, everything went rather smoothly with their wedding. However, their wedding really drove me to solidify my decision to have a small and intimate ceremony with Luciano when the time came. Fuck all that stress with planning and managing a big, fancy ceremony. Wedding planner or not, that was a circus I refused to put on.

"Where are the boys anyways?" Evie asked, peeping up from the couch like a meerkat to scout the empty house.

"Off on their last-minute bachelor party for Luciano." Leah mused with a chuckle and roll of her eyes as she joined Evie and me on the couch with the other girls in tow.

"You really trust them after what happened with Aidan's bachelor party?" Jade, Ares's wife (that's a crazy story for another time), questioned with a raise of her eyebrow as she picked up a glass of champagne off the coffee table.

A chortling scoff from Naomi—Sebastian's wife and Leah's younger sister—had our heads turning towards her as she looked knowingly at Jade. "Says the person whose man is the troublemaker of the group." She remarked smugly at Jade.

"Oh, as if Sebastian is a saint himself." Jade snapped back with a flat glare at the younger woman.

"Listen," Leah spoke up, cutting the rising tension with her authority, "Let's all agree to disagree that we have the worst and best taste in men."

"Says the one who trained her husband to be the perfect man," I muttered under my breath with a roll of my eyes.

"Hey, just because Nikita is younger does not mean I had to teach him shit." Leah defended herself with a sarcastic scoff and click of her tongue. "He was just a little rough around the edges and needed some smoothing out, that's all." She muttered into her glass of scotch before sipping at it sullenly.

"Okay, come on, no more talking about the boys. They can handle themselves out there," Evie said with a clap of her hands. "Tonight is about our little Juliet here, who is about to get married... Again?"

Waving a dismissive hand in the air, I took a few sips of my drink before replying, "It's just the ceremony, guys, nothing to make a big deal or fuss about." Maybe I was a little too nonchalant about this whole thing, but I really didn't see the big deal about it.

Yeah, I was excited and nervous about it, but I wasn't freaking out about it. Granted, Luciano was pretty chill about it all too, kind of. He got snappy a little toward the end, but I wasn't on the receiving end of it. So, I didn't care.

"I strive to be as chill as you for my wedding," Leah commented with a dry chuckle.

"Speaking of your wedding," I dragged my words out as I turned my body to face Leah fully, "Does Nikita plan on proposing any time soon?"

"I mean, we've talked about it..." I sensed a but to follow from how solemn she looked. "He's told me he plans on it... But... I mean... Would it be mean of me to be a little pushy about it?"

Absolute silence filled the area as we all took a gross interest in our drinks. We were probably the worst people to answer that question because half of us got married rather unconventionally. Luciano and I married legally after months of being with each other, and even then, it just kind of happened...?

Luciano did end up proposing to me, the whole getting down on one knee and getting sappy bit, but it was something we both saw coming. But again, legally, we've been married for all these years, so it wasn't a big ordeal of tears, screams, and 'oh my gosh' and shit.

I didn't feel the need to 'push' for marriage per se, so I really couldn't advise Leah on anything. Also, my advice probably wouldn't be any good.

Leah's younger sister and Jade wouldn't be any help either because Naomi was forced into a marriage with Sebastian, and Jade kind of fell into a similar situation as me. Neither of us pushed for anything or needed to, nor did we really think far about marriage because we didn't need to.

Thankfully, sweet Evie broke the ice for all of us. "Uhh no? I mean, if you two love each other and are sure about it all, then I don't see why not?" Evie didn't have to push for anything either because she and Aidan somewhat planned things ahead.

"I just... Nikita is still young, and I don't want to seem like a nag." Leah sighed heavily, running a hand through her hair.

Giving off an unsure hum, I awkwardly shrugged my shoulders. "A little nudge won't hurt him, and he's not *that* young." Nikita was in his late twenties last I checked, so he wasn't 'young' in my opinion. Compared to Leah, yeah, he was young, but she was up there with Luciano and the others.

"Just... Let Nikita take his time unless it's too long and sweet, then shove a ring into his hands and kick him to his knees." I added my final piece before sipping some more of my drink.

"Alright, come on, no more serious talk. It's supposed to be a fun night before our girlie here gets hitched tomorrow." Evie said with a few claps of her hands. "So, everyone, grab some drinks, and let's get wasted!"

And that's what we proceeded to do. Well, what the others proceeded to do. I remained stone-cold sober, along with Leah, who wanted to be responsible for looking after the others. It was probably a good thing we stayed sober, though, because the other three ended up passing out after the long night, and Leah and I had to put them to bed... And we had to help them through their hangovers the next morning.

"I hate alcohol. I'm never drinking again." Evie groaned into the toilet as she hugged it.

"Yeah, we'll see how that goes tonight at the reception," I told her in a sarcastic voice with a pat on her back. "Leah has some kind of hangover concoction for all of you in the kitchen, so go take it and drink some water. Once you are done nursing the hangovers, I'll set out all our stuff for you guys to change into."

"Nope." Leah's voice peeped up from behind me, making me turn my head back. "You don't lift a single finger for us. It's your day. You're the bride. So, you go park your ass in the makeup chair for the makeup artist and hairdresser to do you all up and pretty." I had no choice in this matter, judging by her insistent tone. Either I went willingly, or she'd drag my ass into the chair.

Opting for the less painful option, I went of my own accord. After changing into my little white robe with 'BRIDE' on the back, I parked my sweet ass in the chair to let my face and hair be tortured for the next hour or so before squeezing myself into my wedding dress just as the others finished up with their hair and makeup.

Casual or not, I was rather fond of my wedding dress. It wasn't typical or traditional, being on the short side and not overly fancy, but it was me. The dress itself was an off-the-shoulder, long-sleeved, lace-embroidered dress with a sweetheart neckline that came down to just above my knees. The whole thing hugged my body like a glove and made my curvy body look really plump and sexy. Then, my favorite part of the dress was the removable train made of layers of sheer lace with gems scattered about to match the scattered gems of the dress itself.

I didn't want to have a Cinderella ballgown of a dress or some frilly princess dress. I wanted something a little more on the simple side that still had its flare to it, and I wanted something I could move and enjoy being in for a whole damn day. When Evie suggested getting a convertible dress to me, I nearly blew up with joy because I could have the fancy for the vow ceremony and then the fun and sexy for the reception without having to change dresses.

Also, I didn't have to worry about tripping either because instead of heels, I opted for a pair of fancy sandals—perfect for the sandy ground. Going barefoot did make the list for a hot minute, but the thought of having my feet naked throughout my whole wedding wasn't pleasing though.

"Alright, it's almost time." The planner announced after popping her head into the living room where we were all gathered—all of us girls didn't know where the guys were.

Neither of us has heard a peep from any of the men since they left my graduation party to drag Luciano out to his bachelor party. Luciano didn't come to bed last night, much to my displeasure, and that should have been a sign for me to call and check up on him. But that kind of slipped my mind with everyone throwing up left and right this morning. Besides, Luciano was a grown-ass man. He didn't need me to call and check up on him like that. I trusted him not to get himself into some kind of stupid trouble, knowing our wedding was literally the next morning.

"The men are all down there waiting, and the priest just arrived, so he should be ready in the next couple of minutes. The photographer suggested getting some first-look shots and scenery pictures before everything began. If you want to, that is." The planner spoke with a warm smile on her face.

"I think that would be a great idea." I beamed with an excited smile and bounced a bit on the ball of my feet. "Let's do it!"

Excitement about the possibility of Luciano's reaction to seeing me in my wedding dress for the first time surged throughout my body as I eagerly dragged everyone outside. Surprisingly, he hadn't seen my wedding dress, not because I kept it from him, but it wasn't something I shoved in his face, nor was it something he asked about. If he had asked, then I probably would have shown him. But now, I was glad none of that happened because I actually wanted to possibly surprise him right now.

I carefully watched from behind the patio door as the photographer distracted Luciano. "Mister Agosti, please, can you look that way for me real quick?" The photographer pointed to a random area behind Luciano, making him turn. "Perfect, just some shots of the groom, and just keep looking, getting the perfect shot." While pretending to shoot some pictures, the photographer waved at me to come from behind his back. "Alright, just stay there for another second. I'm going to back away for another angle."

Unable to hold back my elated delight, I let it spread wide on my ruby-red lips as I reached up and placed a hand on Luciano's shoulder. The flinch from Luciano caused my body to jump slightly in response to the surge of adrenaline kicking my body.

Spinning around, Luciano opened his mouth, probably to say something mean to someone about sneaking up on him, but his expression quickly changed to an elated one when his eyes landed on me. Opening and closing his mouth like a gasping fish, all he could do was stare at me in shock while smiling like a goof. "*Amorina*... You... Wow..." His soft laughter cracked as tears welled up in his eyes.

"Babe, don't, you'll make me cry." Needless to say, Luciano never got emotional like this, ever. I could count the number of times he has on one hand.

Running his hands down his face, he looked at me through his sniffling as he dropped to his knees and hugged my waist. "I'm in heaven, I swear." He forced an emotional chuckle through as he buried his face into my stomach.

"Luciano, we can't cry yet. We haven't even started the ceremony or gotten to our vows yet." I mentioned with a cracking voice of my own as I struggled to hold my own emotions back.

"I thought about cutting your dress off later, but now... I don't want to ruin it because I want to see you wear this again and again to remind me what an angel you are to my life." He joked with a laugh, making me roll my eyes and slap his shoulder.

"Yes, please don't ruin this dress." I didn't care about all my other clothes, but this was too special now to ruin.

A soft set of claps interrupted our moment and tore our attention away from each other. "Alright, alright, everyone, take your places. We have a ceremony to get underway." The priest announced with a big grin on his face.

Unhappy grumbles breathed out of Luciano as he got up and forced himself away from me to take his spot at the front once more while I journeyed to the beginning of the aisle. Thankfully, it didn't take long for the ceremony to proceed once everyone scrambled to their seats, and I was down the end of the aisle standing across from my wonderful husband (husband-to-be again?).

As things continued, the priest's voice droned on and on, and honestly, none of what he said registered in my mind because I was too busy staring at Luciano like a schoolgirl on her first date with her long-time crush. Only reason why I snapped out of my daze was because of a nudge from someone.

"Miss Juliet, your vows, if you have any?" The priest urged me with a teasing smile, probably amused at the fact I stood there like an idiot drooling over this handsome hunk of mine.

"Of course, I wouldn't think of going to my own wedding without vows." I joked with a nervous chuckle.

Reaching out to Leah, I handed her my bouquet to take Luciano's hands into mine. "I know you tell me not to say it, but I never listen to you anyway. So, I will say it now and again until you go deaf." A brief pause to chuckle with Luciano as he rolled his eyes at me and looked at me knowingly. "Thank you. Thank you for saving me. Thank you for loving me. Thank you for being my rock, my peace, my comfort, my everything. I really don't know where I'd be if you hadn't run into me that night." Those who knew the circumstances of our first encounter snickered a bit along with us. "And I will forever be thankful that you never gave up on me."

At a loss of words, I forced my mouth to close before stupid stutters could strain out of me. "Thank you for believing in me and giving me a new life, one where you are in it every second of every day. I will forever cherish every morning I get to wake up to your handsome face and every night that I get to be safe in your arms. I swear, for the rest of our life as husband and wife, I will always do right by you, respect you as you respect me, love and care for you in sickness and in health, and be there by your side through thick and thin, for rich or for poor, until death tries to do us part."

A blow of worry punched me in the gut from the empty feeling of air in my hands. Did he change his mind after all this time? Why else would he let go of my hands during this moment?

I was about ready to cry from the rejection until a warmth cushioned my face and forced my attention up to Luciano's tearing eyes. It was as if his amber orbs needed to sparkle and shine more than they normally did—so rude.

"Sweetheart, I only gave you all that you deserved." He told me with a growing smile. "But even then, it is not enough. I won't ever be able to give you enough, even with all the wealth and power I have, but I am going to damn well try my best to. You deserve the world, the skies, the sun and moon, the stars, and all the galaxies. You are such an amazing woman, and I am so blessed to have you in my life. I truly don't deserve you and your good heart, but I'm selfish, so I'm going to keep and guard you like the devil I am."

Waves of comfort and happiness warmed my body until it felt like I would melt like heated chocolate from his words and the feeling of his thumbs stroking my cheeks.

Afraid of falling because of my knees growing weaker and weaker with each word out of that damn kissable mouth of his, I had to reach up and grab ahold of his hands and wrists.

"I will cherish you for now and ever. If anyone should be thanking anyone, it should be me thanking you for all the good you have brought to my life. I thought I had it all until you came along and gave my life the breath of fresh air it needed. You really are the best damn thing to ever happen to me, and I swear on my life that I will love and honor you through thick and thin, in sickness and in health, and rich or poor, until death comes for us. You will forever be my little brat, my *amorina*."

With a tear running down his face, he leaned in and kissed my forehead. "I love you, my Juliet." He whispered.

"I love you too, Luciano." I couldn't wipe the obscenely wide smile off my face if I wanted to.

"Alright, hold on, save the tears for after you put the rings on each other and after I pronounce you guys husband and wife." The priest chuckled softly with a pat on Luciano's shoulder.

I don't think I've seen Luciano move any faster to put something on me until now, with how he nearly shoved my finger off my hand with the force behind him putting the ring on me.

Laughing a little, I took my sweet time slipping the ring on his finger to tease him a little, which earned me a complaining groan and a flat glare.

"With the power vested in me and on behalf of God, I pronounce you husband and wife." Shutting his little black book, the priest stepped back and gestured us together. "You may kiss your bride, Luciano."

And that's when the tear work started for both of us. The moment our lips collided, it was like two missiles to our dams.

"I fucking love you so much. You really are the best thing in my life, and I swear I will always treat you right and love you until I die." He whispered hastily against my lips between kisses.

"I love you so much. Thank you."

The two of us held each other at the altar for a long, sweet moment, crying our emotions out for the world to see.

"God damn it, would you two stop." Ares interrupted our moment, earning a slap to the chest from Jade. "Gonna make me fucking cry and embarrass myself." He grumbled behind his hand while turning his tearful face away from us.

Unable to help it, Luciano and I gave out a good laugh before letting the priest wrap up the ceremony so we could move on to the reception. Which, thank fucking God, because apparently I was starving and didn't know it.

After a good while of sitting around and stuffing our faces with idle chit-chat shoved in between, we finally moved on to popping and pouring the champagne down the pyramid of glasses. "Are you sure you're okay, sweetheart? You never turn down good champagne." Luciano worried over me as we went from the glass pyramid of champagne to our cake.

"I had too much to drink last night, and I'm gonna throw up if I have a drop of alcohol in me right now." I lied smoothly through my reassuring smile as I stood beside him at our wedding cake.

Luciano opened his mouth to say something but quickly shut it with a shake of his head. "I don't want to know what you girls did last night. I'm just gonna be ignorantly blissful." He mused with a chuckle before picking up the knife with me.

"To us." Luciano grinned happily at me for a second before cutting into the cake with me.

Keeping a calm smile on my face, I watched Luciano's face twist with confusion with a bated breath and a racing heart. "What the... Didn't we get white champagne for the cake flavor?" He asked in a small voice as he cut more slices into the cake and pulled them out.

Utterly confused after seeing all three tiers were blue on the inside, he looked at me for an answer. "Why the fuck is it blue?" He wasn't mad or upset, just very confused and concerned.

The calm smile on my face had unconsciously widened giddily at this point, and I couldn't help but feel like I looked crazy with how much my cheeks ached from the smile. With a nervous lick of my lips, I gently moved Luciano's face to the projector screen behind us, which had been playing a slideshow of various pictures of us. It wasn't now.

Inside of a slideshow, the screen remained frozen on one single picture of a grainy black-and-white ultrasound.

Leaning up to my stunned husband, I giggled softly into his ear and whispered, "Happy anniversary, my dear husband."

Now, as happy as I was about the news and the surprise, I couldn't help but grow concerned when he stood there in a stupor. "Luca... Uhh... Honey... Say something?" I softly tugged at his sleeve in hopes of getting his attention.

What I didn't expect was for him to whirl around with a huge grin and spin me around with a happy shout and laugh. "Is it really true? Our baby is inside of you right now?" He asked with a grin that would put The Joker to shame. "I'm going to be a dad?"

All I could manage was a happy sobbing nod of my head in response while I clung onto him for dear life.

"You guys! You see that! That's my son! I'm going to be a dad!" He shouted with glee as he continued to spin me around in his arms.

"Luciano, you're gonna make me throw up if you keep spinning me," I mentioned with a dry laugh while holding back the contents of my stomach from coming up to embarrass me on my wedding day.

Apologizing, he set me down and dropped to his knees to level his smiling face with my stomach. "Hey there, buddy." He spoke to my stomach with a gentle rub. "I already love you so much, and you're not even here yet. I swear, I will be the best dad ever to you."

"Yes, you are." I smiled lovingly down at Luciano as I ran a hand through his gelled hair. "We are going to be the best parents to our child."

Standing back up, Luciano grabbed my face and kissed me deeply. "I didn't think it was possible to love you any more than I do, but... Fuck, I love you so fucking much more."

After a round of applause and congratulations from everyone, the place settled down for Luciano and me to have our first dance. And, of course, I cried like a damn baby because of the emotions, which I blamed the hormones for throwing out of whack.

The two of us took center stage as the lights dimmed and our song, Breathless by Shane Ward, played over the speakers as we wrapped our arms around each other. "Is that why you've been off the past few weeks?" Luciano asked as we swayed softly to the beat of the song.

"Yeah... It kind of took me by surprise because I was still on my birth control patches, but my boobs didn't feel right, along with my appetite. So, I made a doctor's appointment two weeks ago, which is when I found our little bean inside of me." I replied to him with a sheepish chuckle. "Two months, that's how long our little troublemaker has been inside of me."

"Isn't two months a little early to find out gender? How do you know it's a boy?" Luciano questioned with a high raise of his eyebrow. "Not that I mind or care either way, as long as it's our baby, that's all I care about. But you said son on the picture earlier."

"Blood test." I gave a small shrug of my shoulders. "I was too impatient to wait until the scan at twenty weeks, so when the doctor offered the blood test since I already had to give blood for the other lab work, I said yes."

Tightening his arms around me, he lowered his head into the crook of my neck, humming softly and inhaling deeply. "I'm so fucking happy right now I could really die. This day... Just... Fucking amazing." He mumbled into me.

Inhaling a trembling breath, I leaned my head back to look at him nervously. "Would it still be amazing if I make one request regarding our kid?" I asked with a lick of my lips.

"Nothing can dim today. You can tell me to wear a clown suit right now, and I wouldn't be offended." He assured me with a warm smile, stroking my cheeks with his fingers.

"Please don't ever do that. If you ever wear anything remotely clown-like, I will ban you from sex for a whole year." I threatened him with a serious glare before recollecting myself.

Stepping into him, I lay my head on his chest and looked up at him with hopeful eyes.

"Can we name him Gale?"

Epilogue: Luciano

~18 years later~

"Oof! Get off me, old man!"

"Are you going to keep your trap shut to your mother?" Fuck I felt old; struggling around on the floor with my nearly legal son made my damn bones ache as if I'd been slammed against the cage twenty times in a row by a charging bull.

Throwing his elbow back, Gale caught me right in the face, making my hold on him loosen enough for him to slip free. "No! I don't want her ripping my head off after you throw me under the bus. I ain't taking the fall for it this time."

Slightly winded, I panted softly, "You got a new Lambo out of the situation last time," I argued back with him as I scrambled up to my feet and charged after him.

369

Just as he grabbed the door handle, I wrapped my arms around him and threw him backward onto the floor. Quickly, I threw him into a headlock and held him down.

"That Lambo was so not worth Mom's wrath. I nearly shat my pants when she chewed me out! And she locked up the Lambo, so I can't even freaking drive it. Nothing is gonna keep my mouth shut this time." He argued back in a strained voice.

Grunts of struggles, along with the thumping of our bodies hitting the floor, filled the room as we rolled around.

Unfortunately, I stood no chance against my son because I raised the damn kid, and at seventeen, going on eighteen soon, he was already my size. Actually, as much as I hated to admit it, he was bigger than me. I wasn't close to my prime now at a much older age, and with age came its downfalls. By no means was I weak and useless, still picture perfect in terms of health, but I definitely wasn't how I was when I was in my twenties and thirties in terms of strength, agility, and dexterity.

Which my son took full advantage of.

A pained grunt and hiss scratched at my throat at the feeling of something large and hard bashing my face. "Son of a bitch." I cursed out of habit as I reeled back and held my face.

And unfortunately, he had Juliet's smartass mouth. "Wow, that's not nice to say of mom. Then again, that's not nice to call your wife. Though, also, for me to be born, you would have had to..." His word drew out from the stern glare I shot him.

"You're about to be grounded until college at this rate," I grumbled in a stuffed-up voice because of my aching nose.

"Ooooh, what you gonna do? Lock me at home? No technology? You know I can still fuck shit up no matter what." Gale sassed me back with his arms crossed and a smug smirk on his face.

Fucking... I am seriously not doing this right now.

I shouldn't be arguing with my damn kid, nor should I be letting him get under my skin this much. Then again, I had no one to blame but myself because he came from my balls. Granted, he is half of Juliet, but I couldn't blame all of Gale's spunk on her genes because I definitely was a huge asshole like him when I was his age.

God damn it. Parenting was supposed to be easy at this age, not harder.

"Would you just shut up and go to your room already." It wasn't so much a question as it was a demand.

Of course, being the smug little devil spawn he was, he locked his feet down and widened his smirk. "No." I wanted to punch his puffed-out little chest and knock him down a few pegs. "What are you gonna do about it, old man?"

"I'm gonna beat your ass and make it look like an accident and drag it to your room myself if you don't move on the count of three." Okay, I wouldn't hurt him *that* bad, just enough to teach him a lesson on who was in charge around the place.

"I can take you on any day."

Yeah, no, we're doing this.

My cocky ass son needed to be taught a lesson the hard way.

Lunging at him, I easily tackled him to the ground with a grunt and put him in a knee hold down. "Don't forget who taught you how to fight." The extra trainers who helped him when I couldn't were nowhere near my playing field.

Gritting his teeth, Gale threw his hands at me while bucking his body to try and throw me off. "Don't forget that I am your son." I don't know how, maybe through sheer determination or some stupid stubbornness, but he managed to pull one of my legs out from under me, toppling me over. "And that I am better and stronger." A winded grunt punched out of my body from Gale's weight falling onto me.

"Stronger I'll give you. Better?" Just to prove my own stubborn point, I tripped him down by grabbing his arm and pulling him right into me. Not giving him a hair of a second to react, I wrap my arms and legs around him, putting him into a guillotine chokehold.

"Luca! What the fuck are you doing to our son? Let him go, you asshole!"

Uh oh.

"Ooooh, you're in trooooouuuublllle." Gale's strangled voice choked out mockingly from under me.

When I showed no signs of releasing Gale because I was too busy plotting an escape and coming up with a whole list of excuses to lessen the blow from my lovely wife, a swift kick lodged itself into my side. Instinctively, my arms released my son with my cough so my body could curl up to defend myself against another blow.

"The fuck is wrong with you? How many times do I have to tell you to quit doing that kind of hold on Gale? What if you snap his neck or suffocate him with your fat arms?" Juliet had every right to fret over our kid, even if she knew I'd never truly harm him—mother's instinct and all. Well, that and a guillotine choke was rather risky, but it often got my point across to Gale fairly quickly. Of course, I'd never harm him; I was a professional, so I knew what I was doing.

Checking Gale over, Juliet completely ignored me—rude—as I groaned in pain on the floor. It might have been exaggerated to earn some sympathy from Juliet, but I doubt it'd work since she knew her hits could never hurt me unless she went for a cheap shot between the legs.

Huffing, Juliet glared at both me and Gale with her arms crossed. "Why the hell were you tw—OH MY FUCKING GOD! WHY THE FUCK IS MY NEW COMPUTER BROKEN!?"

And that would be our cue to scram.

"Get the fucking keys," I told Gale in a hurry as I scrambled to my feet and made a run for it.

"She'll just hack the car and shut it down." Gale's voice trailed behind me as we ran through the house to the garage.

Stopping at the key cabinet, I trifled through it with Gale. "Not the Camry." Eventually, I grew smart enough in the first few years of our relationship to stash away some old cars that didn't rely on computers and fancy electronics. Juliet couldn't hack something that didn't have Wi-Fi unless she managed to Jerry rig it.

"I thought she slashed the tires on that damn thing last time she caught us." Gale's words were as frantic as his hands as he brushed them through every set of hanging keys.

"Wheels are replaceable." With the keys in one hand, I snatched my son's wrist and dragged both our asses out the door just mere seconds before Juliet got her hands on us. "Get in!" I practically shoved my son into the car when I flung the door open and forced him to crawl across the center console.

Unfortunately, our escape hit a flat before we even started the car. "Holy shit, dad! Mom's got her controller and the drone up!" Yeah, words I never

ever want to hear from my son or anyone. A pissed-off wife with any kind of weapon was a huge no-no, but *my* pissed-off wife with a weapon? Yeah, no, we were fucked.

Three soft pops rang out in succession, and the distinct sound of air hissing out of deflating tires filled my ears and the air around us.

"I'm gonna kill both of you." Juliet's deadly voice chilled the air and my spine.

"Sweetheart," with a sheepish smile, I turned around to face her with my hands up in the air. "It was an accident. I'll replace it like I always do."

"Okay, the fact you broke my expensive, customized shit pisses me the fuck off, but what really threw me off my hinges is the fact I had a program running through there that's taken me weeks to perfect. You potentially fucked it all up! The whole network that the program was going to shut down could potentially be all gone. Yeah, I'm fucking pissed about the broken screen and computer tower, but I'm really fucking pissed and angry and upset about the program and victims who are going to be harmed if this shit fails!"

Juliet kept prattling on and on about how this had been a long project for her and the business and how it was a big stint, and honestly, I felt like a fucking asshole now. Looking over at Gale, I could see his shoulders slumping with his cowering body as he looked at his mother apologetically.

Yeah, this time we fucked up, bad.

Swallowing the lump in my throat, I slowly approached Juliet, taking the gun away from her before pulling her into a tight hug. "I'm so sorry." I was definitely groveling more tonight. "What can we do to fix it. Please, tell us. We really should have been more careful with our roughhousing, and we should have known better than to roughhouse around your systems."

Climbing out of the car, Gale joined in on the hug. "Yeah, I'm sorry mom. I should have just listened to Dad and not egg him. It's my fault the fight started." At least he had our big hearts where it counted. "Please, let us help you fix it. Do you need me to try and run a backup program or a different program to try and patchwork things? Is there anything I can help you recover?"

"I don't know how much of it can be salvaged, or if *any* of it can... Just... Go plug in my spare tower, boot it up, and transfer whatever data you can from the tower you broke. I need a moment to cool off before I rip both your heads off and kick them into the sea." Juliet sighed heavily against us with a deep frown.

"Mom, I promise I won't mess around with Dad in the media room anymore. Just don't be upset anymore, please." Gale pulled his best puppy dog face on Juliet, making her roll her eyes and shove at him.

Struggling to hold back her smile, she covered it up with a scoff as she shoved at Gale. "Don't make that face anymore, and I won't. Seriously, you look like you're constipated."

"That's rude," Gale remarked with a roll of his eyes.

"But the truth, so suck it up." Juliet bit back at our son with gusto. "Go fix your fuck up while I deal with your dad."

Smirking at me, Gale stuck his tongue out and mouthed, 'You're in trouble' like the little turd he was before he turned around and scrammed out of sight.

"You're sleeping in the bushes tonight, mister." Juliet deadpanned at me, jabbing a finger into my chest.

"*Amorina, principessa,* sweetheart, baby, come on. We're going to fix it as best as we can. Gale is fixing the system, and I'll do what I can. If you have a location or area of interest, send me that way, and I'll take care of the rest, no problem." I sweetened my voice, hoping to get in some of her good graces.

Knowing Juliet, she meant what she said about me sleeping in the bushes. It wouldn't be the first time she locked me out of the house and forced me to sleep outside.

Kissing her tense forehead, I looked at her pleadingly as I dropped down to my knees. "Juliet, sweetheart, please, I am sorry. I was being stupid, and I should have known better. I swear, we won't mess around in the media room after today. I just wanted to teach him a lesson for being a little turd, and things got out of hand. I'm really sorry." After hearing about her program and how we possibly fucked it up, in turn fucking up a big operation, I truly felt guilty as hell.

Wrapping my arms around her waist, I hugged her tightly and blessed her body with kisses on her stomach and thighs. "Juliet, please."

"Put that mouth to use elsewhere tonight, and maybe I'll reconsider your sleeping arrangements." She relented begrudgingly with a forced glare. "And your ass better be out there tonight to catch any runaways."

Victorious, I grinned up at her for a second before getting back up on my feet and hugging her with a sway. "I'll gut anyone who moves," I promised with a twisted grin.

"Or you can save them for our coming anniversary trip," Juliet suggested with a dark smile of her own.

"I'm surprised the ocean isn't permanently red from how many bodies we've bloodied it with." I mused with a fucked-up laugh.

Joining with a twisted laugh of her own, Juliet reached up and wrapped her arms around my neck. "At some point, it probably will." She commented.

For a sweet moment, the two of us stood there looking at each other with sheer adoration. "Sometimes, I still can't believe we've been together for twenty-four years and the wonderful life we've created together. And our son," I had to pause for a moment to chuckle and shake my head, "Gale might be a pain in the ass, but I couldn't be more proud of the man we've raised him to be."

"I can't believe it myself sometimes. I mean, thinking back on it after all this time, just... I don't know. It sounds like a dream I might wake up from any day now." Running the tips of her fingers across my cheek, she settled her hand against my face, tilting her smiling face at me. "I really can't thank you enough for saving me that night and taking a chance with me. We've had our mountains in the road, but we made it through them together and became stronger, and that's all that matters. The life we've built is more than picture-perfect to me, and sometimes, I can't believe Gale is our kid because he's just so perfect. We really did good with him, and I can't believe he's going off to college in a few months."

A whole-ass kid. *My* whole-ass kid who I didn't fuck up somehow. Parenthood has been one hell of a ride that had me clenching every step of the way. I had good parents growing up who did a wonderful job of raising me, but I very clearly remembered how much of a rat-ass bastard I was. And lordy, to think of my son as a mini-me, especially in his teenage years—fuck. Thank God Gale was more than a wonderful kid. He had a bit of a temper and complex like me, but it was dimmed enough by Juliet's personality that he was more than tolerable.

"Given who his parents are, I say he turned out just perfect. And hey, I gotta say, we did a damn good job with him." Seriously, I don't know how we fucking managed, but we did. So, we both deserved pats on the back.

"Ugh, I'm not ready to let our baby out into the world." Juliet pouted sadly with teary eyes. "I still remember when he was the size of a stuffed animal in my arms."

"And now he's breaking arms." I snickered, unable to help myself.

"Luca!" Juliet exclaimed, slapping my chest. "Don't ruin my moment. He's already a spitting image of you. Don't remind me that he likes to fight like you."

"He's still a little computer nerd like you, too. He's got both brains and brawns, so what more can you ask for." I remarked with a chuckle, tightening my arms around Juliet and swaying her back and forth a little. "But hey, at least he's not partaking in underground fights and just beating people for no reason like I did when I was his age."

"Fair point, and at least he's not hacking the government and stealing money from people or something," Juliet added with a soft laugh of her own.

Taking a deep breath, I rested my chin atop her head. "Our boy is going to be just fine out in the world. We made sure of it."

"I know. It's just the mom in me being sentimental and emotional. I mean, he's our son, and he's grown now, and I guess the mom side of me that wants to keep him as a baby forever is having trouble with that." Juliet chuckled dryly with a soft sniffle. "Sometimes I wish we could have had more."

Frowning, I pulled away to hold Juliet's face and look at her sternly. "*Amorina*, Gale is perfect, and I will tell you time and time again, one perfect child to devote all our love and attention to is better than a whole army of children whom we can barely remember the names of. I don't and won't ever love you any less because you only blessed me with one child. It really does not matter to me. As long as you are here and healthy with me, that's all I want and need."

Honestly, it didn't bother me one bit that Juliet only gave us one child. Hell, she could give us none, and I'd still love her like never before. As long as I had my Juliet, that's all I cared about.

I nearly died that day at the hospital when the doctor had to rush Juliet into emergency surgery following a complication of her surgery, which then resulted in her needing a hysterectomy. I didn't care one bit for the latter. I would have been a broken man if I had to leave the hospital without my wife by my side.

I was never one to put a quantity to children anyway, so I really couldn't care less about how many children she'd give me.

It was harsh to think and say, but I would have rather left that hospital with Juliet alive and without our child than without her and a bundle of what should be joy in my arms. Functioning without Juliet was impossible after all these years, and if I had to raise our son every day without her by my side, I'd die of a broken heart the moment Gale turned eighteen.

Thankfully, the worst-case scenario didn't come to fruition, but it could have. Even if she didn't have to have her uterus removed, I wouldn't have risked another child with her anyway because her life was more important than having another spawn of mine fill the world. Also, after raising Gale, one of me was more than enough for this damn world.

"Don't ever apologize for that, ever. I don't know how many times I have to tell you." I hated how she weighed that burden on herself so much when it genuinely held no value to me. "I love you and married you for you, not for your womb. I love you because you are a wonderful woman with a heart of gold despite all the shit the world has thrown at you."

Kissing her with a smile, I held her lips against mine to pour every ounce of my soul into her. "I will always choose you over everything at the end of the day because I love you, for you."

I seared her mouth with another heavy kiss before holding her tenderly in my arms. "I love you, Juliet, for now and always."

"Thank you for loving me and having me. I will always love you, Luciano, until the end of time."

Glossary

- **Amorina:** Little love.

- **Anch'io ti amo:** I love you too.

- **Brava ragazza:** Good girl.

- **Cazzo, sei così meraviglioso, principessa:** Fuck, you're so gorgeous, princess.

- **Compadre:** Friend

- **Il Diavolo:** The devil.

- **Lo giuro, non conoscerai mai la sofferenza per mano di qualcun altro con me:** I swear, you will never know suffering at the hands of someone else with me.

- **Merda:** Shit.

- **Porca puttana, tesoro, mi ucciderai:** Holy shit, honey, you're going to kill me.

- **Principessa:** Princess.

- **Sono così dannatamente fregato:** I'm so fucking screwed.

- **Sono così fiero di te. Hai fatto benissimo:** I'm so proud of you. You did very well.

- **Stai zitto:** Shut up.

- **Ti amo:** I love you.

Thank you!

Scan me to leave a rating/review!

IF YOU ENJOYED THE story (or didn't), please take a second to leave a rating/review! Reviews and ratings are so important to authors, especially indie authors like me! So, please take a second to give it some stars!

What's next

Hope you guys enjoyed this first book in my new mafia series, The East Coast Syndicate. I have a lot planned for this series which will contain five books in total, all being standalones. Next up will be Leah's story, which will be a reverse age gap love story that will tie this world into the rest of my mafia world with an introduction of a familiar(ish) MMC.

Leah's story will be set to drop sometime early 2025, so I hope you all stay tuned for teasers as time comes. In the meanwhile, if you are craving more mafia then I have my Volkov Bratva series you can sink your teeth into, or if you want something more light-hearted and a nice laugh then I have my darkish rom-coms.

About the Author

ROSE CHASE, A DEDICATED nurse and loving mother to two boys, discovered her passion for storytelling in middle school on online forums and Wattpad. Despite her busy life, she delves into the captivating realm of contemporary romance, with a particular fascination for dark romance and morally gray characters. Through her skillful storytelling, Rose navigates the intricate dance between love, desire, and the shadows of human nature. When not saving lives or caring for her family, she immerses herself in the world of fiction, inviting readers to explore the depths of love and passion while confronting the complexities of the human heart.

tiktok.com/@rose.chase.author

instagram.com/rose.chase.author/

facebook.com/rose.chase.author

amazon.com/author/rose.chase